the Life and Death
(but mostly the death)
of Erica Flynn

the Life and Death
(but mostly the death)
of Erica Flynn

Sara Marian

Per Bastet

The Life and Death (but mostly the death) of Erica Flynn

Published by Per Bastet Publications LLC, P.O. Box 3023, Corydon, IN 47112

Cover art by Zakary Kendall

Photograph by Ron Perrin

Cover design T. Lee Harris

ISBN 978-1-942166-00-9

This is a work of fiction. Names, characters, places and incidents are products of the author's imagination or are used for literary purpose and are not to be construed as real. Any resemblance to actual events, locales, organizations, or persons, living or dead, are entirely coincidental. The names of actual locations and products are used solely for literary effect and should neither be taken as endorsement nor as a challenge to any associated trademarks.

This book is dedicated to my family, for all the hours spent reading to me when I was too little to read for myself. I would especially like to thank my mother and fellow author, Marian Allen, who walked the tightrope between supporting and challenging me in my formative writing years, and who taught me that the only absolute rule in writing is, "Do what works."

This book is also dedicated to Zakary Kendall, who continually inspires me to greater things. Thank you for always having my back, for making me smile, and for waking me up to my own potential. You're the best friend and the best partner a girl could ask for.

the Life and Death

(but mostly the death)

# of Erica Flynn

Chapter One

the end

If I'd known I was going to be dead less than an hour later, I might have been nicer about the whole thing.

Maybe.

Tact has never been my strong point, and I'd had enough buttons pushed that morning to treat myself to a ride on the high horse of self-justification.

I'd like to think that, if I could've seen twenty minutes into the future, I'd have said, "Dom, you're awesome and I love you and things will work out," or, "Don't worry — you won't be stuck here forever." Something reassuring, thoughtful, and decent. Something he deserved to hear. Something that I meant rather than something I said just to be an asshole.

Of course, if I could've seen twenty minutes into the future, I wouldn't have died in the first place, because I would probably have had the sense to drive more carefully.

You learn a lot by dying. Way more than I learned by living.

So, since I was still a stubborn, temperamental mortal in a moment of unappreciative pique, my actual last words to my husband were, "I am so *sick* of my life with you! I hate it!"

And I slammed the door on my jacket. I had to open it again to get free while Dom stood in the hallway watching, arms crossed. My keys jangled together in my hand as I pointedly slammed the door again, feeling stupid for doing it and angrier at everything because of feeling stupid.

Spring was opening up that morning — chilly, bright, and

scented with the grass Dom had cut yesterday.

The accident was fifteen minutes away, and all I could focus on was the sour prelude to my workday, the clash of words that accomplished nothing, and wanting to kick myself already for what I'd just said.

What a way to go out.

Dominic called my cell about five minutes before the crash, and I was still too angry to answer. I waited till the phone beeped that I had voicemail and listened to the message, my pulse dull and heavy in my throat, my eyes sliding over the graceful, steep slopes of the tree-laced hills along the highway as if they didn't matter.

"Erica. I guess you're not ready to talk." He sounded mad, but I could hear, too, that he didn't *want* to be mad. "I just wanted to make sure you're driving safe. No speeding because you're angry. I'll talk to you later. Love you."

I wasn't ready to make up, but I didn't like the idea of having to wait through my workday, either. I listened to his message again, trying to gauge whether an apology would even matter to him yet. Maybe I should—

And out of nowhere, BOOM.

Trust me when I say you don't want to be doing ninety while fiddling with your voicemail — especially when the highway curves away and your car is suddenly aimed at a gigantic tree, and you're too busy with your cell phone to notice. Trust me when I say that it'll be even worse if you're also right by a big, steep slope when the tree jumps in front of you. So much for the pretty landscape not being important.

The car rolling and twisting, the crack of my own bones breaking, and the warmth of blood welling out of me, and all I can think is, *I hate it when Dom's right.*

~*~

You spend your whole life hypothesizing about what you'd do with your final month, your final hour, your final ten minutes, if only you knew ahead of time that you were going to die. The problem with this is, you don't account for what condition you're going to be in as you slip out of this world.

I'd spent the previous five years telling people, hypothetically, that what I'd do with my time was, I'd profess my undying love to Dom — my method of doing so depending a lot on my mood at the time and how much alcohol I'd had before I answered.

~*~

When the real thing happened, it didn't go quite the way I'd planned.

There were a few waves of blazing, nauseating pain, and then sirens. I was staring out the shattered window, for about a century, at the tiny new leaves of the maple tree my bumper had said an abrupt hello to.

And then the car door creaked open, with the tinkle of glass raining down all around me as what was left of the window fell to the ceiling.

Some guy in a uniform was talking to me while he cut the seat belt away, and I whimpered and grunted and wished he'd shut up and stop trying to console me.

Then I was lifted out, and the world turned right side up again, which did nothing for my nausea problem.

There was a stretcher waiting, and an ambulance waiting, and an emergency room waiting. Somewhere along the journey, my mouth brimming with of the taste of wet iron, I remembered that I was supposed to call Dom. I was pretty sure I wasn't coming out of this alive, what with the blood and the pain and the EMT's yelling words like "critical" and "stat" as they wheeled me through the doors of the ER.

I must've been in shock, because I mainly just felt hazy and numb. My best attempt at getting to a phone was that my hand twitched toward a black payphone, glistening with greasy fingerprints, as we sped past.

Rectangles of icy light flicked by overhead. There was a tinny sound in my ears, everything beyond it muffled and wavy. My hand slid around, feeling for my cell phone, but I couldn't remember where I had left it.

"It's okay, honey," the nurse on my right said. All I could process about her was her arm, stretching up and away toward her body, near my face. Fine, dark hair over a thick scattering of freckles. No jewelry. Probably not allowed.

"Want my phone call." My voice came out weak and wet. I tried to cough, but my abdomen wouldn't respond, so I turned my head. Heat spilled out of my mouth and down my cheek.

"It's okay," the arm's voice said. At the shoulder of the arm was a caduceus — the staff with the two snakes and the wings that you see all over medical uniforms and paperwork. I stared at it, not quite able to laugh through whatever was wrong with my abdominal muscles.

The caduceus is the symbol of the Greek god Hermes, who isn't a god of medicine at all, actually, but a god of commerce, thievery, and messengers. He also guides the souls of the dead to the border of the Underworld.

I wondered, fuzzily, how many people stared at that symbol in their last moments and knew how morbidly appropriate it was. Not even my nerdy fluency in mythology could've prepared *me* for the fact that the afterlife would prove it to be an eerie foresight on the part of modern Upper Worlders . . . but I didn't know that yet, because I was still alive — barely.

"I'm allowed one phone call," I said, more insistent, but my volume wouldn't go up.

"This isn't a jail, honey. This is a hospital. Just relax."

I didn't want to, but it was like my thoughts were no more than liquid swishing around in my brain. With that one command from the nurse, my focus slid away.

I'd pictured a better attempt on my part. Yelling Dom's name and clawing my way through the hospital staff, clutching the phone wildly in my bloodied hand, maybe. After which I'd deliver the most eloquent expression of love ever heard by human ear.

What really happened was, I spent my last hour alive . . . dying.

Chapter Two

the bright side of death

For a while — not a time, because time stops working once you're dead — there was nothing. Not blackness or whiteness or emptiness or antimatter. There was just nothing, not even a sense of myself, and at the same time, there was everything. Which might be the same thing. I don't know.

And then I heard voices, echoing but muffled. I was aware, next, of regular, comprehensible darkness, and I panicked, wondering if I'd survived but lost my sight. I was almost relieved when it occurred to me that I couldn't possibly be alive — everything felt different. No adrenaline reaction, just the emotion of fear. No pain, no itches, no need to breathe. There was no heartbeat throbbing in my chest as I worried that I was blind. The emotion was there, but not the hormones. Not the biology. Weird.

I was lying curled up on my side, face pressed against a hard, rough surface, damp from the humid air. At first, I thought there was something strange about the texture, and then realized that, no, it was *me* there was something strange about. Lying on a rock-hard surface didn't *hurt*.

Slowly, I sat up, and I knew, for certain, that I was dead then. With the abdominal wounds I'd suffered in the accident, I doubted I even *could've* sat up, and definitely not without unbearable pain, if I'd still been a living being.

Escaping from all that physical anguish was a relief, and I'd never particularly feared death — not my own, anyway — so I wasn't sure this was altogether a bad situation to be in. On the other hand, I sure hadn't expected to die so young, and it was lousy timing in terms of Dominic and me. All the same, there was a sort of dreamy, drifting calm to my emotions, even the negative ones.

But I couldn't just sit here in the dark — I had to figure out where I was and what was going on.

I picked myself up and squinted. Maybe, after all, it wasn't all blackness, because it looked a bit less black up ahead.

I made my way up a dank, slick stairway, and at the top was the tunnel you always hear about. Yeah. With the light and all at the end.

My frantic pre-death wish hit me all over again. *I need to talk to Dom! I can deal with being dead, but I need to say goodbye first.*

Facing down the blinding whiteness ahead, I willed myself to be pulled back. *Come on, ER people. You're supposed to have the paddles on me now. Somebody's supposed to be yelling, "Clear!" and you're supposed to try again.*

Any moment now.

As long as I didn't walk down the tunnel and see what was at the end, maybe they could still pull me back.

Somewhere there was a heart rate monitor emitting a steady, high-pitched tone, and I just needed it to blip a couple times. All the ER staff working on me would sigh with relief and go home happy they'd saved an extra life today, and I'd lie in a hospital bed semi-conscious for a few days. Dom would come and sit by my bedside and hold my hand. He'd talk to me even though I couldn't hear him. His dad would come with a fifth of whiskey to "get him through it," which Dom's mother would disapprove of, but put up with, distracting herself by fluffing up any flower arrangements people had sent me. And my family would crowd around my bedside and try to console Dominic.

And of course I'd wake up and throw my arms around everyone and I'd apologize to Dom. All would be forgiven and I'd be a lovely, wonderful person forever after.

Right. Cue violin music.

Come on, doctors, do your stuff. Blip, you damned heart rate monitor. Come on, heart — start beating. Breathe, you stupid lung sacks.

I sat down in the tunnel and waited.

People started coming up the stairs, one or two at a time, straggling along through the damp-walled tunnel, glancing curiously at me as they walked past, but no one stopped to talk to me. I was a little surprised when a fox scrambled up the stairway and on into the light, followed eventually by a turtle who plodded past where I sat — but then, I told myself, what's surprising about it? Animals die, too, and they've got to get to the afterlife *somehow*.

The distant voices continued, their number increasing as people moved on through. I'd always kind of expected that you got your own *private* tunnel of white light, but no. Let me tell you, there is nothing private and personal about the passage to the other side. Everybody dies. Everybody is a lot of people, not to mention animals, and they're all coming through sometime.

A twenty-something couple headed past me, clinging to each other as they walked. The guy was holding onto the girl like he could shield her from whatever it was the afterlife held; her head nestled on his shoulder. I turned to watch them pass into the light, then put my head down on my arms and cried.

Even as despair howled out of me, I didn't feel like my death was final. It wasn't exactly hope as much as stubbornness. I didn't *want* to be dead yet, and damned if I was going to stay dead if I didn't want to.

Did Dom know yet? Had he gotten a phone call from the hospital saying I was in critical condition? That I was dead? Did my parents know? My older brother and my younger sister? My niece?

At some point music started. Jazz. Big band. Through my

sobbing I could hear the slide of trombones, led by a sweet, clear clarinet, with a section of trumpets cutting in from time to time, and I wanted to know what the hell was going on beyond the light.

I finally sat back and wiped my cheeks off on the sleeve of my green sweater — my favorite one. Not what I'd been wearing when I died. I stared at my clothes for a moment, then let out a growl.

"Why do I have these clothes on?" I shouted out loud. "This doesn't make any goddam sense!"

"If it upsets you that much, you don't have to keep 'em on." A guy had come in from the bright side of the tunnel, where the music was coming from. He was extremely scruffy, tall and scrawny, and looked to be around forty-five or fifty. He was grinning at me.

"I'm married," I said stiffly.

"You're dead," he pointed out. "So not exactly. Till death do us part, and all that."

"We didn't say that," I said. "We thought it sounded like a disclaimer, so we cut it from the ceremony." I paused, reflecting briefly on the wedding, then pulled my attention back to the present.

"And who the hell are you?" I asked.

"The ferryman's assistant. You're holding us up, you know." He leaned his shoulder against the tunnel wall and pulled a frayed cigar from the jacket of his tweed suit.

"I'm waiting for them to get my heart started again," I said, pointing randomly upward.

In the flare from his lighter, I got a better look at his face as he gave me a pitying smile. He looked younger by ten to fifteen years than I'd first estimated, though with deep laugh lines around his eyes and mouth, and hollowed cheeks. Steel-grey stubble covered the lower half of his face. "It's not that bad this side, you know. You've just gotta let go of the idea that being dead is going to ruin everything for you."

Considering the upbeat tempo of the music beyond the light, and the fact that it sounded like a party was going on, I was inclined to believe him. But. . . .

"That's not why I have to get back."

"Lemme guess." He scrutinized me as he went on. "You have to get back to tell your husband how much he means to you." The tip of his cigar shone a brighter red as he took a drag.

I opened my mouth, closed it again, and looked away.

"You probably said something stupid just before you died. You're young, so you died suddenly and unexpectedly. You didn't get to make up for what you said, and you want to put it right before you go to rest."

I was glad I'd looked away, and had to wipe my cheeks on my sleeves again before I looked back to the ferryman's assistant.

"Am I right?" he asked.

"How do you know all that?" I asked back.

"You don't ferry people across the river as many times as I have without hearing the same story a few times over, or seeing the patterns of which people have what story." He puffed out a big cloud of smoke and chuckled.

"I'm not going to get back, am I?" I said glumly, knowing the answer.

"Nope." Another puff of smoke.

"Is this Hell?"

"Depends," he said with a grin.

"I never believed in Hell," I commented.

"Good, then it won't be Hell."

"How does *that* work?" I asked.

"This is the Underworld, sweetheart. It's what you make it. It's not Heaven or Hell, it's just a place to be for the rest of eternity. You can enjoy it, or you can make yourself miserable. It's up to you." He extended a hand to help me up.

"And you're sure I can't get back?" I asked.

"Not from here." He patted me on the shoulder in a way that wasn't protective enough to be fatherly, but might be the shoulder-pat of an alternate-reality version of Dom's dad, my father-in-law, Rick. But Rick would a hundred percent never flirt with me, unlike this guy. "Come on, before everybody gets too drunk."

"Drunk?" I said, but he smiled instead of answering. The light got brighter as he led me up the tunnel, his cigar smoke wafting around us and smelling surprisingly good, considering how much I had always hated cigars while I was living.

At the threshold, I hesitated, looking back and wondering if I was making the right decision. But what was I supposed to do? I was *dead*, and if there was any way to get back to Dom, I wasn't going to find it sitting around a tunnel for the rest of my afterlife.

I turned around again, facing forward, and stepped outside. The light dispersed, and I stopped in my tracks. This was not what I'd expected.

A twilit beach spread out below me, bordering a broad river. The bank was narrow, with smooth blond sand and a scattering of ferns and palm trees. Tiki torches glowed and flickered in the evening light, and a boardwalk led up to a flat-topped ferry. Most of the newly deceased had already boarded the boat, although there were a few people still on the shore, most of them holding cocktails, shot glasses, or beer bottles. Here and there someone was crying or looking disconsolate, and most of them had someone nearby, talking to them or proffering a drink. A bunch of people were looking over some kind of pamphlet, too, the slick paper gleaming in the dusky light. I didn't see the fox or the turtle — maybe they'd swum across already, or had a special animal boat or something.

The source of the music I'd heard was a band, situated on the flat roof of the ferry. On the deck below, despite how crowded the little vessel was, several people were dancing — including the couple I'd noticed earlier. They were good dancers, I noted, smiling a little at how happy they looked. In a way, it was sad to think they were dead, but they seemed okay with it, and after all, at least they were together. Guess that was their feeling on it, too.

"You'd think some people would have the grace to stop being cheerful at this point," someone muttered nearby. I looked around to see a slim black woman, not much older than myself, glaring at the couple.

I shrugged. "I think they're cute."

She snorted, and the ferryman's assistant laughed and slapped me on the shoulder again, so hard I almost stumbled down the stairway in front of me.

I turned to look back the way I'd come, and received another surprise.

The tunnel I'd just come out of was actually part of a gigantic statue of a three-headed dog. We'd come through the mouth of the head in the middle, which was resting on the stone platform I now stood on.

"Cerberus," I said, and the ferryman's assistant nodded.

"Don't wake him up," he said with a wink, and jogged off down the stairs.

I followed, and almost immediately was handed a beer.

"I hate beer," I said, and somehow a rum and coke appeared in its place.

I stared at the glass in my hand. Well, did I really expect things to be normal? Here I was in the Underworld, and what I was confused about was how I'd gotten the drink I wanted? That really should be the least of my worries, I thought, and took a couple pulls at it.

Whether I liked it or not, the only way I was getting back to Dom was by finding out more about this place and how it worked . . . and I might as well enjoy the perks while I was at it.

I wasn't sure where the ferryman's assistant had gone — probably onto the boat — but I figured he was my best bet at finding out what, exactly, was going on. He seemed like he'd been here a while, long enough to be comfortable with the whole thing. That made him an expert, as far as I was concerned.

A quick squeeze through the crowd didn't turn him up, though, so I picked a spot at the railing and leaned there, staring out across the water and feeling sad for myself.

Somebody handed me a brochure — one of the pamphlets I'd seen people looking at when I first came out of the tunnel — but I'd barely had time to glance down at it when the ferry started moving, floating gently away from the shore.

Well, I was headed onward now, no matter what, I thought, glancing back at the statue of the hellhound Cerberus. It was hard to be too worried, though. Everything was so weird here, and emotions felt so different without their physical side, that it was easy to drift along with everything, the way you would in a dream.

We'd no sooner pulled away from the boardwalk than the ferryman's assistant showed up at my elbow, his cigar having shortened quite a bit since we'd last spoken.

"What's your name, anyway?" I asked.

He rattled out something long and full of consonants.

I looked at him hopelessly as he finished his fifteenth syllable.

He laughed. "You can just call me Anatol."

"I can just about do that," I said. "I'm Erica Flynn."

He tucked his cigar into the corner of his mouth and shook my hand.

"So where are we going?" I asked.

"Across the river Styx, to the city of Hades." He pointed at the brochure I was holding.

Welcome to Hades, the Liveliest City of the Dead! it proclaimed, in big, cheerful block print. There was a photo of a city skyline covered up by bullet-point info about attractions. I couldn't really take any of it in yet. It seemed easier just to talk to Anatol.

"Is it okay that I'm not Greek?" I said. "I mean, am I in the wrong place?"

One corner of his mouth quirked. "Everybody comes here. I'm not Greek, either — I'm Russian."

"You speak really good English," I commented, at which he burst out laughing.

I was getting more than a little annoyed at my ignorance being a source of amusement, and it was between clenched teeth that I said, "What, exactly, is so funny here?"

Anatol stopped laughing, but the creases at the corners of his eyes were taut with the effort as he looked out across the water. "I can't speak a word of English."

"And I can understand you . . . why?" I asked wearily.

"We're not actually speaking, either one of us. You got vocal cords, gorgeous?"

I hadn't really thought about it until he asked, but, well, I didn't seem to have a heartbeat or adrenaline or the capacity to feel pain, and that said pretty clearly to me that I wasn't a physical being anymore. "Well, no, I guess not."

"Everything here is just thought," Anatol explained, confirming my conclusion. "No substance to it at all. We want to communicate, we do it. Looks like talking because that's what we expect. That's what we're used to." He flicked ash into the crystal-clear water and snickered. "Your Russian is very good, though."

"Thanks," I said. "My teachers always said I had a natural talent with languages."

I thought about what he'd said — about substance versus thought — and looked around at my fellow passengers again. "So that explains the drinks and the clothes."

"What? Oh, yeah. Just what's created out of desire or expectation." He perched on the railing, holding on to a support column. "Here's one of the fun things about that. Here, take a drag." Anatol held out his cigar.

"No thanks," I said. "I hate cigars."

"You're not going to hate this one."

I took it and, after a long hesitation, tried it. My concerns about my situation didn't go away, but within seconds I felt totally relaxed. Everything would work out, and there was nothing tasted better than this cigar. It was like inhaling a good mindset rather than poisonous smoke, which wasn't actually smoke and couldn't actually poison me. (The whole nothing-is-really-anything deal was going to take me a while to adjust to.)

"Holy shit," I said placidly.

Anatol watched my response to the cigar with satisfaction. "I told you you'd like it. It's one of *my* cigars. One of the advantages of living in a world made up entirely of thought and sensation is, you can actually experience something as another person would."

"Uh, sure." I ran that one through my head a few times before it clicked. "So what I'm smoking is not an actual cigar. It's *your* experience of what a cigar is."

"Right."

"Cool." I took another drag and sat down on a deck chair that hadn't been there till I wanted one.

"It's a pretty popular pastime down here, sharing how we experience something we like. It's called joy-swapping. We use it for currency, too, so you'd better think up something for yours." He winked, then hopped back down onto the deck. "I should probably get below and see if Charon needs me to do anything before we dock in Hades." He patted me on the shoulder as he passed by. "You can keep the cigar."

I watched the choppy, grey water of the river flowing past, feeling blessedly distanced from my problems, and more than a little curious about what was to come. I'd find out if there was a way back; that was for sure.

But for now, I thought as I took another puff of Anatol's blithe state of mind, death didn't seem too terribly bad. I could get used to this.

Anyway, I had no choice — I had to figure this place out if I was ever going to get back to Dom.

Chapter Three

the future of the recently dead

With Anatol gone about his business, I turned my attention to the brochure. The front cover boasted about parks, museums, the music scene, and restaurants. Wondering what the hell dead people needed restaurants for, I flipped to the inside.

Down about being dead? Don't be! said the heading on the first panel. *Here in the Underworld, you've got nothing to lose.*

Possibly influenced by the buzz of the cigar, I laughed out loud at that.

With no physical needs, now you can focus on doing the things you enjoy most! There was a briefing on joy-swapping and positive thinking, along the lines of what Anatol had told me.

"Well, at least the music's good," someone said, before I read any further.

I shifted my gaze from the brochure, and found that the speaker was the cynical black woman who'd commented on the dancing couple back on the beach.

I nodded, my mouth too full of smoke from Anatol's cigar to answer her verbally. The jazz band on the rooftop of the ferry was still giving the ride across the river Styx a weird Mardis Gras atmosphere, and my troubles were clouded up in a haze from the joy-swapped cigar. "Got good associations with this type of music." Smoke rolled off my tongue with every word.

"Me, too." She extended a hand and I shook it as she told me, "My name's Latrischa Blake."

"Erica Flynn." I took another puff and a long look at my new acquaintance. Smooth skin, crimpy hair down to her shoulders, delicate chin with a strong jaw, dressed sharp in a bright blue satin top.

"So what are you doing here?" I asked.

"Pretty clearly, being dead." Latrischa's tone was sardonic, but her expression was friendly. Well, friendly by her standards.

"Yeah, I get that part," I said. "But I guess what I mean is, how did you die? You look too young to be dead."

"How old are *you*?" she countered.

I laughed. "Fair point. Twenty-nine. You?"

"Twenty-eight."

We shot the bull for a while, speculating (with no accuracy, as we'd soon find out) about what was to come now that we were dead, and my original question got lost in the shuffle. Since Latrischa had, before her demise, expected nothing — literally, nothing — to follow, she was interested as to what we'd find on the far bank.

"What do you think about all this?" I asked, flicking my hand against the "welcome" brochure.

Latrischa pulled a folded-up copy out of her pocket and took a seat next to mine. "I don't know what to think," she said. "It *sounds* pretty good. I'm glad you can still sleep and eat when you're dead." She pointed at a chunk of text in the middle panel.

"Yeah, but what for?" I said. "If you don't need to—"

"Don't you have any favorite foods?" she asked.

"Yeah, I see what you're getting at," I admitted. "And I guess sleeping is comforting sometimes. Supposedly, you'd go crazy if you didn't dream."

"Check this out," she said, pointing to the small print on the back cover. "This thing is put out by the Board of Tourism?"

"Hey, I guess even dead people've got hometown pride." Then I noticed something just below the mini-map with directions to the Board of Tourism's headquarters. *Comments? Questions?*

Concerns? Direct your query to 4611 Lethos Blvd, Department 2, District of Hades, UW.

Interesting. I certainly did have comments, questions, and concerns. Good to know someone was paying attention. As soon as I got my bearings, I could send off a letter, and maybe satisfy some of my curiosity about the Underworld while I waited for an answer. Easy.

The ferry docked just as I finished the cigar Anatol had given me.

We mounted a set of wide wooden stairs — very creaky and weathered to smoothness — which led up to a boardwalk.

The twilight had darkened to starlight, and most of the illumination along the docks was provided by the glittering, blinking lights of what seemed to be a bustling carnival. Snippets of calliope music sounded along the boardwalk, and with them came the scent of flame-roasted meat and greasy, sugary junk food.

I was still under the effects of the cigar, feeling pretty happy-go-lucky about everything, and I have to admit I perked up at the thought of cotton candy.

The ferry passengers, as a group, had stopped moving forward and we all stood there together, staring ahead at the unexpected spectacle before us. Beyond the glimmer and flash and bright but tattered canvas, the city of Hades towered, sloping upward from the riverbank. It was hard to get much of an impression in the little visibility the stars and streetlights provided, except that the city twisted its way up and around the hillside in precise curves, like it had been designed by a geometry teacher with a thing for landscaping. The city and the hill were clutched together in a weird symbiotic look, visually inseparable, like the buildings had grown right out of the ground.

Anatol came up the stairs and moved through the hesitant crowd. He didn't say anything, just glanced back at us huddled there on the boardwalk and grinned before he disappeared into the mass of tents, carts, and people up ahead.

I think we'd all expected to be guided *to* somewhere, and it was sinking in now that we were just being dropped off. The brochures had explained some of the basics, but still — there were no instructions, no right or wrong way to start out, no judgment, no to-do list for the afterlife. Weren't there any rules here? Laws? Crimes and punishments?

Freedom is a terrifying thing to adjust to.

Latrischa and I shrugged at each other.

"Are we supposed to wait here for someone?" I heard a woman ask.

Somebody else responded in a whisper, "Wait for what? Wait for who?"

I pictured myself standing there on the pier waiting to be fetched like a child by some bearded guy in a white robe, who'd then tell me if I'd been a good girl or a bad girl, and I'd presumably feel pleased with myself or bow my head in shame. It gave me the itch to be irreverent.

"If God shows up," I said jauntily, "tell him he can find me on the carousel." I followed Anatol into the busy carnival grounds, feeling the others watching me as I slipped away into the thrum of the crowd.

It was so much brighter beside the tents that everything outside the grounds just looked black. I was surrounded by color and music and people and movement, and I got sort of a rush from being immersed in it — the kind of thrill I'd always associated with feeling the most alive. I almost forgot that I wasn't.

Carnies yelled for attention from passersby, rides blared music, the rhythmic thud of a nearby ski ball setup thundered away.... I wandered through, marveling at how simultaneously normal and strange it all was.

I found out quickly that Anatol had been right about currency in the Underworld. I watched people trade chocolate bars or homemade-looking gingerbread men, and in one case what looked like an empty bottle, for elephant ears or their passage onto rides. I figured I could probably do it, as I'd made myself a rum-and-coke earlier. It was definitely better than working for money. I watched from a few feet away as the carnie opened up the "empty" bottle and held it below his nose, inhaling deeply. In the faint breeze, I caught the slightest whiff of it myself — the smell of the ocean. Not some skanky, polluted beach, either, but the pure, clean scent of warm sand and saltwater on the wind, with a faint musky undercurrent of seaweed. It smelled both peaceful and energetic, like a weight lifted from the shoulders, like you could just lift anchor and escape into the elements forever.

The carnie nodded to himself as he screwed the lid back down on the bottle, and tucked it into his coat pocket. I moved on, wondering what I could use for my own personal currency.

Anatol was standing in line a few tents away. He noticed me, and waved me over.

"How are you liking the carnival?" he called out as I headed in his direction.

I didn't answer until I was standing next to him. "I've just been walking through," I told him. "Just scoping things out."

"Don't like carnivals?"

"I love carnivals, I'm just a little. . . ." I stopped. How *was* I feeling about everything? Was I okay with being dead now, just because of a cigar and a few rides and booths? I wanted to get back, and there was some part of me that was confident I'd find a way to do it. Not sure how or when, but I was whole-heartedly counting on it. It was the only reason I was feeling remotely okay right now. And what if there *wasn't* a way back?

"Conflicted?" Anatol suggested.

"Very." I looked up at the tent we were standing outside of as the person in front of us ducked inside. It was a fortune-teller's tent. I couldn't help but laugh. "What the hell do the dead need a fortune-teller for? I mean, what can she say, 'You're going to have a long, successful afterlife'?"

"Find out for yourself." Anatol winked and ducked into the tent, leaving me standing there unsure what to do with myself. So I stood and waited my turn. I'd always liked fortune-tellers and tarot cards, although I didn't put much stock in them. I had a bit of a superstitious streak — more because it was a neat idea than because I believed in it — but mine was nothing compared to Dominic's. Dom read his horoscope the moment he woke up. Really.

He'd stumble out of bed, unshaven and bleary-eyed, throw on a bathrobe and slippers, and sit on the stoop with the paper, thumbing through it to the back few pages. That early in the morning, Dom mutters out loud when he reads and follows the print with his finger. Through the doorway, he'd yell across the house to me what his horoscope had to say, then what mine said, then his parents', then my entire family's. Somewhere around midway through mine, I'd give up on trying to fall back asleep and head for the kitchen to make coffee. I could hear him better from in there anyway.

About the time I'd set the coffee on the table and start buttering our toast, he'd stumble back inside and join me in the kitchen, paper still in hand. "Thanks for the coffee," he'd say (every morning, as if I didn't always make it, as if it surprised him it was there), and he'd kiss me on the cheek and set out every flavor of jam in the fridge.

That was our morning routine.

And, to get back to the point, Dom was the superstitious one, and he loved fortune-tellers. On one of our first dates, in fact, we'd gone to a little carnival we just so happened to spot on the way to dinner, and we took turns going in to hear about our respective futures. He came out looking quite pleased with himself, and it wasn't until much later, when we were on our honeymoon, that he finally explained why. "She told me that the green-eyed girl I'd recently met would agree to marry me within the year, and that you and I were soul mates."

"Dom, she'd just told *my* fortune," I said. "She probably overheard us talking and knew we were together, and then when I saw her she hinted about an engagement and I got all stupid and giggly. She knew because of the way I reacted, not because she's psychic."

"Oh, so you got giggly about me?" Dom grinned ear to ear, and I stuck my tongue out at him and then snuggled up closer to him on the couch.

Thinking back on all this was getting me down again, so I was relieved for the distraction of a woman's voice calling me into the tent.

It was dimly illuminated with wavering candlelight, with a cloth-draped table in the center. On the opposite side of the table sat a woman of about thirty-five, round-faced and a bit pudgy, but not unpleasantly so. She was covered in spangles and glitter, and dressed in dark colors — possibly plum and navy, but it was too dark to be sure. She wasn't what I'd pictured beforehand, being on the younger and heftier side of my expectations. Also, she seemed surprisingly pleasant and warm-natured. I'd anticipated doom and gloom and sunken cheeks above a grim, thin-lipped mouth.

"Sit down," she suggested, extending a glittery hand toward the upholstered armchair opposite her.

I sat.

She looked at me with interest, but didn't speak.

"Well," I said. "Tell me my future, then."

She smiled and shuffled her cards, then held the deck out for me to cut.

I did so, and returned them to her.

She turned over a card. I didn't recognize her deck, and in the dim light I couldn't see the card well enough to make out which one it was. I wasn't any good at interpreting the Tarot anyway, that being one of Dominic's areas of expertise. All I could tell was that the picture was a photograph, not a painting or drawing, of a towering black building, windowless and asymmetrical.

"I see that you miss someone very much," she said.

"Well, duh," I said. If I'd still had blood, I'd have flushed as soon as I said it. "Sorry. Rude, I know. Sorry. It's just . . . wouldn't anybody coming through have somebody they miss? I mean, we've all just died and left everybody we know behind."

"Not everyone." She smiled. "Some of the people you know and love are here in the Underworld. That's one of the nice things about being dead."

I hadn't quite thought of that yet, which made me feel silly — and excited, too. My favorite uncle, Jeff, had died about seven years before me, when I was twenty-two. I'd been in college at the time, working toward my bachelor's in history.

He'd left his house to me, as my brother and sister and I were his only younger relatives, and my siblings — even though my sister was my junior by three years — were more established in the world (i.e., more prone to success). I was the one who needed a leg up, in other words. He explained it this way in his will, anyhow. I secretly believed it was because I was his favorite, too.

The fortune-teller returned her attention to the card.

I listened as she guessed a few specifics right — not much more than Anatol had figured out, with the exception that she pegged Dom's hair color (black).

She turned another card. At first, I thought the second photo was of a pair of black horses drawing a chariot, but when I took a closer look, it was a glossy black car — a modernized antique sports car, the kind of thing you see at fairground shows. How I'd gotten horses out of that, I had no idea.

"You will embark upon a long journey down a dangerous road," she told me.

"Bit late for that, isn't it?" I said, trying (really, I was) not to sound or look like I felt (which was along the lines of, "Help me, I've walked into a cliché.")

She gave me another knowing smile, and turned another card.

And then she burst out laughing. Her whole air of mysterious omniscience disappeared, and she just laughed delightedly without stopping. There was a mischievous glint in her eye when she looked up at me again, still clutching her side. What was creepy was, meeting her gaze now, I really did feel like she knew me. Like she understood exactly what sort of person I was, down to my core, and she hadn't had to get to know me to find it out. It would've made my skin crawl if I'd still been physical.

"What's all that about?" I asked, trying to sound undisturbed by the abrupt change of tone. Even *I* recognized the card she'd turned over — the Ace of Wands — although I had no idea what it meant. Like the rest of her deck, it was a photo, the wand a wood-and-bronze walking staff, leaned against a bookshelf.

"I know what's going to happen," she said. "Don't worry, it favors you. I just like your style, that's all."

"Uh, thanks," I said, wondering what I was supposed to do, at some point in the future, stylishly enough to merit such roguish and exuberant laughter.

"I'll just be going then," I said, hopping out of my chair and scooting it up a few inches closer to the table. "Glad things are going to go well for me. Thanks."

"I'll be seeing you again, Erica," the fortune-teller said to my retreating back.

"Okay, then. See you," I called from the side exit.

Anatol was standing there waiting for me.

"How'd it go?" he asked.

"Weird," I said, pointing my thumb back over my shoulder. I forced a lighthearted laugh. "Don't put much faith in that kind of stuff."

"Come on, long-legs." Anatol pulled at my sleeve. "I'll show you how to buy cotton candy."

Chapter Four

a great place to be dead

"Food's the easiest thing to use for your joy-swapping," Anatol told me. "Unless, of course, you have any addictions." He grinned and held up one of his unlit cigars, then tucked it away again. "It has to be something you absolutely *love*. An individual, tangible item, mind you, unless you want to go work in the red light district."

"There's a red light district in the city of the *dead*?" I said.

"I told you it wasn't Hell." He winked. "Now, think of something you can actually hand out that's one of your all-time favorite things. Better if you have emotional associations with it, too."

"Like how cigars relax you?" I asked.

Anatol nodded. "Once you decide on something, concentrate on *wanting* it. Then you'll have it. Easy as that."

"Okay. . . ." I paced in front of the concession stand while the guy behind the counter traded his wares with other souls. Anatol was right — food-based items were the most common — but there were other frequently used themes, too. Scents, for one. The "empty bottle" method was one way of transferring an aroma, and then there were some people who handed smells over via incense or scented candles, or perfume or cologne spray bottles. One guy handed over a sandwich bag full of either cocaine or powdered sugar (I assumed cocaine) in exchange for popcorn and soda. Now and then there was artwork or a CD. Anatol waited patiently on a bench nearby, shuffling a deck of playing cards.

Food definitely seemed the easiest to me, and I needed to figure out currency whether I was stuck here or not. I might have to buy information from someone, or pay a toll to get through the gates of the Underworld — who knew? I thought hard about toasted marshmallows, then did as Anatol had instructed, and found that I had one in my hand.

He jumped up when he saw me holding it. "Good! Here, let me try it."

I handed it over.

"Not bad." He didn't sound impressed, but he smiled encouragingly. "Try it again, though. It *tastes* like you like it, but I'm not getting the emotional factor."

Camping trips, I thought, working on the next attempt. My brother teaching me how to get the marshmallow toasted just right without burning it when we were kids. Uncle Jeff taking us hiking on the weekends. Me taking Dom on the same trails, years later, trying to show him a little of what I'd grown up with and lost with the death of my uncle. Dom and me snuggled up by the campfire, and me trying to teach *him* how not to burn the marshmallows.

"Try this one." I held it out to Anatol, who popped it into his mouth in one bite.

"Ahhhh, there you go!" he said slowly, around the marshmallow. "That's definitely getting there. Keep putting those associations in, and you'll have it down for good."

"What do you get out of it?" I asked, curious.

"It tastes like . . . growing up," Anatol said. "A little sadness in there, but that's okay. It heightens the sweet feelings. Good work." He stood up and put an arm around my shoulders, guiding me toward the stand.

"Now, try it again, and we'll have some cotton candy."

~*~

The glories of the dockside carnival, once my curiosity overcame my love of the Ferris wheel and the ski ball booth, led on into Main Street. It was dark, but streetlights kept Hades fogged in an orange glow. Anatol had returned to the ferry, but we'd agreed to meet back at the carnival once I'd had a look around the city.

In downtown Hades, shops and shrines and bars and music halls jumble together around larger, grander buildings whose contents seem to constantly change — sort of museum-ish, except the exhibits shift around of their own accord when you aren't looking, and nobody staffs them. There's just stuff *there*: paintings and sculptures and books and scrolls. Wall displays full of information that change according to what you're thinking about. The wall displays are my personal favorite. If there were such things as hours in the Underworld, I would've spent them there, in front of those gently-glowing screens.

When I was a kid and still believed in Heaven, they asked us in Sunday school what we thought it would be like. I didn't volunteer my answer, but what I really thought was that, in Heaven, since they said you were one with God once you got there, you'd know everything God knew. You'd have God's omniscience. I was going to know everything, understand everything. How fantastic was that going to be?

By the time of my death, I wasn't expecting God or Heaven anymore. I don't know what I'd expected. Not what I got, that's for sure, although I'm not complaining.

Even without Heaven, though, I had the wall displays. That was as close to omniscience as I wanted.

My first encounter with them was at the Board of Tourism — one of the first places I checked out after leaving the carnival.

Following the mini-map on the back of the brochure, I left Main Street to cross Third and Fourth Streets. Both blocks were taken up entirely by the main library, with four glassed-in walkways bridging the street between the two sections. The sheet-glass windows would've looked perfectly modern, except that they were surrounded by stone gargoyles, big granite columns, cathedral spires, and Latin mottoes carved into the building. Frank

Lloyd Wright meets Edgar Allan Poe, I thought.

On my walk, I passed other pedestrians on their way from one place to another, talking, laughing, griping, singing in slurred voices . . . like any normal city, really. Not that many cars, though, I noticed. There were plenty of cabs around, and I spotted an el station near the library, so maybe here, like in New York, it was easier to get around with public transportation than to deal with the hassles of traffic. Although, looking around, I realized there weren't any traffic lights. No stop signs, crosswalks, speed limit postings. Sweet. Now I'd *have* to try driving here sometime.

From the corner of Fourth and Osiris Streets, I could see the roundabout pictured on the map, with the Board of Tourism in the center — an octagonal brick tower bordered by colorful flowerbeds and a circular green lawn. Its sign, at the entry to the brick-paved parking area, was in the same cheerful block lettering as the brochure front.

Inside, the displays covered the eight walls of the building, although at first I thought they were flat screen televisions. An octagonal wooden case of slick pamphlets for individual venues stood in the middle of the room, and a kiosk nearby was staffed by a middle-aged lady and a guy in his late thirties.

The lady was busy talking to an old Indian couple at the desk, but the guy, sandy-haired and clean-shaven, hurried over to greet me.

"Hi, welcome to Hades!" he said. His words were rapid-fire, but with a twang and a Carolina drawl. He had a boyish face, with wide-set eyes that took the swagger out of his confident handshake. He immediately struck me as the kind of person who can smile all day at one stranger after another, and be genuine about it *every time*. His nametag labeled him *Ben*. "Are you visitin' from another city, or recently deceased?"

"I — what do you mean, 'another city'?" I glanced at the brochures in the stand by the kiosk, and noticed a few of the titles that I'd missed at first. *Nilfhelm, Mashu, Nirvana, Vaitarani. . . .*

Names of underworlds — I recognized them easily. My senior thesis for my history degree had been on world mythology.

"Recently deceased," Ben said, nodding to himself. He smiled sympathetically. "I know, it's all *really* confusin' at first. But that's what the Board of Tourism is here for!" He gestured broadly at the screens and brochures, then laid his hand over his own chest. "I'm sure you have quite a few questions. So ask me!"

I had a *million* questions, and then again, only one I desperately wanted the answer to. But it might be best to warm up to that one, get a feel for how helpful this guy was underneath the welcoming-committee smile.

"Well, to start with," I said slowly, "I get the whole business with having whatever you want, in a way, and everything down here being created out of wishes and expectations. But . . . there are some messed up people in the world. Doesn't that make it kind of dangerous down here?"

He'd obviously heard the question before, and the left corner of his mouth twisted up. "You're not takin' into account two *very* important details. One is, you are *never* in danger here. You left that behind with your mortality. There can't very well be physical danger to a person with no physical body, after all, now can there?"

"But there are things about this place that are still . . . well, that follow certain physical rules." I thought of my own tears in the tunnel when I'd first arrived, and of Anatol's arm around my shoulders, guiding me through the carnival. That had definitely *felt* physical, in a weird, detached way — like how my feelings were still there, but not the hormones that accompanied them. "If someone can, say, touch my shoulder," I said, "why couldn't they smack me one, or something? I can see how dead people are safe from being murdered, but. . . ."

"Easier just to demonstrate," Ben said, and before I could react, he'd grabbed a baseball bat from somewhere and swung at me.

I yelled, cringing away from the blow. But no contact came,

and when I looked up, I was a few feet away from where I'd been standing next to Ben.

"Ben!" The middle-aged lady jerked around from her conversation with the shocked, wide-eyed Indian couple. "I *wish* you'd refrain from alarming the tourists!"

"Sorry, Helen." Ben grinned, shrugging. "Simplest way to get the point across."

She turned back to her couple, trying to regain their attention and get them relaxed again.

"Okay." I eyed Ben warily. "Now tell me *why* that happened."

"Your desire was to avoid the bat," he said.

"Yeah, but I *expected* to get hurt," I shot back.

"But your desire *not* to get hurt outweighed your expectation that you would."

"What if it hadn't?" I asked, a little indignant.

"Trust me, it does with ninety-nine percent of the people down here." He leaned the baseball bat against the brochure case.

"What's with the one percent? Masochists?" I stepped back toward him now that he was unarmed again.

Ben nodded.

"Well, how did you know *I* wouldn't get hurt?" I demanded.

"I was just guessin', to be honest." Ben chuckled. "I've got pretty good instincts about people."

"You said earlier that there were two factors to why screwed-up people don't screw up the Underworld," I said. "What's the second one?" Now that I'd started asking questions, I couldn't help being curious — and curious beyond what was strictly necessary to returning to life.

"Consensual reality," Ben said. "You got a whole lotta people down here who think of the ground rules of bein' dead as bein' one way. There are people who think differently, an' different cities have slightly different ways of workin'. Even right here in Hades, there *is* sort of a spectrum of experiences. So much depends on the balance between consensual reality and individual wants and expectations."

"So sometimes a person can overcome consensual reality, if they want something badly enough?" At last, we were getting around to the point — and quite smoothly, too, I thought happily. This was the kind of stuff I'd been hoping for.

"Depends how far out the person's wishes are, and whether anyone around them wishes just as hard *against* their desires." Ben looked at me quizzically. "Why?"

"I was just wondering if anyone can *leave* here, if they want to badly enough."

Helen shot us a filthy look, and I realized she'd overheard. Ben quickly turned away from her, made a weird face and put a finger to his lips.

He waited until she was involved in her conversation with the Indian couple again before he answered me, his voice hushed. "Well, there's always the other cities, although, personally, Hades will always be home to me."

"No, I meant, leave the Underworld."

"Oh, the Atheists' Graveyard," he said, quieter still, looking nervously at Helen. She was still talking to the couple, but glaring at me.

I filed the reference to the Atheists' Graveyard away as "something to find out about, but which doesn't help right now, so let's not get off-track."

"No, no, no." Taking his cue, I lowered my voice, but I knew I was still talking too loud. Hope and excitement and frustration seemed to up the volume, no matter how hard I tried to be quiet. "I mean, leave the Underworld and be *alive* again."

"Darlin', when you're dead, you're dead." Ben's voice was suddenly gentle. He darted a worried glance at Helen. "That ain't gonna happen."

I sighed. "I'm getting that answer a lot."

"Sooner you accept it, the sooner you'll see what the Underworld has to offer." Ben smiled kindly, perking up as something occurred to him. "How 'bout I show you the information panels? You can take a look around the city quick that way, maybe get you excited about bein' here." He looked over at Helen like he was emphasizing to her that he was doing his best to bring me around about death.

"Okay," I said, but then stopped him. "Can I ask you something personal, first?"

"Go ahead." He squirmed a little. "But nothin' about skippin' town, okay? Helen's defensive as a mother bear about this city, hates anyone who hates it here. An' believe you me, she'll take it out on *me* if she gets in one of her *moods*. She's either sweet as an angel or mean as a snake, an' I like her better as an angel."

"Why *are* you here?" I asked. "I mean, you *personally* — why are you working here, when nobody has to have jobs anymore once they're dead? Especially," I whispered, "if you have such a mean co-worker?"

"Me?" Ben laughed. "That's easy. About Helen, well, she's a doll, long as you don't cross her, and for the most part we see eye to eye. As to workin' here, couple reasons, actually. One, I *love* this city. It's the best place I've ever called home, and I moved around *a lot* when I was alive. Two, I believe in helpin' other people. Always have, but never had the time, topside. Too busy tryin' to make ends meet."

"That's an admirable philosophy," I said, and I meant it, "but don't you care what *you* get out of your afterlife?"

"I don't lose anythin' by comin' here and explainin' things to new folks. I'm here forever, so why not make the Underworld better for everyone? I *do* get something out of that." He looked so earnest it almost made me believe humans could be inherently good creatures.

I smiled. "You're a nice guy, Ben," I said. "Now, you want to show me those info thingies?"

~*~

What impressed me about the wall screens wasn't their size or clarity or even *how much* information seemed to be available through them. What got me was that they were thought-responsive.

Initially, as Ben explained it to me and left me to my own devices, I couldn't help wondering about the other cities in the Underworld.

The screen popped up maps, aerial photographs, and columns and columns of text as I stood there.

Too much to take in, I thought, and things shifted around into a more organized layout — names of cities with branch-off thumbnail images and drop-down menus.

Cool. I wondered about the Atheists' Graveyard, and the thumbnail for it filled up the screen. A panoramic view of a ghost town: empty streets and buildings reduced to mere skeletons, tufts of grass growing up through floorboards and rows and rows of gravestones. I must've speculated about the stones, because text popped up across part of the sky in the photograph.

Like an elephants' graveyard in the Upper World, the Atheists' Graveyard is the place to which firm non-believers migrate in order to cease all existence. Well outside the influence of any other city's reality, the town is ideal for anyone who wishes, after death, to continue to disbelieve in an afterlife. Here, those who wish for the complete nothingness they were expecting beyond the grave can slip peacefully into nonexistence forever, with only a stone to show their passing, as it was when they left the World Above.

Okay, I thought, not going vacationing there. The screen went back to the overview of all the cities, flickering as I realized that wasn't what I wanted to know at all. What I wanted to know was how to get back to Dom. How to be alive again.

The screen went bright red and flashed searing white letters. *BLOCKED! Information request invalid!*

Helen was at my elbow then, so close I could smell her

flowery perfume. Up close, I could see deep frown lines between her eyes, although she also had pretty heavy laugh lines around her mouth. She was tiny, maybe not even five foot, but her anger was intimidating in its intensity. "I suggest," she said, in a clipped, precise voice, "if you can't think of anything better to do with your afterlife than try to get out of it, that you stick with the Atheists' Graveyard."

"Look, it's not that I don't like it here." Thankfully the red screen went away. "I think this city seems pretty cool, actually. I just want to get back to my husband, that's all."

She looked at me like I'd just peed on her shoe, and marched away without another word.

"I warned ya," Ben said, coming over. He shook his head. "I'm tellin' you, darlin', there's no way back once you get here. But if you're determined to look, this is not the only place with these information panels. The library's got plenty, and there's no angry Helen lookin' over your shoulder."

I nodded. "I get the hint. Get out of here and stop pissing her off."

Ben laughed, and I grinned back nervously. He'd been awfully nice about everything, and I felt bad I'd put him in a lousy position with his co-worker. "I wouldn'ta put it that way, but. . . ." He shrugged. "Take my advice. Look up somethin' more *cheerful* on the library's displays. Find out a little more about the city. The sooner you let go of the Land of the Livin', the sooner you'll be happy."

"I can't do it." I pulled out the brochure that had led me here in the first place, pointed to the address on the back. "It says to write to this address if I have questions. Where *is* this address? It isn't here, is it?"

Ben shook his head. "Not here. We take letters, when people want to send 'em, although usually we can answer most anythin' your average new arrival wants to know."

"But you don't know where the letters go once they're sent

off?" I asked.

"I don't, darlin', I apologize."

"Let me write one before I go, anyway," I said. "Then I'll get out of your hair."

Ben agreed and left me with a pen, paper, and an envelope at the desk. He assured me that stamps weren't required in the Underworld, and that until I was set up in a place of my own in Hades, the Board of Tourism would serve as my return address.

Helen had a new set of dead people to take care of, so she stayed away while I worked on my letter.

I stated my plea to be allowed to return to life, trying to make it as much of a tearjerker as possible. When I was satisfied that it was polite, well-stated, and succinct, I took the sealed envelope over and asked Ben where to put it.

"Mailbox is by the parkin' lot." He held the door open for me and pointed. "Good luck with your afterlife, darlin', and drop by again if you need any fu'ther assistance."

"Unless it'll piss Helen off," I said with a little grin.

"Ha, well, in that case, let me know you're gonna piss her off, an' we'll step out for coffee while you ask me your unorthodox questions." Ben winked, and I posted my letter. It'd been a long time since I'd written an actual letter — I was way more used to e-mails and faxes than paper mail — but somehow, it felt more satisfying. As if I were more likely to get a reply to this thing I was dropping off rather than just clicking a button. Or maybe I was just hoping harder for answers than I ever had when I was alive.

Chapter Five

a minister, a reverend, and a priest walk into a bar . . .

Hades, capitol city of the twilight realm on the far side of the river Styx. New York City of the Underworld.

It sprawls, massive, across the fields and hills along the river, bustling in places, ghost-town empty in others, but nonetheless managing to house, entertain, and for the most part satisfy over five billion souls. Most of the departed feel more comfortable in the big city, as if we're afraid we'll fade away if nobody's around to hear our voices or see us walking down the street.

On the outskirts, little communities do their thing. Beyond that, the wild. Animals laze in the tall grass, flit through the thick tangle of trees, tussle in the sunlight. In the city, it's always some shade of twilight, but out in the wild, there are places where it's always day, others where it's always night, and the roads to other Underworld cities pass through, ignored by the animals. They lie on the roads and sleep unhindered.

There are souls who reside out there, generally because they don't want other people screwing up their afterlife, and I can't say I didn't think about joining them. Leaving behind consensual reality definitely has an appeal.

On the other hand, Hades is a great place to be dead.

I'd taken Ben's advice and used the library's screens to find out more about the city. With my letter posted, I felt like I could relax a little, take a look around. If I got what I wanted, then this would be my only opportunity to experience the afterlife until I died again (which, I hoped, would be when I was really old). Dom would want to know everything about this place — I could picture how excited he'd be if we were here together. Of course, that was a mixed bag for me: awful to be apart from him, awful to think even fleetingly about him being dead so young, and at the same time heartbreakingly sweet to imagine his enthusiasm and sense of wonder if he knew about Hades.

So, I had told myself, I might as well explore a little while I waited for answers.

Latrischa and I had sort of latched on to each other since our trip on the ferry. We'd picked up a regular bar — The Dead Man's Chest — and a couple of drinking buddies, including Anatol. Since being dead hadn't answered more than ten percent of my philosophical questions, there was more than enough to bullshit about at the bar.

Heaven was a subject of regular debate in the Underworld. It surprised me at first, hearing people arguing over metaphysical stuff. I guess I'd figured, well, here we are in the great Unknown, and now we Know. So what's there to speculate about?

Not everybody felt that way, though.

The depressed minister who, along with Latrischa and me, frequented The Dead Man's Chest (and who seemed to be permanently in a state of bitter and loud-spoken drunkenness) would sit in the corner and groan out his list of reasons for believing that we were, in fact, in Hell. To him, maybe, it was Hell — when we couldn't get him to shut up, some nights, it certainly was to the rest of us.

Sad thing was, it really did seem like a cloud hung over the guy, or like trouble went out of its way to find him. I suspected it had to do with the fact that he *expected* the worst of everything, like a self-fulfilling prophecy in its most tangible form.

He had a couple buddies, one a Catholic priest and one a reverend from some other denomination, who liked to sit with him and debate. The priest thought we were all in Purgatory, paying off our debt for bad behavior until we'd been purified enough to move up the ladder to Heaven. The reverend thought we were already there.

"Look at it this way," he'd tell the other two. "Here, there's no such thing as money or even ownership, and no need for law because there is no crime. The lion and the lamb, out in the wild, sleep side by side without disturbing one another."

"That was supposed to happen in the Rapture," the depressive minister muttered into his glass.

The reverend waved a hand dismissively.

It was true that nobody owned anything. It didn't much matter since everything was made up of concepts and wishes and thoughts and expectations. We all had places we lived, but they weren't physical places. The same people could occupy the same home without ever even seeing one another, in theory. Space and form, like time, were irrelevant here.

It was also true that there wasn't any crime, because if you can't steal or forge or cheat people out of their stuff, the only thing left to do to them is hurt them — which, as Ben had neatly demonstrated to me, was physically impossible. Even verbal abuse was, to some degree, non-viable, since if you affected someone's emotions badly enough, they'd just stop seeing you and hearing you — essentially *willing* you out of their perception. You'd still exist, sure, but not to the person you'd upset. Eventually, you'd fade back into the person's awareness, as they became less averse to your presence, but you wouldn't stay there long if you upset them again.

If only that had been the case in junior high. . . .

No matter how hard I fought against it, I'd settled pretty comfortably into the afterlife. I kept telling myself I was just waiting for an answer to my letter, but I knew better. The fact is, being dead felt *great*.

The permanent buzz of invulnerability, not having a weak

physical frame weighing you down, being able to shift your surroundings to suit your whims, and having control over nearly everything that could adversely affect your experience of the world — that kind of power and freedom is hard to beat. The feel of a never-ending vacation, doing only what you want to do and never getting bored of it . . . well, that's a perk, too, to say the least.

And no matter how much stuff I looked through in the library, in books and in the info screens, I couldn't find anything about how to get out of the Underworld. Maybe it really couldn't be done, I finally admitted to myself one evening, looking out over the view of the river from the library's fifth-floor window. The clouds were purple and orange, streaked with gold in a slow sunset, the Styx like a river of fire with the reflected colors. There were worse places to be stuck forever, I told myself, but it didn't take away from the emptiness of Dom's absence.

I had a residual nagging urge to find some way to communicate with him, but there were plenty of distractions keeping me from full-fledged desperation.

You'd be surprised at the extensive collection of art and literature the dead produce. Physical buildings couldn't hold it all. Restaurants serve cuisine limited only by the chef's imagination, architects dream up buildings with no constraints of cost or weight issues, and (Latrischa's favorite) fashion designers come up with elaborate outfits that pay no heed to gravity or "what if the wind blows" issues. There's plenty to explore in Hades, and beyond the city limits, where the wild takes over . . . well, there's more than enough to keep an active mind from dulling. I had to admit, as far as being dead went, this was definitely a sweet setup.

The only thing that upset me about the afterlife — aside from being unable to visit the living — was the fact that, on the few occasions when I decided to sleep, I dreamed memories. Bits and pieces of my life would re-play while I slept, and I'd wake up frustrated and confused, halfway sure I'd never died, and with the disconcerting feeling of deja vu.

~*~

I dreamed about the last weekend of college, when my housemate and I decided, on the spur of the moment, to go on this road trip and got stranded when her car broke down. It was almost midnight, we were in a bad neighborhood in Philadelphia, both close to broke, and neither of us had told our parents we were making the trip. We stayed in the car, looking through the manual, and reached the conclusion that whatever was wrong with it wasn't anything we could fix, nor was it anything we could afford, even pooling our money.

"What do we do now?" I asked, as some guys started banging on the window of the car, yelling for us to get out. They were laughing, joking around, but that didn't mean things wouldn't get unpleasant. I shook my head at them and pretended to be calling someone on my cell phone. They backed off.

In the end we called my older brother, Tyler, to come rescue us. He ribbed me about it for a while, but he didn't rat me out.

And I dreamed, too, about the time Dad took us to the Museum of Historical Arms and Armor, and Tyler spent the whole time glued to his Game Boy. He was ten, I was eight. My little sister, Laura, was five, and alternated between fussing and wiping her nose on the hem of her dress, despite Dad's best efforts at the use of tissues.

Dad's enthusiasm put me in awe, though. I stared at everything with him, not speaking at first, just trying to see whatever *he* saw in all that metal and wood, blades and gun barrels and chain mail and helmets. I'd seen photos in books, watched Dad pore over volumes of Medieval and Renaissance art or history — the plague and the Crusades, inventions and modernizations — and the previous summer he and Uncle Jeff had taken Tyler and me to a Renaissance festival to see craftsmen and swordfights, period costume and old-fashioned, campfire-roasted food.

I'd been intrigued by them, too, but seeing the real deal, all the ornate detail that someone had put such care into so many years and decades and *centuries* ago. . . . I was staring at the etching on a humongous broadsword — taller than me, at that age. The thing should've seemed clunky, unwieldy, awkward. But it didn't. Light played across the surface like sunlight on water, the etched vines around the hilt and down the center of the blade rough and glittering. My brain suddenly added two experiences together and I felt I could sense the man who'd done this work all that time ago, just as if he were standing there with us.

I pictured him: a big, brawny guy you'd never expect to create something as delicate as those vines — and were those tiny star-shaped flowers, tucked between the leaves? — carefully adding each delicate, natural curve of the etching. His eyes intent on his work, he didn't know how his lips pressed together in concentration, or how I could see in his face the feeling he had for this piece he was creating.

At that point I also knew that I was projecting what I'd seen of Uncle Jeff at the piano, Uncle Jeff working on the little abstract statues he carved, Uncle Jeff tending to the wounded wildlife he often took in for the conservation program at the forestry division where he worked.

I smiled at Dad, who was watching me, like he knew something had happened in my mind, my way of thinking.

I woke up not knowing where I was at first, reaching for my dad's hand. I couldn't put my finger on why these dreams troubled me so much — they weren't terrible memories — and not knowing why bothered me even more.

"Everyone has those kinds of dreams in the Underworld sometimes," Anatol assured me when I talked to him about it at the Dead Man's Chest. "Especially people who haven't gotten used to being dead. The less attached you are to the Land of the Living, the rarer those dreams get."

"But I don't *want* to be less attached to the Land of the

Living," I objected. "I want to *be* in the Land of the Living."

Anatol shrugged, his expression sympathetic but helpless. "Then you'll keep having dreams that upset you."

"What about my letter?" I'd checked back with the Board of Tourism over and over, even after I gave them the address of my Underworld home, but they hadn't received any mail for me, and I'd gotten nothing at my place. "I haven't had an answer yet. You really don't have any idea where they go?"

"If I did, I'd tell you," Anatol assured me.

"I wonder if that woman at the Board of Tourism is hiding my mail or something," I said.

"You sound paranoid," Latrischa commented.

I didn't grace that with a response. "I've got to find some way back to the Upper World."

"Face it, hon." Latrischa gently squeezed my arm. "You're dead. Enjoy it." It was good advice, and I did *try* to take it.

I'd found myself a little niche, a house near the main library, just a few blocks from the Dead Man's Chest. It was nothing elaborate or large — a living room with a tiny kitchenette in one corner and a hallway that led to a small bedroom and a bathroom. Eventually the toilet disappeared from the bathroom, because I neither needed nor wanted the experiences that necessitated using it. The bathtub stayed, as did the bottles of fancy bath supplies. At first it seemed weird, finding a house and settling into it without paying for it. There was no one to buy it from, since nobody owned it. It was just somewhere safe and comfortable to be when I didn't want to be anywhere else — comfortable by my standards meaning a lot of floofy cushions, an enormous floppy couch, and a bean bag chair. It seemed to favor a red-and-teal, jewel-tone palette. My mom would have politely described it as "a bit loud", but it suited me fine.

Latrischa took in my eclectic pseudo-Asian-hippie decor with approval, which surprised me. "Like the colors," she said, as if she begrudged the compliment.

We headed to the bar together, walking in silence at first. I thought about Latrischa's comment on my new home — or rather, about Latrischa herself. "What did you do when you were alive? For a living, I mean?"

"I painted houses for rich assholes." Latrischa stared straight ahead, sounding bored with the topic. "You?"

"I had a bachelor's in history," I said.

"Yeah? What'd you do with that?" she asked.

I laughed. "Kept it in a drawer and worked at the zoo gift shop."

"I was an art major. Shows what good an education will do you."

I got the feeling she was uncomfortable, like the emotional equivalent of a static charge was building up between us. Sometimes I felt like I knew Latrischa really well already, and other times — like this particular conversation — I couldn't get a handle on who she was at all. I couldn't get any sense of who she'd been as a living person. Trying to imagine Latrischa doing normal banal stuff like grocery shopping and brushing her teeth, answering to a boss, subjecting herself to the daily grind, was beyond me. I knew she'd done all that stuff, but truth to tell, she didn't seem like she'd put up with the mundane world very well. She seemed more likely to shake the world by the shoulders until it stopped expecting her to deal with bullshit.

We'd arrived at the Dead Man's Chest by this point, and as soon as we walked through the doorway, Anatol waved us over to a table.

He stood long enough to pull two chairs out for us, then took his seat again next to me and picked up a half-smoked cigar from the ash tray.

Across the table from me, on Anatol's left, was Matt.

Matt was ten when he came to the Underworld, and didn't look much older than that, despite his efforts to change his appearance. That's something most dead people aren't too good at, no matter what they can conjure up otherwise. Changing how you look usually feels too weird (I tried for a more petite version of myself once, and felt like I'd stuffed myself inside a latex balloon the size of a cat,) so unless you do it gradually, you'll naturally shift your looks back to normal. So I stayed tall and curvy, Anatol was still scruffy and gaunt, and Matt still looked ten. That being said, I *was* able to get rid of the crow's feet that were just starting to show up at the corners of my eyes when I died. You don't see too many little old folks in the Underworld. Old people have an easier time turning themselves young than young people trying to age themselves — after all, old people have been young and they remember how they looked and what they felt like back then. Kids don't have the same advantage.

Of course, Matt knows a lot more than a lot of ten-year-olds, but he still thinks like he's ten. Anything he wasn't allowed to do while he was alive, that's what he likes to do in the Underworld. Except drink. He can't understand why anybody would drink anything, even water, when they could have any flavor of milkshake imaginable.

Let me tell you, if you want a good milkshake in the afterlife, find Matt. If you could own anything, Matt could buy half of the city of Hades just off the quality of the chocolate ones.

On this occasion, his other main interest was plain to see, as well.

"Heya, Matt," I said. "What's up with the eyebrows?"

He pulled something fire-engine red out of his pocket. It looked exactly like a stick of dynamite from a Road Runner cartoon, only in miniature, like a firecracker. "Want to try one?" he wiggled his singed eyebrows.

"No, thanks," I said. "The experience of cartoon-style pain is not one I want."

"That's not so much a joy-swap item as a self-punishment item." Latrischa sat down next to him and did him the favor of looking it over, at least.

"You guys are such grown-ups." Matt rolled his eyes. "It

doesn't *hurt*, that's the thing about cartoons. They're always fine, like, two seconds after they get squashed or blown up or whatever."

"He's got a point," Anatol said. "Although they do seem to be in pain for those two seconds, based on their facial expressions."

"Yeah, but it only hurts if you *expect* it to hurt, here," Matt said. "You've just got to think of it different."

"Kids have no grasp of reality," Latrischa muttered.

"You'd have more fun if you didn't, either," Matt pointed out.

"You've got me there, kid." Latrischa offered a high five, and Matt accepted.

"I'll be right back," I said. "I'm going to the bar — Latrischa, what're you having?"

"Same as usual."

The Religious Guys Anonymous were seated at the counter, their barstools arranged in a triangle near the peanut bowl. Vic, the bartender, was busy with other patrons at one of the tables. He was a tall guy with a terrible walrus mustache and a big, round laugh that could break up every conversation in the room simultaneously. I don't know if he died at the turn of the twentieth century, or just had a thing for the look of the times, but his mustache and his hair gleamed with hair oil or wax or both.

I'd asked him, once, why he'd decided to run a bar in the afterlife. "Always wanted to own my own bar," he had told me. "Never could talk my wife around to the idea — would've eaten up our savings, might've lost everything on it. . . . Now that we're both dead and gone our separate ways, and money's no consideration, well, I can finally do my own thing."

"I'm sorry to hear about your — uh — separation," I'd said.

Vic had laughed. "It's all right. We had a good life together. There's no bad blood between us, just . . . well, after death, you want to explore your options. We both agreed on that."

The idea had bothered me more than I'd let on with my forced smile. If Dom felt that way after he died, I'd be heartbroken. It had been so long since I'd had any inklings of fear on that score with Dom — with both of us alive, I'd had no doubt he'd stick with me through Hell and high water . . . but would Hades and the river Styx be a whole different ball game? Rattled, I'd backed out of the conversation with Vic, and never brought the subject up with him again.

Standing there waiting for him to take my order, I watched the unhappy minister fumbling with a particularly difficult peanut shell. The priest had half-filled a drained pint mug with husks, and was munching away happily in between sentences.

The optimist reverend listened with obvious amusement to whatever anecdote the priest was conveying. The minister looked sour and disapproving, but that could've been the peanut giving him trouble.

". . . and the next morning, he came down to breakfast shaking all over, sure he was going to be kicked out of the order — we almost laughed ourselves sick, but I finally managed to tell him we'd just *drawn* that tattoo on him."

The priest roared with laughter at his own story, slapping one big hand on his massive knee, and the reverend chuckled appreciatively.

"Finally!" the minister muttered, evidently having cracked open the peanut shell. I watched as he fumbled for the contents, then threw them away from himself in disgust.

The shell landed on the counter, close enough to me that I could see that all the minister had found inside it was a worm. It wriggled along the bar, disoriented from its sudden flight through the smoky air.

"God, what did I do to deserve thy eternal punishment?" The minister pounded his fist on the bar, and the reverend patted his shoulder gently to calm him. Feeling sorry for him, I turned away and at least pretended I was minding my own business.

Vic came over, taking a moment to glare at the minister. "Drunk as a skunk," he commented, turning his attention to me. "What can I get you?"

"Cherry and lime margarita for Latrischa — no salt — and for me. . . ." I considered my choices, then ordered my usual rum and coke.

"Why do I bother to ask?" Vic teased me. "You, Latrischa, and Anatol always order the same."

"At least Latrischa and I let you mix something," I said. "With Anatol, you basically just hand him a bottle of vodka and have done with it."

Vic's laugh broke over the room like a tidal wave, leaving a brief silence behind it before the murmur of conversation returned.

While Vic made our drinks, I took the little worm outside where he'd be safe. Don't ask me what the worm was *doing* hanging around a bar in the city of Hades — most animals (even bugs) seem to have better things to do with their afterlives than interact with humans. Since he was in the Underworld, I assumed he was a dead worm and probably safe anyway, but old habits die hard, unlike people and worms, and I've always been the type to put bugs out rather than squash them.

Returning to the bar, I paid Vic with my own joy-swap specialty. I still had to concentrate pretty hard to produce one, but it was getting easier.

"Mmmph," the bartender said approvingly. "You're getting good at these."

"Thanks." I took the drinks back to the table, stealing one more glance at the Religious Guys Anonymous. The priest and the reverend were helping the minister to his feet, where he swayed precariously as they led him out of the bar.

"Poor bastard." Anatol had followed my gaze to the trio.

Taking my seat next to him, I didn't say anything, but I agreed with his sentiment. I was grateful that, despite my longing to return to life for Dom's sake, I was at least capable of enjoying my afterlife. It would be terrible to be trapped here forever, hating it and wondering what you'd done wrong. I remembered Anatol telling me, when I'd first met him in the tunnel, that the Underworld *could* be Hell, if you thought of it that way.

Now I saw what he'd meant.

Chapter Six

don't shoot me, i'm only the piano player, and i'm already dead anyhow

I'd promised Latrischa I'd go with her to this downtown jazz joint she was crazy about. It wasn't much of a place, just a little hole-in-the-wall pool hall and bar with a piano in the corner, but Latrischa had heard good things about their live (no pun intended) music, and that was all it took to get her to scope a place out.

It was dim, as most bars tend to be, and hazed with smoke. You couldn't tell what color anything was through the gloom — it all looked sort of bluish purple. Patrons lined the bar, and most of the tables had extra chairs pulled up to accommodate big groups of obvious regulars. They were so at home in their seats that half of them had their knees propped up on the tables. One group got up to leave, and as they stood, a different set of customers appeared in the seats, a new set of drinks spread out on the table — half-drained mugs of beer, empty shot glasses, wet rings from glasses of ice water — as if they'd been there all along. It wasn't that unusual a sight in a crowded bar in Hades; like I said, when space and time are moot points, multiple people *can* be in the same spot simultaneously.

Most of the guys were in suits — sans ties — and I was glad Latrischa's self-designed flashy, shimmery, Flamenco-style dress wasn't too much for the place. Since she's one of those girls who can't stand to be wearing the same thing as anyone else, though, I was also glad it stood out *just enough*. Otherwise I'd have had to wait for her to re-invent the whole thing.

As it was, she nudged me, casting a glance over my jeans and tank top. I sighed and concentrated, and the tank top lengthened into a cocktail dress, jeans disappearing as it reached mid-thigh. Latrischa made a face, so I made the dress shinier and added ruffles along the bottom. "Good?" I asked, and she gave me a thumbs-up before we wove our way further into the smoke.

I stopped again after only a few steps.

In the corner, on a six-inch-high platform, was the piano, looking beat-up even in the bad lighting. And at the bench was an early-forties guy in a sweater and jeans, slim except for a barely-there paunch at his middle, with untidy brown hair streaked with grey, and small rectangle-frame glasses that were permanently askew. He had laugh wrinkles at the corners of his eyes, but I couldn't see that in the dim light — I just knew they were there.

I stared at him, not moving forward, prepared to be embarrassed if I'd let a wish cloud my perception.

"Oh, a new guy," Latrischa commented from just behind my right shoulder. "He's good, too."

He was joking around with nearby drinkers, playing nonstop as if it were no harder than talking, and after a moment his gaze swung around and met mine. The music faltered, then stopped as he recognized me. Everyone who'd been watching him now turned to me.

"Uncle Jeff?" I said.

Flashes of memories bombarded me — childhood camping trips and piggy-back rides, getting ready for my driving test at sixteen, my first roller coaster at ten, finding fossils together along the riverbank, my sixth birthday when he bought me my very own record player.

All I could smell, suddenly, was cedar wood and pine resin mixed with sharp aftershave, almost like the pre-storm spark of ozone — Uncle Jeff's scent. If he'd had an aura, it would've been made of the air of the woods; a green, easy, honest kind of aura, breezy but dependable, and always moving.

My own form shifted around my consciousness, perspective warping as my shape shrunk around me. I looked down at myself — what there was of me. Grubby jeans with the knees torn and grass-stained. Bright orange tennis shoes, slightly muddy. Hair in a ponytail, spilling over my shoulder. I was eight again, the only kid in the bar, looking up at my uncle in confusion.

I was aware that Latrischa was staring at me, although she was still behind me.

Uncle Jeff leapt forward and picked me up in a hug the likes of which I hadn't felt in twenty years — pure familial safety and love, cradled like a treasure against my favorite grown-up's chest.

How, in a city this big, could we possibly have found each other? And yet, there he was, and it was definitely my uncle, and I wasn't asleep, dreaming this up.

As my shock wore off, my form shifted back to its usual shape and size, the hug changing with me until I stood on my own two feet again, nearly my uncle's height, chin on his shoulder.

We stepped back and looked at each other then, still with an audience.

Uncle Jeff's expression was a combination of delight tempered with deep sorrow, and it took me a moment to realize precisely how this meeting must seem to him. Here I was, his niece, not yet thirty, meeting him in the afterlife. Of course, he'd died at forty-one, himself, when he'd broken his neck. Poor Uncle Jeff was always clumsy, and we as a family tried hard to keep him from ever doing work on his roof or with the trees in his yard, but you can't stop a Shaw from taking risks. It's a hereditary stubborn streak on my dad's side — or at least, that's my excuse.

Uncle Jeff gestured to a guy nearby, who jumped up from his seat and slid onto the piano bench as my uncle departed from it. The new player launched into his music, and everyone except Latrischa turned away from us again.

My regression to my eight-year-old self felt like a weird exposure, so for good measure, I gave her a dark look and said, "Not a word."

Her surprise gave way to a brief smirk, but she spared me. Not once did she ever mention the regression, then or afterward.

"Erica." Uncle Jeff put his hand on my shoulder, pulling my attention back to him. "What happened?"

"Car accident." For some reason it made me smile. Maybe because I was talking to someone I knew, someone who knew me. Anatol and Latrischa had gotten to know me, sure, and a few others I'd met in the hereafter, but it wasn't the same as talking to someone who'd known me topside. And seeing Uncle Jeff so serious felt awkward, like without his usual lopsided grin he wasn't fully dressed. It was hard not to try to make light of my own demise just to take that weird look off his face.

Latrischa was looking back and forth between the two of us, seeming stunned.

I apologized to her and introduced the two of them, and Uncle Jeff and I moved away from the piano, where it was quieter. Latrischa stopped by the bar to order her drink, although I knew she was also trying to give us some space to catch up.

Uncle Jeff hugged me again, squeezing more this time. "I hope it didn't hurt much." He was still preoccupied with the thought of my death.

"Not exactly." I took a seat in one of the plastic-covered booths. "It did at first, but I went into shock pretty quick."

It was true. Such a strange feeling, back in the hospital, when they were cutting away my blood-soaked shirt, looking down at my own damaged body in that hazy, disconnected way. *Well, that's a shame,* I remember thinking, almost casually, as I regarded the wounds. *I've always had such a nice tummy.*

I'd been very okay with dying, really. My body hadn't given me much choice, as it had fairly well shut down my brain before the end.

"How is the family?" Uncle Jeff sat down across from me, his voice eager.

I guess one of the down sides to time not passing is, you feel like you've only just left the world behind. There's no sense of distance from the past — from your life — and you can't tell yourself, as you would on a long trip away from home, that you'll see your family again in six months. You can't count down the days. You don't get letters or phone calls. You don't even know how long it's been.

I was relieved for the change of subject.

~*~

Back when Uncle Jeff died, my brother, Tyler, had come to my apartment to tell me the news. Uncle Jeff fell off a roof and died. Oh, yeah, sure. Tyler sounded so sincere, with that careful note in his voice because he knew how close Uncle Jeff and I were.

Tyler stood in my doorway, clutching his baseball cap and looking mournful.

"Tyler, that's not freaking funny." I actually punched him — as a sister will punch her older brother, which is to say, extremely hard and with full use of the knuckles, preferably right in the bicep. "Don't joke about stuff like that."

I opened the door further. "Well, are you coming in or not?"

He didn't argue with me until we sat down in my mismatched living room, and it was that fact that tipped me off he might be telling the truth.

"Erica." He flicked his tongue against the corners of his mouth before continuing. "It really is true. Uncle Jeff's gone."

"I don't believe you," I snapped, but I did believe him. Aside from the red-rimmed eyes, Tyler didn't know he did that thing with the corners of his mouth when he was nervous, and if he didn't know he did it, he couldn't have purposely done it to fake me out. He also never took that damn ball cap off until *after* he'd come inside. Never. But he had today.

"I'm sorry, Erica," he said.

Too numb to consider my own feelings about it, all I could focus on was how our dad was going to react to his younger brother's death. "Does Dad know?"

"*He* told *me*," Tyler said. "He was there when it . . . you know . . . when it happened."

I was the last in the family to find out. What that meant was, everyone knew I'd take it the worst, and nobody had wanted to be the one to break the news to me. Without anyone telling me, I understood all of this, and that Tyler had volunteered because he wanted to be the one who was there for me.

It came as something of a surprise to me that *I* wanted Tyler to be there for me, too — the person who'd always stuck up for me when the shit hit the fan during our childhood. Sure, we'd fought and picked on each other and teased each other, but when it came down to it, Tyler had always had my back.

If it'd been my sister Laura who'd told me the bad news, or my mom or Tyler's wife, Maci — it would've been all too easy for us to have a good cry together and then change the subject and try to cheer each other up. If my dad had been the one to tell me, he would've made it so easy for me to fall apart and let him take care of his little girl again, even though it was his brother who'd died.

With Tyler, I didn't feel weak, and I didn't feel pressured to cheer up either. He let me cry for a bit, ruffling my hair gently, but then he pushed me onto practicalities. "I'm hungry," he said after about half an hour. "Let's order Chinese food."

Before I had a chance to object, Tyler had already called the number off the magnet on my fridge. We waited for our chicken lo mein and won ton soup over a game of chess — Tyler's only intellectual pursuit — which I lost.

We were both miserable, and neither of us could concentrate on the game, but it was okay. It was acknowledged silently on both sides, and accepted.

And then the funeral, and the will, and the deed to the house

Uncle Jeff had left to me. During all of it, I just wanted to curl up asleep and not wake up until the sadness had passed.

The hardest part about moving into his house was, the upstairs bathroom still smelled like Uncle Jeff's aftershave.

They say scent is the strongest sensory connection to memory. They're not wrong about that.

It was a small house, just an eat-in kitchen and a living room downstairs, with a cramped bathroom stuck under the staircase. Upstairs were two decent-size bedrooms and the master bath. There was a nice brick patio and a manageable backyard, and I'd always loved the place. Tucked into the living room corner was Uncle Jeff's upright piano, probably the only inanimate thing he'd really cared about in his lifetime. I couldn't begin to estimate the hours I sat listening to my uncle playing jazz piano during my childhood.

And it was because of the piano that I met Dominic Flynn.

I gave Uncle Jeff a quick rundown of family events since his death, trying to keep it brief for Latrischa's sake.

"You haven't told me much about how *you've* been," Uncle Jeff pointed out as I wrapped up.

"Well," I said, "I'm still living in your old house—"

"Did you keep the piano?" he asked.

"Of course I did. No way I could've parted with it," I said. "And, well — that's how I met my husband." I couldn't help grinning.

"You got married?" Uncle Jeff looked delighted. "To a musician?"

I nodded. "Chloe started taking piano lessons not long after you died." I turned from him to Latrischa to explain that Chloe was my niece, then turned my attention back to Uncle Jeff. "She took her lessons at my house, since I had your piano. And Dom was her piano teacher." I thought back to those Saturday afternoons of sneaking looks at him from the living room doorway, and the first time he'd caught me at it. Confusion crossed his face first, then the tiniest little smile. He'd asked me out the following Saturday, after Chloe's lesson.

As Uncle Jeff and I chatted about the budding of my relationship with Dom, I realized just how much I'd let myself settle into being dead. What had happened to my plans of getting back to Dom? Of at least speaking to him again? I had to know that he'd be okay, that he knew how I really felt about him and about our marriage. Damn it, I'd gotten way too comfortable.

And now — reunited with my uncle, the person I'd longed the most to see when I'd been alive — things were going to be even more complicated. How could I stand to part with Uncle Jeff again, if I got the chance at getting back to the Upper World?

Typical. The moment I had Uncle Jeff around, I wanted to spill out all my troubles to him, get his perspective and his advice. Nobody else could sift through problems quite the way he could, and I'd have given anything for his help in the last couple months before my death — when Dom and I had started fighting.

Uncle Jeff's expression shifted suddenly as we talked, and I caught the look. Glancing at Latrischa, I saw what he'd noticed. She'd retreated completely from the conversation, looking miserable. I thought back over the exchange between Uncle Jeff and me, but it had been nothing if not cheerful. Still, we had been leaving her out, and I felt bad about it.

"I'm glad you talked me into coming here tonight," I said, nudging her.

She forced a smile.

"I am, too," Uncle Jeff said. "I can't believe—" He smiled and shook his head. "It's incredible, in a city this size, running into Erica."

"Not that incredible," Latrischa said thoughtfully. "One, jazz is a niche scene — it's not that shocking to run into the same people over and over even in a big city. Two, you know, they say you *do* find your way to the people you love the most in the afterlife."

"They do?" I asked.

"Well, they say it about Heaven, anyway. Didn't they ever tell you that in Sunday school?"

I shrugged. "Not that I remember."

"It does kind of make sense, now that I think about it," Uncle Jeff said. "I mean, given that what you want affects the Underworld around you, why *wouldn't* the two of us meet up once you got here? We both wanted to see each other. Somehow we guided the circumstances."

"For once, I don't care about *why*," I said, laughing. "I'm just thrilled to have you back, Uncle Jeff." But the fact that I knew he was the strongest tie the Underworld could've bound me with gnawed at me, even as Latrischa snapped out of whatever was bothering her, and joined us in a round of celebratory drinks.

Chapter Seven

phone psychics

"Dom and I weren't exactly on the best terms when I left," I confessed to Uncle Jeff, in the park near downtown Hades.

We'd decided to catch up one-on-one, and the park was my uncle's first choice for location. I hadn't told him anything about the argument up till then — I mean, who wants to tell someone right off the bat about what's *wrong* with their marriage? You kind of want to put it in a positive light.

Uncle Jeff frowned a little. "You seem pretty crazy about him."

"Yeah, well. Life was trying to get in the way, and neither of us was doing a very good job stopping it." I tucked my leg up on the park bench and watched a pigeon waddle up with a demanding look on its face. Dead pigeons aren't much different than live pigeons.

"What was the problem? Money stuff?" Uncle Jeff looked sad, whether for me or for himself, I couldn't tell — he'd died a bachelor. Not that he hadn't dated, just nothing had worked out for him. He'd been crazy about us as kids — Tyler and Laura and me, and then later, Chloe — and suddenly my memories of that closeness hit me in a new light. I wondered if Uncle Jeff had died regretting the fact that he'd never had a family of his own. No wife, no kids, just an empty nest he sometimes filled by taking in a rescued animal from the forestry where he worked, or having his nieces and nephew visit. Maybe. Or maybe he'd been fine with it. It had never occurred to me when he was alive.

Uncle Jeff repeated his question, thinking I hadn't heard him.

"Some money stuff." I pulled myself back to the conversation at hand. "Stuff about chores. Whether we were going to move away for a job he wanted. That kind of stuff. Mostly petty, but with enough important things thrown in to keep us both on edge."

The truth was that the main thing had been that move, and my primary reason for digging in my heels on that one was, it was my Uncle Jeff's house — a house I had so many fond memories of. It didn't help that I had family in town (far enough away that they didn't get obnoxious, but close enough to give me a sense of belonging and security), or that I actually liked my I-knew-my-degree-wasn't-going-to-get-me-anywhere job — assistant manager at the zoo gift shop. I was absolutely not ready to move all the way out to Chicago for Dom to *possibly* make a living as an actual performance musician, instead of teaching kids piano. Much as I wanted him to be able to live his dreams and all that, I also wanted more definites in the equation before uprooting myself. I was *happy* living at Uncle Jeff's, up until that buddy of Dom's who worked for the performing arts center had to go and give him a lead.

The worst part was how selfish that made me feel. I'd just wanted more time to get used to the idea, really. And now, what did any of it matter? I didn't even have a few minutes to tell Dom I was sorry. Right now I'd gladly be uprooted and out of sorts with my life in Chicago, with Dom, if I could just *be there*.

I wondered how long it had been since my death. Had he moved yet? Were things going well for him? How was life without me working out for Dom?

I have to admit the thought of him moving on without me was a knife to my proverbial heart. But so was the thought that his last memory of me was a bad one, and that he'd have to live with that memory for a long time to come.

"I need to get in touch with him somehow," I said.

"Well, there's always the medium phones. They aren't too reliable, but you could give it a try." Uncle Jeff tossed a few peanuts in the direction of our fat pigeon companion, who gulped them up greedily.

"The *medium phones*?" I repeated.

"Yeah. There's a bank of them over that way." He pointed, and I stared off down the grassy slope. A line of trees that blocked the view beyond.

"So they're, what, how you talk to psychics? Those nutty psychics who're always going on about how your dead granny wants you to know she loves you and doesn't really hate you because you married a wastrel? That kind of medium?"

"Yup. Pretty much." He grinned.

"Oh, great. That's a very reliable source to pass on the most important message I want to communicate." I thought for a moment. "Then again, Dom would probably go in for that kind of thing. I've never known him to go to a psychic, per se, usually just fake gypsy fortune booths, but he *might* go to a medium now that someone he cares about is dead. . . . I don't know. It might be too weird even for him." But a spark of hope had lit within me. Dom's superstitious streak very well might be the solution. "Where did you say those phone booths were?"

~*~

Both the phones and the booths were orange. It seemed an oddly cheery color choice. Intense, but not neon — like the oranges you see at farmer's markets — and perfectly polished, untarnished by our greaseless dirt-less un-biological fingers that didn't have dead skin cells to flake off onto everything we touched.

I slid into a booth and looked out at Uncle Jeff for reassurance. He nodded me on, and I closed the door between us.

The curve of the phone was smooth in my grip, and a wave of nervous excitement came over me. All my hopes rested on this attempt. It could be the answer to all my problems, or it could fail me entirely.

"Calm," I whispered to myself, and looked at the keypad closely for the first time.

There was only one number, one button. The others were blank shiny metal, flat and purposeless. Just a zero.

I picked up the receiver. A dial tone — such a normal, everyday sound.

Beep. I pressed the zero.

"Hello. Operator." A woman's brisk, professionally-friendly voice.

"Operator, can you put me through to the topside?" I asked.

"Which medium in the Land of the Living are you trying to reach?" she asked, as if my question were a completely stupid one.

"Er . . . I'm not sure." At least I couldn't get butterflies in the stomach anymore — just one more benefit to not being physical. "I'm not trying for a specific medium, really. I'm trying to contact my husband, Dominic Flynn. I don't know who he'd be going to see." Surely most people didn't know which *medium* they wanted, right? She had to be able to help me out here. . . .

I was relieved when she answered by telling me she'd direct my call to the appropriate department, as soon as she found it, and put me on hold. Yes. There was hold music, too. Elevator jazz.

And now what? Who knew if the psychic I was getting would actually give a damn about finding Dom for me, or if he/she would get the message right, or if Dom would put any stock in him/her? I didn't know for sure he believed in this stuff.

It really all came down to hoping that my own wishful thinking was well-founded.

The phone beeped softly, stopping the music, and a deep male voice came through a crackling line—"Hello? Who's there?"

Anybody who thinks it'd be creepy to pick up a telephone and find themselves suddenly hearing a voice from the other side, well . . . it's not just creepy when you're the living person. I nearly dropped the phone from the unnerving fact that this voice was coming to me from across the void. I mean, I was just on a damn phone, from my perspective. This guy was communicating with me who-knew-how. With nothing but the power of his brain. Damn creepy.

"I can tell you're there." Static popped at me with nearly every syllable the medium uttered. "Who are you?"

"Erica Flynn. My name is Erica Flynn. I have a message I want to get to someone."

"Yes," he said, "I know. Your husband, Dominic."

How did he know that? Had Dom contacted this guy already, from his end? That would be a weird coincidence . . . or maybe that was why the operator had connected me to this medium. Or he was the real deal, and could read minds — even dead ones? I opened and shut my mouth a few times, then said slowly, "That's right. Can you help me?"

At the medium's request, I gave him what had been my home address, so he could find Dom.

"That's in Albany, New York," I added anxiously. "I hope that isn't far. . . ?"

"Not at all." He sounded weirdly relieved, as if he'd been really worried about that part. Maybe he had some kind of driving anxiety. "I live in Albany, too. Now, what can I tell Mr. Flynn that will assure him that I've spoken with you? Something you've only told him, that he knows for a *fact* that no one else knows about you."

This posed something of a problem for me. I'm not much good at keeping secrets about myself, and Dom knew that.

"Erica?" the medium prompted.

"I'm here," I said quickly. "We came up with names in case we ever decided to have kids. . . ?"

"And you never told anyone? Not your best friend? No one in your family?"

"No." We hadn't told anyone in either of our families for fear of being hounded about it. Both our families were far too baby-eager to be encouraged. Dom's mother would probably have mailed us paint swatches for a nursery the moment we'd shown any sign of interest in popping out kids. Then, if a couple years later we were actually putting a nursery together, she would've broken down crying if we hadn't used the colors she'd picked. Dom could handle his mom's sensitive nature, but it made me feel terrible whenever something we'd decided on upset her. As for telling friends, well, they were almost all single, which meant baby-related stuff either depressed them or scared them.

"What names did you choose?" the medium asked.

"For a boy, he would've been Douglas Jeffrey Flynn. If we'd had a girl, she'd have been Beatrice Nicole Flynn." It felt weird to talk about that now — it was the first time I'd talked about what might've been ahead of me if I were still alive.

"And what do you want me to tell Dominic? The message you want to send him?" the medium said gently.

"I want him to know I didn't mean what I said, that I'm sorry. And that I love him. And that I'm safe, but I miss him." I stopped at that, afraid if I kept going I'd start complicating things. There was too much I wanted to say, and none of it would get across strongly enough unless I saw Dom in person.

"Do you mind telling me what it was you said, in case he asks?" the medium rumbled.

"I don't want to repeat it." I turned away from the keypad, as if it were the one asking me the question. Then, impulsively, I added, "Tell him I'm going to try to come back . . . if I can."

There was a long, uncomfortable silence where neither of us apparently knew what direction to take things.

"Don't worry," the medium finally crackled. "I'll find him."

"What's your name?" I asked. "So I can get back in touch with you?"

"I told you already." He sounded confused — and I didn't remember him mentioning his name — but he told me again anyway: "Chester Wilkins. Trust me, I've done this kind of thing plenty of times."

"With success?" The whole conversation seemed a little

disappointing — more like a telegram than a message from beyond the grave.

"Sometimes," he said carefully.

Then he hung up.

I listened to the dial tone click in, and put the receiver back on the hook.

What the next step was, I hadn't quite worked out, but I did know this — I'd meant it when I'd blurted out my intention to return. I just wasn't sure how to get there.

Chapter Eight

storming the castle (sorta)

Despite my restored determination, I had zip when it came to leads on getting back to the Land of the Living. Wishing was all well and good, but I didn't get a real, honest-to-goodness breakthrough until, by chance, I overheard the three men of God talking one night—

"—went to Hades himself about it," the Reverend We-Are-in-Heaven was saying.

"You spoke with Hades?" The Purgatory Priest raised his eyebrows so far they almost reached his hairline (which, in his case, would have been particularly impressive). He hid the rest of his face behind his mug of ale, darting a glance at the minister, who had traded in his omnipresent expression of despair for something like gleeful condemnation.

"You spoke with a false god?" Minister Doom-and-Gloom cried.

"There are many facets to God," said the reverend. "The way I see it, Hades is just one of them. The one set here to watch over us."

"Hades is the guise of Satan!" The minister's face was aglow as I'd never seen it. The unexpected opportunity to preach fire and brimstone must've had him pumped up. I guess you don't get much chance for it once you're dead. Nobody listens at that point.

The Purgatory Priest leaned back in his chair and took another gulp from his mug. All he needed was a bucket of popcorn, and he'd be ready to settle in and watch the show.

The reverend shook his head and launched into a theological explanation — how Hades could be God could be Yahweh could be whatever he wanted to be — but he didn't get far before the minister interrupted, and the shouting match began.

"Erica, I said could you pass me the pitcher?" This last comment was from my table, more specifically from Latrischa.

Anatol, who was sitting to my left, jiggled my shoulder.

I handed the pitcher across the table and glanced back over at the religious club. "I didn't know there really was a Hades."

"I assume you mean the guy, since it's pretty goddam obvious that the place exists?" Matt drew a smiley face in the condensation on his milkshake glass.

Latrischa gave Matt a severe look that made me realize she'd probably had younger siblings when she was alive. "Did you have a mouth like that on you when you were alive?"

"Not in front of my mom." Matt added an arrow sticking out of the smiley face's head.

"Yeah, the guy." I was still hung up on Matt's mention of the god Hades as opposed to the city Hades. Really, naming your own realm after yourself is pretty conceited, not to mention confusing to your population. The men of the cloth were now standing at either side of their table, bellowing at one another and clenching their fists. I was surprised at the reverend. He was a pretty mellow guy, and tough to discontent — very Zen, for a Lutheran.

"Go to Hell!" he was yelling at the minister.

The minister let out a choked sob. "I can't afford the train ticket." He sank, wailing, into his seat, and wept.

"Great." The priest gave the reverend a disapproving look. "Now you've upset him again. You *know* that's a sore spot with him."

The reverend sighed and sat down next to the minister, trying to console him.

"If I *have* to be condemned by God—" the minister raised his head—"I want to at least be properly punished."

"May as well be damned in style." The priest patted him on the shoulder.

"Yeah, there's a guy." This last was from Anatol, referring to Hades.

I looked away from the Religious Guys Anonymous to stare at my companions. "How many of you knew this?"

Uncle Jeff looked guilty, and tried to hide it by taking a few gulps of beer.

"Not me," Latrischa said. "Who cares, anyway?"

"I do." I watched their expressions as it dawned on everybody what the existence of some kind of official ruler-of-the-dead would mean to me. If there was a guy in charge, there was somebody I might persuade to let me have, if nothing else, a few quick minutes with Dom. Not having to go through a medium to get a message across the void.

"How do I find Hades?" I demanded of Anatol. I expected him to grin, but he actually looked worried before he shook his head and turned to talk to Latrischa instead of answering me.

"I swear, Erica. . . ." Uncle Jeff raised his hands as if I were pointing a gun at him. "I don't have the faintest idea."

"Matt?"

"I'll tell you how to get to Hades' Palace," Matt said without hesitation.

"What would I owe you?" I asked suspiciously.

Matt grinned. "Just come with me next time I go to the thrill park."

The thrill park was the whacko cartoon-physics region most of the kids in the city hung out in. You could let yourself get run over by steamrollers, drop anvils or pianos on each other out of windows, jump off cliffs and squash flat like a pancake, or blow yourself or your friends up with cartoon dynamite. Matt's mini-dynamite was a popular attraction these days, as well. This is a kid's idea of paradise, and every parent's worst nightmare.

"Can't I just teach you a new cussword?" I pleaded.

Latrischa leaned across Anatol to glare at me.

Matt stuck his hand in his glass and licked the last residue of the milkshake off his finger. "Come on, stop being such a boring old grown-up."

"All right, all right, I'll go," I said. "I owe you big, for sure."

"Awesome!" Matt threw me a high five, and I realized that for all his mockery of adults, he missed having somebody to look out for him. Not that he wanted to be told what to do — but he wanted a sense that he belonged to somebody. That was why he hung out with us: we may have had the disadvantage of being grown-ups, but we were *his* grown-ups. I might've teared up, if I'd still been topside and breathing, but that would've ruined my coolness points with Matt, so it was just as well I was dead at that moment.

To get to the palace of Hades, you can take a cab to the east side of town, to the city's other riverbank — the edge of the Lethos River. Take a sip from this one, and you'll forget all about the origins of your soul. What your life was, what your heartaches were, who you miss, why you miss them so badly. All of it gone the moment the water touches your tongue. I was tempted. There's nothing like forgetting your bad experiences ever happened, being blissfully ignorant of pain. Some people can do that without the Lethos River. Me, I'd probably start trying to remember as soon as I'd finished forgetting. Even when I know I'm going to get burned by the answers to my questions, I'll still ask. Ignorance is only bliss unless you can't leave well enough alone. I like to think this makes me a wiser and stronger person, although that could be me bullshitting myself.

So.

I paid the cabbie with a roasted marshmallow. A smile spread over his face as he worked the first half of the confection in his mouth. "I think you overpaid me."

I dug my hands into the pockets of my knee-length jacket, which was whipping around in the gusty air. "Thanks for the ride." I gave the guy my best attempt at a carefree smile, and walked on down to the docks.

It was different from the docks at the Styx. It was empty, weirdly quiet, and grey. The dusky sky was lighter out here on the outskirts, but, at least at the moment, it was a pearly silver, a dull backdrop for a desolate landscape. There weren't any boats docked in the choppy water, and certainly no brass-band-topped ferries or dancing.

Near the waterfront was a sizeable plaque mounted on a rusty metal pole, like those tourist information signs you see at historical sites. Across the top, in large, all-capital letters, was written: PALACE OF HADES. Below, in smaller text, it read, "The Lord of the Dead welcomes you to the Underworld and hopes you will enjoy your stay, which is permanent and non-negotiable. Please avail yourself of the benefits of being dead. If you're not enjoying your afterlife or want more information on the currency, activities, and options available to you in the Underworld, please see the Board of Tourism downtown at the Osiris Street Roundabout."

Well, that was . . . unhelpful. Informative, in its way, but in the way of someone politely saying, "Go away. I don't give a damn."

An arched bridge loomed ahead of me, with steep and irregular stone stairs climbing up one side and down the other. The clumsily-placed stones of the staircase were jagged and rough, as if not many people had passed across it.

I realized that it didn't make any sense for something to have eroded when there wasn't, apparently, any kind of physics at work, but then, not much *does* make sense when physical laws cease to apply.

This wasn't much comfort as I crossed the bridge to Hades' palace.

I hadn't known what to expect of the place, so I wasn't surprised by it.

It looked like it had erupted from the bowels of the earth, torn through the surface of the ground of its own volition, breaking and shattering itself in the process. It was stone, glass-smooth and crystalline, with sharp, crooked spires. How there could be an interior to it, I wasn't sure.

There was a traced outline of a door, about where you'd predict a gigantic front door to be on a palace, just to the left of a serrated column of stone. The outline was ornate and silvery — shiny, but dull compared to the sleek surface of the building. I didn't recognize the symbols decorating the doors — they were twisty and complicated, not like any alphabet I'd ever seen.

"Okay," I said out loud. "So how do I get in?"

I tried to think like a mythological god.

There ought to be a trial of some kind, like having to slay a beastie. Or maybe I had to know a password. Or answer a riddle, but nobody was showing up to ask me any riddles. And there weren't any beasties to slay, either.

Most of the time in the Underworld, if you want to move through a wall, you'll suddenly notice a door further along that you'd apparently missed — very convenient. Technically you could walk through walls, but for the most part people didn't because, well, doors appeared for you and we tend to prefer methods we're used to. But I doubted I'd be able to stroll straight through the wall here. It just wasn't that kind of place. Not cooperative in the least. Or, at least, that was what I assumed.

I reached out to trace the strange letters with my finger, and as my skin touched the surface, the space inside the outline filled with a flat, bird's-eye view chessboard.

"Seriously?" I said. "The old 'playing chess against Death' bit?"

Sighing, I moved one of the white pawns. The black knight moved out. "At least I'm decent at chess, thanks to Tyler." If I made it back to the Land of the Living, maybe I should be nicer to my brother. "It could be worse — I'd never get in if I had to win a game of backgammon."

Instantly, the chess board disappeared, and a backgammon board appeared in its place. A pair of dice, the same stone as the palace, fell from the top of the column nearby, rolling to land at my feet.

"I should shut up now," I said after a moment of disgruntled silence.

A dozen games later, I managed to get enough good luck with the dice to win. "Yes!" I jumped up and down as I rolled double sixes and watched my last four pieces clear off the board. The door had only two pieces left — one more turn without those doubles, and I'd have lost yet again. "I win! Now, let me in already!"

The board disappeared, leaving the blank surface of the outlined door again.

I pressed a hand to it, wondering what the next step was.

The stone gave, like cool, thick liquid. I jerked back. The doors rippled, as if I'd stuck my finger into Jell-O that hadn't finished setting.

It was disorienting to the point I had to close my eyes for a moment. When I looked back, the surface was still and solid again.

All right. Just walk through the wall? That easy?

"Easy" is not the right word for it, as I discovered shortly afterward.

As disorienting as one fingertip had been, pushing my whole self through what seemed to be solid stone was exponentially more so. Of course, none of it was physically happening — there wasn't a physical *me* for it to happen to. Who knows what sinister metaphysical substance my poor little immortal soul was actually pushing its way through?

When I emerged on the other side, I was standing in an immense room (although "room" is a horribly inadequate noun for the space I'm describing), so vast and so dim I couldn't see the ceiling or any of the adjacent walls. The columns scattered across the floor were the same smooth, gleaming dark stone as the outside of the structure. The floor itself looked like black marble, so shiny it was reflective.

I stared down at myself in its dark surface. Same old me there — long-nosed and sharp-chinned, slim and pale. Even the same haircut I'd had when I'd died, shoulder-length and swept over and back from my face. I looked the tiniest bit younger, maybe, with the subtraction of the barely-there laugh lines around my eyes.

Hm. Looking pretty casual for a visit to the Lord of the Dead, I realized. I focused my attention on my jeans and sweater, and a knee-length navy skirt and a crisp white button-up were the result. I looked like I was interviewing for a job.

I gave myself a little wave to pluck up my courage, and glanced behind me at the wall I'd walked through. As I'd expected, there was no trace of a door there.

So. Off into the dark recesses of Hades' creepy palace.

As I took my first few steps further, I had the terribly unsettling feeling that the room was revolving just a bit with each of my footfalls. I stopped, braced myself in case it happened again, and moved forward.

It did happen again.

I was glad I wasn't physical anymore, because I was dizzy as it was, but at least I wasn't sick into the bargain. Walking faster made the room spin faster, so as much as I wanted this whole business to be over with, I moved slowly.

A faint glow caught my attention, off to the right — well, further right now, and — damn. Now it was behind me.

What would happen if I walked backward? I wondered, and tried it. The room spun the other direction.

Unpleasant.

But it did mean that I could keep one point along the walls in my sights. I walked backward until the glow was slightly to my left, then turned in place on my heel, and moved forward so the light swung back over to my right. And turn, and back, and turn and forward, as the room moved left and right. I wasn't a bad dancer back when I was alive. I was kind of getting into the swing of it by the time I reached the wall — and the glow, which was a doorway. Maybe.

It was shaped like a doorway. It was rough quartz or diamond or something. Just a big lump of crystalline rock, set into the wall, with a light source behind it.

I tried the walking-through-it trick, but nothing happened, aside from me bumping into the door.

So, maybe it was time to try a password?

I couldn't help thinking of that part in the *Lord of the Rings*, where they have to get through the doors into the mines. It was my dad's favorite part in the whole series, where they realize that the entire time they've been trying to solve a riddle that *wasn't even a riddle*. Speak friend and enter. Dad used to say that to me whenever I was overthinking things.

"Friend?" I asked the doors, but it didn't work. Not that I'd expected it to.

"Cerberus."

Nothing.

"Persephone!"

Nothing.

Okay, so that stuff was probably too obvious. Nobody who's actually worried about security makes their e-mail password their pet's name or their wife's name.

"Pluto." The Roman name for Hades. "Pluto17. Pluto with a zero in place of the *o*." Okay, so maybe the e-mail password theory wasn't going to get me anywhere. I could stand here forever and guess. Really, *forever*.

If there were a password, wouldn't Matt have told me?

Maybe, unless he wanted to see how easily I'd get it on my own. He was a competitive little twerp — he might want to see if it took me more guesses to figure it out than it had taken him.

I sighed and sat down on the slick black floor, facing my challenge.

At around my four hundredth guess (I lost track of the exact number), I figured I was doing something wrong.

If there wasn't a password, what was the trick? What was so obvious Matt wouldn't even think to tell me about it, assuming he wasn't in a twerp mood?

Things usually worked in the usual way in the afterlife, because it was what we expected. Was my expectation that this palace was different the very thing that was *making* it different?

I stood up and did what I'd normally do when confronted with a door I had no business opening without permission — I knocked.

A chunk of the crystal moved, with a grainy shifting sound, until it stuck out at about doorknob level, about doorknob size.

I grabbed the knob and turned, and somewhere in the recesses of the stone, a latch clicked. I pushed, expecting it to feel heavy, but it opened as easily as any normal door.

A slim, clean-cut man stood a few paces away, looking mildly intrigued. He had the sort of face that doesn't often wear intrigue, and if it does, it's only ever mild. He looked like he'd been pacing, lost in thought, or possibly he'd gotten up to adjust the stereo.

There was music coming from somewhere, with the soft hiss and crackle of a vinyl record. Classical-esque, with violins and cellos dominating the piece, but definitely nothing traditional. An edgy minor key, an exotic beat that might be a tango.

The room looked like a study — there was a desk and lots of bookshelves, everything very wood-tone and polished to gleaming. A cheerful fire glowed in the hearth on the opposite wall from the door. Half the room was raised about a foot higher than the rest, with a low, wide pair of stairs set at an angle. The style was what you'd maybe get if you explained a late-1800s English-style study to a twenty-sixth century man, or possibly an alien.

"You wanted to speak with me?" the man prompted. He looked both very average and very unusual. It's hard to explain the contradiction away. It might be clearer if I said his *features* were very average, but the sum of all that nondescriptness was a strange thing. I couldn't decide if he was handsome or not.

"You're Hades?" I asked.

He nodded.

"Shouldn't you have guards or something?"

"What for?" He looked genuinely perplexed by the idea.

I shrugged. "I don't know. This is a palace, right? I just expected more . . . panache?"

"You wanted it to be more complicated?" There was a smile somewhere behind those Spartan features (if I may use the word in application to a god of Greek origin without sounding trite).

"No, it was complicated enough," I said. "You make it damned unpleasant to get here."

"If I welcomed people with open arms, everyone would come and ask me for things." Hades turned his back on me to mount the stairs. He walked to his desk and sat down with his hands folded in front of him.

I gave him a dirty look. "That doesn't sound very godly."

"Not from your point of view, no."

I didn't answer, although a few sharp retorts came to mind. Mainly because I still hadn't heard his answer to my request, although I was getting the feeling I knew what he'd say, and that I wasn't going to like it.

"What brought you here?" Hades asked.

"I want to go back up," I said. "Or whatever direction it is. Land of the Living."

He broke into a smile that surprised me in its warmth. "Don't you all?"

I was not encouraged by the kindness in his manner. Somehow it made me feel even less like he gave a damn what I wanted. It reminded me of a cat holding its claws in just to keep the mouse wondering when they'd be unsheathed.

"Well, not for long." I realized I was fumbling and looking away from him, which irritated me. "I just need a few minutes, really."

And what the hell? I gave him my sob story. I might as well. I didn't have anything to lose by it, as I could already tell he'd say no regardless.

". . . So really, I just want to have a quick word with Dominic and then I'll come right back down. That can't be too much to ask. . . ?" I trailed off as I finished.

"Unfortunately, it can. I'm not in the habit of letting people *out* of the Underworld. It's rather the opposite of what I'm here for."

"But I just need—"

"Now, Erica, if I made exceptions, I'd have to make so *many*. Do you think you're alone? *Thousands* of souls who want one last moment with their living loved ones." He stood and strolled back down the steps to stand before me, his hands folded behind his back, and I noticed for the first time how *tall* he was. "I really don't understand it. Your going back would serve no purpose."

"It would to *me*," I said. "And to Dominic."

"You all end up here. It makes no difference which world you have your conversation in." He smiled as if he were bestowing some gift by telling me, essentially, that my concerns meant nothing to him. Well, maybe they didn't. Maybe they seemed small and petty to a big important deity, but by that standard, what I was asking for was small and petty, too — so why not grant it? What would it cost him?

It was then that I noticed the fireplace — really noticed it. As we'd been talking, I'd taken note of a steady movement inside the fire, but hadn't paid much attention. Now I saw that it was a stream of sealed envelopes, arriving one after another, appearing in the fire, burnt up almost the instant they materialized. Somehow I managed to catch a glimpse of the address on one of the envelopes. *4611 Lethos Blvd, Department 2* — was all I saw, but that was all I needed. This was where my letter had gone.

That lazy bastard. He wasn't even *reading* the letters people sent. They got here and were destroyed in the same moment, and he didn't have to make so much effort as to toss them in a trash can.

And here I'd been doing my best to patiently await a reply, letting myself get comfortable. Letting myself get attached.

Resentment welled up in me like an animal trying to climb out of a pit trap. Maybe he *was* some kind of alien. He didn't seem to understand how people worked, or decided to stop working.

"You can say it doesn't matter all you want," I said. "That doesn't make it *not* matter." I knew if I'd been physical I would've been shaking, and more from fear than I would've admitted. But there was no way, now, that I'd back down from him. Not after seeing the letters in the fireplace.

"I won't let you out of the Underworld." He loomed over me. "The end." He flicked a hand vaguely in my direction just as I was about to object, and—

I was standing outside again, on the other side of the Lethos River, staring back in the direction of Hades' palace. Wind whipped at my hair and my jacket, smelling strongly of rain. I took one last look over my shoulder at the palace, wishing I had one of Anatol's cigars, and then hurried to lose myself in the city again.

Chapter Nine

show me the way to go home

"I guess I'm stuck just passing messages through the medium," I told Uncle Jeff glumly.

We were sitting in his little efficiency house that was mostly studio. Under one table was a camp cot he pulled out when he wanted to sleep, which wasn't often. He didn't even have a kitchen — he never was crazy about cooking. He still enjoyed food, but he liked the excuse to go and mingle with other people, so he went out for his meals. Other than the cot and the workspace, he had the obligatory piano (a baby grand, way nicer than anything he could've afforded while he was alive) and a book nook with a couple of recliners angled nearby.

Uncle Jeff looked up from his carving.

"What?" I said defensively.

"I know you." He smiled and went back to whittling away at the piece he was working on. "You're scheming something, aren't you? What've you been reading up on all that Greek mythology at the library for?"

"All right, so I'm trying to figure out a way to get around Hades," I admitted. "Or persuade him, if I can."

"Look, do me a favor, okay?" Uncle Jeff sighed and set his carving aside. "Don't do anything crazy? At least not until you've tried something *not* crazy."

"Okay, all right, I'll call the medium," I grumbled. "Maybe he's talked to Dom."

"Good." Uncle Jeff hugged me. "Come on, I'll walk you to

the park. Latrischa said she'd be there, anyway, and I thought maybe we could all go to a show tonight or something. Or dinner."

"Let's see how this goes, first," I said.

~*~

"Chester?" I asked when the phone clicked over.

"Who's there?" came Chester's deep voice.

"It's me again. I asked you to speak to my husband, Dominic Flynn. Have you contacted him yet?" I fidgeted with the orange coils of the phone cord.

"What is it you need to tell your husband?" he asked.

"I *told* you that already." I gripped the receiver tighter. "You mean you haven't even contacted him?"

"I need more information," Chester said. "I need to know who your husband is, where I can find him, who you are. I need to know what to tell him. I'm willing to help, I just don't know how. You have to tell me."

I was stunned. My emotions were in turmoil, even without chemicals and hormones to course through me. What was he saying? There couldn't be more than one psychic Chester Wilkins, and even if there were, they wouldn't have the same voice. Could he really just have forgotten?

A forgetful psychic — now that would be ironic, I thought, somewhere beneath my confusion. He *had* been sure, the last time we talked, that he'd given me his name up front, and I was almost positive he hadn't until I asked him for it.

I felt soul-sick as I realized the guy was probably crazy. That was all there was to it. Just a crazy man who happened to have *real* voices in his head, but what did it matter, since he was crazy? No one would ever listen to him. It seemed like the kind of thing a god from the old myths would do. They're big fans of irony and tripping humans up with fate and all that other stuff that makes being human miserable. Sadistic streak a mile wide, all to prove a point to us poor lowly shades — that they are superior.

Chester was asking me questions I'd already answered in our first conversation, and I could hear the low rumble of his voice even as I moved the receiver away from my ear and toward the flat silver slat that would cut us off. And then, Click. He was gone.

Latrischa and Uncle Jeff were waiting on a nearby park bench as I emerged from the phone booth feeling crushed.

"How'd it go?" Latrischa asked, with her usual lack of insight into other people's mind frames.

"Not so hot," I said. "I think my medium is crazy."

"Oh." She threw a few bread crumbs out to the pigeons as I took a seat on the opposite side of the bench, next to Uncle Jeff, and we watched the birds waddle around fattening themselves.

One of the nice things about Latrischa, she doesn't really lay on any pressure for you to explain yourself. She assumes you don't want to talk, but with an unspoken agreement that you'd pour your heart out if you felt like it. Usually, I'm a talk-it-out type, but it was nice to know that, with Latrischa, it was up to me when and where I let my feelings loose.

Uncle Jeff played along, turning the conversation back to what they'd been discussing before.

"So, Latrischa, you were saying something about how you ran a business, back in the Upper World?"

"You did? I had no idea what you did before you died." I felt somewhat guilty that this was the case. Guilty, and a little bit hurt that Latrischa hadn't told *me* — she barely knew Uncle Jeff. But then, he always could get people to talk about themselves. He had such a deliberate attentiveness when he listened, it made you feel like whatever you told him, he'd be curious to know more.

I was interested despite myself, although part of me just wanted to go straight to the library and work on an escape plan. But it wasn't often Latrischa was willing to talk about her life, and I wasn't so self-centered I could pass up the chance to find out more now.

"You've said before that you painted houses," Uncle Jeff said. "You didn't say it was *your* business, or that it wasn't just 'ho-hum, time to paint a solid beige wall,' or something."

"I'm good at texture detailing and inlay work." She shrugged. "I used to do that kind of stuff on rich people's houses. I had a business called 'The Finishing Touch,' and got paid shitloads of money for doing tedious stuff builders don't want to be bothered with. People would pay me to inlay existing floors or texture walls to look like marble. They didn't want to actually remodel, or they wanted to *look* like they could afford solid marble columns leading into the dining room, but they didn't actually want to pay for solid marble."

"We should collaborate," Uncle Jeff suggested. He elbowed me to prompt my agreement. "Wouldn't some inlay look good on my carvings?"

I agreed, and Uncle Jeff turned back to Latrischa. "You aren't sick of it, are you? I mean, you still enjoy doing it?"

"I liked doing it when I started out." She looked miserable in a non-grouchy way for the first time since I'd met her. "But right about the time the business took off and started paying enough to be a good living, it hit me how fake all of it was. Fake textures to make stuff look more expensive, fake people to work for, fake people to impress. Fake fake fake." She avoided looking at either of us. "It might've had something to do with the fact that I got engaged to one of my clients and then, three weeks before the wedding, found out he'd been cheating on me for six months."

Uncle Jeff and I offered our condolences and outrage at the offending fiancé, and Latrischa seemed to cheer up with the increasingly unkind words Uncle Jeff offered up to describe the guy.

When we'd finished abusing the fiancé, Latrischa smiled. "I'd like to see your sculptures," she told Uncle Jeff.

"Oh, they're just little carvings, really." He ducked his head.

"I wouldn't call them sculpture. Just a way to unwind, something to do with myself."

I was only half-listening by now, but in retrospect, it was incredibly lucky I was present for their little chat. "Look," I said, "why don't you two go on to a show or something? I'm going to the library."

Uncle Jeff groaned. "Again with the library."

"I've got research to do," I said.

"Come on, Erica," Latrischa wheedled.

"No, I'm not much company right now anyway." My mind had wandered off to thinking about the way *into* the Underworld, and wondering if Anatol, who knew so much about the route in, would know of a route out.

Uncle Jeff put an arm around me and kissed my temple. "We'll figure something out, don't worry. Right now, though, I want some dinner and some jazz. C'mon!"

"Later," I said.

"You sure?"

"You guys have fun." I stood up, pushing a pigeon aside with my foot, and forced a smile. "I'll come with you next time."

Uncle Jeff turned to Latrischa. "How about dinner, then? Somewhere new?"

~*~

I had a favorite spot in the downtown library, on the third floor by the windows overlooking the River Styx, behind the History section. There were potted palms at either side of the bay of windows — not technically *live* palms, but to tell you the truth, I could never tell any difference between live plants and plastic ones anyway.

Uncle Jeff and I habitually met there over coffee, chatting or perusing books, as we'd often done at the library in Albany, back in the Upper World, while I was in college in the years before he died.

I sat alone by the view of the Styx on this particular occasion, with my feet propped up on the table, staring at the info screen on the nearest wall.

Photos of ancient Greek pottery; breakdowns of the architecture of temples to Hades; a classical painting of Hades on his throne, with his scepter in one hand and his Helm of Invisibility in the other, a cornucopia of precious gems at his feet; pages and pages of myths and references to myths scrolled by.

"There has to be a way out," I muttered. "A road back." It was in the myths, after all. People had come down here and gotten out again.

Did they really, or were those just stories — and if they were stories, how did they get started? How did the living know anything about the Land of the Dead, unless someone really had escaped from the Underworld?

I wasn't turning up anything new here, and I felt restless. I grabbed my raincoat and headed down to the river.

"Sure, there's a road back to the Land of the Living," Anatol said, "but I wouldn't recommend you try to get back that way."

"Well, that's what a road is *for*," I said. We were sitting on the empty ferry, down at the dock. It was in between trips across the Styx at the moment, rocking gently in the lapping water. Ropes of white miniature bulbs coiled around the ironwork of the railings, and the music of the dockside carnival drifted down to mix with the clank of the chains that kept us in place. A gold-and-pink horizon stretched down to the water and lit it up to a warm glow.

"You don't understand." Anatol shook his head. "It's guarded. It's dangerous. It's also the path back to pain and sickness and mortality. How do you think all that is going to feel after you've experienced invulnerability?"

I chewed on that one for a while before responding. "Not so good, I wouldn't think. But I *have* get back. You know that. It's not like you can say, 'No one who's traveled that road has ever been seen again,' right?"

Anatol sighed, smiling a little despite himself. "You've got the chance of a fish out of water."

"What happens when someone travels back to the Land of the Living?" I said. "How does it work?"

"Work?" He shrugged and scratched the stubble on his jaw with the end of his unlit cigar. "How should I know how it works? You don't know, nobody else knows. I don't even know if Hades himself knows how it *works*."

"What I want to know is, what's going to happen to me when I pop back up topside?"

"Different things happen to different people. Depends." Anatol shrugged again. "Better to just forget the whole thing. It's not bad this side, is it?"

"No," I conceded reluctantly. "But look, is there or isn't there a way back from the dead?"

"No." He lit up and leaned back in his deck chair. "Well, yeah, but — not the way you're talking about."

"Okay, what's the yeah?" I pressed.

"Well, you can get your soul up there, sure. Sometimes you're just a drifting spirit, can't even be seen or heard. If you're lucky you might get strong enough to show yourself or speak aloud, or you might be able to take over an animal nearby, maybe even a person. Takes a lot of time, though, usually. A *lot* of time. Years, at least. A lifetime or two if you've got lousy luck."

I made a face. No way was I counting on luck or fate in a mythologically-based scenario.

"Or," Anatol continued, "you manage to get your old body back, but of course it's *dead*."

"Like . . . zombie movie dead?" I interjected. "Rotting flesh and stuff?"

Anatol nodded without stopping his litany of horrific scenarios. "Or you reincarnate and don't remember your old life or your old self, or you reincarnate and you *do* remember, which is worse by far." He took a long, deep drag off his cigar.

"But is there any way to control it?" I tried not to dwell on the possibilities he'd just laid before me, although most of them had already occurred to me and kept my thoughts churning before now. You don't want to show up on your husband's doorstep to profess your love in a damaged body, a lack of a body, or somebody else's body. Chances are it'll scare the piss out of him, and if it doesn't, you know there's something wrong with the guy. Especially if he's okay with you suddenly having a different person's body — that's just hurtful. "Isn't there any way to go back and actually *live* — as yourself, I mean, in your own living body?"

"No," he repeated.

"There *has* to be," I insisted, thinking about the mythology again. "Hades can do it, can't he?"

"Yes, but he's *Hades*. He's not technically dead . . . at least, I don't think so. And besides, he's got—" Anatol stopped abruptly, with a curious change of expression. He tried to cover it up by not looking at me, sticking his cigar back in his mouth and clamping his teeth down on the end. "Anyway, things work differently for Hades."

"Hang on." I moved around to try and force him into eye contact. "What was that about?"

"What was what about?"

"You thought of something, didn't you?"

"No, I didn't. There's no way to do what you're suggesting. End of story." He crossed his hands over his stomach, tapping his fingers nervously.

"Anatol, don't screw with me." I wasn't sure if I was mad at him or not. "This is more important to me than . . . well, more important to me than *me*. If you don't help me I'll just try by myself and probably get into worse trouble. I'll probably try something crazy, so you might as well give me an edge, if there is one."

"There's one thing that would do it." Anatol looked at the sky, so purposefully askance from me that I could *feel* he was trying to tread carefully. The sensation hung in the air between us, as tangible as humidity or summer-sun heat. "If you had Hades' scepter."

"If I had Hades' scepter," I repeated flatly.

"It's the only thing that'd guarantee a safe return to the Land of the Living, and the only thing that'd let you control how things worked out." He finally let himself look at me, but only from the corner of his eye.

We were silent for a long while, Anatol taking in his cigar and the sunset, and me lost in my thoughts and schemes.

"I doubt he'd let me borrow it," I said at last, sighing. "And I guess sneaking away with it is too stupid to contemplate."

"I wouldn't advise you to try," Anatol said, by way of agreement.

"Could you just show me where the road begins?" I asked.

"You'd be better off trying your medium again."

The mere idea of talking to Chester Wilkins the Madman again depressed me, but I could see his point. I didn't have a whole lot of good options. I might as well take Uncle Jeff's advice: start with the least dangerous idea and work my way up to the stuff that bordered on insanity.

"You're right," I said. "But if Chester's got nothing, can you take me to the road?"

Anatol gave me a sideways look that clearly said, "It's your afterlife," offered me a puff of his cigar, and nodded as he blew a long tongue of smoke across the sky.

Chapter Ten

metaphysics causes miscommunications

"It's me, Erica Flynn," I said, the moment the phone clicked over from the operator.

Chester was evidently distracted, because he didn't answer. All I could hear was background noise, followed by a phrase from him that I couldn't make out, then another voice (also too indistinct for me to catch the words), more background noise. . . .

A click, like a car door being shut, and sure enough, the familiar rhythmic dinging that reminds you to fasten your seatbelt.

"Sorry," Chester rumbled. "I was at the grocery store. Now, what is it you needed?"

"Right," I said. "It's me, Erica. Have you spoken with my husband yet?"

"Briefly." Chester's tone was evasive.

"Well, did you tell him what I asked you to?" I was pleasantly surprised that his memory seemed to have returned.

"I did," the psychic said slowly, "and then he threw me, literally, out of the house — with many a nasty curse word, I might add. Seemed to think I was running a scam."

"Yeah," I said without thinking, "I can understand that."

"Thanks a lot for the sympathy," Chester snapped.

"Oh. Sorry. I mean, I really am. Just a bit single-minded at the moment," I said. "Didn't you give him the names, to prove you'd talked to me?"

"That was just before he grabbed me by the shirt collar." There was a great deal of surliness in Chester's voice.

Reflecting on it, I could see how using the names Dom and I had picked out for our potential offspring, when I was now dead along with all our future plans, might not have been the easiest thing on Dom. It made sense that it would upset him — it was probably like having someone pour salt into an open wound. The question was, even if he flew off the handle at first, why hadn't it sunk in that Chester *knew* those names?

"So he just threw you out?" I asked. "He didn't even listen?"

"No," Chester said. "After that, I left."

"Hm. I was hoping he'd be at least somewhat prepared when I show up back from the dead," I lamented.

"Well, look," said Chester. "There's no way I'm going back to talk to him, so you'll just have to tell him yourself. However you do that is *your* problem."

He hung up.

"That could've gone better," I said into the flatlining receiver, and hung it up.

~*~

"What happened to *you*?" Uncle Jeff glanced up from his book. "You look like you've been in a war zone."

I sat down across from him at our usual spot in the library. "I went to the theme park with Matt." I caught my own reflection in the dark window next to us. "You weren't kidding," I noted, eyeing the soot stains on my face, left there by Matt's mini-dynamite. "Although you're lucky I didn't show up boneless or squashed flat."

"You *are* boneless," Uncle Jeff pointed out.

"True." I laughed.

"Weird place, huh?" he asked.

I nodded. "Voluntarily getting things dropped on you is harder than it sounds. At least, when you're dead. It's hard not to flinch — if you flinch, you move out of the way, and then you don't get any prize coins."

"That's your incentive to let someone drop an anvil on you?" Uncle Jeff asked.

"There are special rides if you get enough prize coins," I said. "Matt wants to get a thousand, so he can get into the water park."

"What's so great about the water park?"

"They use super-chocolate chocolate milk instead of water," I said. "You know how Matt is about chocolate. So I got as many prize coins as I could and gave them to him when we left."

"Why doesn't he just *make* some prize coins?" Uncle Jeff asked.

"I asked Matt the same thing." I took a moment to fix the scorch marks and generally smooth out my bedraggled appearance. "Matt told me, 'What's the fun in *that*? I'd miss all my chances to get blown up and stuff!'"

"Better you than me." Uncle Jeff laughed.

Helping me sift through things was one of my Uncle Jeff's specialties, and I turned the topic to my last conversation with Chester.

"Okay, so wait a second." Jeff closed his eyes and raised his brows, holding his hands out in front of him in the universal gesture for, "Bear with me, I'm trying to think here."

"I'm waiting." I stared vacantly at the info screen that took up the wall to my right, where my train of thought instantly pulled up an image of Hades' scepter. I looked away quickly. Nothing crazy yet, I told myself.

"So Wilkins knew things you hadn't told him about yourself, right? The first time you talked to him?" Uncle Jeff opened one eye to squint at me.

"Yeah, he knew Dom's name, and that he was the one I wanted to get a message to. So? Maybe he's psychic, but that doesn't mean he's not also crazy." I skimmed a paragraph on the screen about

Hades' apparent love of music, which I didn't think was much help to me, since in the same story he ended up screwing over the poor bastard he'd made a deal with.

"Did you mention any of that same information in another conversation, later on?" my uncle asked.

I looked up from the book, frowning as I thought back to my talks with Chester.

"Yeah, I did. When he didn't remember me, I was trying to jog his memory. I told him my name again and mentioned Dominic by name again and asked if he'd given Dom my message. He didn't remember anything."

Uncle Jeff looked excited now, as if that'd been exactly what he hoped to hear me say.

"What?" I said, perplexed.

"I think I know what's going on. And I think Wilkins might not be crazy."

"How's that, then?" I asked.

"There's no such thing as time here, right? Here in the Underworld, it's just eternity. We don't experience hours or minutes, we don't get tired or bored, now is just always now, and any part of now could keep on being now indefinitely, right? If we so chose?"

I took a beat to run that through my head again in slow-motion, as Uncle Jeff had fallen into his usual habit of talking at light-speed when excited.

"Right," I agreed, after processing.

"But in the Land of the Living, time is going forward in its friendly, comprehensible, linear fashion, just like normal, right?" Uncle Jeff continued.

"Yeah, sure."

"So when you contact him, you're calling from a non-time state, where there isn't any linear time, but he still experiences events in terms of sequential time."

"Okay."

"So what if the conversations are happening *in a different order for him* than they are for you?" Uncle Jeff looked like he'd just found the ultimate Christmas present under the tree.

"Oh." Weird as it sounded, the more I thought about it, the more it made sense. "Armchair quantum physics," I said. "Very clever."

"So maybe you should talk to him again?" Uncle Jeff prompted.

"I always knew you were brilliant." I swept by with a quick kiss to my uncle's cheek as I passed him.

~*~

But Chester was done with me. I called seven times, with no luck. He wasn't answering. He was shutting me out.

I wasn't sure where to turn or what to try, and I was too frustrated to think of anything. This is the kind of situation where sleep feels great.

Tucked under my red paisley comforter, I drifted pleasantly away from the woes and irritations of conscious thought.

I dreamed I was standing in my own living room, back in the Upper World. It was raining — I could hear the steady, rhythmic patter of it along the porch roof, and turned to look out the tall double windows that faced the street. Someone in a raincoat thumped up the porch steps and out of my view right as I looked out. I watched the tip of an umbrella appear and then shake, as its owner tried to dislodge the excess water.

The room smelled of ozone and wood, tinged with cinnamon air freshener and Dom's cologne. There was an empty whiskey bottle on the coffee table, its lid discarded on the floor nearby, and one of Dom's and my wedding photos on the end table, next to a shot glass.

The doorbell rang, and in the stillness of the house, it sounded intrusive, breaking the peace of the rainfall's rhythm.

And then I heard Dom's footsteps on the stairs.

I stared toward the entry hall, through the double-wide

doorframe that separated it from the living room, but from this angle I couldn't see the bottom of the stairwell or the front door.

The door was opened and I heard Chester's voice rumble Dom's name out as a question.

"That's me." Dom already sounded suspicious. "How can I help you?"

"My name is Chester Wilkins. May I come in? I'd like to speak to you about your . . . your late wife."

"Oh." Dom's voice was tired and flat. "Of course, come in. Is this about the funeral arrangements, or. . . ?"

I could hear Dom rattling the hangers in the coat closet while Chester asked, "When did your wife pass away?"

"Three days ago," Dom said. "Come into the living room."

I'm dead, I thought with sudden panic. *I'm dead and they don't know I'm here, and how did I get back?* I couldn't feel my heart beating as I looked around desperately for somewhere to hide. The compulsion to conceal myself was entirely illogical, since I wanted to talk to Dom, but faced with it like this, knowing he would be afraid of me, I couldn't deal with it. I was dreaming, after all, although I didn't know it at the time, and you can't expect logical thinking in a dream.

So I ducked behind the floor length curtains just as they came into the room.

"Sir," Chester said to Dom — I heard the rustle of cloth and the creak of springs as they both sat down and settled in — "first of all, let me tell you how sorry I am for your loss."

No answer — Dom had probably just nodded his acceptance of Chester's condolences.

"What I'm going to tell you will probably sound impossible to believe," Chester went on. "But I have spoken with Erica three times in the past three days."

A pause. Then Dom said sharply, "What?"

"I'm a medium," Chester explained. "I have contact with the deceased, usually initiated by the deceased themselves, on a regular basis, Mr. Flynn. And your wife, sir, chose to contact me. She asked me to come and speak to you."

"What?" Dom was louder this time. "What kind of scam are you pulling?"

"Mr. Flynn, I am not a scam artist. I was asked by your wife to come talk to you."

"Erica doesn't even believe in mediums!" Dominic snapped. "She would never contact a medium — even *dead* she would think this was a load of horse shit! And if you'd talked to her, you would've known when she died without having to ask me."

"Please, Mr. Flynn, I know you're upset, but I do have some proof that I've spoken to her." Chester's voice was steady and soothing, but I could've told him that would only piss Dom off more. If you want to make Dom hopping mad, all you have to do is sound calmer and more reasonable than he does.

"Look, mister," Dom growled, "I've just lost my wife. I'm hung over *and* I'm drunk, I haven't slept in three days, and the last thing I want is some psychic coming around and prying into my head for the information he needs to fuck with it."

By the end, he was yelling, and I heard both of them jump to their feet. I'd only heard Dom drop the F-bomb once before — that was more my style than his — and even without adrenaline I felt jumpy with Dom this upset.

"Douglas Jeffrey Flynn." Chester's firm voice cut Dom off as he started to yell some more. "She told me to say that was what you'd have named your son, if you'd had one. Beatrice Nicole, for a daughter."

"You get the fuck out of my house." I heard a violent scuffling and Dom panting for breath, obscenities I'd never heard from him escaping between every inhalation, Chester's protests barely audible as his voice moved out of the room and into the entry hall again.

I peered out from behind the curtains just as Dom slammed the door and clicked the lock on.

He tore something up — I couldn't tell what — then screamed another obscenity, rattled Chester's raincoat out of the closet, and threw it out after him. Out the living room window, I could see the umbrella slip past, but I never did get a glimpse of Chester.

Maybe I'd better talk to Dom myself, I thought. That's what I'd wanted, after all — and things had to go better than Chester's attempt.

"Dom?" I called.

I could hear his breathing in the other room.

"Dom?" I found him sitting on the fourth step, shuddering, his head down so I couldn't see his face.

Surely he had heard me? I was standing right next to him. But he didn't look up.

I touched his shoulder gently, but he still didn't move. I couldn't even feel him beneath my fingertips. This must just be a dream, I finally realized. That's all this is.

"I love you," I whispered, because it felt good to say it to him, even if he was only a figment of my dream and not my real husband in the Upper World. "I hope you're taking better care of yourself than this. Don't drink so much, and get some sleep." I kissed the top of his head, which I couldn't feel at all against my lips, and just as he was about to look up at me, just as I was about to get to see his face, I woke up.

I lay awake for a long while in my king-sized bed, feeling way too small with all that space to myself.

Chapter Eleven

notes from the underworld

"You're gonna drive yourself nuts with this stuff," Latrischa said, when I told her about the dream. We were walking from my place to Uncle Jeff's studio, which took us along the ridge of Cypress Lane, overlooking the sweeping view of the lush park and the riverside below us. "Get a grip, girl — you're dead. Things are good here. Why do you have to hang on to life so hard?"

"You *know* why," I said. "And it isn't my fault what I dream."

"No, but it's your fault you dwell on it so damn much," she sighed. "You have dreams about the Upper World almost every time you sleep. It's a fresh start, being dead. Take advantage of it."

"It *would* be a fresh start, if I didn't remember my life."

"Well, there's no help for that," Latrischa said.

"There is, I just wouldn't want to do it." I kicked a stone along in front of me as I walked, thinking about the Lethos River near the palace of Hades. "Anyway, what if it wasn't just a dream? I have all those dreams of memories from my life. Those things really happened, so what if this really happened, too?"

"I don't know. I think you're grasping at straws," Latrischa said. "And what do you mean, there's a way not to remember your life?"

"The Lethos River," I said impatiently. "But about this dream — what if I was actually seeing what happened with Chester and Dom? Like Uncle Jeff said, time is different up there than down here, so it doesn't matter that Chester had already been there the last time I talked to him."

Latrischa shook her head. "I don't think like that, Erica, sorry. You'll have to talk to Jeff about all that time jazz."

Which I did, once we arrived at his studio. While I explained, Latrischa wandered around the room, studying Uncle Jeff's carvings, browsing the titles of the books on his shelves, and looking through a coffee table book he had on nature reserves of the world.

"What do you think?" I asked Uncle Jeff. "Do you think I have some kind of link to Dom in the Upper World now, or something?"

He shook his head. "You started the dream out just as Chester arrived, and woke up almost the minute he left, am I right?"

"Yeah," I said.

"Then, if anything, I think you may have formed a psychic connection with *Chester*." He looked apologetic. "He's the medium, after all."

~*~

"Chester!" I gripped the receiver and hissed into the phone. He was trying to ignore me, block me out, and I wasn't having any of that.

I guess this is what they call haunting.

"Chester!" I rapped my knuckles on the mouthpiece with my free hand. It echoed with satisfyingly noisy thunks within the receiver.

"I know you can hear me, you pain in the ass. Come on! If the worst thing that's happened to you all week is some guy threw you out by the shirt collar, then. . . ." I stopped, considering. "Okay, so that sucks, but worse things could happen."

"Like what?" Chester's voice finally rumbled through the line.

"Uh . . . he could've brained you with a poker? He and I could've been mad serial killers in cahoots to lure you to his house and do you in? A live badger could attack you when you open the mailbox?"

"Look, just leave me alone," Chester cut in, before I could think of anything that would top the badger. "My son just finished moving back in yesterday, and I don't want him knowing about all this."

"All what? Aren't you a professional psychic?" I asked.

"Yes."

"Doesn't he know that?" I said.

"Yes, but he doesn't know any of it's *real*," Chester explained.

"O . . . kay. . . ." I struggled with where, precisely, to start untangling the logic at hand. "So you'd rather he thought you were a fraud than that he thought you were—"

"Crazy," Chester supplied.

I sputtered for a few seconds. "But this is *real*. I'm really dead, and you're really talking to me. You aren't crazy. I mean, I always thought you people were, but the point is — well — you aren't." I didn't add that I, myself, still had doubts about his sanity.

"I know that, but my kid doesn't. He's all about logic and being rational. The supernatural just doesn't happen in his world," Chester said. "And he and I have had enough problems between us without me dragging spirits into it. Just leave me alone and let me finally be on good terms with my kid, all right? That's all I ask."

"But I need your help!" I said.

"Why me? There's plenty of other psychics out there."

"Because. . . ." I stopped because I didn't exactly know. "Because I know you. Sort of. And, look, I'm sorry about the way Dom treated you. He didn't mean it." I decided to leave it at that. I didn't really want to go into the fact that I might have witnessed the scene, partly because I wasn't sure I had, and partly because I didn't want to seem like I was spying on anybody — even dead, you don't want people to think you're a big snoop.

There was a long silence, so long I got to thinking he was blocking me out, but finally he spoke again. "What do you need from me?"

"I need you to perform a séance so I can talk to Dom myself."

"You do realize that involves me speaking to your husband again?" Chester growled. "I'd have to be in his physical presence, otherwise I'd have to conjure you up and then go to wherever he is without losing my concentration. That's assuming I even knew where he was every minute of the day."

"But what if you called me up somewhere we knew he'd be, and then waited for him?" I asked.

"I just *said* I have to hold my concentration the whole time," Chester said. "You think it's easy to keep a piece of someone's soul in the wrong world? It's not even easy to *get* it here."

"Whoa, wait." I was suddenly sidetracked entirely. "A *piece* of someone's soul?"

"That's right," Chester said. "You'll be aware of both worlds at once. I don't know how all this works, but my assumption is that your soul is either in some transcendent state that I can't understand, or your soul is split in two — one in this world, and one in your world."

"That's going to be uncomfortable, whichever of those is the case," I commented, but pressed on. "Okay. Split soul or not, I want to do this thing, and I need your help."

"I doubt your husband is going to be receptive to my company," Chester said. "And frankly, I'm not receptive to his. For all I know, he'll call the cops the minute he sees me. That's the last thing I want — my kid having to pick me up from jail two days after he gets home."

"Can you perform a séance or not?" Through the glass walls of the phone booth, the park had darkened into shades of blue and purple, and little swarms of lightning bugs provided transient illumination between pools of lamplight.

"All right," Chester snapped.

"Uh, okay," I said. "So you can do it? You can bring me back?"

"Fine. I'll raise your spirit, but only because I already promised to. Given everything that's happened to me on your account, I wish I hadn't. Unfortunately for me, I already gave my word." I could practically feel his glower through the phone. I racked my brains trying to remember when he'd done anything like promise me a séance, and realized that he meant he'd given his word *prior* to this conversation. In his timeline, we'd already talked about this before. That explained why he was acting like I already knew about his son.

"Oh." I pulled out a mini notebook and a pen from my jeans pocket, and wrote myself a reminder: *Make Chester promise séance*. Then I tucked it away again and re-gripped the orange receiver more firmly. "When can you do it?"

"I don't know yet. I have to make arrangements. I need *someone* that you know to be part of the ceremony, for one, and your husband is one thousand percent out, in my book," Chester rumbled.

"Right." It was a damn shame that Dom had assumed Chester was a crank. Things would be so much easier all around if he'd accepted that I really was sending messages to him from beyond the grave. "I don't know who else you could ask, though. I mean, Dom's the most superstitious person I know. If he doesn't believe that I have anything to do with you, I have no idea who would. My parents are pretty down-to-earth, my brother — well, Tyler's not the sharpest knife in the drawer—"

"What about your sister?" Chester cut in.

"Laura?" I tried to remember when I'd mentioned Laura to him, but I didn't think I had. I scribbled myself another note and stuffed the notebook back in my pocket.

"Do you think she would agree to a séance? Is there anything that only you and she would know about, that I could use to get her to believe me?" Chester asked. "Something that wouldn't get me thrown out of the house this time?"

I laughed. "Laura? A séance?" My little sister, who was hard-wired for business. She could make money the way other people could gain weight — without trying, without thinking, and completely by her natural habits. Laura was the epitome of worldly, and the last person I'd associate with something as ooey and intangible as a séance. I could more easily see Tyler being sucked in — all you'd have to do is find a video game where somebody raised the dead and let him play it for a couple of hours, then tell him you wanted to do it for real.

"I can't quite see that," I told Chester. "You can try, if you want. What other 'arrangements' do you need to make?"

"Just let me handle that." He sounded annoyed, but reassuringly committed to fulfilling his promise.

Chapter Twelve

where not to go for a picnic in the afterlife

Anatol and I had plans. Ever since he'd told me about the Road to the Land of the Living, I couldn't get it out of my head. I wanted to see it, to know it was real. A Road that really could lead me back home, back to Dom.

Without Hades' scepter, there was probably no point even thinking about it, but what if I *could* get my hands on the scepter? What if the fortune-teller back at the docks had known I was *going* to get it, and that was what had impressed her? The more I thought about it, the more I was sure that was what she'd seen in my future. Maybe I was kidding myself, trying to bolster my own confidence, but it felt good to think that she'd seen it happen already, that I had a guaranteed success ahead of me.

Anatol and I met up at the Dead Man's Chest, and walked to the northeast edge of downtown.

"I'll tell you again," Anatol said as we walked, "you don't want to go down the Road."

"I know it's not a picnic," I said.

I expected him to laugh, but he didn't.

"Have *you* been down it?" I asked.

"I tried once," he answered. "Here, turn right at this intersection."

We'd left the hub of the city behind now, and the buildings here looked older. I didn't see anyone else on the street except one nervous-looking guy in a long raincoat who crossed in front of us.

"What happened?" I asked Anatol.

"I turned back." He paused at the next crosswalk to strike a match and light up. Shielding the flame from the wind, his voice muffled from talking around his cigar, he said, "I decided to be patient instead." Smoke curled out of the edges of his mouth.

"That's why you work the ferry," I said slowly. "You're waiting for someone."

"Best chance of finding someone in the afterlife." Anatol held the cigar out for me and I took a puff.

Handing it back to him, I said nothing for a few blocks, thinking about that. I could stand missing Dom until he showed up — it wasn't like I'd even be aware of time passing, and he'd be able to affect his apparent age with a little effort — but for *Dom*, his life would go on, presumably painfully, and knowing him, he'd feel guilty for years about our argument contributing to my death. I wasn't just going back for my own sake.

"Who—" I started to ask.

Anatol guessed my question and answered before I'd finished asking. "A woman, of course."

"Your wife?"

He blew a smoke ring. "No. I made the mistake of not telling her my feelings until she was already married to someone else."

"Oh." I suddenly saw Anatol in a whole new light.

"It turns out she loved me, not her husband, but it was too late for all that by the time we exchanged confessions." His smile had none of its usual humor.

"That's awful," I said. "For all three of you."

Anatol shrugged. "Life is sad."

"So you're waiting for her," I said.

"So we can spend our afterlife together." The gleam came back into his eyes, his smile broadening. "I can't tell you how happy I was when I died and realized we would have a chance here that we never would have had while we were alive. She would never have divorced, not unless her husband had been a bad man — and he wasn't."

He was putting so much faith in someone who could so easily let him down. What if she fell in love with her husband after all? What if the husband wanted to be with her in the afterlife, too, and she felt obliged to stay with him? What if she got to the afterlife and didn't want either one of them? All Anatol's devotion would be for nothing. I'd never pictured him at the mercy of anyone or anything—his gruff, easygoing swagger put him in the "tough guy" category in my mind — and this sudden revelation of tenderness made me scared to see him hurt.

"That's really sweet, and at the same time kind of creepy," I said, choosing to keep my other thoughts to myself. "I mean, you're waiting around for the woman you love to drop dead."

Anatol laughed. "I'm waiting for her to be reborn," he corrected. "That's how *I* think of this place. But enough of all that — we're here now."

He stopped walking before I did, and I stood at the threshold of the Road to the Land of the Living, Anatol waiting a few paces behind me.

The edge of the city just dropped off here, as if even the buildings of Hades themselves didn't want to get too close to the Road. An abandoned train station, all glass and steel and brick, heavily decorated with birds' nests, was the nearest structure, and even the birds seemed to have left it behind.

The cracked pavement of the street finally broke up into a scattering of black rubble along the ground, and a few yards later the wild took over, the Road cutting through it in a twisting, writhing line through the underbrush.

The vegetation was strange — sparse in places and thick elsewhere, some of the plants looking as if they belonged in a jungle and others more like what I'd imagine in the Kalahari. The Road ran through a tunnel of trees, mostly of a single kind, thick with blackish-green leaves, many of their branches choked into strange angles by masses of another plant's vines. The leaves shivered in a wind that whipped my hair around my face, and in all the rustle it was hard to tell, but it seemed as if things were stirring up in the branches.

"Seen enough?" Anatol chuckled as I took a step back, closer to him.

I attempted bravado, flashing him a grin over my shoulder, but I found the Road far more disturbing than I'd expected. It wasn't so much what I could see, or the fear of the things I couldn't see, along the way. There was a certain sensation in its presence — a creeping awareness of vulnerability. I hadn't realized how far removed I was, having settled into the Underworld, from the feeling that I could be harmed. That I could get sick. That I could starve.

Looking at the Road, I remembered what it had really felt like to be alive, but not the good sensations. Only the fears.

Before my death, I'd always enjoyed the stories of Greek mythology. They were entertaining, and they offered a whole different perspective on the human condition than the slog of the everyday modern world. The humans were often petty, but the gods were even worse — jealous, small-minded, temperamental brats throwing tantrums, misusing their powers to squabble like children among themselves.

All very amusing, of course.

I hadn't much thought about it until I'd stood there talking to Hades, but at some point in that conversation, it had clicked with me that this fantastical realm was, in fact, *actually ruled* by one of the gods from those stories.

The question was, how accurate were the myths on the whole vengeance thing?

Lying in bed in the Underworld, I thought over the dangers involved in traveling the Road. I could probably face that, when it came down to it, but even so, I'd still have to steal the scepter of Hades, and to do that, I would need help. It was all well and good for me to take risks with *my* immortal soul, with *my* eternal afterlife, but if I brought in accomplices, would Hades punish them, too?

I thought about Tantalus from the old myths, doomed to suffer eternal thirst while standing up to his neck in water. Or Sisyphus, forced to roll a boulder up a hill, only to have it reappear at the bottom, over and over, forever and ever. Granted, I'd seen no evidence to support those stories, but the Underworld is a big place.

If I was only risking myself, I could brush all of it aside as tall tales, go on with my plan, and hope for the best, but in order to get away with this, I'd need all the help I could get. Assuming I could even pull it off.

I'd have to content myself with whatever help Chester could offer me, I decided. If he could do one séance, surely he could repeat the process. Maybe if he got one right, and had another witness to tell Dom about it, we could do a second one and Dom would come around. That way I could have my conversation with him, at least. It wasn't as satisfying, but it was less risky this way.

But I'd have to really push Chester to get him to go through with it.

Chapter Thirteen

revenge is a dish you should follow the recipe for very carefully

"Where's Latrischa?" Uncle Jeff asked when I next arrived at the Dead Man's Chest. Matt and Anatol were at the table with him, playing Slapjack with Anatol's card deck, and the Holy Dead Guys Trinity was at the bar — Vic was re-making a drink for the minister — but Latrischa was nowhere to be seen.

"I thought she was already here," I said. "I stopped by her place on the way over, and she wasn't home."

"We thought she was with you," Anatol said. He and Uncle Jeff traded glances.

"That's weird," I said.

"Maybe she's at the Fashion Exchange." Matt shrugged, and since his game with Anatol was paused anyway, went to the bar for a fresh milkshake to modify.

"Maybe she had a date," I suggested.

"I doubt it." Anatol darted another glance at Uncle Jeff.

"She's probably just at the Fashion Exchange, like Matt said." My uncle smiled nervously, trying to shrug off the cloud that was gathering between the three of us. "Anyway, she's dead — what do I think's going to happen to her?"

I had a nasty sinking feeling as I thought back to the conversation I'd had with her on the way to Uncle Jeff's — when she'd been talking about the afterlife being a fresh start. She had asked me what I meant about forgetting about life, and I'd mentioned the Lethos River. I hadn't given it a second thought, I'd been so preoccupied with my dream about Dom and Chester's argument. *You big dummy,* I thought at myself.

"I can think of quite a few unfortunate things that could happen to a dead person." Anatol had caught my expression.

I sat down hard. "Oh, guys. . . ." I put my hand over my forehead and leaned on the table. "I think I did something really stupid. You know about the Lethos River, right?" I knew Anatol did, because he was the one who'd told me that its mythological powers were true.

"Yeah," Uncle Jeff said. "It's supposed to make you forget everything if you drink from it. By Hades' palace, right?"

I nodded.

"Does it really work that way, or is it just a story?" Uncle Jeff looked to Anatol for his answer.

"It really works that way," Anatol said.

"And you think she—" Uncle Jeff's eyes widened. "But that's like—"

"Like suicide for the dead," Anatol finished for him.

"She wouldn't really do it." Uncle Jeff crossed his arms. "Not Latrischa. She's a tough customer — she's not the type to take the easy way out. Right?"

We all looked at each other. No, she wasn't the type. But that didn't mean it couldn't happen.

"Well, let's *go.*" I jumped out of my seat. "Maybe we can stop her before she drinks from it."

Chairs clattered as the three of us scrambled out the door. At the last second, I yelled back to Matt, "Gotta find Latrischa — we'll see you later, okay?"

"Great, so I'm stuck hanging out with *them*?" He jerked his thumb at the Religious Guys Anonymous, looking disgruntled.

When we jumped out of the taxi, we could already see Latrischa sitting on the bank, staring into the water.

She looked up as we approached, and I was relieved to see

that she recognized us instantly.

"What's up, guys?" she said awkwardly, letting her hair fall forward so we couldn't see her expression.

Uncle Jeff sat down next to her, his worn penny loafers scraping the pebbly ground. A few pebbles broke loose and scattered across the rocks and into the water. "That's what we came to ask you."

I took a seat on a big rock on the other side of her, and Anatol leaned against the bridge and smoked.

"You weren't planning on drinking that, were you?" Uncle Jeff motioned toward the water.

Latrischa shrugged. "I was thinking about it. I just wanted to see it, think it over a little. I hadn't really made up my mind yet."

"Are you mad we're here?" I asked, and she finally tucked her hair behind her ears so I could see her face.

She just looked worn-out, frayed and listless, but she forced one side of her mouth upward for my benefit as she shook her head. "No, I'm not mad."

"You know you'd forget us, too." I turned to Anatol. "Wouldn't she?"

He nodded his confirmation, tapping ashes off his cigar against the stone bridge behind him.

"I didn't know that part," Latrischa mumbled.

"Even if you didn't," Uncle Jeff said, "what happened in your life is part of who you are — you wouldn't be the same person without those experiences, however bad some of them might be."

"And they can't all be bad memories," I added. "I've had those sugar cookies you use for joy-swapping. Those are some seriously happy-tasting cookies."

She actually smiled then. "My granny and I used to bake those together. She always let me put as much icing and sprinkles as I wanted on them after they cooled off, too."

"Is she still—"

"Topside? Yeah."

"See, you don't want to forget her," Uncle Jeff said. "She'll probably be excited to see you again when she gets here."

Latrischa nodded.

"And your brothers and sisters," I pressed.

"How did you know I have brothers and sisters?"

I grinned and bumped her shoulder with mine. "The way you tell Matt off for his language."

She laughed. "You got me there. Oldest of six: two sisters, three brothers. You know, guys, I wasn't actually set on going through with this." She gestured at the water.

"Okay." Uncle Jeff clasped her shoulder. "We're just trying to tilt the balance in our favor here."

"I guess you guys really like me, huh?" Despite her smile, she looked embarrassed and fragile, which I wasn't used to from her.

"Duh." I bumped her with my shoulder again.

"You like me, too, Anatol?" she called teasingly.

"Nah." He winked and gestured at the barren, grey landscape surrounding us. "I just came along for the scenery."

"Can we all go back to the Dead Man's Chest now?" I asked. "Before Hades comes over and tells us to get off his lawn?"

~*~

"Are you ever going to tell me what happened?" I asked Latrischa, when I had her to myself again — back at my place, after a few rounds at the bar with the others.

Her guard went up instantly. "What do you mean, what happened?"

"I mean, how you died. You've dodged the question every time I've asked," I said. "Does it have something to do with you going down to the Lethos today?"

Latrischa's mouth tightened and she drew herself up, then

sighed and sagged back on the couch. "Yeah. I guess in a way it's got everything to do with it."

"Why are you so secretive about it?" I asked. "I mean, your whole life. I have to guess almost everything about you, and I'm your best friend — well, your best dead friend, anyway. I think."

"Yeah, yeah, yeah." That was, I thought, probably the most warm and fuzzy answer I'd get out of her.

"So what gives?" I said.

"Look, it's embarrassing, all right?" Latrischa looked annoyed again. "I was being stupid. A dumb, heart-broken little girl trying to get back at the guy that hurt her. That's not *me*." She paused, and a small, wicked grin crossed her face for a moment. "*Me* would be a well-thought out, successful, premeditated, first-degree murder."

"You know that's redundant, right?" I put in.

"Yeah, whatever. Anyway, I do things right and I think things through," she said. "That's why I hadn't decided what to do about forgetting everything when you guys showed up today. If I want to get back at someone, I don't just fly off the handle, and I sure as hell don't do anything that would cause *me* more trouble than them."

"Remind me not to piss you off," I muttered.

She stuck her tongue out at me. "Do you want to hear this or not? Because if you want to know, I'd rather get it over with now you've got me started."

I gestured that my lips were zipped, then folded my hands in my lap and batted my eyelashes innocently.

"So I found out Travis — that was my jerk fiancé — was cheating on me. I told you about *that*. I cried for a day or two and acted all soppy and pathetic, and then I just sort of switched it off and was *furious*. I was even madder that I hadn't decked him the last time I saw him, because I'd been too busy crying to be angry at that point."

I nodded. I could understand that sentiment — there were a couple of ex-boyfriends who still had a punch in the face waiting for them if I ever saw them again, although now that I was dead that might pose a problem. It was like the comeback line you think of later, when you wish like hell you could reverse time and *use* it.

"He *loved* his house," Latrischa continued. "His big, swanky house with all that inlay and all that paintwork *I* did for him, and his big, swanky garage with his sports cars. So one night, he dialed my number — he said accidentally — from some night club where he and his—" she made a horrible face.

"Floozy?" I suggested.

"I was thinking more like hussy," she said. "Anyway, he called me from a night club where the two of them were enjoying themselves. He was drunk, so maybe it was accidental, but all I could think was how he was rubbing it in, calling me like that."

She looked over at me and then away. "I knew they were out, and nobody else lived there, so I knew the house was empty."

I thought I could see where this was going, but I didn't interrupt.

"I burned down his house," Latrischa said, slowly, every word delivered precisely. "Starting with the garage. There were gas cans in there, too, which helped. I'm not sure whether the house was gutted or not, but I *know* those cars didn't make it."

"But you died in the fire?" I said.

"Yeah." She nodded. "I got trapped. Things went up faster than I expected, and the smoke got to me."

"And you're ashamed because you think you shouldn't have done it?" I asked.

She snorted. "No, I'm ashamed because I didn't plan it well enough to live through it — and I would've gotten caught if I hadn't died . . . which might actually have been worse, to tell you the truth. If I'd lived and gone to jail for it, my granny would've given me an earful for doing it. As it is, I *died* over that dumb chump, and if you think *I'm* bad, trust me, you don't want to be Travis if my granny gets hold of him now."

"Again, remind me never to piss you off." We were silent for a moment. "Still, he deserved it."

"You think so?" Latrischa searched my face, as if it were up to me to forgive her.

"Hey, he's rich — he can buy another house and more cars. He probably got plenty of insurance money for it. You can't get back the time you spent with him while he was cheating on you." I shrugged. "Plus, I'm biased because you're my friend."

"You don't think I'm a lousy person because of what I did?" she asked.

"No." I didn't think it was the pinnacle of morality, but at the same time I was kind of awed by the whole thing. Talk about grabbing life by the throat — burning down someone's house and sports cars for revenge sure wasn't pussyfooting around the issue. I had to admire the extremity of it. Besides, she obviously felt worse about what she'd done than she was admitting to.

"I think," I said carefully, "that for somebody who talks so much about letting go of life, you're dragging around a lot of baggage about this Travis guy. Maybe you need to let go of *that*. But that doesn't mean you've got to forget the good parts of your life."

"Look who's talking, Miss Gotta Make Up For One Mistake," Latrischa said, rolling her eyes.

"Shut up." I threw a pillow at her, but of course it missed.

Chapter Fourteen

death is taxes

When I next spoke to Chester, he knew me, but not my name, and although he knew Dom's name, he displayed none of his previous animosity toward my husband. My only guess was that we (from Chester's point of view) had spoken before, but not much, and apparently they hadn't been very revealing conversations. Which conversations they were (from my point of view), I wasn't sure about.

The one thing Chester seemed clear on was my desperate desire to get a message to Dominic.

I waited until I'd built up a good amount of sympathy from the medium, then opened up the question of the séance.

He was reluctant. "I'm not sure about that," he said. "My son just graduated college, and he'll be moving in here in a few days. It's the first chance I've had in years to patch things up with him."

"And you're afraid that raising the dead might put a damper on your relationship with the young man?" I couldn't help thinking that at least his son sounded like a reasonable human being, capable of logic and sanity.

"It's not something your average teenager or college kid has to explain away to his friends, you know," Chester grumbled. "It's also why his mother divorced me."

"I'm sorry." Okay, stamp *Jerk* on my forehead now, I thought. Sure, I had a nagging suspicion that Chester Wilkins was a flake, however authoritative that booming voice might sound, but it was still sad to think of him standing in a doorway with his bags all packed, looking up at what had been his happy family home, and knowing he was losing it just because dead people could talk to him for some reason. And seemingly, he was trying to help us dead people out, with no benefit to himself in my case. Being a professional medium, he presumably got paid by his living clients — since I was dead, I guessed this was pro bono.

But I *needed* his help, so I couldn't let myself feel so sorry for him that I couldn't be pushy about it. *For Uncle Jeff,* I thought, *who wants me to try something* not *crazy.*

"It doesn't have to be elaborate or anything," I coaxed Chester. "I just need to come back for a few minutes. All I want is a few minutes."

He let out a long sigh that said, without words, how much he really, really wanted to tell me no.

"Please?" I pressed.

"Look, maybe I can work something out," he said.

"I need an answer," I said. "This is eternity here, on this side. Can't you at least give me a sure answer, so I won't be in suspense?" Okay, so I was playing it like 'eternity' meant the slow passage of time forever and ever, which I knew to be the exact opposite of what it was, but I had that reminder in my notebook that I needed to get Chester to give me his word, and I was going to get it.

And because he wasn't yet set against me, he said, "All right, I'll do it."

"Do you swear to me that you'll bring me back? You won't change your mind?"

"I won't," Chester said.

"I need your word."

"I swear I'll perform the séance, but I can't promise it will bring you back to this side, or for how long." He had the sure tone of evasiveness in his voice. He'd love to wiggle out of it already, but he must've been tender-hearted, because he wasn't saying no.

"Just promise you'll perform the séance," I wheedled.

"I said already, I promise. You have my word," Chester said solemnly.

"Great." I flipped open my notebook and put a check mark by my finished task. Glancing at the page, I added, "Oh, yeah, and I have a younger sister named Laura." I flipped the notebook closed again and stuck it in my pocket.

If he was confused by my last statement, he didn't say so, and the phone disconnected a moment later, leaving me with a dial tone. I hung up the receiver.

I'd gotten Chester to agree to one séance, but to talk to Dom, I'd probably have to coax another out of him. And that was even assuming that Dom would be willing to come for the second one, if a second witness of my ghostly presence was enough to convince him of Chester's integrity.

I would press on with Plan B, I decided, despite the dangers involved. I didn't *have* to go through with it, if things worked out with Chester, but there was no reason I couldn't have things in place to carry it out if Plan A fell through.

Time to visit Anatol at the ferry.

It was docked at the moment, on the Hades side of the Styx. I looked around as I passed through the carnival, but I didn't see the fortune-teller, and her tent was empty — a sign across the front claimed, "Out For Lunch."

The boards creaked as I made my way up the dock. Anatol stood at the railing, looking across the river, but he turned as he heard my approach, and waved.

When the ferry was docked, I found it to be an immensely soothing place. The River Styx shimmered with light spilling down from the carnival, and Anatol and I sat back in our deck chairs taking in the scenery and a peaceful breeze, chatting.

Eventually, I wound my way around to my object.

Anatol sighed and ran a hand through his short, coarse hair.

"What?" I demanded. "*You* were the one who gave me the idea."

"I didn't think you'd really decide to try to steal the scepter of Hades." Anatol sighed again, then laughed affectionately. "I should've known better, with you. I thought I was talking you *out* of your daredevilry."

"I guess you just convinced me to raise my sights," I said. "I'm serious, though. I've got some ideas hatching about how to pull it off — the only problem is, I don't know where the scepter itself *is*."

"I do."

I jerked around to see who had spoken. The voice was unfamiliar, gravelly, and nasal. The speaker himself was short and broad-shouldered, his cheeks sunken and his eyes protrudent. How a dead person can seem greasy, I don't know, but he did, with oily wisps of grey hair that seemed to hang at random lengths, and ill-kept stubble that made Anatol look like a clean-cut, upright gentleman by comparison.

"Charon," Anatol said, half as an introduction for me and half, it seemed, as an admonishment to Charon himself.

"I know where he keeps it." Charon addressed me exclusively, purposely ignoring Anatol's displeasure with this turn of events. His grey-blue eyes bored into mine, like he was sizing me up for the task at hand.

I glanced nervously at Anatol. If this guy was in the Hades Fan Club, I was pinched for sure.

"Don't worry," Anatol assured me, reading my expression correctly. "Charon's not fond of Hades."

Charon spat, realized he'd spit on his own vessel, and seemed annoyed by the fact. He pulled a grubby handkerchief out of his pocket, tossed it down, and used his foot to rub vaguely at the spot he'd offended. "I used to get *paid*, you know, for ferrying you people across the river. Until that overbearing tyrant forbade me to refuse passage to the souls who couldn't pay the toll. *Now*, I've got no authority whatsoever. On my own ship, I have no say who can board and who can't."

"Why did he change the rules?" Privately, I thought well of Hades for the first time since I'd met him. It seemed very modern and kind-hearted, making sure even the poor had safe passage to what was, admittedly, a great place to be dead. When I'd read Greek mythology, I'd always thought Charon was a jerk, leaving poor lost souls on the wrong side of the river to wander aimlessly, just because they didn't bring him a couple gold coins. It's not like he could even *spend* them, here. Some people are just greedy, a fact that Charon himself further underlined with his next statement.

He smiled hideously. "Because he wanted as many souls in his realm as possible."

"Why?" I said. "Does it feed his power, or something?"

"How should I know?" Charon shrugged.

"Would you be willing to tell me where Hades keeps his scepter?" I asked.

"I'd like to take a swipe at Hades any way I can," Charon said with another shrug. "But what's in it for me?"

"You already pointed out it's going to make Hades unhappy," I stalled. "Why do you still ferry people across, if you're not getting paid, anyway?"

"Oh, occasionally, someone still turns up prepared. People from good, old-fashioned countries with good, old-fashioned values, who understand that there's no such thing as a free ride, Upper World or Underworld. Death *is* taxes, missy." Charon laughed. "And I'd be on my boat anyway, so I might as well pick up what fares do come along. It ain't like when the ancient Egyptians came through regularly — now *those* folks were loaded! 'Course, they mostly don't stick around the capitol, anyway. . . ."

"This boat's about the only thing he loves," Anatol put in from his perch on the railing, stopping Charon in mid-ramble. "That and money, of course."

The wheels of devious thinking turned quickly in my mind, and an idea came to me. "You don't spend much time on the land, do you?" I asked Charon, trying to sound casual.

"Nope." He shook his head adamantly, not seeming suspicious about my line of questioning. "Just pop up to the carnival from time to time — I do enjoy that whatchacallit, the boat ride that goes upside down?"

"The Viking Ship?" I suggested.

"That's the one. But I don't go past the carnival, no sir. Don't want to lose my sea legs." He patted the column behind him affectionately.

"Are you particular about where your coinage comes from?" I asked. Anatol looked at me sharply.

"If it's gold, I don't care what country's seal is on it." Charon's greedy expression conjured up images of blood-spattered gold coins with swastikas on them, although honestly I didn't know what Nazi money had looked like. I wondered how Anatol was still such a nice guy, being in close proximity with this weirdo for so many trips across the Styx.

"Well, it happens that there's a place I know of here in the Underworld that uses gold coins for tender," I said. "I could probably bring you, say, five hundred?"

Charon produced another horrifically unpleasant smile. "Tell me more about how you're going to put one over on Hades."

Anatol listened, too, and by the time I had finished my explanation, he looked more impressed than worried.

However risky I knew my plan was, I found that comforting.

"The one thing I'm worried about," I told Charon, "is that I'd be endangering the people who'd help me, should I go through with this."

Charon shook his head. "Nah. If I thought the repercussions would be bad, I wouldn't have put my two cents in to start with."

"You don't think Hades will punish me?" I was skeptical.

"I didn't say that." Charon laughed a harsh, unpleasant laugh. "He won't bother with the people who help you. It's *you* he'll be after."

"How do you know that?" I glanced at Anatol, but he was leaned against the railing of the ferry with his arms crossed, not looking at either of us.

"I know how Hades works," Charon said, in answer to my question. "I've seen enough of him to know pretty well what he'll do and who he'll do it to."

On one level, I felt incredibly relieved. On another, not so much. "And what do you think Hades will do to me, if I go through with this?"

Charon shrugged. "Not even I know how much of that stuff from the myths is true. There are those who say it's all stories he spread himself, just to rattle people and make them obey him. Some even go so far as to say he let a few souls loose, gave them passage back topside in exchange for them agreeing to tell those tales."

"And is that true?" I asked.

"How should I know?" Charon said again. "You bring me the five hundred gold. When I've got it, you'll know where the scepter is." With another grin, he turned away and stumped off down the stairs to the engine room — or whatever was below deck.

"What, exactly, are you doing?" I asked Matt, peering over the edge of the skyscraper. The two of us stood looking out over the city from one of the highest roofs available, the sprawl stretching away in all directions.

"I'm jumping off roofs," Matt said matter-of-factly. "It's fun." At which, he stepped up on the ledge and then swan-dived off, hurtling toward the asphalt below with an exhilarated, high-pitched whoop that echoed back up to me.

I watched him fall, getting smaller and smaller, until he

appeared to bounce, his whole form seeming briefly to morph, and he sped back up until he was back at eye level with me. He hung in the air for a moment, and I extended a hand. He took it, and I pulled him back onto the roof, marveling again at how little reality seemed to mean to kids around here.

Matt grinned at what must have been a very disoriented expression on my face. "I like not having physics," he said.

"Agreed." I took a seat on the ledge, my back to the steel and glass chasm of the city street.

Matt sat down next to me. "What's up?"

"Two things," I said. "One, how many more of those prize coins do you need to get into the water park?"

"Two hundred and forty-three," Matt said without a moment's hesitation.

"How about I try to get Uncle Jeff, Latrischa, and Anatol to go with us to the theme park, and the five of us try to earn your coins plus five hundred more?" I suggested.

"I'd get in a lot faster that way." Matt's face lit up. "You're the only one that's helped me with it so far — nobody else will go with me. Whatcha need the five hundred for, anyway?"

"A bribe," I admitted.

"Okay, so what's the other thing you wanted to talk to me about?"

"I may need a favor," I said. "If I *do* need this favor, I want to know if I can count on you for it."

An abrupt "What?" was the response, but he listened, his smile widening, and nodded vigorously at my conclusion.

"You'll do it, if I need you to?" I asked.

Matt spit on his palm and held it out. I spit on my own, and we shook on it.

And thus part two of my plan fell into place, even as I hoped I wouldn't need to use it.

Chapter Fifteen

the séance

Luckily, the next time we talked, Chester and I seemed to be on the same page. He remembered everything I remembered, and he didn't reference things I didn't yet know about.

More importantly still, he was ready to bring me across. I hoped this would solve everything — then I could forget all about Hades and his stupid scepter, Charon's greed, and earning almost eight hundred prize coins by letting kids run over me and drop pianos on my head.

I didn't even bother to ask Chester where he was or who he'd gotten to help him, I just told him I was ready, and I took my first trip back from the Underworld.

Being called up for a séance is one of the weirdest experiences a dead person can have.

One minute you're on the phone to the medium, clutching the orange plastic receiver and listening to him intone ridiculous mumbo-jumbo formalities. How much of what's said is to get the medium in the right mind frame — to get his focus together — and how much of it really has to do with cosmic planes or dimensional shifts, I don't know.

At any rate, just when you're starting to think this is a big fat joke at your expense, things start to change.

The first thing I noticed was that the Underworld around me didn't look quite right. Squinting out of habit, as if I had eyeballs that squinting would make any difference to, it took me a beat to realize I was getting more than one visual image, one fainter than the other. The green grass of the park outside the phone booth was distinct, charcoal-colored sky stretched above it and textured with clouds, a few trees scattered around. But just barely, I could see something else — a room with tall, arched windows, the arcs traced faintly across the dark Underworld sky. They were so bright I couldn't distinguish anything around them, but I knew where Chester was. My younger sister's condo.

"Is she here?"

I almost cried, hearing Laura's voice. The rush of overwhelming love I felt for her, hearing her ask for me, was only matched by the shock of it.

"Laura!" I yelled into the receiver. "Laura, it's me. It's really Erica!"

"Well, is she?" my sister insisted. Obviously, she couldn't hear me yet.

Her condo was becoming more distinct. The light coming in through the windows was full, bright daylight, and now I could see the plum drapes framing them, the gleam of the brushed metal coffee table, and the reflection off the wall-mounted TV. Vaguely, there were still the trees against the sky, the skyline of Hades rising up in the distance. Chester went on intoning nonsense in his deep, rumbling voice.

"Oh, I feel weird." I clutched my head with my free hand. There was the sensation that "me" was in a different place than "I". If I'd still been physical, I would've said it felt like my head and my brain were in two different places.

"Erica! I can hear you!" Laura said.

And now I could see her, tensed on the edge of the couch, a tissue clutched in her right hand. She looked drained, her nose and eyes red from crying. My heart went out to her.

"This is weird." I realized that although I was holding a phone in the Underworld, my hands were free in the Land of the Living. I still felt the plastic against my hand, could feel my hand curled around it, but I could also feel that I was holding my hand up in front of me, fingers out straight as I stared at the indistinct, grey-white of myself. I stepped toward Laura, and at the same time was still within the phone booth.

"Tell me about it," Laura said. "Your funeral is tonight."

I looked over at Chester for the first time. I caught myself boggling, and tried to tone down my expression.

He was a big, sturdy guy. Not fat, but hugely tall and very, very solid. Imagining Dom, who was an inch or two shy of six foot and slender, throwing this guy out by his shirt collar — well, let's just say Dom's emotions must've been doing most of the work. He'd only come up to Chester's chin.

Chester's short, wiry black hair was streaked white above his left temple, his skin coffee-brown and smooth, with no wrinkles across his forehead or at the edges of his eyes. I knew his kid was old enough to graduate college, so maybe in his mid forties? Early fifties? Other than that white streak in his hair, he just didn't look that old, even in his serious dark suit and little wire-frame glasses.

"Wow," he rumbled, looking back at me. "I've never actually managed to do that before. I mean, I've never had a spirit manifest."

"A medium who's never seen a ghost," I said before I could stop myself. "That's a good one."

Chester glowered at me and my sister stared at me, still trying to get hold of the idea I was there.

"Sorry," I told Chester. "That came out a little more snotty than I meant it."

"Yeah, I get that that happens a lot with you," he growled, but his expression shifted back into one of curiosity rather than anger.

Laura stood, her eyes wide, as if she thought blinking would make me disappear. She moved slowly toward me, reaching out with one hand.

Laura and I do share an uncanny resemblance. People have

thought we were twins, though we're far from identical. Laura has one of those cute, pretty heart-shaped faces, with a cute, pretty heart-shaped mouth and a small, elegant nose. My face is longer, narrower, and harsher, although Laura's secretly the one with a mind and heart like a steel trap. We're both slim, but soft in the curvy bits, if you get my meaning, with the same medium-brown, wavy hair, although Laura keeps hers longer and streaks it with blonde highlights.

Without thinking, I'd raised my hand to meet my sister's, palm forward, fingers curled slightly toward each other's hands. Hers trembled, mine drifting forward like smoke in a draft, until—

A split-second of sensation — organic rhythm and a sort of liquid heat — and suddenly the Underworld was firmly back in place around me, with no hint of another place beyond it or within it.

There was a hand gripping my arm none-too-gently. It was a long-fingered hand, with clean, well-trimmed nails and pale skin. It was attached to Hades himself, who was wearing a dark shin-length coat and an intense expression that was nonetheless blank. He didn't look angry, disappointed, or surprised. Just intense, and extremely tall up this close, as we were both crushed into the little orange phone booth.

I was still trying to adjust to being in only one world again and feeling woozy with the effort as I stared gormlessly up at his pale, narrow face.

"You belong *here*," he said pointedly. "You have been told that. I thought I had made myself clear when I told you that you were not to return to the Land of the Living."

"Oh, you were clear." Honesty seemed to pour out of my mouth without my consent as I held his eye contact. "You were clear. I just don't care."

I had done it. I'd made it back topside. Only for a moment, but I had *done* it.

"The only thing that matters to me," I continued aloud, "is

going back up and talking to Dom."

"You can't." Hades released my arm. It occurred to me that he'd managed to make direct contact with me, and I wondered if it was because I'd been distracted at the time, or if it was due to his godly status. "I do not make exceptions."

The phone booth was feeling pretty small for the stare-down we were having, especially with Hades' propensity for towering over me when he didn't like how the conversation was going.

"But I *can*," I pointed out. "I just might not like the consequences you come up with."

He inclined his head ever so slightly in assent.

"Thing is, though," I said, "even if you punish me, the more unpleasant things are for me here, the harder I'm going to try to get back up there."

I could see in his eyes that I'd stated exactly what was on his mind, and also that he wasn't sure what to do about it.

But he said nothing, and in a flicker, I found my surroundings changed. I was now standing on the sidewalk outside the Dead Man's Chest, the wind gusting sheets of newspaper along the lamp-lit street.

Chapter Sixteen

What could go wrong?

After that, every time I tried the medium phones, I got a high-pitched triple-beep and a stilted, recorded message: "We're sorry, but the number you have dialed is not available. Please check the number and dial again." As annoying as those messages are normally, I found it far more so when the only number on the phone at all was the zero.

"Figures," I muttered to Uncle Jeff. "The phone company's in on it."

He smiled, but he looked worried. "How about I give it a shot? Maybe I can get through, pass on a message for you."

I sighed, thinking that sending a message through Uncle Jeff to Chester, who'd then, if I was lucky, pass it on to Dom, seemed awfully far off from having a heart-to-heart with my husband in person. But it was worth a try. "Sure. It's Chester Wilkins you want to ask for. Tell him thanks for the séance and—" I stopped, realizing that unless I could use the phones myself, I had no idea how Chester could call me up for a second séance. The whole point of the first one had been to bring Laura in on convincing Dom to be there for a second séance, and if we couldn't do it, I'd been wasting a lot of both my own efforts and Chester's. "Just tell him thanks, if you get through," I said.

But Uncle Jeff didn't get through. The connection to Chester seemed to be severed from the Underworld.

"Why do I have this unsettling feeling that you have something up your sleeve?" Uncle Jeff asked me. We walked in silence for a while before I answered, along the banks of a slow-moving brook that ran through the park, both of us listening to the water trickling its way over the stones. I could see flashes of coppery orange here and there — goldfish swirling in the currents.

"I've been talking to Anatol about how I can get back topside," I admitted, as we stopped to lean on a bridge railing, side by side.

"Can't you—" Uncle Jeff started, then shook his head.

"Just drop it?" I suggested, a little sharply.

"I wasn't going to put it that way, but. . . ."

"I kind of wish I could," I said. "I mean, I like it here, and — I've missed you."

"Missed you, too." Uncle Jeff put one arm over my shoulders and kissed the top of my head.

"I've got to go back, though."

We stood there watching the fish, and then Uncle Jeff said, "Tell me this plan."

~*~

"This is *really* starting to sound like a bad idea, Erica." Uncle Jeff was uncharacteristically giving me the dire-warning-of-an-older-relative talk, and now, of all things, he was looking at me over the top of his maroon-framed glasses.

We'd adjourned to our usual table at the library, me spilling out my plans while we walked, gathered a few books, and settled into our seats by the big window.

"It doesn't matter what kind of idea it is." I scanned the index of yet another book of Greek mythology. "This is something I have to do. Consequences are beside the point."

Uncle Jeff ground his teeth. "You never *did* listen when anybody warned you about anything. You're determined you can do whatever you want, and never get hurt."

"Oh, look who's talking!" I said indignantly. "You'd still be alive if you hadn't *insisted* you weren't going to fall. Everybody but you knew how clumsy you were, but you just *had* to go up on the roof and fix the satellite dish yourself." Wow. I was deep down still kind of mad at him for that. Sure, I'd done stupid, risky stuff in my life and gotten away with it. The time my housemate and I got stranded in Philly, for one, but there were plenty more scrapes I'd escaped from unscathed. And yeah, that can make you cocky. The last warning I hadn't listened to was when Dom told me to stop speeding, ten seconds before I'd slammed into that tree.

"Okay, look, maybe you did learn it from me, in part," Uncle Jeff snapped. "But if I was being stupid then, listen to me when I'm telling you you're being stupid *now*."

"This is different," I said. "I'm dead already. What's going to happen to me?"

"This is your immortal soul we're talking about, here. Eternity. Do you really want to risk screwing it up? You can't mess with metaphysical stuff and hope it works out okay. I mean, what if you just — vanish — or — stop existing entirely? What if Hades decides to punish you somehow?" Seeing he wasn't getting my attention (or at least, that I wasn't showing it, as I continued to peruse the books laid out on the table between us) he tried a more aggressive tack. "Does Dom really mean that much to you?"

I looked my uncle square in the eye. "Yes."

And then returned to my book.

Uncle Jeff let out a frustrated groan and sat back in his chair. "Maybe that's not the right question to ask. I get that you love him—"

"I *did* marry him, you know," I pointed out.

"—But I'm sure he *knows* that you love him, and that whatever bad times passed between you two before you died, you still loved him and cared about him. What I'm saying is, he's going to forgive you. In the long run, whatever arguments happened, they're trivial."

I set my book aside and put my leg up on the corner of the

table, leaning back to stare at the ceiling as I answered. "He might be able to forgive me. It might have been okay, if I'd lived long enough to talk to him again. I'm not sure it ever would've become trivial to me, though — it would've been a long time before I forgave *myself* for saying some of the things I said, even if they'd rolled off Dom's back. And I don't think they *did* roll off his back. Otherwise, I might be able to relax and just enjoy my afterlife. I know I'll see him again, but I feel like I've abandoned him, and I can't stand that."

"You *died*, Erica. It's not like you had a choice."

"If he'd died suddenly, and right after a fight, I don't know how I would've stood it. I can't imagine how he's feeling right now." I stared down at the table, frowning. "He called me and wanted to make up, and I didn't take the call. And then I died." If I'd been alive, I couldn't have stopped myself from crying. I felt the pain now, but not the sting of tears starting up, not the suddenly-unresponsive vocal chords warbling toward a sob. I was angry enough that I didn't want the tears to come, though, so they didn't.

"He'll be fine. It'll just take a while," Uncle Jeff said gently. "People get over that kind of thing all the time. People die unexpectedly — it happens."

I thought about how Dom had thrown Chester out by his shirt collar — a very un-Dominic reaction, since he was generally both extremely polite and even-tempered. Thought about the empty whiskey bottle and the pain in Dom's voice when he'd told Chester off. Clearly, emotions were running high in the Flynn household, assuming that hadn't *only* been a dream.

I didn't like being cross-questioned about my feelings for Dom, especially by Uncle Jeff, who generally sat back and watched a situation until he understood it before he gave his own opinion. I wished he'd do that now. I wished he could have *seen* how much Dom and I meant to each other, because then I wouldn't have to explain anything.

His expression darkened in response to my obvious frustration, and my uncle and I sat staring each other down across the big oak table, the tension between us almost palpable.

Our glowering was interrupted by Latrischa, who breezed in unexpectedly and with unusual cheeriness. "Hey, guys." She pulled a chair up next to Uncle Jeff, then noticed the atmosphere between the two of us and said, "Oh."

Uncle Jeff broke off the stare-down to greet Latrischa, and I gave her a curt nod. I was glad she'd come in, if nothing else because it took the spotlight off of me and my hare-brained schemes for a while.

"So what's up with you guys?" she asked. Ever since she'd finally told me about her death, Latrischa had been a lot different. More like her old self, and then again, not nearly as bitter. They say confession is good for the soul, and apparently I wasn't the only one she had told — Uncle Jeff knew about all of it, too. He'd been sympathetic, even going so far as to say the guy had gotten what he deserved, which I still had mixed feelings about, myself.

"What's up?" Latrischa repeated.

"Erica's being stupid," Uncle Jeff said bluntly.

"My uncle is being a bossy pain in the ass," I shot back.

"I see," Latrischa said. "So, everything's nice and cozy here, then." Despite her jocular off-handedness, I knew her well enough to see she was confused and not a little concerned. Everybody was used to Jeff Shaw and his niece Erica getting along so incredibly well. It didn't help that *we* were used to it, too. I'd always felt like Uncle Jeff had my back, and to be at odds with him now, of all times, had an especially nasty sting to it. Fighting with him felt like turning the world inside out — it was just *wrong*.

"So what's up with you?" Uncle Jeff asked Latrischa, clearly as eager as I was to put off the rest of the unpleasant conversation, although we were bound to continue it at some point.

"Oh, nothing much. I knew you were coming down here, and thought I'd drop by." She gave him a strange little smile, darted a glance at me, and then gave me an even stranger smile, very bright and very fake.

I shot a quizzical look back at her, but she looked away.

She and Uncle Jeff turned the conversation friendly and casual for a while, chatting about some musician at some club, then musicians in general, music in general, and so on, getting more animated as they talked. I sat with my arms crossed, a book in my lap, trying to ignore them so I could read up on artifacts associated with Hades.

The trouble is, everything that's actually been *written* about the gods is *just made up*. This makes research into concrete facts about them difficult. I really wished I could get my hands on Hades' legendary Helm of Darkness, in addition to the scepter — it would make for a much better getaway. It didn't just make the wearer invisible, it made the wearer *undetectable*, even to the gods, according to the myths. Definitely something that would come in handy to someone trying to sneak out of the Underworld after stealing from the Lord of the Dead.

But I didn't even know if the helm was *real*.

Besides, I had enough on my hands just trying to get the scepter.

All of this was doing nothing for my frustration level.

"So how are you being stupid, Erica?" Latrischa asked me suddenly. I realized there had been a pause beforehand, but I'd been too engrossed in my book to notice. I had finally found a good-sized, detailed illustration of the scepter.

I told her, with many interruptions by Uncle Jeff, the rough outline of my plan ("rough outline" being — to be honest — all there ever was of the scheme).

"Doesn't sound stupid to me," Latrischa said when I'd finished. "Sentimental, maybe, but I get that." She may be cynical as hell, but at least Latrischa understands that not everybody is.

"But it's incredibly dangerous and has no guarantee of accomplishing anything whatsoever, plus it's entirely unnecessary," Uncle Jeff pointed out.

"Sounds fun to me." Latrischa grinned. "And anyway, she's twenty-nine years old, not to mention dead. She doesn't need her hand held."

"You won't have a *body*. How are you going to talk to him?"

"I *will* have a body," I said. "That's the whole point of getting the scepter."

"How do you know it works like that? How do you know you aren't just going to turn up as—" he waved his hands around— "a ghost or a lost soul or whatever?"

"Anatol told me." I turned the book around so that it was facing them. Despite himself, Uncle Jeff leaned forward to see what I'd spent all this time searching for, and I could see in his expression that he was sizing it up, trying to see how he could do what I'd asked of him.

"I can't," Uncle Jeff said after a moment, and he sounded genuinely apologetic. No matter how set against me he'd seemed this whole conversation, deep down he wanted me to succeed. He just didn't want to lose me forever if I failed. I felt such affection for my uncle as that thought occurred to me that my irritation ebbed away all at once, and I determined to be all the more clever about what I was doing. I had left behind one person I loved, a whole world away, and I wanted to fix that. I wouldn't mess things up and leave another loved one in another world to mourn for me.

Uncle Jeff spoke again, though, pulling me back to the issue at hand. "Even if I wanted to, I couldn't. We have no idea if this is anything *like* the real artifact." He waved a hand at the illustration between us. "There's no point even *trying* unless we know for certain *exactly* what it looks like."

Latrischa shrugged helplessly at me, and I knew they were both right — which made me angry again. "I *need* your help," I said to Uncle Jeff, pleading.

He wouldn't look at me. "I'm sorry." He folded his arms across his chest.

I walked out, fuming. It hurt too much to be at odds with Uncle

Jeff, felt too awkward in front of Latrischa, was too frustrating to be held back at every turn.

And the person who knew best how to soothe me when I was upset was the very person I couldn't have. Dom was a world away, and everything, it seemed, was set against my getting back to him.

I walked quickly at first — an old habit from being alive and needing to burn off the adrenaline of anger. Gradually, I slowed down, realizing I didn't have any destination in mind. The Styx flowed along to my right, uptown high-rise condos to my left. The riverfront here was lined with a strip of neatly trimmed grass and blossoming fruit trees, with park benches at regular intervals facing the water.

I sat down and stared out over the Styx. Downriver, noise floated over from the carnival, but the only sounds nearby were the soft shifting of leaves and petals in the trees, the gentle passage of the water on the other side of the railing, and the muted voices of people on their balconies behind me.

Somehow, I had to find out exactly what the scepter looked like. But so far, I hadn't even gotten the bribe together for Charon, which meant I didn't even know where Hades kept it. And even if I knew, I wasn't going to risk being found looking it over *and then* go back and steal it later. The last thing I wanted was for Hades to know what I was up to.

I thought about the various illustrations I'd seen of it. They all showed an elaborately carved staff, topped with the head of a bird with rubies for eyes. That much was consistent. But what the carving looked like, what kind of bird it was, and for that matter, the cut of the rubies, varied a lot between depictions.

So why did I have this instinctive sense of what looked right or wrong about each one? All the drawings I'd looked at, I realized, I'd been comparing to something. The illustration I'd shown to Uncle Jeff — when I'd first looked at it, I'd thought, *A vulture's head, that's right.* But the carvings hadn't seemed right to me. There should be more detailing, and the wood should be accented with bronze. The vulture was the right bird, but the features were off. The rubies were the wrong cut, the wrong shape, and the wrong size. How in the world could I have such a distinct idea for what it was supposed to look like?

Where had I seen that image? It wasn't a drawing or a painting. Not one of the images off of Greek or Roman pottery, photographed for art or history books. It was way too detailed for that.

I frowned, trying to remember, listening to the calliope music drifting over from the carnival — and that was when it hit me.

The fortune-teller's tent. The tarot cards had all been illustrated with photographs. There had been three cards before her weird outburst. The first one had been the towering black building, and now I realized it was Hades' palace. The second had been the pair of black horses pulling a chariot, which was supposed to be another of Hades' prized possessions in the myths. Then she'd turned over the Ace of Wands, and started laughing. The Ace of Wands.

And the card had been a photograph of the scepter.

If the cards' depiction of the palace had been accurate, was their depiction of the scepter accurate, too?

My suspicion that the fortune-teller had foreseen my successful theft of the scepter now turned into full-blown conviction.

I needed to see her — and more than that, I needed to get that tarot card.

Chapter Seventeen

bad god! no biscuit!

The carnival was crowded, as it had been my first time there — I had the impression it was always swarming — and the tent didn't stand out. It was the same brightly-striped, somewhat-the-worse-for-wear canvas as every other tent, similarly glittering with flashing lights and signs, but nonetheless I walked right to it, shouldering my way through the teeming masses of souls, most of them fresh off the ferry and looking confused or eager, depending on the person.

But the fortune-teller was away. She'd left a sign hanging across the entrance that said simply, "Out."

I stood outside, wondering what to do next. I was too excited about the scepter card to just come back some other time, and besides, I was anxious to pull the excuses out from under Uncle Jeff's refusal to help me. If nothing else, I had to at least get another look at that card.

And maybe it was good that she wasn't here. If I was wrong and she didn't know I wanted to steal the scepter, she might go to Hades and tell him what I was planning. I didn't really have any reason to think she'd be on my side. I didn't have any choice about trusting Charon, but the fewer people who knew what I was up to, the better.

I paced around near the tent, struggling with my conscience over the idea of sneaking around when the fortune-teller was away, but I knew I'd do it, no matter what Jimminy Cricket might've had to say about my morals.

A quick, guilty look around reassured me that nobody was paying any attention to what I was doing, and I slipped into the tent.

It was dark, of course, and I fumbled in my pocket until I produced a book of matches. Lighting one, I hurried to the table. There was a fat white candle in the center of the tablecloth, and I lit it and shook the match out.

The flame wavered and grew, then steadied to cast long shadows around the room. A small, narrow set of shelves stood by the table, next to where the fortune-teller had been sitting the last time I'd been here. Books lined the shelves, punctuated here and there by trinkets — no, looking closer, I saw the "trinkets" were various forms of divination. A crystal ball, a set of jade I Ching wands, a glass box full of rune stones, a porcelain tea set with a mesh ball for holding the tea leaves. And the tarot deck, on the top shelf.

I took it and sat across from the fortune-teller's chair, riffling through the slick cards. Yes, they were definitely on the theme of Hades' possessions. There was even a photo of his stereo system on one card, just as I'd seen it in his study.

His study, I thought, as I found the Ace of Wands. There was the scepter, in a crystal-clear photograph. It was wooden, highly polished and inlaid with enough bronze patterning that, at first glance, I'd thought the entire piece was metal. The scepter was crowned with a bird's head, its eyes marked by two glistening rubies like beads of blood. It was leaning against a set of bookshelves, and I realized now that they were the shelves in his study. I recognized them from my visit there.

I slid the card out of the deck and into my pocket.

Before you get all "thou shalt not steal" about that, don't forget — you can't steal anything in the Underworld. I flipped back through the deck, and sure enough, there was still an Ace of Wands card among the rest, identical to the one I'd taken.

I put the cards back where I'd found them, double-checked the card in my pocket, then blew out the candle and slipped out of the tent.

Glancing around at the crowd, everything seemed copasetic.

That is, until I noticed Hades himself standing about twenty paces off, and staring right at me.

"I've been looking for you." Hades smiled as he closed the distance between us.

"You have?" I was exceedingly unnerved to hear it. "I'd have thought you could just zoom your god-senses in on anyone you wanted to."

Hades looked amused. "I didn't say I couldn't. Walk with me."

"Where to?" I said suspiciously.

"The park, where it isn't so . . . crowded." His lip curled at the masses of souls around us. He smiled at me again. "You're dreadfully distrustful of me — you'd think I had done something to deserve it."

He was walking off whether I followed or not, which didn't leave my curious self much choice. I caught up with him in a few quick strides, trying to read his expression and failing completely. He just looked passive and serene, the corners of his mouth curved gently upward in a creepily benevolent way.

The park was only a block away, and the gazebo was deserted, which apparently appealed to Hades.

He leaned with his elbows and back against the railing, and I stood nervously nearby — but out of arm's reach — looking around to make sure there were a few other people in line of sight. Some teenagers were playing Frisbee on the lawn, a couple was having a picnic at one of the tables by the brook, and two or three passersby wandered the paths.

"I've been thinking about our last conversation," Hades said.

"You mean after the séance, when you told me I could never go back to the Upper World again?" I said bitterly.

"Well, yes, that conversation." Hades put his head to one side.

"I've been thinking that was somewhat unfair on my part."

I looked at him in surprise.

"I've decided to let you go back to the Land of the Living," he said, "for a visit. You'll have to come back, of course." Hades smiled and wagged a finger at me.

I found myself smiling back. "Of course," I agreed, then frowned. "What's the catch, though?"

"Catch?" Hades looked confused, as if he were searching a mental dictionary for something he didn't quite understand. "Ah, I see what you mean. No, no, there's no catch. At first, obviously, I was set against the idea, but on further reflection, it seems a small concession to make. As you pointed out yourself, you will give me no end of trouble otherwise, which shows a certain admirable determination on your part, after all. I value my peace and quiet. To me, that is worth making an exception — provided that you don't tell anyone I've done this for you." He laid a hand gently on my shoulder. "I don't want it to get around, or I'd be barraged with other requests I would rather not grant."

I couldn't believe he was giving in so easily. Was he honestly moved by my pleas, or were his godly powers so weak that he couldn't stand up to a resolute mortal? Or was this a trick? But as we stared at each other, trying to read one another's expressions, I couldn't help it — I believed what he was saying. He was going to let me go back.

"So I have your permission to go?" I asked hesitantly.

"Better than that. I will send you back, myself." Hades' dark eyes gleamed with a kind smile, and from the inside pocket of his long coat, he pulled out a small blue bottle. "All you have to do is drink this."

Something in the back of my mind was screaming for my attention, but the thoughts felt muffled and indistinct, and I wasn't interested in warnings right now. Not even from myself. I wanted to believe him. This was great! Hades was going to make this so easy for me. Finally, I could go to Dom and make things right, and when I came back, I'd be able to relax and enjoy the afterlife. And Uncle Jeff and I would stop arguing about my safety, because I'd have no reason to risk myself again.

Slowly, I reached for the bottle Hades was holding out to me. I hesitated for one moment, frowning as I tried to remember something, but Hades caught my eye, and I returned his smile, feeling silly for worrying. Soon, I'd have nothing to worry about ever again.

"Thanks." I took the bottle and unscrewed the lid. "I can't tell you how much this means to me. I don't know what to say."

Hades looked incredibly pleased — almost eager — but I put it down to good feelings brought on by a philanthropic deed.

I tossed my head back and drank down half the bottle in one gulp.

Something strange was happening. I felt weird.

"Drink up!" said the man standing next to me. He was familiar, but who. . . ? He pressed his hand over mine around the bottle and pushed it toward my lips.

"Wait — what is this?" But the man looked so caring and compassionate as he repeated that I needed to finish drinking the liquid that I did what he asked.

Everything went black.

Chapter Eighteen

the deadest little town this side of the styx

I opened my eyes.

Where was I? For that matter, where had I been before this? I felt like something had happened to me — something bad, the way you feel when you wake up from a nightmare but can't remember the events of the dream at all. Briefly, I considered the possibility that I *had* simply had a nightmare, but that didn't explain why I didn't know where I was.

The room was sparsely furnished. I was lying on a narrow, brass-framed bed, and as I sat up, the springs squeaked. A battered wooden chair stood in the opposite corner and a broken mirror glittered above a chipped washbasin in a splintery wooden stand. The floor and walls were rough, bare wood, and overhead, the exposed beams slanted toward the window next to the bed. There was no glass in the window, and one of the shutters was loose, swaying and creaking in a shifting wind.

How had I gotten here? I couldn't remember anything before I'd awakened in this room. Had I been sick? Drunk? Attacked?

Maybe if I looked around, it would jog my memory.

So I got up, moving quietly in case there was someone around who shouldn't know I was awake. There was no door in the doorframe, and I stepped out onto a sort of indoor balcony — a catwalk, really, with a long row of rooms opening onto it and a view of a large central room downstairs. Sort of a saloon or an Old West inn or something. There was a bar counter down there.

But no people.

And again, almost no furniture. What there was wasn't in good shape, all battered wood and chipped paint. Very plain and rough, like the building itself. Dusty, too.

This obviously wasn't my home or anything. I poked around the empty rooms, but found nothing helpful. Checking my pockets, I found no indication of anything about myself, either. No wallet, ID, keys, candy wrappers, loose change, coupons — not the tiniest clue about who I was or where I'd been before I woke up here.

I headed outside into a gritty late afternoon, the sunlight stark and aggressive. The whole street looked abandoned, lined with greyed wooden buildings, their windows broken, boarded up, or missing altogether. Quite a few of the buildings had collapsed, leaving just their foundations and rubble, or a partial frame, filled with golden-brown grass and thorny brush. And there were gravestones everywhere.

In some places, they were neatly lined in rows, but others were scattered seemingly at random — inside the collapsed buildings, in the middle of the street, blocking the doors to the few intact structures.

Wherever the hell this was, it was definitely a place for stray tumbleweeds and the ghosts of cowboys, I thought.

As I walked down the packed dirt of the street, I checked out a few of the gravestones. Some of the names and dates fit my expectations, but others seemed completely out of place. I mean, it's a little weird to find a tombstone dedicated to *Starshine Peacechild, 1964-2003* in an Old West ghost town. Or *Li Wu Zhang, 1341-1423.*

A T junction with another road ended the street, so I turned left. This little town was strictly in a grid pattern, nothing but empty countryside stretching away on the opposite side of the road. A couple of blocks further, a train track curved off into the distance, and eventually it curled around to run parallel with the road.

Up ahead, facing the town, was a train station — a small

wooden platform and a ticket booth with the glass busted out of the window. Across the front, in huge ironwork letters, was the name of the station, which brought me up short, trying to process what I was reading.

The Atheists' Graveyard, the sign proclaimed.

What *was* this town, and what was I doing here? Sure, I had a name to attach to the place now, but that didn't put it any recognizable context for me. If I could just remember *something* from before I'd woken up. . . .

To one side of the busted-up ticket booth, a sign listed other stations along the railway. I wondered if the other stations were like this one — derelict and abandoned. I frowned. These were all names of places for the dead. Different names for the Underworld or the afterlife. And this place?

I looked around and caught sight of another sign.

Welcome to The Atheists' Graveyard!

I stepped closer to read the smaller print under the big block lettering.

Didn't believe in an afterlife, and don't want to face one even though it's here? If you're a firm disbeliever, feel the Underworld is all just an illusion, or you're just plain tired of existing, you've come to the right place to escape it all. Here in The Atheists' Graveyard, you can slip out of existence without a fuss. Enjoy your stay, and rest in peace.

Wait, so I was dead? I sat down on a bench and thought about that. Okay, that seemed . . . right. I didn't remember dying, but I knew that things were different now than they had once been. Time had worked differently, and things had *felt* . . . not the way they did now. Was that what had happened to me before I'd found myself here? Did you just wake up in the Underworld with no memory of yourself or your life?

I didn't have an answer to that, of course.

Atheist seemed to fit me, I thought, but something about this didn't sit quite right. Not believing in a divinity was one thing, but not believing in the Underworld when you were in it — that just seemed silly. Fact wasn't something you could ignore.

So, what if I hadn't just turned up here by metaphysical mojo? What if I'd come here with intent? What had been my reasoning?

Tired of existing?

That didn't sound like me. Unless . . . unless something really bad had happened to me. Something that maybe I didn't *want* to remember. If people could come here and just . . . die . . . that sounded like some kind of magic. Had I come here to die, and magically forgotten who I was in order to escape some kind of emotional anguish?

There were no answers to any of my self-inquiries.

So what should I do? I wondered. I could stay here at the station and see if a train showed up, maybe go to one of these other cities, where maybe I could find out about myself — and the afterlife. But was there something awful I'd rather not know about, lurking and waiting to surprise me the minute I figured out who I was?

And what about the feeling that something bad had happened to me just before I woke up? Was I in some kind of danger if I left here?

Maybe it would be better not to find out. Maybe I should assume I'd come here with a purpose — to disbelieve myself out of existence — and maybe I ought to follow through with that.

Or I could go back to the abandoned saloon and think things through before I did anything else. That seemed sensible, which seemed unlike me, but I opted to follow my sensible instincts.

The barroom seemed huge, deserted as it was, and with so little furniture to fill it. Aside from the counter, there was one broken stool and a dinged-up player piano. Overhead, sheathed in dust, was one of those gigantic wood-and-iron chandeliers that always falls on the bad guys in old movies. Behind the bar was a long panel mirror speckled with tarnished patches, and quite a few whiskey bottles caked with dust. I buffed one up enough to see the date on the label — 1839.

I wondered if it had aged well, or, since this was the Underworld, if it had aged at all. Putting it back on the shelf, where it clinked merrily against its fellow bottles, I turned to look in the mirror.

So this was me, I thought. I felt no attachment to my reflection, didn't recognize myself or feel any familiarity.

Surely there were people who cared about me, who remembered me, who were dead, too. I must have a family somewhere — dead or alive, and probably some in each column. Unless they didn't know who they were, either.

But even so, I had to *try* to find them, I thought, idly looking over the player piano. Huh. Looked like it might still work.

I wished I knew if it was normal to have no memory after death, and pushed a button at random.

The piano started up, tinny and out of tune, but not bad for something that *looked* so neglected. It was some old ragtime piece, and I recognized it.

Why that, and not my own reflection?

The mind is a strange thing.

I closed my eyes and listened, straining to remember. It *upset* me for some reason, this music — a cheesy, light-heartedly mournful piece, as contradictory as that sounds. But my associations with it were anything but light-hearted, and it was being played *wrong* somehow. The tempo was off, or something — it was more than just the out-of-tune piano.

I sat on the broken stool and popped open the bottle of whiskey. The song went on as I sipped straight from the bottle.

It *had* aged well, and I took a couple more pulls before the music stopped.

I brought the stool over next to the piano and pressed the button again, making my way slowly down the neck of the whiskey bottle.

And when it ended again, I started it up again.

The fourth time through, I started crying, the tears flowing easily with me in a tipsy state, and then I stopped in mid-sob.

Because *I remembered something.*

I used to know someone who played the piano. Someone who'd died — no . . . someone who was still alive, that I'd left behind. I frowned, confused. Which memory was right?

This song — who had played this song?

Someone who had died. A man. Who? What was he to me? Friend, relative?

I couldn't remember anything more.

The piano stopped.

I stared at it, then pushed the button again and drank some more.

Cry more, I told myself — which was also, I knew, not like me, whoever I was.

Somewhere in there was a deep and terrible pain, and even though I didn't know what it was, I could feel it there, and I found plenty of tears in it.

And the more I cried, the more I remembered.

Things were still patchy. There were empty places where there should be memories, and things that were hazy or didn't connect properly that I knew I should know more clearly, but what I recovered was this:

I wasn't new to the Underworld, and it wasn't normal to lose your memory. Somehow, someone had *made* me forget everything — and had dumped me here *hoping* that I'd figure out what this place was for, and that I would assume I was supposed to slip into nonexistence.

I knew I was Erica Shaw — wait, was that right? — and I knew I had friends in the capitol city of the Underworld: the city of Hades. There was something I was trying to do, somewhere I was trying to get to, when I'd been sideswiped by whoever had put me here.

No . . . there was *someone* I was trying to get to. I was fuzzy on the details here — a name or an exact relationship was beyond me — but it was someone I was in love with, I knew that. I could remember his eyes, and the expression in them when he looked at me, and I knew it was someone who loved me, too. But that was all I knew about him, me, us, or the reason I was trying to defy death to get to where he was.

Whoever this guy is, I thought, he better be worth it.

But I knew, even without really remembering him, that he *was* worth it.

I started out the door, then checked. I would need some kind of payment for train fare. Well-aged whiskey might do the job, I reasoned, and grabbed a sealed bottle before heading for the station.

The train pulled up while I sat at the empty station, trying — and failing — to remember more. "Hades South," I told the uniformed ticket-man as I handed over the whiskey.

He took it, considered it for a moment, then nodded. "Decided you're an agnostic, have you?" He gestured toward the deserted town.

"I guess so." We shared a laugh as the train thundered up to speed.

Hades South. I wondered where the hell that was, or whether I could find my friends before I found my enemy.

Or how I would know which was which.

Chapter Nineteen

soul searching

I'd been hoping that prior experience in the city of Hades would come back to me on arrival, and in that hope, I was sorely mistaken. It didn't help that, although I didn't realize it then, I had never been to the Hades South station. I'd barely used the subways, let alone the overland trains that went between cities. I'm a pedestrian at heart; always have been.

So when I got to the platform, I looked around to no avail, searching for memories. I did find a city map, though.

Vaguely, I recalled that I'd regularly checked for my mail at the Board of Tourism at the Osiris Street Roundabout, around six blocks from the station.

That was the best lead I had on myself, so that was where I headed.

Unfortunately, the train station and the library were in opposite directions from the tourist center — otherwise I'd have walked right past the library and probably picked up a few memories upon seeing it.

As it was, I arrived at the Board of Tourism with only a shadow of a memory of the place. The woman at the desk was middle-aged, snub-nosed, and steely-eyed. Her long brown-and-grey streaked hair was pulled up into a knot at the back of her head, and by her expression upon seeing me, I gathered we weren't friends.

I hesitated to approach her, trying to gauge how strong her dislike was — had she had a hand in my turning up in the Atheists'

Graveyard? But then, wouldn't she be surprised to see me back here in Hades?

Besides, she didn't strike me as the conniving type. If this woman hated someone, she'd come out and say it. Her nametag labeled her *Helen*.

"Where's the other guy?" I asked her, unable, for the present, to remember Ben's name.

"Ben is out for lunch." Helen pursed her lips in disapproval — at the idea of lunch or the idea of talking to me, I wasn't sure which.

"Any mail for me?" I asked.

"I thought you had moved in somewhere," she said pointedly, but looked in the mail cubbies.

"I did?" I asked, which got me a weird look for an answer. "I haven't been getting any mail. I wanted to make sure none came here for me. Can you make sure you have the right address, in case anything does come through?"

Helen flicked through a stack of files and pulled one out. Her thumb covered up my last name, but I'd been right about my first — Erica. "1804 East 27th Street?" she arched an eyebrow. "Correct?"

Repeating the address to myself in my head, I nodded. "Yeah, that's right. Thanks for checking."

"Are you — all right?" Helen narrowed her eyes. I wasn't sure, but I thought she might've been feeling a little sorry for me just then.

"Fine." I thanked her again, and left.

~*~

But when I got to 1804 East 27th, I wasn't sure I was fine, after all. There was an apartment there, all right — a little red brick place sandwiched between two taller buildings — but it was vacant. The door wasn't locked, so I walked right in, but the place was empty, bare hardwood floors and echoing rooms full of sunlight from the long, narrow windows. Dust motes danced in the light as I tried to picture what the place had looked like furnished.

I didn't know what I wanted it to look like. What I wanted was to know what I *would've* wanted if I had known anything about myself. If I'd stopped making it so complicated and just wanted what I *wanted*, I'd probably have wanted what I'd had before, but I didn't know that.

So I stymied myself.

Reasoning that maybe a walk around the neighborhood would turn something up, I headed up 27th Street a block and turned onto Three Furies Boulevard — which, although I didn't know it right then, is where the Dead Man's Chest is located, four blocks from my apartment. I wouldn't have walked that far — I'd planned to circle around and come back — except that I saw the neon signs in the dimming evening light.

The place looked busy, and I figured I was bound to know some of the patrons in an establishment this close to home. Somebody would recognize me, and maybe I'd even recognize them.

So I went in.

I don't know if you've ever walked into a bar where everybody knows everybody else, except you, and everyone looks up when you open the door. It's not high on my list of favorite things, but the moment was short-lived in this case.

"Hey, Erica!" someone yelled in a friendly way, and a trio of older men waved hello from their barstools. A few other random and vaguely familiar faces smiled or nodded their greetings, but one group looked up in shock.

"Erica! Where have you *been?*" One of them jumped out of her chair. "We've been looking everywhere for you!" She was about my age, black, and stylishly dressed. Her expression wavered between relief and ironic, low-key irritation.

"Thank goodness you're all right!" Someone in his mid-forties with maroon-framed glasses stepped around the girl and hugged me. This guy was crazy-familiar, but I couldn't pinpoint his identity. I also had an unnerving sense that he and I had argued not long before I'd wound up lost in the Atheists' Graveyard. Was his relief real, or a front to hide what he'd done from the others? Somehow, he was connected to the player piano song — and why it had made me cry. I could see in his face he was hurt that I wasn't more responsive to his greeting.

"I told you she was okay," said a kid sitting at the table. "Erica can take care of herself."

The last person at the table, a tall, hollow-cheeked man in his late forties, his jaw dusted with stubble, carefully folded a pack of cards and put them in his pocket. He looked at me intently as he drank the last of a glass of vodka, and I knew he could tell something was wrong. They all could — I sensed that — but he had some idea of what it was. The odd part was, it didn't make me distrust him. I knew he was okay.

"Can I talk to you a sec?" I asked, my glance flicking away from the group.

"Sure." He stood, pushing his chair in.

He followed me outside, where I turned my back to the window. I didn't want to see the others — I felt guilty for not knowing who they were, for not remembering them and caring about them the way I probably should. For suspecting their reactions, their relief at seeing me again.

I stared into the grey-blue eyes of the man I almost remembered, trying to bring back where I knew him from. "You — you were there when I first . . . died . . . weren't you?" I asked. The first person I'd trusted after my death. My first source of information in the Underworld, and one I had depended on.

"What's going on, Erica? You disappeared. None of us could find you. Your Uncle Jeff was in a complete panic." The man gestured back toward the bar, the table.

"My . . . Uncle Jeff," I repeated in a whisper. The man in the glasses. We'd fought, yes, but over what? I felt even worse for suspecting him now. Why couldn't I connect everything up?

"Look at me, Erica," the stubbly guy said.

I looked up.

"What did you do?" he asked.

I shook my head. "Nothing!" What had someone *else* done, was what I wanted to know. And who had it been?

"What's my name?" he asked.

Tears welled up in my eyes, and I let them spill over. "Anatol," I said, remembering. "Anatol."

He took my chin in one hand, rubbing gently at the tears with his thumb. "What happened to you?"

"I can't remember," I admitted. "I don't know how or why, but someone did something to make me forget . . . *everything*." I told him what had happened — waking up in the Atheists' Graveyard, the piano, the tears, the recovery of part of my memory, and how I'd wound up here, trying to find the friends I didn't remember.

"Lethos water," Anatol murmured. "Has to be. But how you've recovered even this much—" he shook his head. "I don't understand it."

"Do you know who — who gave me Lethos water?" I asked.

"I don't know how he got you to drink it, but I'd stake my afterlife it was Hades that did this to you."

"And I can trust . . . all of you?" I nodded toward the group inside without daring to look at them.

Anatol smiled gently. "Yes. You can trust all of us — and don't let Jeff hear you talking like that. It'd break his heart, even if you're not quite yourself at the moment."

So we went back into the Dead Man's Chest and filled the others in on what had happened — as well as we could, since a lot of it was guesswork.

"Do you think he found out what you were planning?" the girl — Latrischa, that was her name — asked.

"What I was planning?" I repeated. What *was* I planning?

They all exchanged glances with one another, except the kid, who looked thrilled. "This is *awesome*. You are totally on the run from the big, bad Hades. You gotta have a secret identity now, so he won't find you."

"Y'know, Matt, that's not entirely a bad idea," my uncle said. "Erica *should* probably lie low for the moment. If Hades finds out she's made it back and recovered some of her memory, he may try something else."

"*Now* don't you think we should help her?" Latrischa asked my uncle. "I mean, if she can make it back topside, Hades can't mess with her, right?"

"She *would* be out of his jurisdiction, so to speak," Anatol agreed.

"Okay, so wait," I broke in. "What are we doing?"

"Your plan!"

"Right. My plan." I cocked my head. "What was that, again?"

"There's got to be some way you can fully recover your memory," Uncle Jeff said. I could see our family resemblance, but I couldn't connect any associations with him. It was unnerving, because I could tell he and I had been close. There was a certain protectiveness in the way he sat on the edge of his chair, near me but facing the door, like he was just waiting for Hades to walk in and try something.

"She recovered more than she should have, by all normal standards," Anatol commented.

"It was when I was crying," I said. "That's when I started to get stuff back — and then, when I was talking to you," I nodded to Anatol, "I was upset that I couldn't figure out who any of you were, and it was when I cried over that, I remembered your name."

"Is it possible that she was *crying* out the Lethos water? That it came out of her system as tears?" Uncle Jeff asked Anatol.

Anatol shrugged. "I don't know. She's the only person I know of who's been forced or tricked into drinking it. Maybe if you drink it involuntarily, and *want* your memories back, it's possible to reject the liquid and expel it from the soul."

"It's like those fairy tales where tears cure curses," Latrischa said. "You know, like the witch curses one person blind, and the person who loves them cries for them, and when the tears fall on the blind eyes, they can see again?"

I didn't remember whether I'd ever read such a thing or not, but Anatol nodded.

"I don't think I can cry all my memories back," I said. "I'm not much of a crier, for one, and for another thing, I seem to be gaining back less each time. Last time, all I got was Anatol's name. Back in the Atheists' Graveyard, I was getting back whole chunks of information about myself."

"And telling you stuff about yourself isn't helping," Latrischa added. "We *tell* you stuff, but you don't have any of your own memories of it."

"Right," I said. "It's all disconnected. No associations. I mean, okay, so my favorite color is green, but *why* is my favorite color green?"

"Associations," Uncle Jeff repeated slowly. "Memories and associations. . . . What about your joy-swap item?"

"I don't even remember what I use for joy-swapping," I said.

"Marshmallows," Latrischa answered. "Marshmallows with associations and memories built into them."

"But she can't make one unless she already has those associations to put into it," Anatol pointed out.

"But *I* know who has one." Latrischa stood.

"Who?"

"Vic." She jerked her head toward the bar, where the kid — Matt — was talking to a tall, beefy guy with a walrus mustache.

"Won't he have eaten any she's given him?" Uncle Jeff asked.

Anatol, grinning, shook his head. "Latrischa's right. Vic's a collector. He keeps at least one joy-swap from every customer. That's part of why he runs this place."

"What, just to *have* them?" Uncle Jeff asked.

"He says it's stocking up happiness for gloomy days," Anatol explained as Latrischa hurried off to ask Vic for one of my marshmallows. "You know how collectors are."

"Will he be willing to give up part of his collection, then?" I asked anxiously, not remembering Vic's generous nature — but my anxiety was abruptly halted when Latrischa waltzed back, immensely pleased with herself, and handed me a jumbo-sized roasted marshmallow.

"This is it, then." I stared at the little golden-brown confection. "The rest of my afterlife depends on this marshmallow."

"Pretty much." Sympathy and cynicism vied for dominance in Latrischa's voice.

I popped the marshmallow into my mouth, chewed—

Chapter Twenty

friends in low places

—And remembered.

Everything.

My whole life and afterlife tumbled back together in my mind, along with a good, strong dose of guilt for ever having forgotten certain elements of it — namely, Uncle Jeff, Dom, my family . . . well, pretty much everyone I loved.

I also remembered Hades' little trick, and wanted to kick myself for falling for it. Sure, he'd been using some kind of godly powers of persuasion on me, but I knew, too, that it had only worked because I'd wanted to believe him. I'd been more focused on wanting to get back to the Upper World than on resisting Hades' weird hold over my capabilities of judgment and logic.

I'd lost the tarot card I'd taken from the fortune-teller's deck, and I could only hope that, like the furnishings of my apartment, the card had actually disappeared along with my memories. Otherwise, Hades had found it on me while I was unconscious — which would mean he was onto my plans.

Uncle Jeff reassured me that the card *should've* popped out of existence as soon as my memory of it was gone.

"Okay. So the only bad news there is that I've got to get another copy of that card," I said.

"Are you sure the picture on that card is accurate to the real scepter?" Uncle Jeff asked.

"I'm pretty sure. I mean, the deck has photos of the palace and

Hades' stereo, and *they're* accurate."

"Does that question indicate that you're going to help her make the fake?" Latrischa asked slyly.

Uncle Jeff half-smiled and sighed. "I don't have much choice. Erica's gotten herself into so much trouble as it is, I've *gotta* bail her out." He ruffled my hair, trying to be jovial, although I could see how worried he was. "That's my niece, all right."

"So we're all in?" Anatol asked solemnly. "We're all going to help with this?"

Uncle Jeff and Latrischa met Anatol's gaze, then each other's, and nodded firmly. Matt was wiggling around in his seat, thrilled to be a part of so major a mischief-making, and added vigorous nodding of his own.

"Don't any of you want to go back topside?" I asked. "I mean, I've already got everything set up. If anybody wants to come with me...?"

I looked around at each of them. Latrischa shook her head, her expression souring. Matt hesitated, but his answer was firmly in the negative. Anatol smiled, but I knew what he meant by it was *no*. None of their answers surprised me.

But when I met Uncle Jeff's gaze, I realized I'd been halfway hoping he'd say yes. The other half of me knew better, but it still hurt more than I'd have admitted aloud to watch him smile sadly and say, "No. Thanks, but no. This is where I belong now."

He and Latrischa exchanged a look, and Anatol patted me on the back, letting me know he was aware of how I felt.

"Then, Erica," Anatol said, pulling me out of my fleeting self-pity, "tell us what you've got planned. We'll see what we can do to make these hare-brained schemes of yours as practical as possible. It's us against the Lord of the Dead, girlie, so let's put up a good fight."

I cheered up, thinking of the support my friends were offering, how much they cared about me, and how much trouble we were going to cause for Hades. "Well, I've got a bribe to earn.

I know the scepter is somewhere in the study, but I still need Charon to tell me *exactly* where Hades keeps it. So . . . you guys want to go to the thrill park with Matt and me?"

Matt grinned, and everyone else at the table groaned.

We agreed to meet up for the thrill park after we'd all had a chance to relax beforehand — it had been one damn thing after another for everybody since Hades had wiped my memory. For me, well, you already know that story. For the others, worry had given way to panic when they found all my stuff had disappeared from my apartment, and Uncle Jeff had been frantic, given our falling-out just before my mysterious vanishing act.

So I was supposed to be relaxing, too, but I was restless, anxious to get on with getting out of the Underworld. I went back to the fortune-teller's tent.

She was open for business, but there was no line. I'd been hoping she'd be out, and I'd be able to just slip in and take another copy of the Ace of Wands. No such luck, though, so I stopped at the entrance and called out to her. "Hello? It's Erica. Is it okay if I come in?"

Instead of the verbal answer I'd expected, I felt her hand on my shoulder, gently guiding me into the dim flickering of the candlelit tent. She had that "I know more than you've told me" look again. She unwound the tasseled cords that held the flap open, and the carnival lights were shut out by the thick material, further darkening the room and completely silencing the noise and bustle from outside.

Somehow that simple act brought it home to me for the first time just how serious a thing I was undertaking. I'd known, sure, and I'd weighed the risks. Certainly Anatol and Uncle Jeff had tried to hammer it home to me, but it occurred to me now that I'd been letting them do the worrying for me. I'd been so busy proving my determination and feverishly trying to pull a plan together that I hadn't stopped to process how I felt about the dangers ahead of me. It was odd to feel the excitement and nervousness without the zip of an adrenaline rush, the heavy rhythm of a quickened heartbeat — but even without the organics, I realized I was fidgeting, tapping my fingers against each other in an old nervous habit.

"Sit down," the fortune-teller said softly, and I did, still feeling bewildered at what I was plotting. The fortune-teller took her seat across the table from me, her pale hands all the paler against the dark velvet tablecloth.

"I know what you're looking for." Her eyes had that same mischievous glint I'd seen the first time I'd sat across this table from her. "I can help you get your hands on it."

Maybe Dom was right to believe in psychics, I thought. She could just be guessing well, and being cagey so as not to give herself away, rather than being careful about taking part in an extremely shady and dangerous act. But maybe she really could read my mind, knew about the scepter, maybe even the helm, and — most importantly of all — maybe she could provide me with the information and the means to get one or both items.

We all possessed abilities in the Underworld that, aboveground, would have constituted super-powers. Every one of us was something out of a comic book, in a way. And it was true that the longer you were dead, the more you let go of your old conceptions of how reality functioned, and therefore the more you could do whatever you wanted. There's no such thing as time, but there is always such a thing as change. I didn't know when this fortune-teller had died. She could've developed psychic powers, sure. Why not? It's not like we had anything else to do. Just get better at things.

I thought it was time to force her hand, though.

"What, exactly, can you help me get my hands on?" I asked, as casually as I could.

"You want the helm of Hades." The fortune-teller kept

smiling, and now looked me directly in the eyes. "But that's not everything you're looking for."

I raised my eyebrows in genuine surprise. "Wow. You really can read minds, then, huh?"

She laughed, and flicked her hand across the empty table, leaving the card — the Ace of Wands — in the center of the pool of candlelight.

I stared at the card, then at her. She knew everything, then. She'd seen this from the very beginning. I *would* succeed, I thought excitedly.

"You already have a good idea for keeping Hades from realizing the scepter is gone once you've got it," the fortune-teller commented. "You've even planned an excellent distraction for him to keep him busy while you steal it. And you know who'll tell you exactly where to find it. This—" she gestured to the photograph on the card, "—will prove useful in replicating it well enough to trick Hades, at least until you get to the Road."

My suspicions abruptly crowded to the surface of my mind in a jumble, each one racing to beat the others to the punch. "How do I know you're really trying to help me, not just set me up? What is it you expect from me in return?" I stared into the fortune-teller's pale green eyes, and they gave nothing back. All I could tell was that she was sure of herself — sure I'd believe her, at least, although I was hoping she was also sure of her information, and that she was telling me the truth. She didn't even bother to answer me, just stared back at me with that look of self-assurance.

"How did *you* find out so much about it?" I asked.

At that, she shifted the topic.

"If you're carrying this scepter when you cross back into the Land of the Living," she said, "you'll re-emerge as a living being. Your former self. You'll remember everything that happened here, and everyone up there will remember your death. It does exactly what you need it to do."

"Okay, great, assuming it really does," I said. At least what she was saying matched up with what Anatol and the books had told me.

"It does," she said. "Even if you aren't sure, you'll go anyway, but for what it's worth, I *am* telling the truth."

"All right, what about the helm? You said you knew where the helm of Hades was, too."

"You'll need the scepter to get that far. It's not *just* for getting aboveground without winding up undead." And she told me about the Road. The Road to the Land of the Living is a dismal, treacherous, confusing, winding thing, its wayside heavily occupied by all manner of unpleasant (and highly territorial) inhabitants. It's easy to get lost along it, and most people who do get lost, if they manage to get their bearings, head back into the Underworld, where things are a lot more pleasant and comfortable. Other people don't get their bearings, and wander around in fear and peril long after the rest have returned and got used to the fact that they're dead, and it's really not so bad.

"Wait, so I won't have the helm until I've gotten well out of the city?" I asked.

"Right."

"Won't Hades catch up with me by then?"

"He won't come after you while you're on the Road." She shook her head.

"Bullshit," I scoffed. "You're telling me he's not going to come after me for stealing his scepter?"

"Not as long as you're on the Road. There is plenty of danger between here and the end of the Road. Hades won't bother to act personally unless you overcome the obstacles already in place." She shrugged. "Why should he? There's more than enough to bar your way without his having to lift a finger."

"I don't know if that's reassuring or not," I said darkly. "So, back to the Helm of Darkness. . . ."

"If you make it far enough along the Road," the fortune-teller said, "you'll come to a grove of white poplars by a river gorge—"

"I'm not going to know a white poplar when I see one!" I interrupted.

"Are you going to know a gorge when you see one?" The fortune-teller sighed and shuffled through her tarot deck. "Here." She flipped a card onto the table.

In the photograph was a stand of greyish-trunked trees with diamond-shaped pocks in the bark, and taking up the mid- and background, a chasm with a nearly dry riverbed at the bottom. There were rough stairs hacked into the walls of the bank, but no bridge. Hopefully that river *stayed* dry, if I needed to cross it — and I guessed right by assuming I'd have to.

"Cross here," the fortune-teller continued, "and you will encounter the hydra—"

"Wait, what?" I cut in. "The *hydra*?"

"A seven-headed dragon, and the guardian of Hades' helm," she explained.

"I *know* what it *is*," I said impatiently. "But, seriously, a *dragon*? This is real life, not mythology. . . ." I trailed off as I realized how stupid that sounded. It *wasn't* real life — it wasn't life at all; it was the afterlife, where anything was possible. And I was working on stealing the scepter and helm of Hades, Lord of the Underworld, God of the Dead, so what was shocking me about a mythological creature standing in my way?

"If you defeat the hydra," the fortune-teller said, smirking at my objection and subsequent silence, "you'll find its den nearby. The helm will be there, but it still won't be easy to get. You'll need the scepter every moment of the journey, from the first step you take along the Road."

And, as she continued to explain, once you do get back topside, *if* you get that far, and *if* you manage to manifest physically, there's the whole issue of readjusting to mortality, biologically-based emotions, and illness.

Not to mention the wrath of Hades.
I had fair warning going into it. I can't say nobody warned me.

Chapter Twenty-One

cause of death

"What happened to you guys?" Vic asked, as the five of us — Uncle Jeff, Latrischa, Matt, Anatol, and I — straggled through the doors of the Dead Man's Chest. Everybody looked up, including the Religious Guys Anonymous, who were sitting at the table near ours.

I glanced at the others, who were, like me, covered in scorch marks and red ooze, and pointed at Matt. "We went to the theme park with him. He's invented a paintball gun that shoots fake blood at the target."

Matt grinned. "I'm working on one that, when you get shot, it makes you look all zombie-fied where it hits you. That's my next project."

"I'll get doubles for each of you," Vic said sympathetically.

"Thanks."

We sat down, Matt bouncing in his chair. He plopped the huge bag of prize tokens on the table and dumped them out. "Muahahaha!" he gloated, which was kind of scary coming from a ten-year-old.

"You going to count out my five hundred for me?" I asked.

He nodded vigorously, not taking his eyes off the tokens.

Latrischa glared at me. "I can't *believe* I let you talk me into that."

"I don't think I want to *see* a piano until I've had a stiff drink," Uncle Jeff said.

"Haha!" Matt nudged me. "Stiff drink — get it?"

I rolled my eyes.

Anatol had quick-puffed half a cigar by now, and leaned back in his chair. "At least Matt enjoyed himself, right?"

"Yup. Thanks for helping me win my tokens, guys." The coins clinked against the table as he counted out stacks of ten.

"Anatol," I said, "did you smoke this much when you were alive?"

"What do you think killed me?" He smiled, and smoke came out from between his teeth.

Vic arrived with our drinks, managed to find space for them in spite of the coins, and departed again.

"No, no," the priest was saying at the next table. "If this were Hell, I'd still be stuck with those crazy superstitious witch-hunters from the Dark Ages."

"Didn't he die *during* the Dark Ages?" I whispered to Uncle Jeff.

"I think that's what he meant," Uncle Jeff whispered back.

"Well it was *your* Church that made them that way," the minister said primly. "The Reformation was the best thing that could've happened to the Western world."

"Here they go again." Latrischa rolled her eyes.

"Did they ever stop?" Anatol grinned.

When Matt finished counting out my five hundred coins — which left him with almost three hundred; more than enough to buy his permanent ticket to the water park — I went to give my bribe to Charon.

"Well, well, well," he said, tossing one of the tokens in his left hand as he held the bag with his right. They were golden, which I figured passed for gold in the Underworld, since it was all just an illusion anyway. On the front of each coin was a mallet, and the backs of the tokens had various cartoon characters' heads on them.

"They're gold coins," I said. "You said you didn't care where they were used for currency."

"True, true." Charon nodded, rubbing his beard. "Yes, I suppose these fit the bill, so to speak. I'll take 'em."

"And where, then, can I find Hades' scepter?" I asked.

"One thing first." Charon held up a finger and stepped closer than I was entirely happy about. "You make sure you cause plenty of trouble for Hades."

"I think I pretty much have to, to carry this off," I said.

"You promise?" Charon insisted.

"Scout's honor," I agreed.

"All right then." Charon nodded to himself, then gave me another of his terrible grins. "Hades keeps his scepter in his desk."

"In his desk? How does a scepter fit in—" I began.

"No, no, I mean it's made to look like part *of* the desk," Charon explained. "You've seen the desk in his study, right?"

"Yeah."

"Look at the carvings along the front, where you'd be facing if you were sitting behind it. There's a little catch where it slots in, right at the front of the underside of the desk."

"Great." I thought how hard it was going to be to sufficiently distract Hades while I fiddled around with his desk long enough to find a catch *and* replace the scepter with the fake.

"Thanks," I told Charon. I hoped he was telling me the truth.

It really helped that time wasn't a factor.

Uncle Jeff had always had a pretty long attention span, and now that he didn't have to stop to sleep or eat or take care of himself in any way, he was perfectly happy to just sit and work on a project until it was complete. That, and he wanted me out of Hades' reach as soon as possible.

"How's it going?" I asked him when I went over to his studio one evening. I looked around the work surfaces, but didn't see the fake scepter.

"Oh, I finished my part of it," Uncle Jeff said. "It's in

Latrischa's hands now."

I nodded. "Thanks a lot for doing this for me. I can't tell you how much it means to me." I hugged him, and he rubbed my shoulders.

"I know, I know. I just wish there was something safer you could do. . . ." he trailed off.

"Too late for that," I said, and he forced an understanding smile.

I sighed and sat down in one of the armchairs by the book nook, while Uncle Jeff grabbed a pair of mugs from a cabinet and imagined hot chocolate into them. He makes *really* good hot chocolate, and I took a couple good long gulps of it right away. My mood lifted, and I felt suddenly very tender toward everything — it was a weird, bittersweet feeling, like looking at family Christmas photos from when you were a kid. It's happy, but there's this twinge to it where you know it'll never be quite that way again.

Uncle Jeff sat in the other armchair and took a sip of his own cocoa. After a moment, he set his mug on the side table and sat back, looking thoughtful.

"Since you *are* going back," he said slowly, "there's something I want to talk to you about. . . . It's about my death."

"Your death?" Even now, with him in the Underworld, it still upset me to think about Uncle Jeff's fall. I guess it's hard to break your associations with an event, no matter how illogical it is later.

"You know your dad was there when it happened, right?" Uncle Jeff asked.

I nodded. "He went over to watch a 'Star Trek' marathon with you on TV."

"Yeah, and the satellite dish had gotten misaligned from the wind the night before," Uncle Jeff said. "So I went up on the roof to fix it. I went up before James got there, because I *knew* he would do it himself rather than let me get up on the roof — yes, because I was clumsy when I was physical—"

I couldn't help a tiny smirk, and we had a quick laugh before Uncle Jeff went on.

"So when he got there I was still fiddling with the dish, and he tried to get me to switch places — to come down and check the signal inside and he'd go up on the roof instead. I was irritated with him because he didn't trust me to do it myself, but I said I'd come down. That's when I fell."

I wrapped my hands around the cup and stared at the mini-marshmallows swirling around the top of my drink. I didn't know what to say.

"The last thing I saw was James' face," Uncle Jeff said. "I still have nightmares about his expression, that last instant of my life. He looked like he'd just been hit with a hammer, right between the shoulders. Shocked and helpless. I don't remember hitting the ground afterwards — the next thing I knew, I was in the tunnel. I just wanted to turn back long enough to tell James that everything was going to be okay. Not to kick himself because he didn't manage to catch me or something."

I nodded. "I know how Dad is."

"As protective as your dad was about me, his little brother," Uncle Jeff said with an affectionate smile, "I can just imagine what it's like to grow up with him as a dad."

"I knew he was *there* when it happened," I said. "I didn't know he was *right there*, looking up at you when you fell. I always thought he was inside the house, and saw it through a window or something. He didn't talk about it much, and we didn't ask. We didn't want to upset him."

"Can you do something for me?" Uncle Jeff asked. "When you go back up — if you see your dad — can you tell him I said that there was nothing he could do? It wasn't his fault. I know him . . . he's blamed himself all this time because I just so happened to fall when he tried to get me to come down. I could've fallen anytime. *I* got up on the roof in the first place. I knew it would worry him if I did it, and I did it anyway. I could just as easily have fallen before he got there. Can you tell him I said the only thing that still bothers me is that I'm afraid he thinks it was his fault?"

"Of course I can." I put my hand over Uncle Jeff's.

"Make sure he knows this is a good place." He gestured to encompass the Underworld in general.

"I will," I promised.

"Thank you, Erica." Uncle Jeff patted my hand and smiled.

Chapter Twenty-Two

farewell and goodbye

To tell you the truth, I wish now that I hadn't been so single-minded about my return to the Upper World, that I'd focused more on the people I cared about in the Underworld. My mind skipped over the fact that we'd be saying our goodbyes, and that even though, sooner or later, I'd be back to rejoin them in the afterlife, I had no idea when or under what circumstances that would happen. There was the concern, too, that Hades would find out I was back in town and in full possession of my memory, adding pressure to all of us to rush through the preparations for my theft of the scepter. And once things were set in motion, we wouldn't have a chance to give our parting the thought and attention it deserved.

The closest I got to a proper parting with any of my Underworld friends and Uncle Jeff was the last afternoon I spent at the Dead Man's Chest, and it was that same afternoon I set out for Hades' palace, intent on pilfering his most powerful weapon.

I came into the bar excited — Latrischa had called me at home from Vic's phone to tell me that It Was Ready.

"Do you have it?" I whispered over her shoulder as I took my seat next to her. Uncle Jeff sat on her other side, Matt and Anatol across the table from the three of us.

Uncle Jeff nodded and moved his jacket aside — the fake scepter was leaned up against his chair.

I rubbed my hands together in anticipation and exchanged a

look with Matt. It worried me a bit that I felt as giddy as Little Mr. Anarchy about what we were preparing to do — a bit, but not enough to take the edge off my excitement.

"Ready when you are." Matt set aside his emptied milkshake glass.

"Hold up, kid." Anatol laid a hand on Matt's arm, then looked at me. "Are you *sure*? Once we start this thing, you won't have a chance to change your mind."

"I'm sure." I held his gaze steadily. "I'm ready."

After Matt left, we were silent until Vic turned up with my drink — I didn't even have to order anymore.

"You folks are as bad as the minister today!" he teased us, grinning beneath his prodigious mustache. "Too serious. Drink up, drink up — I want cheerful customers!"

He glanced up as the door opened, and the Religious Guys Anonymous walked in together. "Speak of the devil," Vic said in an undertone to us, and his booming laugh cut through the room.

It was hard not to laugh along with Vic, especially with the mix of nervousness and elation I was experiencing. Even Uncle Jeff cracked his old sideways smile, looking more like himself than he had since I'd first proposed the whole scepter business.

Anatol managed to stop my edgy giggling by sharing his cigar with me.

We'd just gotten back to a steady stream of conversation when I noticed the minister leave the Religious Guys Anonymous' table.

Anatol nudged me. "Now's your chance."

I took the minister's seat at the table with the other two, and Anatol followed Doom and Gloom to the bar — he'd hold him off with a friendly chat to give me more of an opportunity to talk to the reverend and the priest.

They greeted me amiably, and after the usual pleasantries,

I jerked my thumb toward the minister. "He's still pretty set on getting to Hell, isn't he?"

The reverend and the priest exchanged looks. "Moans about it every time we see him," the priest said.

The reverend shook his head. "He won't be content until he's been punished as he expected."

"Maybe you guys should go talk to Hades." I watched Anatol trying to cajole the mopey minister. "The three of you. Maybe get some closure to your argument."

"Oh, that." The priest waved a hand dismissively. "We've finished arguing."

"What?" I sat up straighter, alarmed. Anatol's brilliant idea of having multiple distractions to take the heat off me while I nabbed Hades' scepter was suddenly in serious jeopardy. Sure, I'd still have Matt's diversion, but I agreed with Anatol that chaos was definitely my friend in this instance.

"We've sort of agreed to disagree," the reverend said. "And, well, he's finally going to go see Hell for himself."

"I thought he couldn't afford the fare for the train?" I said.

"He can't," the priest grunted. "He's too miserable to conjure up even a basic joy-swap, let alone anything special — the kind of thing you'd need for a train ticket."

"Why do you think *we* buy his drinks?" The reverend flashed a wry smile. "We bought him a ticket. We're just having a last drink together before he heads down to the station."

"You're sending your friend to *Hell*?"

"He *wants* to go," the priest said defensively, and the reverend nodded.

Great. So now I wouldn't have their big philosophical yelling match, which I'd been sure we could count on, to help me. Or maybe. . . .

"You got him a visa, too, right?" I said.

The priest and the reverend exchanged looks. "What?"

"To travel between cities, you've got to have a visa," I lied.

"Hades has to approve them personally."

"Do they cost much?" the reverend asked with concern.

"No, it's just that it's not always easy to get Hades' approval." I felt guilty for lying to them, especially since the minister seemed to have enough problems without me making up more for him. But, after all, in the Underworld, you couldn't miss your train — without time, it's hard to enforce set deadlines on tickets — and delaying entry into Hell didn't seem like such an awful thing to do to a guy. Still, to make up for it, I conjured up a couple of well-thought-out marshmallows and gave them to the priest and the reverend. "Make sure he gets a return ticket, okay? So he can come back if he doesn't like the fire and brimstone."

The reverend beamed a smile at me and laid a hand on my shoulder. "You're a kind person, Erica."

Feeling even guiltier, I thanked him.

"I guess when he gets back," the priest said, "we'd better go out to the palace."

The reverend agreed. "I'll show you both the way to Hades' study," he assured the priest. He, of course, had been to see Hades before — a fact Anatol hadn't forgotten when he'd suggested the three men of God for our purposes.

Anatol and I swapped a look from across the room, and I gave him the tiniest of nods. We both returned to our table, where Uncle Jeff and Latrischa were waiting for us.

"All set?" Uncle Jeff asked.

"I hope so." But I had a bad feeling that things weren't going to go smoothly.

The Religious Guys Anonymous conferred briefly and then left hurriedly, hailing a cab outside our window.

"That's them off to the palace," Anatol commented.

"You'd better get going," Latrischa said mournfully.

It tugged at me to hear her actually emotional about my departure, but she was right — I had to go while things were lined up for me.

"Wait." Anatol stopped me as I swept past the table. This was no time for elaborate goodbyes, unfortunately. I knew, logically, that if I succeeded, this was probably my last shot at a real farewell, but I couldn't stop now.

Still, I looked down at Anatol as he held onto my elbow, each studying the other's expression. The laugh lines at the corners of his eyes were dormant in this moment of seriousness, his concern for me so intense that I couldn't look away. It was a shockingly tender feeling on such a craggy, roguish face.

"Change of plans," he said softly. "I'll meet you at the Road when you get there."

"You're going back?" I asked, surprised.

"No . . . but I want to help you get started." He squeezed my arm gently. "Once I'm sure you can take care of yourself, I'll head back here."

"I—"

"No time to discuss it," Anatol interrupted. "I'll see you there."

I was way more relieved than he knew, but he was right — I needed to get going. Later, we could consider the dangers or benefits of his coming with me. Now, I had unfinished business with Hades.

Uncle Jeff and Latrischa took their turns at quick goodbyes and hugs, and then, without giving myself time to think about it, I left the Dead Man's Chest, accepted the false scepter from Uncle Jeff, and hailed a taxi.

"Hades' Palace," I said to the driver, and off we went.

Chapter Twenty-Three

the big switch

Outside the door to Hades' study, I paused. There in the vast, dark spinning room, lit only by the refracted light coming through the crystalline door, I listened to the chaos that I'd instigated.

Matt stepped out of the darkness nearby, and I almost yelled, but contained myself.

"I did it!" He grinned. "Hades will have more than enough to deal with now."

Matt disappeared into the wall, then popped his head back out. "Now! Come through now!" And he pulled me by the elbow — into the surface of the black, curved wall. It was like stepping into a giant block of super-firm Jell-O, pushing through the stone surface. From inside it, I listened to what sounded like dozens of voices all clamoring over each other from Hades' study, and felt Matt squeeze my arm.

I let him lead me through and into the study, where we arrived entirely unnoticed. Matt had managed to bring us through right behind Hades' desk, and the crowded lower section of the two-level room was angled so that, crouching down, we were blocked from sight. I ducked under the desk, my view of the room now limited to what I could see through a small slit where the back panel and the underside didn't quite meet up.

Matt slipped back into the fray, joining about thirty other kids he'd rounded up from the theme park — he was paying them off with his blood pellet paintball guns. They all looked around eight to ten, and they were all wreaking havoc, some of them having a shootout with the fake blood guns, others throwing mini-dynamite at each other, and six or so demanding from Hades that he let them go see their parents in the Land of the Living. One little girl was doing a particularly effective job of wailing — long, drawn-out sobs that warbled at the peak of their volume, and gigantic tears streaming down her face as she howled. "I want to see my mo-o-O-o-o-m!" she cried at Hades, who looked like he needed an aspirin or ten.

The Religious Guys Anonymous were there, too, trying to have a serious conversation with Hades regarding the minister's visa while sidestepping kids and explosions.

"Visa?" Hades dodged a lit explosive as it arced toward him.

"To travel to Hell," the minister yelled.

The little girl wailed again, her actual words drowned out by the cacophony of shouting kids and the Religious Guys Anonymous trying to shout explanations to Hades.

"You don't need papers to travel here." Hades looked puzzled at the idea. "This isn't a bureaucracy, this is an afterlife."

"But—" the reverend began in confusion.

Oh please oh please oh please, I thought, *don't let them mention it was me that told them about the visa.* I should've known anything I came up with on the fly would backfire on me.

Luckily, a little boy threw himself against Hades' legs at that point and bawled up at him.

Hades looked down with obvious aversion as he said to the Religious Guys, "As long as you stay *in* the Underworld, I don't care what you do. Just please go do it somewhere other than my study."

"You two never get *anything* right!" The minister turned on his friends. "Visa! What would the Devil have to sign a visa for?"

Hades drew himself up indignantly. "The Devil? Mortal, I'll have you know that Satan isn't half the poker player I am. Don't confuse me for *him*."

The priest roared with laughter, which ticked the minister off even before the reverend started arguing with him.

Waist-deep in screaming children having an all-out war, the Religious Guys Anonymous hit full philosophical yelling match within inches of the god of the Underworld.

This was my chance.

I slipped back out from under the desk, until I was crouching behind it, facing it, and there, where Charon had assured me the scepter would be, was . . . nothing. There was a rounded hollow there in the woodwork, which something obviously was meant to fill, but the scepter itself was gone.

Shit!

I looked around in a panic, but the scepter was nowhere nearby.

I ducked back under the desk to peek through the slit.

In the pandemonium, it was hard to look for a stationary object, but I figured Hades must have the scepter close by him if he had it out of its hiding place.

The minister was shouting over the noise of the kids, preaching at full volume in the reverend's face while the priest — who was paying more attention to Hades' mood than his companions — tried desperately to shut him up.

"Stop!" Hades sliced horizontally through the air with one hand. The room fell silent, although everyone was still going through the motions of shouting. And that was when I caught sight of the scepter.

Hades was holding it.

Now what? How could I possibly pull the big switch when the object to be switched was in its owner's hand?

Worse still, Hades pushed through the now-silent mayhem of the study and headed my direction. He was coming over to the desk!

If he sat down, I was screwed.

Matt looked on with momentary horror, but quickly recovered his capacity for troublemaking. He gave a hand signal to the kids, and silence doesn't stop fake blood pellets or miniature dynamite detonations, all of them directed toward the desk . . . and me, and Hades, who, unlike me, wasn't huddled safely under the furniture.

Hades was instantly covered with masses of red goo, and the room roiled with smoke from the soundless explosives.

Cursing profusely (despite the presence of "innocent" children — for shame!) Hades lost track of keeping the place quiet, and the sound in the room rose again, shouts and cries and gunshots steadily increasing in volume.

Under cover of the smoke and noise, Hades approached the desk, and I didn't dare move even to try and better conceal myself, afraid the smallest rustle, this close to him, might give me away.

But then, as I watched with mounting excitement, Hades slipped the scepter into its place across the front of the desk. His fingers pressed the latch into place and slithered away to rest on the top of the desk. He wasn't going to sit down — he was suspicious of losing the scepter to one of the kids or the Religious Guys Anonymous, or at least he was taking precautions against it, I figured. He wanted it in a safe place in all this madness, and he'd waited to put it away until everyone else was distracted.

Now, if Matt could just get him back *away* from here. . . .

But I shouldn't have doubted Matt's ingenuity, even briefly.

The crazy kid reached into the fireplace and started grabbing the letters that continually fell toward the flames.

With a fistful of envelopes, he tore into the first letter and yelled out the contents.

"Dear Sir or Madam who is in charge of the Underworld," Matt read, and the kids who weren't mid-battle or mid-tantrum giggled derisively at Hades about the "or Madam" part. "What kind of afterlife are you running here, where a man can't fish anymore? I know all about how the animals are dead, too, and how they're supposed to be enjoying their own afterlives, but fish got barely any brains to begin with. What do they need to enjoy anything for? So, you that's in charge, I want to know where's my hunting and fishing rights now that I'm dead?"

The kids who were paying attention during the reading of the letter were quick to conjure up rubber fish, which they proceeded to use as projectiles at one another and, in the case of braver kids, at Hades himself.

The reverend and the minister shouted at each other, and the priest tried to get Hades' attention by waving his arms. "We just want a visa for our friend, and then we'll leave!" he bellowed.

Matt opened another letter and started to read as Hades bore down on him.

Hurriedly, I slipped the catch off the scepter, replaced it with the false one, and was just congratulating myself internally, when I realized that the smoke had cleared and the fish were no longer flying across the room.

I huddled back under the desk, afraid to even peek through the crack in case Hades looked straight at me hiding there, and listened.

The priest yelled.

The minister yelled.

The reverend yelled.

Matt set off a whole chain of mini dynamite. The kids all screamed in unison.

There was still no way I could be sure of getting out without someone — or everyone — seeing me.

That's when the fortune-teller showed up.

From my hiding place, I was at just the right angle to see her come into the doorway, and even though she didn't so much as glance in my direction, I knew she knew where I was and what I was doing there. I felt safe enough for the moment to glance through the slit at the back of the desk.

"I hope you're going to clean all this," she said to the Lord of the Dead.

Hades looked up, his height allowing him to see her over the heads of the Religious Guys Anonymous (who had cornered him again), and actually smiled. "Persephone," he said gently, breaking off the argument with the change in his tone.

Everyone looked at her.

Persephone? I gaped. *Persephone?!* The wife of Hades, the Queen of his realm, was the dockside carnival's fortune-teller and my *ally* in stealing his scepter?

Considering her mythological story, it was possible — Hades *had* kidnapped her and held her against her will, after all — but my suspicion overshadowed everything.

Was she my ally? Was she really helping me, or had she gotten me this far just to trap me? Or was I her way to get back at Hades for trapping her in the Underworld for half of every year? If I was, what did *she* want from me?

"Don't think your charm will get you out of it." Persephone wagged a finger playfully at her husband. "I just *cleaned* this study the other day. I even waxed the woodwork." She sure didn't seem like she was holding a grudge against Hades, from her manner, but she still wasn't giving me away, either.

The Religious Guys Anonymous clamored to regain Hades' attention, but his eyes were all for Persephone now. "Duck!" she warned him, as a kid took aim at him.

She managed to spin him around, facing away from me, as the blood pellet shattered against the wall behind him. Amid all the yelling and wailing, she hugged him, and over his shoulder, she met my eyes through the crack in the desk. She winked.

I crept out, reassured that I could trust her. *Why* she had helped me was a question for some other time — sometime when I wasn't in the middle of a brazen theft.

I was about to make a dash through the wall when Hades started to turn around. Too far out to get back under the desk, and too far from the wall to get out unseen, I froze, completely panicked.

Matt was on his toes, though. Before Hades was halfway

through his turn, the kid conjured up a cherry bomb the size of his own head and threw it straight at me. Reflex jerked me away from the blast, pulling me inside the stone wall even as the explosion and smoke covered my exit. I was out — well, I was *in*, rather . . . inside the solid wall and past the risk of being spotted.

I ducked out into the spinning room, and silently thanked everything I could think of that, for whatever reason, Persephone was on my side.

I had the scepter.

"Run!" Matt whispered from inside the wall, next to my ear.

"Thanks, kid!" I whispered back.

Then I took his advice.

Chapter Twenty-Four

approaching death from the wrong direction

Getting out of the palace was a dizzy little dance through the cavernous spinning room. The subway didn't stop anywhere near the Lethos, and I wasn't going to wait around for a cab, so I hurried on foot over the bridge and toward the edge of town — toward the Road — with many a glance over my shoulder.

But either Hades still had his hands full and hadn't noticed the absence of the scepter, or the Big Switch had worked and he thought he had the original, or the fortune-teller — Persephone — had been right, and he wouldn't bother pursuing me unless whatever the Road threw at me failed.

I wasn't over the shock of finding out that my co-conspirator was Hades' wife. I should've been more careful . . . I was lucky she'd come down on my side. I'd probably want to take a dig at Hades, too, if he'd tricked me into marriage over six measly pomegranate seeds — although she seemed to like him well enough. *Let's just hope I don't do anything to piss* her *off, too*, I thought.

The further I got from the palace, the more I worried. Flying monkeys could suddenly burst from the towers and come after me. Hades could run me down with his chariot. Persephone could catch up with me and demand some terrible price for her help. Matt and his crew and the Religious Guys Anonymous could be in danger for all the trouble they were causing Hades, and it would be my fault if anything happened to them. Uncle Jeff was probably miserable right now. And Latrischa?

I couldn't help smiling. Latrischa could take care of herself. She'd miss me, but it wouldn't bring her down — not for long.

What I needed to worry about now, I reminded myself, wasn't what I was leaving behind. If Anatol and Persephone were right, I'd have enough trouble waiting for me up ahead, once I reached the Road.

And if Anatol was determined to come with me on the first leg of my journey back to the Land of the Living, that brought up its own mess of worries. Now that it was too late to turn back, I felt afraid for him again — the way I had when he'd told me about his married sweetheart.

There was a cab stopped by the curb up ahead, and I flagged it down. Swinging into the back, I told the driver where I wanted to go.

"I'm not going to *that* edge of town." He shook his head. "I'll drop you over that direction, though."

"Good enough for me." I glanced out the back window to check for hordes of flying monkeys. There weren't any, but that didn't make me feel any better. The smoothness of my own getaway actually made me *more* tense. It could only mean one thing, to my mind — what was ahead was going to be far worse than I'd ever imagined.

It took me three tries to get a decent marshmallow to pay the cabbie with. I was too preoccupied and nervous to direct the emotional associations, and in the end he accepted a pretty mediocre specimen.

"People never pay well this side of town," he told me sympathetically. "Too distracted. Guess you've got a lot on your mind when you're headed — out there." His gaze flicked toward the street that dead-ended by the abandoned train station, next to the Road.

I nodded, but said nothing as he rolled up his window and drove off, leaving me alone in the silent street.

I shifted my grip on Hades' scepter, turned my back on the city, and rounded the corner with a forcibly steady, confident stride.

Anatol was leaning against the brick wall of the train station, with one lanky leg propped up as a makeshift surface for shuffling his cards. He saw me coming and tucked the deck back in his pocket. "You did it! Everybody okay?"

"So far, so good."

"Ready?" he asked.

I considered arguing with him about whether or not he should come along, but didn't. One, it wouldn't have done any good, and two, there were an awful lot of questions about the Road that I should've gotten the answers to before now . . . and hadn't.

So I just said, "I'm ready," and fell in step with Anatol.

I faltered only slightly when the asphalt crumbled away into the red clay of the Road, and the black trees loomed overhead. Like the first time I'd seen it, there was a disconcerting sense of weakness and futility here, as if the place itself were a presence, conscious and spiteful, whispering doubts in my ear.

Mind games, I told myself, and clenched the scepter tighter. If Hades were responsible for the unsettling feelings surrounding this place, it made me all the more determined to overcome the Road's challenges, and also made me swagger a little with the knowledge that I'd stolen his prime artifact. If the Road was just a function of the Underworld itself, and this creepiness was a natural, undirected occurrence . . . that seemed worse. I'd rather have someone to be mad at — it gave me more reason not to yield to the fear. *Mind games*, I thought again, more boldly, and kept walking.

~*~

We moved in a companionable silence until Anatol headed off the path, and I checked. I looked from the tangles of underbrush he was seemingly oblivious to, to the clear, albeit muddy, expanse of the Road before me.

"Is it a good idea to leave the Road?" I called after him.

Anatol raised his eyebrows. "I didn't know I was." His gaze flicked down to the scepter, and he smiled. "How many branches are there to the Road ahead?"

I gave him a funny look.

"Just answer," he insisted.

"There's just a road. No forks, branches, or spoons about it," I said.

"So it *does* guide its bearer," Anatol muttered.

I hesitated, stuck the tip of the scepter into the red clay of the Road, then released my grip on the artifact.

There were three Roads — or I should say, three branches.

I grabbed the scepter again. One Road.

Persephone had said I'd need the scepter every step of the journey, and this had to be one of the reasons. It *was* guiding me. I just hoped it was guiding me to the right place.

"Where else do these branch-offs lead?" We started walking again — with me as the trailblazer now.

"Other cities in the Underworld," Anatol said. "The Road links to all of them, usually in the most roundabout way possible."

"Then this is the *only* road that leads to the Land of the Living?"

"Only one I know of." He shrugged. "Although, I got lost so many times when I tried to go back topside, who knows how many different roads I ended up on? I sure don't."

"If you got so lost," I said with a mixture of irony and affection, "what made you think you'd be a good guide for *me*?"

"Well, I was hoping the scepter would keep us from getting lost," he admitted. "I'm not tagging along because I thought you'd get lost."

"Two questions, then," I said.

"Shoot." Anatol put his hands in the pockets of his tweed jacket.

"Well, you're not going back to the Upper World, right? So you're going part way with me and then head back to Hades. How are you going to get back without the scepter? Won't you get lost?"

He shook his head. "It's easy to get *back*. It's only hard if you try to go forward, toward the Land of the Living. That was three questions, technically."

"No, that was one big question," I said.

He laughed. "Well, I'm not charging you for 'em. What's your so-called second question?"

"If you're not coming with me to keep me from getting lost—" I glanced at him — "why *are* you here? I mean, I'm glad for the company . . . but what is it you're worried I can't handle?"

Anatol stared straight ahead, his expression hardening without his features actually moving. "The monsters."

I swept a quick glance around at the shadowy undergrowth. "Define *monsters*."

"Mean, ugly, scary sons-of-bitches who'll try to stop you from getting where you're trying to go . . . and possibly eat your soul."

"Like demons?" I asked.

"Or like giant possums," Anatol said. "At least, *one* time I got attacked by a giant possum. With a scorpion tail."

"Wait, they can actually *eat* us?" I stopped walking to stare at him. "How did you manage to get away from a giant possum-scorpion demon?"

"I wounded it and got away." He shrugged, and we started walking again. "It was that, or let it kill me. After that, I went back to the Styx and asked Charon if I could stay on the ferry if I helped out. I figured, why risk losing my whole eternal afterlife to get back to the Upper World? If I managed to get back, it wouldn't do me any good, anyway. She's still married, up there. If I got myself eaten by Underworld monsters, I wouldn't be here when she arrived in the afterlife. So I turned back."

"So you're saying I'm going to have to fight these things?" I asked.

"Definitely," Anatol answered. "Maybe kill them."

"Aren't they already . . . well, dead?"

"Sort of. The rules are a little different along the Road than they are in the rest of the Underworld." He swept a hand in front of himself to indicate the Road in general. "It runs between death and life, invulnerability and mortality. You've got to expect things to be kind of strange in a place like this."

"And these demon-things, they're, like, animals?"

"Kind of, some of them," he said.

"I can't kill animals!" I'd been brought up to take *care* of animals, and even stronger than my instinct for self-preservation was my revulsion at the idea of cutting into flesh and spilling blood, damaging organs and slicing through muscle and sinew. *They won't have that stuff!* I reminded myself. *This is the Underworld; they're as dead as I am. They* must *be.* Still, I felt firmly opposed to slaying beasties. "Look, no matter how ugly they are, I can't kill animals. I work at a zoo gift shop — I sell soft fuzzy panda toys, okay?"

"They're not just animals," Anatol said darkly. "And they definitely aren't soft fuzzy panda toys. They're *monsters*."

"And a komodo dragon hasn't ever been called a monster?" I countered.

"I *knew* the monsters were going to be an issue for you," Anatol sighed.

Chapter Twenty-Five

can't judge a book by its color

We stopped in a clearing at the top of a hill for a quick break, even though, technically, we didn't need to rest. Despite the lack of muscles to feel sore, bones to ache, or cells to need sleep and regeneration time, I was weary. It was the fatigue of homesickness. I missed Uncle Jeff, Latrischa, Matt, the religious fanatics in the bar, the twilit streets, the view out the dark window of the library — a panorama of glittering city lights with the glow of the dockside carnival in the distance.

I looked back the way we'd come, and the city of Hades was far enough away that it looked faded with the distance — washed out and bluish and indistinct on the horizon. Between it and us, the blackish-green trees swayed in an ever-changing current of wind. The twilight of Hades hung over the city like a storm cloud, looking strange to me as I stood in a blazing afternoon sun. The further in any direction you got from the city, the lighter it was. Certainly there were more pleasant parts of the wild than what lay along the way to the Land of the Living, however — on my train trip from the Atheists' Graveyard back into Hades, I'd seen places where the sunlight was cheerful and luxurious.

Here in the clearing, I could almost get that feeling, but along the Road, beneath the black-leaved canopy, the light seemed stark and confusing. The extreme darkness of the trees and the pattern of shadow and bright sunlight was dizzying. It was nice to get out from under the branches, under an open sky, even temporarily.

I sat on the ground in the sunshine, glad to rest from the

monotony of walking. Anatol perched on a log nearby and fumbled in his pocket for his matches.

"Pretty quiet so far," he commented. I wasn't sure whether he meant *I'd* been quiet, or that there hadn't been much excitement in the journey yet. We had both been pretty somber, it was true — especially since he'd told me I was going to have to slay beasties that might or might not be monsters.

For the first time since I'd decided to travel the Road, I wondered if I was doing the right thing. Not that I'd turn back after all the work it had taken just to *start* the journey. That was why I could afford to let myself think about my doubts. I *knew* I couldn't turn back now that things were already in motion, and I had to carry through on my own crazy plans.

But here was Anatol, who was probably just as eager to see his lost love as I was to see Dominic, and he had turned back before getting to the end of the Road. Like the proverbial hiker lost in the woods, he was staying in one place so he could be found — the smart thing to do, if you're lost in the woods, as my Uncle Jeff had often told us when we went camping with him as kids.

Time means nothing in the Underworld, so how did I know how soon it would seem like to me, when Dom showed up? For that matter, how did I know when, in linear time, I'd show up in the Upper World? It could be a hundred years in the future, for all I knew. Sure, I'd been told otherwise by Anatol and Persephone, but they could be wrong.

"What are you thinking about?" Anatol asked, as if he sensed the question that had popped into my mind.

I looked over at him, watching the first drag of smoke from his cigar as it unfurled from his nose and mouth. "Do you know who the fortune-teller really is?"

"You found out, did you?" He sounded casual, but he didn't give me his roguish grin. He was afraid I'd be mad at him for not telling me.

I wasn't sure that I *wasn't* mad about it, but I figured he had a good reason — even if I didn't consider it a good *enough* reason — to hold out on a friend. "Yeah. While I was stealing the scepter," I said. "She helped keep Hades' attention off the desk. He called her by name. Why didn't you tell me?"

"If I had told you, would you have trusted her?" He watched me closely as I considered my answer.

"I trusted Charon on your say-so," I said. "Maybe. If you'd said she was okay, I'd probably have believed it."

"You put a lot of faith in my say-so." Anatol gave me a little bow with his hand over his heart. "But," he added, holding up a finger, "I didn't know what she would do. Whether she would help you or not."

"Well, a warning would've been nice!" I said.

"Without her help, you didn't stand much chance one way or the other." Anatol moved to sit on the ground, facing me. "I didn't want to jeopardize your chances of gaining her favor. If she hadn't liked you, she simply wouldn't have told you what she knew about the scepter. She'd never even have shown you that Tarot card if she hadn't felt some affinity for you."

"So you knew right from the start that she'd be on my side?" I asked.

"Not from the start," he admitted. "I didn't know about the Ace of Wands card until later, when you finally explained the details of what you were planning — you never told me exactly what happened when she read your fortune."

"What if she'd been against me?" I demanded.

"Then you'd have been screwed already, no matter what you did or didn't know about her." Anatol patted my cheek. "You forget, little one, she's a fortune-teller. She knew what you were planning from the beginning. Before I did. Before *you* did."

True. Which was what had freaked me out about her. He was probably right. If I'd known who she was, I would've gone out of my way to avoid her . . . and what goddess goes chasing down a smart-mouthed mortal, determined to help them out whether they like it or not? None that I'd ever read about — unless the mortal was a hot young man, which I wasn't.

"I'm sorry I didn't tell you, Erica," Anatol said softly. "Please, no anger."

I sighed. "No anger. You're right, anyway. It wouldn't have done any good to tell me who she was."

"Good. Friends, still?"

I nodded.

He slapped me heartily on the back and passed me the cigar, and we relaxed into wondering out loud what the others were up to, back in the city . . . back in the Dead Man's Chest.

I hadn't felt calm since Hades' trick with the Lethos water, and I got so wrapped up in enjoying the tranquil conversation with Anatol that I forgot, temporarily, to worry about anything — angry gods on my trail, monsters hiding in the shadows, looming mortality ahead. Until we finished off the cigar, we just enjoyed the moment, chatting and playing a half-assed game of Crazy Eights.

Then I heard a rustling in the underbrush.

I jerked upright, trying to see the source of the noise, and then relaxed.

"There's something hot pink hiding in the bushes over there," I said quietly to Anatol. He scrambled to his feet, leaving the cards on the ground and backing away from where I'd pointed.

"Get the scepter out," he said with urgency.

"What is it?" I lazily unslung the scepter from across my back.

"I don't know, but I doubt it's anything good."

I grinned a little. "I've never heard of anything scary that was *hot pink*."

And then it came out from its leafy cover, and Anatol and I both took several steps backward as fast as we could.

A centipede as long as a minivan, about two feet high, with a huge pair of spiky pincers by its mouth, is still pretty damn unsettling, even if it's pink — just so you know. It didn't seem to have any eyes, but it had a couple of antennae twitching around unpleasantly in our direction.

I'd been stung by a centipede once, on a camping trip with Uncle Jeff. Aside from the initial fire-shock pain of the bite, there'd been the aftereffects of the poison to deal with — the fever, chills, and all-night pukefest.

I tried to reassure myself that, being dead, this thing wouldn't be able to hurt me, but my feelings weren't about to be persuaded by logic, and made themselves clear as my sweater and jeans transitioned into crude leather armor and a visored steel helmet. Suddenly, I was grateful for the practice Latrischa had forced on me with her demanding attention to fashion — and for my father's obsession with historical armor.

"I don't know whether it will make a difference that you've got the scepter," Anatol said into my ear, pulling me back a few steps further away from the Pepto Bismol Monster. "I'm not sure if the monsters are subservient to Hades, or if they're just convenient obstacles barring the way to the Upper World."

"So they might obey me as the bearer of Hades' scepter?" I turned slightly toward Anatol, but never took my eyes off the centipede.

"We can hope," Anatol answered, nodding me on.

"Shoo." I waved the scepter at the creature and stamped my foot.

Its antennae twitched eagerly and its head turned toward the sound of my voice.

"Get!" I shouted abruptly, leaping forward and batting at it with the scepter. I jumped back just as quickly. The "it's more afraid of me than I am of it" theory was rapidly being disproved.

I wished I had a sturdier weapon than a staff, even if it *was* the scepter of the god of the Underworld.

And the scepter shifted in my grip. Momentarily distracted from the monster, I watched as the staff transformed into a one-handed sword.

"Nice trick!" Anatol said. "I didn't know it could do *that*."

"Wouldn't a gun be more convenient?" I asked. But then again, it made sense — between Dad's Renaissance festival hobby and my own background in history, blades were more my style. After all, I'd handled a blunt sword before, but I'd never shot more than a water pistol.

Before I could experiment with my options, though, the centipede came for us. It darted forward in a hideous flurry of legs, hairless body surfing toward us on a wave of undulating appendages, antennae flailing wildly to make up for its lack of vision.

It was lightning-quick.

Darting out of the way was something that only occurred to me after the fact, and luckily, my instinct was faster than my logic.

All I had time to do was stick the tip of the scepter-sword into the mud, blade vertical, and brace it with both hands to take the impact.

Half of the centipede went to my left, the other half, to my right, and pinkish-black gunk splattered through the middle.

Anatol's hand was on my shoulder — he'd tried to pull me out of the way, but not fast enough.

Both halves of the centipede were still twitching.

It should've stunk hideously, but it didn't. Whether that meant the monster hadn't been real, or whether it was because neither of us was physical, or what, I didn't know, but I was grateful that at least I'd been spared *that*. Bad enough that my armor was covered in the stuff. Man, was I glad I'd thought to include a helmet with a visor! The gunk that had managed to get through the slits was gross, but minimal.

"Are you okay?" Anatol asked shakily from behind me.

I turned around and took off my helmet, wiping my face on my sleeve. I'd taken the full extent of the monster goo, and Anatol was very nearly untouched by the stuff. "Well, I'm glad I can't feel nausea right now. *That* was a revolting experience I hope never to repeat."

But Anatol was staring at my hand — the one I'd raised to take off my helmet. I looked down.

Two of the fingers on my right hand were missing.

It didn't hurt, and I was too confused to be horrified. I'd felt something brush against my hand in the course of the impact, but there had been no pain — nothing to indicate I was losing bits of myself.

"Is this what you meant when you said the rules were a little different along the Road?" Surveying the still-trembling remains of the centipede, I tried to figure out whereabouts my fingers might've got to in there.

"I didn't expect *this*, exactly," he said. "All I meant was, you aren't invulnerable while you're here. You can get hurt. Damaged."

"Eaten," I added. "But it doesn't hurt." I flexed my remaining fingers to illustrate. "What does that mean?"

"Maybe you're not very far along in the process of returning to a semi-physical state. We haven't traveled that far yet."

"Help me find them?" I looked back to the dead centipede.

Anatol stared blankly at me for a second, then half-smiled. "Maybe I was wrong. You very well *might* be okay on your own out here." He looked down with obvious revulsion, sighed, and squatted to examine the left half of the body. "I'll take this side," he said with resignation. "You did great, though. At least you can't feel bad about killing *this*. Can you?"

"No," I said. "It just makes me want to take a shower. And I do feel a little bad about poking around in its dead insides."

"Erica, it *ate* two of your fingers," Anatol pointed out. "Ah, here they are!"

"Great!" I extracted my hand from the jelly-like substance it had been submerged in and got to my feet.

"They're a little messy." Anatol pulled a clean handkerchief from his jacket and carefully wiped the pink gunk away before he handed them back to me.

It was harder to believe things into existence now than it had been in Hades, but I could do it. A bottle of hydrogen peroxide probably wouldn't make any difference in the Underworld, but it would make me feel better, so I doused my damaged hand and the severed fingers in antiseptic and waited for it to finish bubbling.

Anatol watched with morbid curiosity as I stuck the fingers back on, wiggling them to make sure everything was in working order.

"I'm glad that happened while I was dead," I commented.

"It's not every finger that's been inside the guts of a yard-long centipede," Anatol said.

"I guess that makes you guys special," I said to the fingers.

Anatol rubbed at the sleeve of his jacket with a leaf, trying to get some of the pink venom off. "Come on, let's get out of this bug."

Chapter Twenty-Six

monsters are people, too

Even after we wished ourselves clean of centipede goo, I still felt gross, and jumpier than ever.

"You know, the others aren't going to be that easy," Anatol said as we walked on.

"Very cheerful," I said dryly.

"Just warning you." He shrugged. "They aren't all bugs, and they're not all blind, either. That thing was pretty easy to take down — all ways around."

"Aside from it eating me," I said.

"Well, aside from that, yeah."

"Hey, is that a pond over there?" I craned my neck. It was a little off the path, but only barely out of the way, shielded by relatively inoffensive underbrush and ferns. "Maybe we could wash up better—"

Anatol pulled me back by the arm and shook his head. "Still water is bad. Running water's all right, but ponds and lakes — don't go near 'em."

"Monsters?" I guessed.

"Rusalkis."

"Who?"

"Kind of half-ghost, half-zombie. They live underwater, look like corpses. Enjoy drowning people." Anatol looked sideways at me. "Old Russian folklore monster. Scared the hell out of me when I was a kid. Wasn't too pleased to find out that they're real, down here in the Underworld."

"Okay, no cleaning up," I agreed quickly.

We encountered a few more centipedes (all hot pink) as we forged ahead, but we avoided them. It helped that they were blind — as long as Anatol and I stayed still and didn't make any noise, their antennae didn't flick in our direction, and eventually they'd move on. Once the coast was clear, so would we.

Whether it was the atmosphere of the place, or a change within me, or the fact that I'd killed that monster centipede, I wasn't sure, but I felt different. A weird sensation, a sort of tension, was gradually growing in my shoulders and neck — something like the feeling of being watched, but not quite the same.

I tried not to think about it. With most things in the Underworld, that was the best way to make unpleasantness disappear.

Even as I thought this, something unpleasant appeared that *wasn't* going to go away just because I wanted it to.

It began as a massive shifting of leaves and branches, up ahead and to the right. Too close to us for any hope of avoiding a scrap.

Anatol and I traded worried glances, then tried to outrun its progress — at least then it wouldn't be blocking our way forward — but the thing came crashing out of the undergrowth just a couple of yards ahead.

It was a man — no, an animal — standing on two legs. It was huge, covered with matted red-brown fur up to its waist, and a strip of fur continued on up its bare chest to just below the neck. It had a bull's head, shaggy and with wicked points on its horns, and eyes like a goat's, the pupils slit instead of round. Its hulking, muscular frame trembled in apparent fury, an impression driven home by its clenched fists and the sharp, cloven hoof it stamped as it glared at us.

It wasn't quite how I'd imagined a minotaur, but it definitely was one.

And just as I shoved Anatol behind me and pulled out the

scepter, something else unexpected came flailing through the bushes beneath the green-black canopy.

The minotaur and I turned at the same time to see what was up. To my surprise, a thin, scraggly man in clothes no better than rags stumbled out of the tangle of underbrush, seeming not at all frightened by the beastly form of the minotaur as he flung himself in front of it.

"Don't kill him!" The man lifted his arm with his palm upright toward me, as if he were a traffic cop warding off a car from hitting a small schoolboy.

I lowered the scepter, which had switched into sword form in preparation for a fight.

"All right." I spoke quietly, as if keeping my voice down would lessen the beast's anger.

The minotaur glared at me over the man's shoulder, but seemed content to follow along with the "not killing each other" rule.

The man held eye contact with me for a moment, as if to reassure himself I wasn't going to sneak and kill the monster if he didn't look hard enough at me. He seemed satisfied with whatever he saw in my expression, and turned to the creature behind him.

"Octavius!" He held his arms plaintively before him, fingers curled toward his own chest. "Octavius, please! I know you're still in there."

"Who is Octavius?" Anatol asked, as the creature stared at its advocate with intense incomprehension.

I'd been about to ask the same thing.

"*He* is Octavius," the man said woefully, waving an arm in the minotaur's direction.

Now the minotaur and I both stared at the man in confusion. Anatol raised an eyebrow to me when the guy wasn't looking.

"He doesn't look like an Octavius," I observed, for lack of anything else to say.

The minotaur seemed bored with our conversation, and, giving Anatol and me a long, dubious stare out of its red-gold eyes, it stomped a few yards off, fists still clenched, and sat down by a tree, looking sullen. It was clearly waiting for the man, who watched the creature with a terrible expression of sadness.

"He is my brother," the man said.

"Your brother?" I suppose after everything I'd experienced in the Underworld, I shouldn't have been surprised.

Sebastian (the minotaur's brother) proceeded to tell us how he and Octavius had both died when a bridge collapsed with them on it, and found themselves in the tunnel, still together. The two of them had crossed the River Styx on the next ferry (he showed no recognition of Anatol, and I wondered if the two brothers had been here longer than he had). Like me, Sebastian and Octavius had been determined to get back to the Land of the Living, and they'd decided to take the Road together. Sebastian was set on getting back to his wife and little daughter; Octavius, on helping his brother. His only other vested interest in continuing life was that he'd been cut down young, before he'd accomplished any of the things he'd wanted to, or started a family of his own.

"So what happened to him?" I asked. We were sitting just off the path on the mossy ground, facing each other and leaning against the rough bark of the trunks of nearby trees. Octavius was grinding his horns against a tree a few yards off, occasionally grunting as animals will when they satisfactorily scratch an itch. "I assume he didn't start out as a minotaur."

Sebastian's haggard face was eloquent with sadness. He looked as if he were accustomed to the feeling, as if he had been nothing but sad for ages.

"We were making good progress, we thought," he told me. "It seemed like we'd gone so far along the Road, and, of course, with two of us together it was far less difficult to fight off the creatures that we encountered along the way than if we'd attempted the journey individually."

At this, he paused and seemed to take stock of us again, as if wondering what Anatol and I had come through to get this far.

"He began to change," Sebastian said. "I don't know at what point it started . . . sometime after we lost our way."

I thought back to when Anatol had wandered off into the underbrush, thinking it was the way forward. I nearly said something about the scepter, but Anatol gave me a warning glance as he spoke up.

"Go on," he prompted Sebastian. Anatol didn't trust him yet, then. And why should we? I wouldn't have trusted a complete stranger with information about valuable property when I'd been alive. I was going to have to get out of the habit of thinking like a dead person.

"At first, I thought it was nothing more than the effect of the Road — the sense of returning mortality—" Sebastian stopped, glancing at each of us in turn, as if to assure himself that it wasn't just him who experienced the sensation.

Since I knew exactly what he meant, I nodded him on.

"But then he would have these strange . . . episodes . . . times when he was completely unable to understand something, or would forget things. Not amnesia — he never forgot anything from our lifetime, and he didn't forget things that were said or done. He would forget how to *do* things. Once, we gathered wood for a fire, thinking the light might cheer us up after a dismal day, and I asked him to start it while I gathered more wood to keep it going. I came back and found Octavius squatting by the site, staring down at his tinderbox, holding the flint and steel as if he'd never seen them before. 'What's wrong?' I asked him, and he frowned and threw the tinderbox away from him, as if it were at fault. Now, I know my brother well enough to know when he is ashamed that he can't figure a thing out, and when he is using anger to cover up his shame, and that is precisely what was happening then.

"There were more incidents in the same kind, or times when I would tell him something and he would stare at me, frown as if vexed and distracted, and ask me to repeat myself. When I did, he would pretend he understood me, but would head exactly the opposite direction I'd suggested, or in some other manner give away that he could no longer comprehend my meaning.

"He would often clench the sides of his head as if in pain when we stopped to rest and reorient ourselves, and, at last, one day I moved his hands aside to see if I could find the cause. I said, 'Octavius, have you hit the side of your head? It's swollen here, right above the temple.' He merely stared at me, and I turned his face to see the other side. That side, too, was swollen, and in just the same place. But not only swollen — there was a hard lump just beneath the surface of his skin at the center of each swelling point. And as I examined this, it also occurred to me how different his hair was than what I remembered. It had become wiry, less like hair than fur, and its color had deepened and changed.

"I thought little enough of that at the time, and it was only later, when he was so far out of form that he no longer cared for the human notion of clothing and modesty, that I connected that with his overall change. The painful lumps at his temples, as you might guess, eventually broke through the skin and became the horns you now see." Sebastian gestured toward his brother.

I was aghast at the thought of how Sebastian must have felt during Octavius's transition. What a terrible progression that must have been to watch.

"Why do you think it happened?" I asked. "I mean, you're all right." Looking Sebastian over, I felt he looked far from "all right," between his haggard face and his obvious exhaustion, but I was speaking in relative terms here. At least he wasn't covered in dark reddish fur, grunting and scraping a pair of horns against a tree trunk.

"I can think of only one difference between his experience on the Road and my own." Sebastian gazed steadily into my eyes as he spoke. "I never struck the killing blow against any of the creatures we fought. Octavius always had to kill them; I could never bring myself to do it."

Out of the corner of my eye, I saw Anatol sit straight up, alarmed, and stare at me.

"The only difference?" I asked weakly.

"The only one I've been able to think of."

Chapter Twenty-Seven

dead man's hand

None of us felt up to dealing with monsters right then, so I conjured up some firewood while Sebastian manually added kindling, and Anatol used his lit cigar to get the campfire going. Anatol and I sat on a log Sebastian dragged over, and he settled on the mossy ground at the foot of a tree, across the fire from us. His minotaur brother hunched on a rock, further back from the flames.

The sunlight had faded into an overcast dusk, and crickets of indeterminate size and disposition sang all around us. It was a peaceful sound, although all those individual chirps added up to one exceedingly loud chorus.

"What do you think about what Sebastian said?" I asked Anatol, and the cricket-song gave us privacy to talk openly.

"About killing monsters turning his brother into a monster?" I nodded.

"First I've heard of it, but it's not impossible. Or improbable." Anatol looked grim. "The Road is a strange place."

"I don't *feel* monster-y," I said.

"Well, to be on the safe side, maybe you'd better just wound 'em from here on out. You're much too pretty to grow snakes for hair." Anatol winked, trying to lighten the topic.

I answered with a slow smile. "I'd hate to turn into a satyr — think how often I'd have to shave my legs."

Anatol laughed, then took my hand to pull me to my feet. "Let's play a game of poker against this Sebastian. See if we can get to know him."

"I thought your cards got centipeded?" We'd left them on the ground at the first attack.

"That was that deck." He pulled a pack out of his inside pocket. "I made a new one." It looked identical to the old one, the worn blue-and-red box with the dog-eared cards, a green-and-gold fleur-de-lis printed on the back of each.

"Card game?" I called to Sebastian.

He smiled, a little shyly, and nodded.

Anatol sat on the ground halfway between our log and Sebastian's tree, and I joined him.

I jerked my head toward Octavius, who watched our relocation with mild, passive interest. "Can he. . . ?"

"No." Sebastian shook his head as he settled across from Anatol, to my left. "He used to love to play, but that was before his transformation."

"Poker?" Anatol held up the deck and flicked the cards against each other. Sebastian nodded, and Anatol's broad smile made his eyes gleam in the firelight. The tip of his cigar brightened as he inhaled, holding in the smoke until he'd finished dealing. He kept his cards and his cigar both in his left hand, watching Sebastian like a hawk. "You and your brother were pretty close," he commented.

"We are still." Sebastian frowned. "He isn't gone. Some part of him knows who I am. Otherwise, I could never have stopped him from attacking the two of you."

"Good point." I made a face at my cards. "Echhh. Can I get two?"

Anatol obliged me, then gave Sebastian a single card. "Do you think he'll change back into a human if you get to the Upper World?"

"I hope so."

I felt bad about the centipede now. Whose brother or sister or son or daughter was it? What happened to a monster-fied dead person when they got killed, anyway? I wondered. If you were double-dead, were you wiped out of existence altogether, like the souls in the Atheist's Graveyard? Or did killing the beastie release the soul trapped inside, and they reappeared as their human selves back in Hades or something? But not even Anatol had known about the creatures being transformed people — it seemed like we would've heard about it back in Hades if that were true. Unless they couldn't remember, or reappeared somewhere else altogether.

"Erica, it's your bet," Anatol said.

"Sorry." I had a pair of threes. "I'll see your two cigars with two marshmallows and raise you one."

Sebastian sighed, but called my bluff with a trio of three-inch-tall green glass bottles. "The scent of home," he said, when Anatol and I both looked at him for an explanation of his joy-swap item.

I figured he'd sighed to throw us off a really good hand, but his cards were worse than mine. Two two's? I glanced at Anatol, who laid down Aces and eights, and raked in the winnings with a grin.

Sebastian lost just about every hand — and consistently gave away his feelings about what he'd been dealt. He couldn't have bluffed to save his soul, and this is coming from me, who's no Maverick at poker, either.

Anatol ended up with more joy-swap items than would've fit in his pockets, topside, but in the Underworld, it wasn't an issue.

Sebastian went to sleep, Octavius following suit soon afterward. Anatol and I returned to our side of the campfire to talk.

"Let's check out this joy-swap of his." Anatol pulled out one of the green glass bottles, the firelight casting a shimmering emerald shadow over his stubbly cheek.

I scooted closer as he uncorked Sebastian's memories of home.

The scent was warm and golden-green, with undertones of sweetness and damp earth. It smelled of summer and ripening fruit, of running through fields and playing hide-and-seek amid sun-drenched leaves. With my eyes closed, I could sense the familial ties that Sebastian associated with this fragrance, tinged with a homesickness he hadn't been able to filter out when he remembered it from the afterlife.

"I think this guy's okay," Anatol said, and I opened my eyes to see him smiling wistfully. "I think you should travel on with these two."

"Without you?" I realized his wistfulness wasn't about Sebastian's memories. "Why don't you come with me? You've come this far, and you won't get lost this time. Don't you want to go back to your life?"

"My life was a lonely bachelorhood ended by my favorite vices." He laughed gently. "I was the black sheep of my family, and my friends pitied me more than they liked or respected me. I'm enjoying myself in Hades. I like the trips across the Styx, the crowds, the red light district, the ability to smoke and drink to my heart's content with no danger to myself, and most of all—" He thumped me on the shoulder. "Most of all, the friendships."

We exchanged a long, heartfelt smile.

"I was always a malcontent, in life," Anatol said. "I'm happy here, waiting for my girl to show up."

"What if it's not the way you want it to be, when she gets here?"

"Then I'll have forever to get over it and find myself a new girl." He re-corked Sebastian's bottle and grinned.

"So you trust Sebastian now?"

"Yep."

"Why? The joy-swap?" I asked.

"Serial killers have beautiful memories, too." Anatol wagged a finger at me. "No, it was the poker game that convinced me. That's one reason I suggested it."

"What do you mean?"

"He's a terrible liar. He's got the clearest tells I've seen, outside of University first-years." Anatol sounded pleased. "Sebastian is the worst poker player I've ever met."

"So, he's such a bad bluffer that you trust him?" I said.

"What better way to tell if you can trust somebody?" Anatol lifted his palms, face-up.

"But *you're* good at poker," I pointed out.

Anatol gave me a Look, then pretended I hadn't made the comment. "He can't lie worth a damn, so I figure he must not do it often. And you're sharp enough to pick up on it if he tries."

I smiled at the compliment. "And he's obviously got enough influence over his brother that I won't be in any danger from him."

"Having a minotaur on your side can't hurt," Anatol agreed.

"So . . . you'll be going back . . . tomorrow?" It seemed depressing even to say it. I'd have company, sure, but . . . Anatol had been with me from the beginning of my death. The idea of traveling the Road seemed a lot bleaker without Anatol along.

"Tomorrow. Now, let's both get some rest."

Sebastian seemed pleased with the suggestion of joining forces. Having human company probably had serious appeal after being lost in the wilderness with a minotaur, even if the minotaur was relatively friendly.

"You aren't going on with us?" he asked Anatol, obviously confused, as we prepared to go our separate ways.

"I just came to see Erica off." Anatol was talking to Sebastian, but looked only at me as he spoke, smiling sadly. He handed me three cigars from the inside pocket of his tweed jacket. "Take these. As a farewell present."

"Thanks, Anatol." I hugged him. "Thanks for — everything."

"Good luck, hot stuff," he said. "Hope things work out for you and your man."

"Good luck with your sweetheart, too," I said. "I hope you find her soon."

He didn't give me a chance to get overly sentimental. A quick shoulder-slap, a sideways hug, and he was off, his long-legged stride taking him rapidly away. He turned back once to wave jauntily and blow me a smoky kiss with his cigar clenched between two fingers. I couldn't help but smile when I waved back.

Then he was out of sight, and I was keenly aware that Sebastian was looking at me, waiting for me to be ready to continue our journey.

"Let's go." I tried to sound cheerful.

My last tie to the city of Hades was gone. I was so homesick for the place I'd worked to escape, I was almost tempted to catch up with Anatol and go back with him.

Almost.

But not quite.

Chapter Twenty-Eight
it's a long hard road out of hades

Sebastian, Octavius, and I traveled on until they both started off the path.

"I think we should head this way." I pointed at what, to me, was clearly the only road in sight, knowing that they were probably seeing branch-offs that led away from our destination.

Sebastian hesitated, but moved to oblige me. "As many wrong turns as my brother and I have taken, I'm more than willing to follow your lead." His tone was good-natured, but humorless.

"I guess you've been to a few of the cities down here." I looked at him curiously as we got moving again. Octavius didn't seem too sure about my trailblazing skills, but eventually shuffled through the underbrush to get back onto the Road, following behind us at a steady, plodding pace.

"I've only been to Hades, Nilfhelm, and the Field of Reeds," Sebastian said, "although there are many more."

"Hades and the Atheist's Graveyard are the only ones I've seen. What's Nilfhelm like?"

"Full of violent sport and drunken feasting." Sebastian looked off into the distance for a moment, then added, "Not entirely unlike home — in all its worst elements. Not my *family* home, you understand. I mean 'home' in the broader sense, my time and place in the Upper World."

"When was—" But before I could finish the question, I was startled by another voice, somewhat muffled, calling my name. It was an eerie sensation, and I must have reacted noticeably, because both Sebastian and the minotaur halted in their tracks.

The voice spoke again, a little more distinct, sounding as if it were right in my ear, though there was no visible speaker anywhere along the path, and certainly no one hovering by my left shoulder.

"Chester?" I faltered, as recognition of the voice itself set in.

"Erica," he repeated.

Sebastian looked at me as if I'd started to sprout horns, and I realized that he couldn't hear Chester — he was merely reacting to my reaction.

"Erica," Chester rumbled again, and I clenched my hands, trying to reorient myself as reality shifted around me. It wasn't quite like when I'd been called up for the séance, but the strange sensation of two whole separate worlds connecting through the small and relatively insignificant vessel that was "me" was there, and overwhelming.

"Chester? How. . . ?" I trailed off, knowing he couldn't answer my question any better than I could. How he was contacting me without the phones, I decided very quickly, didn't matter. The point was that he *could*, and I wondered next if I could contact *him* without external props, should the need arise.

"Erica, your sister is here with me. She asked me to contact you again." His voice sounded strained, as if it were taking a great effort to connect with me — much more so than when we'd talked on the medium phones.

"Can she hear me?" I asked eagerly. "Laura? Can you hear me?"

There was only silence, and I was afraid we'd lost one another across the void.

But then Chester spoke again. "She can't hear you. She wants to know if you're all right, though."

"I'm fine," I said. "I'm coming back."

"What do you mean, coming back?" Chester asked.

"I mean I'm on my way back to Life," I answered.

"Your funeral was two days ago," Chester said slowly, as if

trying to break bad news gently.

"I'm coming back," I repeated, and contact broke.

Something wrenched — somewhere. Whether it was within me or around me, I'm not sure.

All I know is I gasped for air — the first time I'd done so, even out of habit, since my descent into the Underworld.

Sebastian crouched next to where I lay on the ground, and Octavius, up ahead in the near distance, plodded along as if nothing had happened.

"Are you all right?" Sebastian asked, placing his hand on my shoulder.

I raised myself up on my elbows, but I'd plainly collapsed — onto the scepter, which was still strapped to my back. Hades was nowhere to be seen, but either reality was tired of me twisting it around, or he had just delivered one hell of a metaphysical bitch-slap for my continued disobedience.

I wasn't sure which instance would be the worse for me.

"Fine," I gasped, though I clearly wasn't.

"What happened?"

I tried to explain. If we were going to travel together, I felt like I owed it to Sebastian to let him know about my theft and Hades' probably-impending wrath.

As I spoke, I sat up, reoriented myself, and started to feel better.

"What you're telling me," Sebastian said slowly, when my explanation wound up, "is that you have stolen the scepter of Hades, and that you plan on using it to gain possession of the Helm of Darkness, that Hades surely knows you have stolen from him, and that he knows you are on your way back to the Upper Plane?"

"Yes," I said.

His eyes fell on the scepter, a look of dread crossing his face. I hadn't thought about the danger I was putting Sebastian and Octavius in when I'd taken up with them — not until now, as I saw

Sebastian realize it for himself. Somehow I'd gotten comfortable with the idea that Hades was probably on my trail one way or another, and that he would most certainly catch up with me at some point. . . . Sure, Charon had reassured *me* that Hades wouldn't punish my accomplices, but that didn't mean *Sebastian* would feel safe with me. Not to mention that he and Octavius, too, were trying to escape the Underworld, which I doubted Hades would approve of.

"I'm sorry, Sebastian," I said. "If you and Octavius would rather go your own way—"

He shook his head. "We have wandered this Road aimlessly, with nothing to show for it but grief, through endless troubles. Perhaps because you have the scepter, your direction seems truer than ours has been. If my brother and I are to return to the Land of the Living, I think we must do so alongside you, Erica."

A true smile crept across his gaunt features for the first time since I'd met him. It filled out his hollowed cheeks and lit his dark grey eyes, and I was struck by the realization that he was, in fact, quite a good-looking man — one who had been through far too much hardship to be at his best, yes, but handsome as a rule. I realized I was grinning back at him stupidly, and hastened to clear my expression to something more neutral.

I was getting lonely. Back in the city, I'd been so focused on my grief for Dom, my determination to get back to him, that I had felt, in some way, his presence, all along. Out here, I was no less focused on my mission to return to him, but the path was before me — literally — and now, it seemed, I had the mental energy to actually feel lonely at last.

None of that, I told myself. Sebastian has a wife to get back to, and I have a husband. Sure, we're both dead, and sure, they're both a whole plane of existence away, but still — none of that.

As quickly as the impulsive feeling toward Sebastian had come, it was gone, and an almost tangible ache for Dominic was left in its place.

Sebastian offered his hand to help me up, and I took it with a sad smile, withdrawing as soon as I'd regained my footing.

If he'd caught the momentary attraction, he had the good grace to pretend he hadn't, and we walked on side by side in a reasonably comfortable silence. Octavius had stopped to rub his horns on a tree, so we caught up with him easily.

I reflected on the conversation I'd had with Chester.

My funeral had been two days ago, he'd said. And he hadn't experienced any contact with me between the séance on the day of my funeral, and the exchange just now — nor had I.

I was curious about the fact that three conversations in a row with Chester seemed to have gone in the same order for both of us — right before the séance, then the séance itself, and just now. Was it possible that I was becoming subject to linear time again? And was it possible that the more contact I had with the Upper World, the more aligned I was with its timeline?

Certainly I was getting more vulnerable, and in more ways than one. Exhaustion, the actual gut-shock of sudden fear, and now that momentary urge for Sebastian. Whether I was actually regaining my mortality, or whether one of the functions of the Road was to simulate the miseries of physical existence as a way of keeping people here in the Underworld, I was changing.

Chapter Twenty-Nine

a meeting with despair

The rustling in the green-black leaves of the trees grew more and more ominous — restless and loud, punctuated by odd creaks and flickers. Sebastian and I repeatedly twitched as the strange, sudden darting movements crossed the edges of our vision. Even Octavius seemed to feel the oppression that was settling around us. He held his ears down low, close to his head, and his already-hunched shoulders were even more so now.

I felt strange, as if something were pushing at my soul, weighing it down.

Something flitted past me, less than an inch from my ear, gone so quickly I didn't even catch a glimpse of it before it merged with the mass of dark, moving leaves.

My hand ached for the feel of the scepter — the sense of security it would give me right about now would be worth a lot. But I was afraid to use it. I had a feeling that I had to get back topside if I wanted to avoid turning into just another guard for Hades — another monster along the Road, one more spook to scare off others who were determined to reach its end. I didn't know if it mattered whether I killed again or not, or how the process of my impending change could be accelerated in a place without time. But on the off chance that slaying any more beasties would change me quicker, I wasn't about to test any theories. My instinct told me not to kill again, so I kept the scepter where it was, strapped securely to my back.

"Has this happened before?" I asked Sebastian quietly.

He shook his head.

"I was hoping you knew what was up there," I said.

Sebastian didn't answer, but continued to look around warily as we walked.

The clicking, creaking noises and the rustling of the leaves kept getting louder, the branches actually swaying now in a breeze that didn't reach us down below on the forest floor.

And I felt stranger and stranger, too, but I couldn't pinpoint what felt wrong. I felt somehow too aware of myself, although that didn't make any sense to me.

One of the darting shapes landed in the middle of the road. Sebastian and I stared at it in a moment that seemed to hang in the air, both of us trying to process what we saw.

It was a small bird — sort of — about the size of a chickadee or a sparrow, so black you could see other colors within the blackness, iridescent and glossy. My first thought was that he was a cute little guy, until I took in the fact that he didn't have a bird's head. Instead, there was a thin, ruffed neck ending in a small, round head that was almost entirely taken up by a small, round mouth full of long, sharp teeth. To either side of the mouth was a protruding black eye, set at about ten-o'clock and two-o'clock positions. A little forked tongue flicked from its gaping mouth, and it blinked at us.

I opened my mouth to speak, but the moment of stillness shattered at precisely the same instant. With an earsplitting creak that came from a hundred little round mouths full of teeth, the swarm began. The wind from their wings was strong enough to whip my hair across my face, and beside me, Sebastian put an arm up to shield his eyes. I couldn't even see Octavius through the cloud of bird-things.

Little clawed feet dug at my exposed hands, pulled my hair, tried to pry apart my leather armor to get at me. I batted them away from the visor of my helmet, trying to see how Sebastian was faring. I caught a glimpse or two of him — now in armor, as well, the gold of his helmet gleaming amid all that black — but how he was coping with the little bastards, I couldn't tell. I was too busy trying to figure out what to do about them, myself.

If I couldn't kill them, what options did that leave?

"Hey!" I yelled at a creature, who'd latched on to my flailing left hand. "Let go!"

He didn't seem to be up for conversation. He just turned toward the sound of my voice and hissed, raising his wings in a threatening gesture.

"Excuse me." I tried to ignore the rest of them pelting their bodies against my armor, clawing at me, and making those horrible clicking, creaking sounds at high volume. "I'd appreciate it if you could please not try to hurt me?" I watched my own blood drip out of the wounds where his claws were still firmly in my hand.

His only response to my polite inquiry was to dig in further, and next, to my horror, he plugged his hideous little mouth into the back of my hand and started sucking.

Everything went weird.

My entire being felt like it was being pulled out, as if the Underworld itself was sucking me out of my own form. I fell to my knees, the way you do when you're alive and the wind gets knocked out of you.

It stopped for a moment, and I shook my head, dazed. More of the bird-things latched on to the only part of my skin that was exposed — my hands — and I could still feel others trying to get to the back of my neck.

I had just enough time to process that before the pulling began again, and this time I screamed. All I was aware of at this point was that I wanted it to *stop*.

I threw myself against the ground, crushing a couple of the bird-things. I tore them out of my hair, pummeled my bird-covered hands against the ground, wrenched and screamed. I could feel their bones crunch against my fists, and

I knew I was killing them, but I couldn't bear it.

The little soul-sucker who'd managed to attach itself to my hand had somehow survived, and he paused again. But another had latched on now, and although they were both badly wounded from my thrashing, they hung on.

All I could do in my brief respite was gasp for breath, too confused and tormented to think farther ahead than that instant.

Before I regained any sense, they both started at the same time.

I was beyond any thought whatsoever — I was all reaction and no intelligence. I smashed my hand over and over against the ground, until feathers were plastered against my fist, smeared with blood, shards of shattered bird bones embedded in my skin.

I tucked my hands under my arms and curled around myself there on the ground, more bird-things raining down on my huddled form.

There was just too much pain for me to handle, and giving up felt so easy, so inviting. I went with it.

It wasn't the most heroic thing to do. It wasn't particularly smart, either. For all I knew, my soul would be shredded right then and there, and Sebastian and Octavius along with me.

Why didn't I listen to Anatol? I thought as I lay there being pelted by bird-monsters. *Why do I never listen when anyone warns me?*

I could hear Octavius bellowing in fury in between the piercing shrieks of our attackers, but I couldn't bring myself to move. The creatures *pinged* off my helmet and I shivered every time I felt one hit me.

Sebastian shouted something and I caught sight of him — a flash of red and gold in the blizzard of black feathers. He had a big branch in one hand, with a bunch of dead leaves and twigs stuck onto the end. "The tinderbox!" he screamed again, and this time I understood him.

I didn't know what had happened to the tinderbox, but I had a book of matches in my pocket for the cigars Anatol had given me.

I'd have to expose my hands to the bird-monsters, though. And I'd have to let the top half of my armor go back to being just street clothes, because the pocket with the matches was in my leather jacket. I couldn't possibly concentrate enough to conjure up a lighter on my own, not with the chaos and fear swirling around me.

Not moving, I watched Sebastian a few yards away, flailing desperately and almost dropping the branch. A second later he dropped to his knees, howling. One of the creatures had managed to get its teeth into him.

He struggled to his feet and went on trying to find the tinderbox amid the bedlam.

I forced myself to roll over, staying in a fetal position to protect my hands as I worked a pair of leather gloves into my armor. My movement caught the attention of more bird-monsters, and they swarmed me — even though they weren't making it through, I screamed out of sheer terror at having them crawl all over me. It took every ounce of willpower I had left to change back to my sweater and jacket, but I had to get those matches for Sebastian.

I knew I was well past saving all of us, but this much I could do — get a book of matches out of my own pocket and get them to Sebastian.

The bird-things went for my throat the instant it was exposed, and I clawed and ripped at their bodies as I tore them away. I pulled up the collar of the jacket and did my best with one hand to hold it around my neck, using my other hand to grab the matches at last.

"Sebastian!" I yelled. "Sebastian!"

I felt him grab the matches, and in the same instant one of the bird-creatures found its mark and dug in.

I screamed and tried to pull it away, but it was too late. I felt it tearing at my soul as more of them latched on, and then I slipped out of all awareness.

~*~

I opened my eyes to find Sebastian kneeling beside me, still in gleaming — though mud-spattered — red-and-gold armor, a scarlet-crested helmet tucked under his arm.

"Erica?" He spoke tentatively, apparently unsure how aware I was of my surroundings. That made two of us.

Beyond Sebastian's concerned face, branches criss-crossed a pearl-grey sky, a few dark leaves shivering in a breeze.

I sat up before Sebastian could advise me otherwise. I was in full armor again, probably thanks to a subconscious defensive mechanism. The ground was littered with shattered, black-feathered bodies, smeared into the red clay of the Road. My hands were filthy, stiff with blood and caked-on clay.

Octavius didn't look much better off than I felt, hunkering disconsolately against a boulder a few yards away, the fur down the middle of his chest matted with feathers, mud, and dried blood.

"How did you get rid of them?" I asked, still hazy about recent events. I knew we couldn't have killed all of them — at most there were a couple dozen of the bird-things' corpses lying around, although it was hard to tell, since a lot of them had been completely pulverized.

"Fire." Sebastian pointed behind me, and I twisted around to see the large, now-smoldering branch that he'd obviously lit with my matches. I noticed that a few of the bird-things' bodies nearby were charred, now that I looked again.

I vaguely remembered that in my last few moments of consciousness, I had heard screeches rising up all around me — probably as Sebastian had stormed over with his torch ablaze to drive them away from me.

"You didn't—" I glanced at Sebastian's hands, but other than a few black marks from the burning wood, they were clean. He hadn't killed anything unless it was with the torches.

He seemed to know what I was thinking, and shook his head.

"A few of them flew into the fire in confusion, but I killed nothing intentionally."

I was amazed at his resolve. No amount of willpower or logic could have overcome my need to stop those little bastards from — whatever it was they had done.

Did I still have all of my soul? I wondered. I felt like myself. I couldn't see any parts missing. I did feel weird, but then, I had before the attack, too.

"I think we should move on before they come back." Sebastian looked uneasily at the canopy overhead. It was almost bare now, only a few leaves — real leaves, not a whole mess of bird-monsters that *looked* like leaves from a distance — blocking the view of the sky.

Still, I was inclined to agree that it was a good idea to move on.

Anatol's gone five minutes, I thought, *and, literally, all Hell breaks loose.* I wasn't even amused at my own joke. Not after what had just happened.

Chapter Thirty

transformation

Octavius came over to help me up. I stumbled with the awkwardness of the scepter being strapped across my back.

"Hang onto this for a sec, would you?" I handed the scepter to the minotaur so I could readjust my imaginary armor into a more comfortable position.

I was in the middle of pulling a chunk of clay off my knuckle when I heard Sebastian gasp, and looked up.

"What?"

He pointed.

I looked at Octavius, and then *I* gasped.

The fur on his face was receding, his bull's face realigning itself into human features, the strange, unnatural red of his hair softening into a dark auburn. I carefully avoided looking below his belly-button, as I was pretty sure he was in the process of becoming a naked guy below the waist, as well as above it.

He stared down at his own much-less-hairy chest, looking just as amazed as we were. "What—" he stammered.

"How—?" Sebastian began.

"The scepter!" I said. "It's the scepter that's changing him back!"

Sure enough, the changes seemed to flow through his body from where his hand gripped the inlaid wood, until his transformation back to a fully human form was complete.

He was taller and more athletically built than his brother, and clearly younger, though not by much. I was glad to see that he'd realized the need for clothes, and his need duly provided him with an outdoorsy-type outfit that nonetheless left his chest partially exposed.

"Octavius!" Sebastian rushed forward and embraced his brother, who hugged him back awkwardly with one arm, still holding the scepter in his other hand. I was a little twitchy about not having it in my immediate possession, now that another *human* had it. Somehow a monster seemed more trustworthy to me, which was probably weird, but there you go. Feelings don't always make sense.

At any rate, I was terribly aware of the fact that Octavius was a big, burly guy, and no way could I forcibly take the scepter back from him if he decided to keep it. I wouldn't entirely blame him, either, if it kept him from being a monster.

"Here," Octavius said to me, when Sebastian let go of him a moment later. The previously-a-minotaur held the scepter out to me.

"You won't change back or anything, will you?" I tried to combat my own distrust, now that he'd offered the scepter back willingly. It was strange to exchange words with him after all this time. I was so used to him being around, but beyond communication.

"I don't know," he said, not moving. "But this is yours."

Slowly, I took the scepter from him. Nothing happened. Horns didn't re-sprout from his head, fur didn't re-grow the instant the scepter left his hands. Nothing.

"Does this mean I am cured?" His voice trembled.

"I don't know." I looked at Sebastian, as if he could answer any better than I could.

"It would seem so." Sebastian's tone was hopeful.

Octavius regarded himself further and said, "I am really quite filthy."

Sebastian actually laughed — the first time I'd ever heard him do so.

All three of us were feeling pretty grungy from our travels and our battles, and of course Octavius had the bonus of having become (and then un-become) a big, hairy animal with very little brain.

"Maybe we can find a place to wash up," I said, then remembered Anatol's warning about rusalkis lurking in ponds. "As long as it's running water. We can celebrate your transformation with a good water fight." I grinned, although I was still jumpy, and slung the scepter across my back again.

"Now let's get going before those bird-things come back for another round."

Sebastian shuddered, and Octavius murmured his agreement. On we went, our moods lifted.

~*~

"There's got to be a stream or something around here somewhere," I grumbled, at some point that felt much later on.

"The sooner we find somewhere to wash up, the better," Octavius agreed. I still wasn't used to his husky voice. It was strangely light for someone of his build. I also hadn't gotten used to seeing intelligence and comprehension in his face; it surprised me every time I made eye contact with him, which made me feel rude, but hey, I'd met the guy as a hulking brute with no understanding of language. It took me a while to adjust.

"Over there." Sebastian pointed, and sure enough, through a gap in the trees up ahead, I could see the shimmer of light on running water, just a couple dozen yards off the path.

All three of us picked up the pace with anticipation, and soon we were on the bank, splashing water over our faces and forearms.

"Do you think we lost part of our souls?" My mind was still locked onto the bird-things.

Octavius frowned, rubbing water across the back of his neck, but he didn't answer.

"I think not," Sebastian said thoughtfully. "Of course, I don't know for sure, but I would think we would know if we had."

"I guess so." I had my doubts, but I kept them to myself. I tried to focus on the cool, crystal-clear water running over my hands, loosening the blood and clay from my fingers. And then I frowned for a totally new reason.

"What is it?" Sebastian asked.

I held up my hand for him to see.

There, where the creatures had latched onto me, were two small, scabbed-over cuts, each surrounded by a dime-sized bruise. And I finally realized what the strange feelings I'd been having were. I was feeling *pain*.

Not the anguish I'd experienced when the bird-things had attached to me — this had started before that — but, well, *physical* pain. That weird feeling between my shoulder blades was an ache; the odd distance from myself, exhaustion. . . .

But I couldn't really be physical. I could still affect my own clothing just by thinking about it, and the scepter still changed forms for me.

I turned to Octavius, knowing Sebastian would refuse what I was about to demand. "Hit me," I said.

Octavius stared at me.

"Do it!" I felt my own heartbeat quicken with the expectation of pain — a sensation that I'd grown unaccustomed to since my death. It scared me that I could experience it again. *Was* I physical?

Octavius licked his lips, looking uncomfortable, and glanced at his brother's horrified expression before turning back to me. He seemed to understand the logic I was working with, but he didn't look happy about honoring my request.

Nevertheless, he swung at me without warning, and I have to admit I cringed. Octavius was a big, muscular guy.

But he didn't connect. When the impact didn't come, I looked up to find that I'd moved several feet away.

"That answers that, I guess." I let out a long, shaky breath.

"Does it?" Sebastian looked up at me from his kneeling position by the stream's bank, his expression grim.

"What do you mean?" I asked.

"It seems to me this only raises more questions," he answered. "The creatures that guard the Road can make contact with us whether we like it or not. Why can't we make uninvited contact with one another? And Octavius—" Sebastian glanced at his brother apologetically— "has been one of those creatures, able to attack other souls, yet now, it seems, he no longer has that ability."

I shrugged. "The scepter cured him," I suggested, although that only answered a fraction of what none of us understood.

"The creatures lost along the Roadside are suspended somewhere between the physical world and the metaphysical."

Sebastian and I both turned toward Octavius as he spoke. He regarded us stoically from where he sat on a flat rock, dangling his bare legs into the water. He had wet his hair, and it dripped down onto his bare shoulders.

I didn't know how he could be sure about what he'd said, but I believed him. Anatol had said essentially the same thing, and it made a weird Underworldly sense to me. The self-assurance with which Octavius spoke, too, gave the explanation credibility. After all, he'd been through the strangest transformation I had ever experienced — in life or in the afterlife — and to me, that gave him a sort of authority on metaphysical stuff.

Sebastian seemed to be thinking the same thing. "I suppose no change is simple, here or in the Upper World. We are coming closer to mortality."

We were quiet for a while, and then finally I said, "Hey, weren't we supposed to be having *fun* for a minute?" I splashed Sebastian.

"Oh, you call that fun, do you?" He flashed a broad grin I'd never seen on him before. He really was good-looking, I thought, just before he pushed me into the water.

I yelled and yanked him in after me, and we weren't long in joining forces to bring Octavius down with us.

It felt good to horse around, and to see Sebastian happy and Octavius human.

After a while, though, I slipped out of the water and wandered a little way off from the others — still in sight of them, but far enough that their conversation didn't carry. Sitting down cross-legged on the ground, I tried to distance myself from the Underworld and the Road.

Chester had contacted me once without the phones, and I wanted to know if I could do it, too. I wanted to know what was going on topside. How my family was doing, and if Dom had come around about talking to Chester.

I concentrated, closing my eyes and trying to block out everything around me. I focused on Chester, willing him to sense my presence and help me with the leap from Underworld to Upper World. I thought about his deep voice, his dark suit, what little I knew about his torn-up family life — anything to spark a connection.

But nothing happened.

What was there for me to say, anyway?

Deep down, what I really wanted right now was a moment, even the merest glimpse, of Dominic.

"Erica, are you all right?" Sebastian put a hand gently on my shoulder, and I opened my eyes.

Octavius stood at the side of the Road, waiting. They were ready to go.

I forced a smile. "Fine. I'm fine. Just . . . resting before we head back into it."

Sebastian knew better, I could tell by his expression, but he didn't reply. He squeezed my shoulder, then helped me to my feet.

"I'm sorry about — back there with the bird-monsters," I told him.

"What do you mean?" he asked.

"That I left you to fight them alone," I said.

He smiled. "You got those matches to me. Without those, we would *all* have been in a predicament. Besides, you've done plenty for us." He gestured toward his brother, who nodded solemnly.

"I am proud to have been able to help *you*." Sebastian gave me a little gentlemanly bow.

I was glad I couldn't blush. Why was I such a dork around this guy? *Dom*, I reminded myself.

"Once more into the breach." I firmly pointed the way forward.

Chapter Thirty-One

other side up

I dreamed about Chester the next time we rested.

The house I found myself in was an old, creaky place with high ceilings and dark woodwork, the hardwood floor warped with age. I was in a living room that was half library, with floor-to-ceiling bookshelves making up an entire wall. My first suspicion that this was Chester's house came when I noticed a couple of shelves full of paranormal and metaphysical writings.

I heard voices and turned the corner, wandered through the dining room and into a big old-fashioned kitchen. Chester stood at the bulky iron stove, cooking eggs sunny-side up. He wore a very manly pinstripe apron over his taupe three-piece suit.

At the kitchen table, a younger guy — early twenties, I guessed — leaned over the career ads in the morning paper.

This had to be Chester's son. He was almost as tall as his father, but with a leaner frame, all muscle and no padding, broad-shouldered and clean-cut. His skin was a shade lighter than Chester's, but their eyes and the set of their faces made it clear they were father and son.

"I don't understand how you can do it," the son was saying. "I mean, you're making a profit off these people's credulity."

"Garrett, let's not get into this again." Chester jiggled the pan to keep the eggs from sticking.

"Why can't you just get a *normal* job?" Garrett insisted.

Chester's grip on the spatula tightened, but he didn't raise his voice. "How about you worry about getting *you* a job, son?"

"I know, I know, thanks for letting me stay here, Dad." Garrett sounded genuine. "I just wish you had something more . . . I don't know, dependable? You could start some *other* kind of business, make some steady money, fix this old dump up." He gestured at the kitchen, which admittedly had some cracks in the plaster and the ceramic tile, but was tidy and well-kept and *enormous*.

"Son," Chester sighed, transferring the eggs onto two big plates already heaped with fried potatoes, "you live your life and let me live mine. That's the deal." He set Garrett's breakfast in front of him and sat down across the table. "Whether you believe in what I do or not, my clients do, and it's very important to them."

"But you're *lying* to them!" Garrett said angrily.

I couldn't help thinking, *Dude, you're a grown man and your dad just made you a homemade breakfast, you spoiled little punk. Show some gratitude, or at least shut up.* I may have thought Chester was a bit of a weirdo, but he was, in a sense, *my* weirdo, and I didn't like seeing him get picked on.

Chester set his fork down and, still without raising his voice, said, "Garrett, I don't get on your case because you believe science is the only explanation for what happens in the world. Don't you accuse me of being a liar because my views are not the same as yours. And I am tired of having this conversation with you. I wanted you to stay here until you got on your feet because I hoped we could patch some things up, not to make things worse."

"It'd be easier to patch things up if I could respect what you do," Garrett said flatly, and went back to his breakfast.

I couldn't help myself. I marched over to the table and got right up in Garrett's face. "What's *wrong* with you, kid?" Of course he didn't hear me or see me, which just made me madder. "You could at least show some respect for your dad because he didn't throw those freaking eggs at your *head*, because that's what *I* would do if you were *my* kid and you talked to me like that."

I backed off a pace or two and added, "And he's not a fraud — I'm dead, I should know." He had no idea I was talking to him, of course, but Garrett's guilty conscience must've gotten to him, because his expression softened.

"I'm sorry, Dad," he said. "I shouldn't have said that."

"That's okay," Chester said, but he sounded distracted. I turned to see his expression and was startled to find him looking *straight at me*.

I jerked awake in the Underworld.

Sebastian was still asleep nearby, Octavius keeping watch. "Nightmares?"

"Not exactly," I said. "Just . . . weirdness."

Apparently Uncle Jeff had been right. I *did* have some kind of bond with Chester.

I was glad I hadn't said anything bad about him while I'd thought he couldn't hear me, even just to be funny.

"There." Sebastian parted his brother's hair so I could see.

Octavius kept his head bowed — he was kneeling so that the two of us could see the top of his head. "Have they really returned?" His voice was a little higher than usual.

"Unquestionably." Sebastian looked to me for confirmation.

He was right. I could see the tips of two horns, maybe an inch long each so far, coming up through Octavius's skull. His hair might've been going red again, too, but that could've been a trick of the light, or my imagination.

"Didn't you feel them growing back?" I asked.

Octavius looked apologetic, like a little kid who'd accidentally wet his pants. "I felt *something*, but I hoped by ignoring it, I could stop the transformation."

"It gets harder the more you wander around out here, doesn't it?" I glanced at Sebastian, then back to Octavius. "That's why you both do so many things Upper World style. You don't conjure up a campfire, you gather firewood by hand. Your clothes get torn up, they stay that way — unless you're in serious danger. *Then* your willpower kicks in enough to put you in armor, but only in response to a threat."

Sebastian nodded.

And I was finding it harder to conjure stuff up, too, or change things just by *wanting*. It had started with the bird-monsters, when I'd had to dig for matches instead of just imagining some into existence. And afterward, it hadn't been only Sebastian and Octavius who'd felt the need to wash up, rather than simply wishing to be clean. I'd needed the stream, too.

I had to admit the Road was doing a good job displaying the crappy side of existence among the living. Everything was so much *easier* in the Underworld.

Well, everything except getting *out* of it.

Poor Octavius, still kneeling, rubbed the swollen scalp around his newly-grown left horn, and winced. "Ow! Damn. They itch."

"Maybe I can change you again." I pulled the scepter out and held it across my palms. He looked up gratefully, and put his hands to either side of mine, so that we were both gripping the scepter.

Help him! I thought, willing it to work.

The horns shrank slowly back, disappearing into his hair. I watched, wide-eyed, and then let go of the scepter with one hand to move Octavius's hair aside. They were gone without a trace.

"Well," I said, "at least we have a cure."

"It's a shame it's only temporary, though," Sebastian said.

Octavius rose to his feet and thanked me.

"I wonder what I would turn into," I said. "If I didn't have the scepter, I probably would've changed by now."

"Let us hope we never find out." Sebastian shuddered.

I was about to make a joke about the possibilities when I noticed something about one of the trees nearby. "Is that. . . ?" I jumped over a clump of underbrush, excited. The bark was greyish-white and flecked with diamond-shaped indentations.

"Erica?" Sebastian sounded curious.

"A white poplar." I pointed.

"Of what significance is that?"

"None, maybe." It was only this one, alone, after all. But it was the first one I'd seen, which might mean there were more nearby. Like a grove of them, maybe. And possibly a dried-up river gorge with a hydra on the opposite side. . . .

I hurried back over to Sebastian and Octavius and herded them on, craning my neck to look for more grey-trunked trees.

"I think we're getting closer to the hydra's lair," I explained to the two brothers, who were patiently following after me, asking nothing, but probably wondering plenty about my sanity. "Look, there's another!" And two more, beyond that.

And there it was, just like in the photo on Persephone's Tarot card — the stand of diamond-marked trees, the dry riverbed, the precarious-looking steps cut into the red clay cliffs.

I let out a whoop.

Octavius half-smiled at my reaction, but Sebastian looked worried.

I should've been worried, too, but I was elated to have found the place. I hoped, too, that it meant we weren't far from the end of the Road.

The only thing nagging at me was — I'd have to leave the Road itself to find the hydra's lair. What if the scepter didn't guide me back, once I strayed off the path? Yeah, there was also the actual hydra to deal with . . . but that was cake compared to the idea of getting lost out here.

Chapter Thirty-Two

plight of the living dead

"So how are we gonna do this?" I asked Sebastian and Octavius.

"We'll go with you," Sebastian said.

"Are you sure? I don't want you guys to get eaten by the hydra or anything because of me."

"If we become separated, Sebastian and I will never find our way home." Octavius paused, glancing at the scepter. "And I'll return to minotaur form."

"I don't know what'll happen if we leave the Road," I said. "I may not be able to guide us back to it."

"We have to take that chance," Octavius said firmly. Sebastian said nothing, but I could tell from the look on his face that he agreed with his brother.

"Okay, then. I'll do my best not to stir up more trouble than necessary," I said.

One corner of Sebastian's mouth lifted. "You?"

"Hey!" I laughed, more surprised he'd made a joke than offended that I was the butt of it. "You haven't known me long enough to know how much trouble I can get myself into!"

Octavius cleared his throat. "I'd venture to say that's one of the first things a person knows about you, Erica."

He and Sebastian looked at each other, then back at my expression, and both burst out laughing.

I grinned, since I couldn't honestly deny it.

"So," Sebastian said, when his usual air of solemnity returned. "We have to cross?"

"Yep." We moved to the edge of the chasm and looked down. It was about a thirty-foot drop down to the smooth beige stone of the riverbed. The stairs were clay, slick with damp, and crumbling at the edges. Fun.

"I wish this didn't involve the potential for falling from an uncomfortable height," Octavius commented.

Of course — they'd died falling off a collapsing bridge. I looked at each of them apologetically, in turn, but neither of them seemed inclined to turn back.

"We'll just take it easy, and be extra careful." I tried to sound reassuring.

Tree roots sprouted out of the gorge's walls, between chunks of water-smoothed stone, providing useful handholds for the descent down to the riverbed.

"See, this isn't so bad," I said cheerfully, about halfway down.

Sebastian, in front, seemed to feel the same way, his movements more confident as the drop lessened with our progress. "It really is pretty easy going, once you get started," he called back to me.

I turned a little to see how Octavius was managing. I expected him to be only a couple paces behind me, trying to be polite and patient with my cautious advancement, but I was wrong.

He was only two steps down from the top, hunched as close to the wall as possible, and hanging onto a tree root with his right hand and shielding the view of the chasm with his left. He panted, which I hadn't seen anyone in the Underworld do, obviously in a panic.

"You okay?" I asked, although, clearly, he wasn't.

He swallowed and shook his head. "Don't know . . . what . . .'s come over me." He spoke between heaving breaths. "Never . . . this way . . . before."

"I think you're experiencing a newfound fear of heights," I said gently. "Maybe since that's what killed you. . . ?"

"Sebastian—" He gestured to his brother, who was nearly at

the bottom of the stairs now, oblivious to our conversation. Octavius shuddered as his own motion exposed the view of the drop to his left, and closed his eyes.

"Stuff hits people different ways," I said. "It's funny, though. He's more the worrier than you are. I would've expected *him* to develop a phobia, not you."

Octavius managed a sickly smile, but he looked embarrassed.

"You'll be okay." I went back up to the step just below his. "Stay low to the ground, and take it as slow as you need to."

I reached out for his hand, and after a few gulps of air, Octavius let go of the tree root and grabbed onto my forearm. "There you go," I said. "Now just ease on over. Take it one step at a time."

Nodding and shuddering at the same time, he lowered himself onto my step, while I scrooched backward onto the next one down. *Good thing* I'm *okay with heights!* I thought as I felt my way blindly along the next few stairs, encouraging Octavius to keep going.

Sebastian waited for us at the bottom, surprised, as I had been, to see Octavius's terror. Finally, with only three steps left to go, Octavius relaxed, let go of my hand, and stood to his own full height, squaring his broad shoulders.

"Don't worry about it," I said, because he still looked so ashamed of his fear. I patted his arm. "I know lots of people who are scared of heights in the Upper World." That wasn't exactly true — strictly speaking, I knew *one* person who was scared of heights: my boss at the zoo gift shop, who, strangely enough, was also a tall, buff guy you'd never expect to have such an intense phobia. Inventory days involved a lot of ladder usage, so they'd been exceedingly stressful times around the store.

"And we still have the other side to climb *up*." Sebastian looked sympathetically at his brother.

"I think, actually, that going up seems easier than going down." Octavius stared up at the cliff face. "There will be less temptation to look over the edge when the focus is above me."

We made our way over the pebble-scattered riverbed, our voices echoing off the gorge walls as Sebastian and I did our best to bolster Octavius's spirits for the climb.

At the base of the stairs, Octavius looked up nervously and fought to keep his breathing normal — which, for the Underworld, meant nonexistent. "Erica, would you go first?"

The unspoken plea in his eyes added, "And help me along, like last time?"

"Of course," I said.

"And I'll be behind you," Sebastian told his brother. "If you should slip, you know I won't let you fall."

Octavius nodded, and I started up the steps.

True to his own prediction, he had a much easier time of it going back up the cliff. He was clearly afraid, but put a cheerful face on it and kept his pace steady, if not quick.

"There." I helped him up the last step to the top. "See, we did fine."

He moved back from the ledge and I stayed where I was to help Sebastian steady himself as he joined us.

"There's still going back," Octavius said miserably, as we trekked forward into unfamiliar, unmarked wilderness.

"We'll cross that — er. . . ." I realized what I'd been about to say, and said, instead, "We'll deal with that when the time comes. Right now, I—" I began, but halted mid-sentence again. "What's that?"

"What is what?" Sebastian frowned.

Octavius was looking beyond me, and I turned the same direction.

"That sound," I said quietly.

"I heard nothing," Sebastian said, and Octavius shook his head at him, holding out a hand for silence.

"There it is again," I breathed.

There was definitely something out in the woods nearby, slowly coming toward us. Something not very small.

Another rustle, and then a great loud wrenching sound as a tree was ripped out of the ground between us and whatever was out there. The three of us watched in terrified silence as the treetop went from vertical to diagonal, then disappeared with a thunderous crash as Whatever It Was dropped it. A whole lot of rustling sounds and smaller snapping noises followed.

We still didn't have a clear view of what was out there, but we'd all three swapped our street clothes for armor.

"This does not bode well," Octavius said softly next to me.

"Nope," I agreed.

There was another twisting, snapping scream of wood, and we watched another tree go down.

Now I could see a little through the gap. Coppery scales glinted in the cool, greyish daylight that filtered through the clouds overhead, and I could just make out a thick, clawed foreleg that was nonetheless dwarfed by the thing as a whole.

There was a low rasping sound — a deep inhalation — and something peered between the remaining trees at us: a huge, feathery-scaled head with pointed nostrils like a pit viper's, darting its sinewy neck this way and that to find us.

With a creeping sensation, I noticed two other heads, alike but far from identical, peering from between other trees. One was hooded, like a cobra, with a sleek nose and a darting tongue. The third was beakish, sharp and angular. Their similarity was in their orange eyes, slit pupils, and coppery coloring.

"Look out!" Sebastian pulled me aside as a tree crashed down, its trunk smashing the ground where I'd been standing.

The thing had swatted it out of its way, advancing on us, but slowly.

I could see it fully now — seven heads stemming from one thick, four-legged body.

The hydra.

Chapter Thirty-Three

meeting the hydra

Sebastian's hands were still on my upper arms, and I could feel him trembling. Octavius was slack-jawed next to us, poised as if he couldn't decide which side of the fight-or-flight response was the better deal.

I'd known this was coming, but I still hadn't figured out what the hell I was going to do about it. A little late for a planning session, now that the monster was right in front of us.

It wouldn't be easy to kill the hydra if I wanted to, and it was pretty clear that it wasn't a good idea to do so anyhow. But we didn't just need to get *past* it. I had to get to its lair. *Into* its lair. And back out again.

A few of the hydra's heads glared at me, the others preoccupied with glaring at my companions. It looked pissed, but unsure if it should bother with us. We were awfully small compared to it. Until we approached, I had the feeling it would leave us alone.

I switched to my leather jacket and rummaged in my pocket for one of the cigars Anatol had given me, pulled it out, and lifted the visor of my helmet.

"What are you *doing?*" Sebastian asked.

"Trying to keep a level head," I said, lighting up.

A couple of the hydra's mouths huffed and growled, their nostrils glowing as if they were filled with embers.

I took a deep puff from the cigar, switched back to full armor, and considered the beast before me.

Somehow, it didn't seem nearly as bad as those horrible little bird-things. One big thing — even with seven heads — felt more manageable and less freaky than a horde of small, creepy things all going for us at once. It seemed even easier to deal with now that I'd had a couple of lungsfull of Anatol's cigar. My fear had evaporated.

The hydra lowered several of its heads and puffed flames out of its various nostrils. Some of its heads bared their teeth at me.

"Do you think we can get around it?" Sebastian whispered in my ear.

"Can't," I said. "I have business with it, remember?"

"Business, yes," Sebastian said faintly.

I took a step toward the hydra and slipped the scepter out. I kept it in scepter form, the smooth wood somehow comforting in my palms. I held the cigar between my teeth and took in another puff.

"No—" Sebastian began, putting a hand on my shoulder to pull me back.

"I'm not going to kill it," I assured him, my speech a little hampered by the cigar, and I continued my advance.

He let me go, too afraid of the hydra and too confused by me to pursue the matter.

Another three steps, and I had the hydra's full attention. All seven heads jerked in my direction, weaving the way snakes do when they're warning before a strike. I recognized the gesture from the reptile house at the zoo. I'd watched plenty of kids tap the glass until a cobra got irritated enough to rear up, neck arched and hood flared. They struck with enough force to injure themselves against the glass, and so fast the kids didn't even manage to scream until after the strike was over with.

The cobra-style head of the hydra sure looked reminiscent of those snakes at the zoo. And the other six were giving me the same threat.

I pulled in another drag from the cigar, not breaking stride.

I dodged the first strike.

Another followed instantly. I flipped the scepter and thwapped the attacker across the top of its head.

The whole hydra seemed to flicker and then re-solidify.

Its seven heads glared and hissed, spitting sparks.

Great. Now it was mad.

I dodged another strike almost immediately.

I knocked one head hard with the scepter. The hydra's whole frame flickered again. I had to keep it in contact with the scepter for longer, though.

It was in earnest now — striking with more than one head simultaneously, faster and faster.

I ducked, dodged, kicked, and flailed with the scepter, but I wasn't going to last long at this rate.

"Some — help — here?" I gasped, rolling underneath a strike. The viper-like head unstuck its teeth from where they'd gouged into the red clay, and the beaky head crashed down right where I'd been about to roll. Luckily I'd changed direction and leapt back to my feet.

Something hit the cobra head just as it reared back to strike. It reeled backward, and came up bleeding from its mouth.

I whacked a dragon-looking head across the snout right as another projectile knocked the viper head sideways.

I wasn't about to look away to see what Octavius and Sebastian were up to.

Now the hydra's attention was divided. Two heads looked left, two right, and three stayed trained on me. All seven opened their mouths, and I had just enough time to realize that was a bad sign before the fireballs exploded from them.

Heat flared across my right shoulder and back as I threw myself to the ground, then rolled and jumped back to my feet.

The three central heads were still trained on me, poised to strike.

They came down. I ducked.

Two crashed into one another.

The third swerved.

Its teeth grazed my arm as its mouth clamped shut. The armor tore — along with some of my arm. I nearly bit through the cigar, and clenched my other hand over the wound.

No. I didn't have time for this. Pain would have to wait.

I sucked in a drag off my cigar and flipped the scepter back into a two-handed grip.

Just in time — the cobra head struck and got a mouthful of scepter.

There was a moment when the hydra was gone and a person stood in its spot, but I couldn't take in any more than that before the monster was back, the cobra head rearing away from the scepter.

I'd been distracted.

The viper head hit me square in the chest, and I flew backward from the force.

I came up choking for breath, scrambling to get my hands back on my weapon.

Sebastian and Octavius were doing their best to keep the hydra occupied, throwing every rock and branch within reach. Now that I wasn't in hand-to-hand range with it, it had turned more of its heads to them, advancing on Sebastian, who (very wisely) retreated from it. Fireballs flew through the air, trees burst into flames, and branches snapped from the heat and rained down to ignite the dry leaves on the forest floor.

We had to stop this thing before the whole place went up.

My first instinct was to rush back in, but I held off.

Octavius heaved a boulder the size of his own head at the hydra. It hit the creature's spine, making it stagger. Its heads hissed, and all but one of them jerked in his direction.

Now, I leapt in.

I knocked the beaked head hard with the scepter in the midst of my dive toward the hydra's body. Again, the full-body flicker.

I got beneath the curve of its chest, in a spot that was awkward for any of its necks to reach. My own chest heaved for breath, sternum aching agonizingly with every movement. The ground trembled as the hydra stomped its huge, taloned feet — far too close to where I crouched beneath it.

I held the scepter against the hydra's underbelly and willed it to change the beast.

The hydra screeched angrily. It was smaller already, its heads writhing in confusion as their necks became shorter and shorter, shrinking back into its body.

The body itself shrank and realigned, the scales smoothing into skin, and the heads became a single unit at the end of a normal-length neck, somewhat crooked, the serpentine features shifting together and then changing further — until finally what stood before me was no longer a beast, but a human.

To be more precise, a little old lady in a polka-dot dress and navy blue heels.

She turned an angry, pinched-up face in my direction. "Who the goddamn hell are you?" she demanded.

I introduced myself with quite a lot of stammering.

"How'd I get changed back?" The former hydra inspected her own skinny, wrinkled arms.

"I don't know," I lied, covering up as much of the ornate bird's head carved atop the scepter as I could with my hands. I leaned casually on it, as if it were a walking stick, and laughed nervously. "One minute, you were a hydra, the next — well, here you are! The Underworld is such a weird place, right?"

Sebastian tactfully cleared his throat and stepped up beside me, introducing himself to the old woman. "You have yet to tell us who *you* are," he pointed out.

"When you aren't the hydra, that is," I added.

"The name's Liza-Mae." She extended a gnarled hand, and Sebastian and I took turns shaking it. She narrowed her eyes toward Octavius, who was still hanging back, a couple yards away.

"That's Octavius," I said. "He's Sebastian's brother. He used to be a minotaur, but I — he changed back, too."

Octavius waved.

Now, knowing that, would she tell us whose side she was on? Was she a servant of Hades, or a victim of the Road? When Persephone had told me about the hydra, I'd assumed the former — but since then, I'd met Octavius, and that changed the game up.

"A minotaur, eh?" She looked him over and then nodded decisively. "I could see that. And you three are headed back topside, yes?"

Sebastian and I traded glances. Well, we couldn't very well deny *that* — why else would anybody subject themselves to the worst of both worlds? "Yes." Sebastian gave her a guarded half-smile.

"*Tsk*," she hissed, then sighed, her expression suddenly forlorn as she looked around at the scorched trees and, beyond them, the blue, sunny sky. "I *was* headed back up to the Land of the Living. . . ." She trailed off, and didn't seem inclined to finish the thought out loud.

"So . . . you're not in cahoots with Hades?" I asked, relieved.

"Hades?" Liza-Mae snapped. "Hades be damned, the bastard!"

Ah, good. I relaxed into a warm, genuine smile. "I know, right? What's your beef with him?"

"I was *trying* to get back to the Land of the Living against his wishes, like I said. He sends all these—" she waved her hands around as if she could smack language into properly expressing her thoughts — "*things* after me to stop me, so I killed a bunch of 'em, and next thing I know I'm growing scales and extra heads."

"Killed them how?" It wouldn't have surprised me if she'd said she'd done it with nasty looks, but she reached into her enormous flower-print handbag and hauled something out.

"Holy crap!" I stumbled back a few steps. Octavius and Sebastian tensed, but didn't move.

I don't know much — scratch that, I don't know *anything* — about guns, but what this looked like was a miniature machine gun. Miniature in the sense that a little old lady could heft it one-handed, but it was still a pretty big hunk of mean-looking black metal.

She gave me a toothy grin and returned the weapon to her purse.

"Why're you headed back topside?" I asked. "I mean . . . well. . . ." I looked her over, trying to figure out how old she was. Pretty old, I could tell that much. Mid-eighties at the youngest. I wouldn't have batted an eye if I'd found out she was a hundred.

Liza-Mae caught the meaning of my look, and glared back at me. "You think young people are the only ones got reasons to live, girl?"

"No!" I said defensively. "I didn't say anything like that!"

"You young people," she grumbled. "You're all the same. Conceited little—"

"What do you plan to do now?" Sebastian interrupted helpfully. "Now that you are . . . yourself again?"

Liza-Mae's face, already lined with permanent belligerence, twisted into a disconcerting half-smile, half-grimace. "Tell you what I plan to do. I think I'd like to pay Hades a visit. I've had enough of this damn Road. I think it's time I made him realize that the Underworld without me is easier on him than the Underworld *with* me."

"You'll change back into a hydra," I said, before I could stop myself.

"What makes you say that?" Liza-Mae snapped her flinty gaze onto me.

"Well, I . . . uh . . . ." I looked at Sebastian, who was making the "you just cut your own throat" gesture behind the old lady's back. I shrugged helplessly.

Liza-Mae swept a suspicious glance over me, then turned to look at Sebastian. She could tell we were hiding *something*, after my slip-up, but I hoped she wouldn't have any reason to suspect my "walking stick".

Before I could dig myself any deeper, though, Octavius spoke up. "I changed into a minotaur again after my recovery." Not *entirely* true, as he'd only re-grown his horns, but I wasn't going to argue the point.

"Well, you ain't one now," Liza-Mae pointed out.

"I got better." Octavius smiled blandly and handed me something.

It was the last half of my cigar, which I'd lost when the hydra had knocked me over. It had gone out on its own, and I relit it with glee. "Thanks! So, anyway," I said, huffing smoke, "if you go back to confront Hades, you're going to turn back into a monster."

She grinned. "Won't that be fun for Hades to deal with? A hydra in his palace?"

"Won't he be able to control you?" Sebastian asked nervously. "When you are a guardian of the Road again, won't you be under his influence?"

"I ain't *guarding* anything," Liza-Mae cackled. "This just got to be . . . well, it's different when you're a beast. This is my *territory*. I wouldn't fight for *Hades*." She said his name with deep disdain.

Did she really not know about the Helm of Darkness? Or was she just saying that so *we* wouldn't know about it? After all, we were hiding the scepter from her . . . why should she trust us any more than we trusted her?

But then . . . it fit, in a way. Persephone had told me that Hades wouldn't bother with me personally unless I managed to overcome the obstacles on the Road. He tended to take the easy way out — whether that was logical or just lazy, it was hard to say for sure. Why *wouldn't* he hide the Helm in the lair of a dangerous, territorial creature, rather than hiding it and *then* putting an obstacle in place? No creation or training necessary, and no risk of betrayal by the guardian of his artifact.

"You could join us." I had to offer — having helped her once, I felt obligated to keep her in her own form as long as I possibly could. It seemed unfair to leave her like this, knowing she'd become the hydra again. Besides, I felt bad for keeping secrets from her, bat-shit crazy stranger though she might be.

"I'd rather try the direct approach." Liza-Mae grinned. "You'd all do better to come with me than risk the Road any further."

I shook my head. The afterlife was too tempting to stay in, and Hades wouldn't willingly send me back topside now — not after I'd stolen his scepter — even with a hydra as backup. "I'm too far along to turn back now." I looked to Sebastian and Octavius. "Guys? You want to keep going, or head back to confront Hades?"

"We'll continue," Sebastian said, and apologized to Liza-Mae.

She shrugged, apparently just as happy to raise Hell on her own as with company. "I'm off, then," she said, already walking away.

"Wait—" I called. "Where's your lair?"

"What you want to go there for?" Liza-Mae turned back to me with a distrustful squint.

"A fortune-teller told me I had to go to the hydra's lair if I wanted to succeed on my journey." I was proud of myself for my slick delivery. Anatol's cigar seemed to make dishonesty a lot easier.

Liza-Mae laughed at me, then shook her head. "One dies every minute," she muttered to herself, but I was fine with her thinking I was an idiot if it got her to tell me where the helm was.

"It's back that a-way." She pointed further into the forest, away from the chasm and the Road. "Then hang a right. It's a big gaping cave entrance between two boulders. Hard to miss."

"Thanks!" I felt guiltier than ever, now I had the information I wanted, for not being straightforward with her. "Be careful — and don't drink *anything* Hades offers you, no matter what he says."

She stumped off down the Road, back the way we had come, toward the city of Hades. We watched her in silence. She turned around and called back to us. "Don't worry about me. It's Hades you oughta feel sorry for." She cackled, and disappeared down the stairway into the river gorge.

Chapter Thirty-Four

unpleasant discoveries

Sebastian seemed wary of straying even further from the path. Inwardly, I agreed with him, but I mustered enough bravado to tell him that he and Octavius could go on without me or wait at the Roadside for me if they wanted.

"Of course we *will* come with you!" Sebastian was quick to assure me. "It merely concerns me. If we lose our way. . . ." He trailed off, and it seemed to me that too many terrible possibilities had occurred to him at once for him to go on.

"I wouldn't blame you if you two stayed here and waited for me."

"And then we would be cowards." Octavius stepped up, glaring off into the trees at our right. "We have gotten this far together. We should continue together."

"It's up to you guys," I said with a shrug. "I *have* to go. You don't."

"Yes, we do," Sebastian said firmly.

I tried to hide my relief. "Let's get this over with, then."

Finding the cave entrance was easy enough, just as Liza-Mae had told us it would be.

Her directions had been vague, but, staying within sight of each other, the three of us spread out and searched a much wider area than I could've done quickly alone. It was made easier by the wake of ripped-up trees the hydra had left between the Road and its lair. Some people have those little squishy "stress ball" things to relax — apparently the hydra had much the same use for large vegetation.

"Over here!" Sebastian called, and Octavius and I hurried to join him.

Just inside the entrance, the ground sloped down so steeply that I had to grab the knobby walls of the cave to keep from sliding right into Octavius, who was in front of me, holding three torches. Sebastian was behind me, and I turned back to warn him. The stone floor was slick with clay mud, and by the time we carefully set foot on level ground again, the temperature had dropped a good twenty degrees or so.

It occurred to me that I hadn't noticed temperature during my entire stay in the Underworld.

Nor had I noticed anything smelling *bad* since my death . . . until now.

The lair was rank — eye-watering in its stench. There weren't any bones or corpses lying around, although there were some suspicious stains on the cave floor. I wasn't sure if that was because the hydra had eaten the bodies, or if your corpse just disappeared when you were already dead. Or when you'd never been alive, or were suspended between the two states. I missed the simplicity of believing that everyone was either one or the other — dead or alive. All this metaphysical mumbo-jumbo was harder to keep straight.

Regardless of the reason, the only things scattered around the floor were layers and layers of leaves — swept in from outside or collected by the hydra for bedding — and broken-off stalactites. The stalactites looked distinctly chewed-on. I took a torch from Octavius and bent down for a closer inspection. Tooth marks raked across the surface of the stone, and I shuddered at what those teeth could've done if they'd gotten a better swipe at me. Bad enough as it was, I thought, my lacerated arm throbbing.

Water splashed in the nebulous darkness nearby. Sebastian

lifted his torch, and I glimpsed a flash of firelight reflecting back from a rippling pool. I wondered with more than a little discomfort if the sound and the ripple were just from the dripping stalactites above the water, or from something under the surface. I tried not to speculate too much about it, although I couldn't help but think of Anatol's rusalkis — drowned ghost-zombies lurking in the water, waiting for us to get too close to the edge.

We went over the cavern three times, all of us peering closely at the dark walls, holding the torches as close as we could to any irregularity in the stone. But we found nothing. No helm.

"Are you sure your information was good?" Sebastian broke the silence we'd fallen into.

"Pretty sure." It had been a while since I'd doubted Persephone. After all, I wouldn't be holding the scepter if it weren't for her. If she'd wanted to screw me over, she could've done it long before now. I *knew* she had ulterior motives, and that I didn't know their exact nature — although I had a hunch it was some kind of game she was playing with her husband. It should've made me more suspicious of her, I guess, but somehow the fact that she'd never bothered to hide it was reassuring.

I was a lot more worried about where the helm could be. There was only one place we hadn't looked yet, and I didn't the idea of searching it at all. . . .

The pool's surface glistened black in what little light our torches cast. "I have a bad feeling I know where the helm is," I said.

From their faces, I could tell Sebastian and Octavius had already thought of the possibility, and that they dreaded the prospect, too.

I couldn't see how deep the water was, even when I held the torch directly over it. I tossed a small stone in and it vanished into the darkness, leaving nothing but ripples to show it had ever existed. At least I didn't see any faces in there, or clawed hands reaching upward. The surface shimmered with a warped reflection of me. Sebastian stepped up to look over my shoulder, studying my face in the water, and I met the gaze of his reflection, too.

"I dislike this idea," he said softly.

"That makes two of us," I said. "But I have to wade in. I've got to find the helm. Without it, Hades will catch up with me as soon as I'm back topside."

"He will catch up with you anyway," Sebastian said.

"I know. But as long as I make it back to Dom first, this'll all be worth it." I turned to face him directly. "You understand that, don't you? You're going back for your wife and daughter."

"I want to return to Life," he said. "I want far more than just a moment. But if a moment is all I succeed in getting, then . . . yes. It will be worth it." He looked away, and I took the opportunity to act.

Before he or Octavius could try to stop me, I knelt at the edge of the pool and put one foot down into the water. Even with my leg fully extended, I couldn't touch the bottom. Great.

"Erica—" Octavius said warningly.

"I know, I know," I said. "I'm being careful."

The brothers stood at the water's edge. I could see in their stance and their expressions that they wanted to stop me, but neither of them did. I took it as a sign of respect, and smiled.

"Take my torch for a sec. I'm going to have to step in to see where the bottom is." Sebastian obliged me, and then I handed over my two cigars. "Take these, too. Don't want those babies getting wet."

"Erica," he said, his voice almost pleading. "I think you should stay here with us."

"I can go," Octavius offered. "Sebastian never learned to swim, but I am a strong swimmer. It would be better for me to go."

"No," I said adamantly. "I'm the one going after the helm. I chose this. I should be the one to face the consequences . . . but thank you both."

I stepped fully into the water.

And didn't touch bottom.

I jerked at the shock, splashing the surface as I flailed out. I hadn't imagined for a moment that the water would be any deeper than my height. Surely the bottom wasn't much further down. Cave pools didn't have sheer drop-offs like this, did they?

"I'm all right," I assured my companions, treading water and trying to get my heart rate back to normal. Strange to have it back again at all, let alone racing.

"I'm going to duck under," I said. "I have to find out how deep it is. The helm *has* to be at the bottom."

I tried to ignore the fact that we didn't even know how big the pool was, that this could just be a small visible part of a water system miles and miles wide.

Sebastian called out to me, trying to advise me not to go under.

"I know it's a bad idea," I agreed with him. "I'm pretty sure that's why Hades put the helm in here in the first place."

"Just be careful!" Octavius called.

"I will," I said, and pushed myself underwater.

When I forced my eyes open, the only thing I could see was the flicker of the torches overhead, small and wavering, and illuminating nothing under the surface.

My heavy armor had changed, without my intending it consciously, to a swimsuit — *my* swimsuit, in fact, from my living days. I plunged deeper into the water, my arms extended in front of me, feeling for a surface below. I must've been ten feet down, and the darkness was so complete I couldn't even see my own arms or hands. I kicked to propel myself forward — downward — and kept kicking until I felt the urge to breathe. Shit. I'd forgotten about breathing.

It had been so long since I'd felt the *need* to draw breath. And chances were, I didn't actually have to. I still didn't have a body, after all — I just *felt* like I did.

I hung there in the water, wondering if I should rush for the surface or keep going.

And in that instant, any remaining air in my lungs was thrust out of me. The water itself seemed to be pulling at me, the pressure of it squeezing a stream of air bubbles from my throat. I screamed, water pouring into my mouth, and the pressure continued and mounted until at last I had to take a breath.

I was torn between the awareness that I was being sucked further down and away from my companions — with extreme rapidity, I might add — and the crushing desire for air. I closed my eyes and told myself, *it's just like pushing through the wall of Hades' palace. You just have to believe you* can *breathe water.*

I gasped in water, the weight of it strange and cold in my lungs. But I could do it. I didn't need to worry about getting to the surface for the moment.

Which was good, because I wasn't just being *swept* away. It was as if a huge vacuum that affected only *me* had opened up below. I slid through the water so fast it actually hurt as pockets of different temperatures of water struck me on my way down. I flailed around helplessly for something to grab onto, but nothing was there. Just the black water thrashing my fingertips until they ached.

And then, with more force than I could possibly estimate, I hit the bottom.

Red drifted through the water, floating across my vision.

I lay there, watching the silt re-settle around me, my hair and my blood dancing around my face, shivering in the icy cold and trying to overcome the searing pain in my head and my arm, which had partially blocked my face from the impact.

I was so stunned that it didn't occur to me at first to wonder why I could see.

I couldn't see much, and only very dimly. There were tiny, phosphorescent fish around me. They didn't look nice. They were covered with spikes, and their fins looked razor-sharp. Beyond them, the water was pitch-black.

I struggled to my knees, groaning with pain, and realized I'd been lying on top of the scepter again. At least it was still with me, I thought gratefully. It was amazing it had stayed strapped to me through all that.

How the hell was I supposed to find the helm underwater, with only glowing spiny fish to light the search? And who knew how much area there was to cover?

I didn't even know for sure how to get back to Sebastian and Octavius, although my instincts said to swim back up and to the left, almost on a straight diagonal. But could I? Would that suction still be there? Still drag me back down here, no matter how hard I swam?

For that matter, what was I going to do about light?

If I just had some way of harnessing those fish. All I had was the scepter. It could change into different weapons — could it become something else? A lantern shape that would hold a few of those fish?

I thought long and hard about it, but the scepter didn't change shape.

But. . . .

Something had changed. The bird's head at the top . . . it looked different somehow.

I held it close to my face to see it better in the shifting light of the spiky fish.

There was a catch on the side of its head, where the beak met the rest of its face. I pressed it, and the beak separated so that the top half of the head flipped back, revealing a hollow just big enough for one of the wicked-looking little fish.

It would have to do.

I would have to grab one.

This was going to hurt.

They weren't particularly concerned with me, milling around lazily as I reached for them. Once my hand closed gently around one, though, I had to grit my teeth to keep from letting go. Barbs sank into my fingers, and the fish thrashed in my hand, digging the spikes further in.

I managed to get him in position without releasing him, and then it was just a matter of flipping the bird's head back down and prying my fingers apart. Wisps of blood swirled around my hand, and with the other I clicked the bird's head into place.

Reddish light streamed from the ruby eyes of the bird now, not much brighter than a flashlight beam, but stronger than the fish alone had given off. It looked creepy, those glowing red eyes burning under the water.

I shivered with the cold, making the light quiver.

Other than the fish, there didn't seem to be much around. I'd just have to pick a direction and go with it. Hopefully I could maintain a straight path, and find a wall to follow. I still felt like I was in an enclosed cavern, though what gave me that idea, I couldn't have explained. It *seemed* like there were cave walls around me, that I was in an underground lake within a cavern.

Still, I felt tiny and vulnerable in the dark, cold water, with no way to know how much ground there was to cover — or what might be lurking in the blackness.

I glanced behind me, but of course I couldn't see anything back there. I'd walked too far away from the glowing fish to be able to see them anymore.

Every once in a while, I would pass another group of them. Just as I saw the third school of phosphorescent fish, I noticed the wall. They were swimming close to it, the surface intensely bright with them hovering near it. I laid one hand gratefully on the wall, marked it as best I could with the scepter, and kept it to my right as I moved on.

Blood still streamed in lazy, smoke-like ribbons from somewhere above my left eye, though the wounds in my fingertips had turned out to be mere pinpricks. Occasionally, the water nearby seemed to shift and swirl, and I'd whip around, thinking something was behind me, but I could never see anything there.

I hadn't had any sense of time since my death, but I know, at least, that I did walk for a very long *way* there in the cave lake, growing colder with every breath of icy water. And the further I went, the more my sense of vulnerability increased. My sense of helplessness, too. It was the first time I'd really felt that I couldn't achieve my goal. Sure, I'd felt like the underdog all along — there was no doubt in my mind that Hades had the upper hand, and would, no matter what I did or who I had on my side. But I'd been so determined to get the better of him that I'd honestly believed I could do it. Now, it seemed silly, even childish, to think that I could find one relatively small object in all this blackness, alone and unaided. The only chance I had was if the helm was somewhere along this wall, and that seemed improbable to me even as I moved along it. It was out there in the middle somewhere, in a spot that would be difficult to navigate to.

At last, I came back around to my own mark on the wall — I'd left a crooked X scraped into the algae that covered part of the stone. So the place was big, but manageably so. It wasn't *that* unlikely that I'd find the helm, as long as the pool wasn't incredibly deep.

I followed the wall up, testing the dimensions of the space I had to search.

I'd covered what I thought was about fifty yards up when I felt the water shift below me. Pointing the red beam of the scepter downward, I peered into the darkness.

There was something down there.

A chill that had nothing to do with the water temperature swept over me.

Below, I could see another red light gleaming in the blackness.

Confused, I tried to work out what I was looking at — and saw my own reflection in a convex, inky mirror.

No, not a mirror — a round, black eye stared in the red light, and a mouth gaped open, revealing — not teeth — but what looked like solid *blades* attached to the jaw. A flat-nosed, rough face and a glimpse of a fin was the rest of my impression of the beast.

My own scream was heavy in the water, and for a nightmarish moment I was too terrified to move.

Go!

I don't even remember turning away from the thing, starting to swim.

All I know is that, once I got started, I swam *fast*. My legs pumped against the water, my free hand scooping great swaths of it behind me, and I shot through the darkness so fast I couldn't even see where I was going.

But the gigantic fish — shark — whatever — was gaining on me. I didn't even have to look to know. I was hampered, too, by the fact that I had to keep the scepter in one hand.

I changed directions, dove down, sped up.

It took a second for the beast to match my maneuver — it was big, and it wasn't so easy for it to overcome its own momentum.

Somewhere below the terror, I told myself, *Good. That is good.*

I thought I would explode with fear.

There was the bottom of the lake, silt wavering lazily in the water's currents, just another five yards ahead.

I kept going at top speed until the last possible instant, then jerked to the right.

The beast crashed headfirst into the lakebed, and I didn't wait to see any more.

Gasping with fear and exertion, I turned away to try and get my bearings.

And there it was, just drifting along the bottom of the lake, covered in algae and crusted with mineral deposits.

The helm of Hades.

Chapter Thirty-Five

a hell of a hat

The helm was an old Greek-style helmet, with a T-shaped opening in the front. Under the grunge, it was probably bronze, but that was just my educated guess.

I grabbed the helm, and my fingers closed around layers of slime and grit. Even so, I was fully aware of the gigantic prehistoric-looking fish recovering right behind me, and, gross or not, I lowered the helm over my head.

Theoretically, assuming this was the genuine artifact, I was now invisible — better yet, *undetectable*. I turned toward the creature that'd been chasing me, and landed with both feet on the silt of the lakebed. At first I was worried, because I could see myself, but then I moved one foot to the side and noticed that there weren't any footprints under me. I should definitely be leaving an impression in the soft, sandy ground, but it was perfectly smooth.

Still, watching the fish-creature blink that horrific black eye, regaining its bearings, I had to fight the urge to swim as fast and far as I could.

I froze, afraid to move the water around me in case it found me that way. Could it smell me? There was still a thin wisp of blood trailing near my head, and I knew sharks could smell blood from miles away underwater.

It circled the area twice while I stood there, terrified of moving. The big slits in its blunt nose flared as it sniffed for a trace of me, but it didn't react, even when it came so close to me that I started to shake.

Sure I'd given myself away, I braced myself against the ground to push off, but the monster swished right past me.

Not even the current of the water around me had exposed me. I couldn't even be smelled, presumably heard, or run into anyone by accident and reveal myself that way.

I wasn't pressing my luck, though — I shivered, terrified that the beast would come back for me, or, worse, that there were more of them lurking in the black water.

~*~

I headed back the way I thought I had come — up and to the left — checking over my shoulder for the giant fish. I didn't feel the suction that had dragged me down here, but then, I was wearing the helm, which made me impalpable.

When I broke the surface, it didn't make the slightest ripple. Water poured out of my mouth, and I coughed until at last my lungs accepted air.

Sebastian and Octavius were standing right next to the edge, watching for me, but neither of them saw or heard my return.

I wondered if they could hear me if I intended for them to. "Can you hear me?" My voice came out quaky and weak, but they both jumped and stared into the water, looking for me.

I took the helm off and Sebastian gasped. "Erica! You got it!"

Octavius leapt in and helped me to the water's edge, pulling me up onto solid ground with Sebastian's help.

I was shaking all over, and thankfully the laws of physics were suspended enough to provide me with warm, dry clothes within a few moments.

"Could you let the fish out of the scepter?" I asked Sebastian.

"Excuse me?"

I showed him the catch on the head of the bird, and warned him about the spikes.

Once I'd recovered enough to relay to them my underwater

adventures, they were shocked that so much had occurred during our separation. From their perspective, barely any "time" had passed — they had only just begun to wonder whether Octavius should go in after me.

"Let's get out of this place." I eyed the black pool with a shudder.

Together, we headed up and out of the hydra's lair, back into the ravaged forest.

It felt good to be out in the open again, and even better to be able to see. And not being chased by gigantic lake monsters — that, too.

Now that I wasn't numb from the icy underground water, though, I realized I was aching all over. *It's all in your mind,* I told myself. *If you just ignore it, it'll go away.*

But getting the helm had taken its psychological toll on me, too. I didn't feel ready to face anything, not until I'd had a chance to collect my thoughts and recuperate.

Sebastian and Octavius, too, were feeling the effects of fighting the hydra with me, and poor Octavius was far from ready to cope with the gorge again.

"I'm worried we won't be able to find our way back to the Road," I said, "but, honestly, right now, I don't know what I'd do about it if we couldn't."

Sebastian nodded his understanding, and we all agreed to take a break, leaning against the trees the hydra had so conveniently thrown to the ground.

"After all," I said, "with this being the hydra's territory, the other monsters probably avoid this place. This may be the safest place we *could* stop to rest."

"Let's hope you're right," Octavius said.

"When you return to the Land of the Living," Sebastian asked me, "what will be your first act?"

I considered a moment, rubbing at the helm with a scrap of cloth torn from my imaginary sleeve. I was thinking of that question's opposite — how the living speculated about their final act, and how few people managed to make the most of their last hours. Mortality probably worked the same way from both ends of the spectrum.

"I don't know that I'll have a choice," I said. "If rising from the dead is anything like dying in reverse, I'll probably be busy just trying to keep up with the changes."

"But if you had a choice." Sebastian lay on his back, one arm behind his head, his face turned sideways to look at me.

"All right," I said. "I'd eat a big, fat, juicy California orange."

Octavius chuckled.

"What about you?" I asked Sebastian.

"Hold my wife and daughter, one in each arm." He looked up at the canopy of the trees.

I smiled a little.

"I expected you to say something like that about your Dominic," Sebastian said, looking at me again.

"I think I'm going to need to be prepared for that," I said. "I don't know how he'll react to me coming back from the dead. He'll probably be afraid at first. I sort of want to steel myself for a bad initial reaction."

We fell silent.

"What about you, Octavius?" I turned to him.

"Go to the nearest bathhouse and have a long, hot bath." He closed his eyes as if savoring the very idea.

I had to admit it sounded good after the lack of temperature in Hades, and even if I didn't have a body, I felt grubby as hell right now.

We talked as the light changed around us and the sun set, I smoked one of my two remaining cigars to calm my still-shaky nerves, and in the end we built a campfire.

I finished cleaning the helm by its light, chatting with my companions about their family and mine, listening to Octavius as he talked about the countryside around their family vineyard, and to Sebastian as he described to me his little girl's first steps, which had been into his own arms.

I had the means to return to the Land of the Living. I'd come all this way successfully, and, for the first time since I'd entered the Underworld, it seemed like Dom was just around the corner, waiting for me in another room rather than another world, and that I could enjoy this one moment among friends without guilt.

Later, we slept, too tired to care that we were dead, and so could have pressed on despite our exhaustion.

Chapter Thirty-Six

the end of the road

The sky was glowing pale gold when I woke. One good thing about being dead — you don't get that horrible taste in your mouth in the morning.

As soon as we were all awake, we headed for the gorge, the helm strapped at my waist and the scepter across my back.

At the precipice, Octavius hesitated, and I pulled out my third and last cigar from Anatol. "Don't know why I didn't think of this last time," I told him, handing it over.

"You don't want to keep it for yourself?" he asked, reluctant.

"Take it." I offered him a light, and he leaned the cigar into the match flame, puffing to get it going.

Sebastian gave me a grateful smile, out of sight of his brother, and I shrugged surreptitiously.

We managed to get Octavius down to the riverbed with as little trauma as possible, although it took some encouragement at first, even with the cigar.

"That's weird." I looked around at the stony floor of the chasm. Yesterday, it had been completely dry, but there were pools of water scattered across the surface now. "It didn't rain on *us* last night."

"Underworld weather." Sebastian shrugged, and he and Octavius kept walking across, toward the stairs on the opposite bank.

I peered into one of the shallow puddles, and instead of my own reflection, saw a white, hollow-eyed face leering up at me. A bony hand reached up, and I jumped back as it broke the surface and grabbed at my ankle.

Apparently, the technicality that this was a riverbed didn't make any difference if the water in it was still, not running.

"Bad rusalki!" I smacked its knuckles with the scepter, and the hand retreated back under the water's surface. "Breaking the rules."

I peered into the pool again, but nothing looked up at me from it now. Nothing to show anything had ever been there, aside from the splashed droplets of water from the hand's sudden emergence.

"Watch out for the puddles!" I called to Sebastian and Octavius. "There're monsters in there."

Octavius sank gratefully to his knees, once we'd made our final climb out of the gorge. "Oh, I could kiss this ground," he sighed, patting the forest floor affectionately. "I admit, though, it was much better with your cigar than without."

"Hopefully, no other cliffs will need to be scaled on this journey." Sebastian leaned a hand on his brother's shoulder.

"I'm just glad the Road's still where we left it. Look." The grove of poplars to either side of us partly shielded the view, but there was the Road — a wide ribbon of rusty clay through the dark green forest. I'd been more than half-afraid that it would disappear or move while we weren't looking.

But it hadn't, and now I had Hades' helm in my possession. If I could make it back to the Land of the Living, not even Hades would be able to find me while I wore the Helm of Darkness.

Sebastian, who'd somehow ended up with the cigar, helped Octavius to his feet.

At length, we reached a bridge.

I was surprised, as it was the first *built* structure we'd encountered on the Road, and also reluctant to cross it with two guys who'd died together on a collapsing bridge. They seemed okay with it, though — even Octavius — so on we went. Maybe it was because the bridge wasn't very high, or maybe because there was water flowing under it, but Octavius didn't even pause before starting over it.

"I wonder what river that is." I peered over the edge.

"I couldn't say," Sebastian answered noncommittally.

But halfway across, I stopped in my tracks.

Up ahead was the three-headed statue of Cerberus.

"What the—"

"We came all this way, only to return to where we came in?" Sebastian cried.

"It seems appropriate, I think," Octavius said, with infuriating lack of surprise.

"But no." I started forward again, slowly. "This isn't where we came in — at least not where *I* came in. It was a beach." I gestured off to the left, where it would've been, but we were in the middle of the forest.

"It was the same for us," Sebastian said.

"There must be two statues," I speculated, but I felt nervous.

Warily, the three of us approached the triple-headed dog.

It was positioned right in the middle of the Road, and beyond it I could only see layers and layers of dark branches, as if the path ended here.

The statue was bigger than the hydra, the tops of its paws at my eye level, or chin level for Sebastian and chest high for Octavius. Cerberus was depicted as a hunting-dog of some kind, wide-muzzled and intelligent-looking, and all three of his heads were identical, as far as I could see from this far below them.

We didn't notice the creatures at first — not until they'd crept into the edges of the clearing and loosely surrounded us. The shifting shadows at the tree line had disguised their movements, and the creatures themselves were a dull, greyish-rust color that blended nicely with the red clay mud of the Road.

By the time I realized something was wrong, there were a dozen or so of the fat, squat creatures watching me from the edges of the clearing, inching forward. They made no noise at all on the soft clay.

To say that the fat little monstrosities were toad-like would be akin to describing a saber-toothed tiger as cat-like. Imagine a toad crossed with a rhino, then add some shark to the mix. They were roughly three feet high in their squatting position, with long, powerful legs and thick tails. Now that I could distinguish them from the background, it was readily apparent that they had long, sharp teeth set in their protruding lower jaws, and I didn't relish the idea of their getting any closer.

Their back legs were clearly made for jumping, despite their bloated underbellies, and I noticed little clawed hands at the ends of their forelegs. I'd spent enough time around animals of all kinds, working in the zoo, to know the difference between curious behavior and threatening behavior, and these guys were definitely set to attack.

"Monsters," I said, and Octavius and Sebastian looked away from the statue to see the rhino-toads slinking up from the riverbank.

I pulled out Hades' scepter, trying to make no movement sudden enough to provoke an equally quick response from the fat monstrosities.

"Perhaps you *shouldn't* transform them." Octavius gently laid his hand on the scepter.

"I agree." Sebastian's glance darted over the approaching beasties. "There are too many. If any one of them decided to take the scepter from you by force, we couldn't hope to overpower all of them."

I hadn't thought of that.

"What do we do, then?" I asked. "We don't even know where to go from here!"

"Intimidate them?" Sebastian suggested.

I took a step on the diagonal, slightly forward but away from the nearest toad-monster.

It tensed instantly, poising to jump.

The creature opened its mouth to reveal a triple row of sharp, crooked teeth.

Oh, please tell me this thing couldn't spit poison or anything. . . .

Still, with a gun I'd be able to shoot *near* the rhino-toads and maybe freak them out. Scare them into leaving us alone.

The gun I came up with was an old-fashioned derringer pistol, another museum piece that had left an impression on my imagination. With my back against the gigantic paw of the Cerberus statue, I aimed at the tree above and behind the closest toad-monster, and shot.

Zing! Thok! The tree shivered and let loose a cloud of dark leaves. The toad-thing squatted there glaring at me, unmoved. If anything, just more annoyed with me. The others continued to creep toward us.

Okay, so maybe I needed something bigger. A two-barreled shotgun grew from the little pistol, and I squeezed the trigger toward the packed clay next to the closest monster.

BOOM! Schluuuk. Mud exploded from the ground and rained down over all of us, splattering the nearby trees liberally. The rhino-toads flinched, but didn't back off.

"Oh, come *on!*" I yelled. "That scared *me*, and I'm the one with the gun! Don't you have any sense of self-preservation?"

And then . . . a rumbling began.

At first I thought, illogically, of an earthquake.

"Hey, at least *that's* scaring them off!" I watched excitedly as the toad-monsters turned tail and started hopping back toward the water. They slunk back in as silently as they'd left it, raking claw-prints into the slick mud of the banks.

"What *is* that?" Sebastian frowned, moving back toward the bridge. "The river. . . ?" He turned to look at us, and his eyes widened.

"What?" Octavius felt his temples, checking for horns.

Sebastian grabbed both of us and hauled us away from the shelter of the statue.

The rumbling subsided slightly, which seemed weird to me at first.

But it *was* the statue. It wasn't rumbling — it was *growling.*

And it wasn't a statue.

"*Seriously?*" I threw my arms out in frustration. "I've already *had* the monster with multiple heads. Isn't one enough?"

"We're not going to be able to outrun that!" Octavius shouted to Sebastian, who was trying to run while pulling two people who weren't making any attempt to follow suit.

"We're really not." I put the scepter back in its proper form. "At least there's just one of him."

The left head swung toward me, and, as with the hydra, I gave it a good solid smack with the scepter.

Cerberus didn't change.

He wasn't like the others. He wasn't a soul transformed — this really *was* his true form.

Cerberus snarled in fury at my attack, and I backed into Sebastian and Octavius.

"Maybe it's time to *try* running?" I squeaked.

But we had nowhere to go — one huge forepaw blocked us on each side, and the only other choice was to turn our backs and run the other way. I knew he'd catch up to us, probably before we even took two paces.

Sebastian and Octavius seemed to be thinking the same thing, and we huddled there together with the huge dog's three heads snarling and slobbering at us.

It tried another swipe, this time from the right, aiming for Sebastian, and the scepter met it right in the teeth.

No, I thought. *You are not allowed to hurt them.*

If it weren't for me, they'd still be wandering around lost. And lost was better than eaten, the way I saw it, even if one of you was trapped in the form of a monster.

One blow to the right again, another to the left, and again we tried to back a little further away. Maybe if I could just hold him off long enough, we'd get some room to make a break for it.

No such luck.

The middle head came at me while I was expecting another blow from the side.

And it got me.

"Octavius!" I screamed from behind the beast's teeth. "Sebastian!"

The jaws parted slightly, and for a moment I glimpsed the two brothers, their faces rigid with shock.

"Take the scepter!" I tried to push it out to them. It was their only chance, and if I was going to be eaten, the scepter wasn't going to do me any good.

But Cerberus clamped his teeth shut again, and tried to swallow.

I screamed in fury and panic, whacking at everything in reach, trying to get him to open his mouth enough for the scepter, or me, or preferably both, to escape.

And then he tossed his head back, and I plunged into darkness . . . and slipped out of all awareness of myself, the world, and everything.

My last thought was, *Now, I am really, finally* **dead**.

Chapter Thirty-Seven

a sudden sympathy for zombies

There was a time of complete peace, when I was nothing and nowhere.

And as I drifted back into awareness of myself, I felt happy.

Gradually, this gave way to curiosity. I knew clearly that I was no longer a snack for Cerberus, that somehow I had transformed rather than been eaten. Or the world had transformed.

I could hear nothing.

I couldn't move.

I couldn't open my eyes.

Beneath my fingertips was something soft and smooth — some sort of fabric. In the quiet, I listened to my own breathing, and from the sound of it, I could tell I was in an enclosed space . . . a *small* enclosed space. The humidity of my own exhalations was beginning to feel oppressive. The air was flat, unsatisfying. I couldn't seem to get enough in to fill out a breath.

At last, my eyelids lifted, and it was just as dark beyond them as it had been behind them.

I tried to sit up.

Banged my head against something only a few inches up.

"Shit!" I rubbed my forehead. Whatever I'd hit was cushioned, but it had surprised me.

I extended my arms as far as they would go, pressed them into the velvety lining above me.

I'm in my coffin, I realized, and my heartbeat ramped up to a rapid, powerful thumping. My breath quickened. In my coffin and *alive*.

Three reactions hit me at once.

One was fear and a desperate urge to escape, the second, an attempt to logically calculate the best way to go about escaping, and the third was—

I laughed. A good, hard belly-laugh.

I was back. I had shuffled back into the mortal coil. I had made it back to the Land of the Living.

Of course, I wasn't going to *stay* living for long if I didn't get out of this coffin. It would really suck to suffocate here and now, after all I'd been through to get here.

I realized one of my hands was still holding the scepter, and I felt around until I found the helm next to my hip.

They'd made the journey across the void with me, then. Good thing, since I'd been counting on it.

My mind tried to race with questions about what would happen once I got out of the coffin, but I firmly pushed all that onto the back burner. The first order of business was not to suffocate.

Would the scepter still change from one form to another?

It took more concentration than it had in the Underworld, but it still worked. I changed it into a knife, and turned it up on its end so that it was vertical. I wondered if I popped it back into full scepter form, it would burst the lid of the coffin. Surely it wouldn't break the scepter — I mean, weapon of a god and all that.

But wait — maybe . . . if the helm had allowed me to move through water without disrupting it, would it allow me to climb right through the lid of the coffin, through the dirt, and out of my grave? It was worth a try.

I fumbled in the awkward space, but managed to get the helm on, and slowly sat up. It was too dark to see anything as I got unsteadily to my feet. Theoretically, I was now standing partly in my coffin and partly in the earth around it.

I'm going to need a bath before I see Dom, I thought.

I had to keep my eyes closed as I climbed . . . and I had to try not to breathe, as doing so invariably resulted in me getting dirt in my mouth. The helm didn't help the problem that inhaling dirt rather than air isn't particularly good for a living being. It was not a pleasant experience, let me tell you. Digging out of your own grave is not the optimal way to spend your first minutes back from the dead. Keeping hold of the scepter, still in knife form, didn't make the process any easier.

I should've asked to be cremated, I thought. *Then, at least, I'd just pop out of a little urn in my own living room.* Like a genie coming out of a lamp.

When I finally surfaced, full sunlight streamed down on my upturned face. I pulled myself out of my grave and took a moment to catch my breath.

I'd expected, without reason, to come back to life in the middle of the night — in the still, quiet night — and broad daylight dazed me. I rested my back against my own tombstone and thought I'd just let myself be dazed for a while.

I wondered what had happened to Sebastian and Octavius. I missed them already — it felt like I'd been away from them for ages, not mere moments . . . and maybe I had. It wasn't like the Underworld obeyed any of the usual rules of the space-time continuum.

Everything felt strange. The sunlight warming my skin, the air moving in and out of my throat as I breathed, my own heartbeat and the feeling of my blood traveling through my body. To suddenly have nerves and tendons and muscles where before there had been only a *self,* even if that self had experienced the *sensation* of having all those physical components . . . it wasn't the same as actually existing within a constantly-changing, always-decaying, always-regenerating, organic shell. The mechanics of this thing that was a body! The chemistry! It was amazing to me that it functioned at all. How could it? It was too complex.

The grass they'd laid gently atop my grave was warm and slick beneath my bare calves, the satiny, dark purple dress I'd been buried in hot from the sun, and covered with dirt. I used to wear this dress on dates with Dom. I'd been wearing it when he proposed to me, just in from a trip to the symphony — his favorite place to spend an evening out, if he could afford it. I'd had wine at dinner afterward, and I was brimming with self-confidence, feeling luxurious and sexy as Dom opened the door of the car for me. We'd come back to my house — Uncle Jeff's old house — and on our way from the driveway to the door, he stopped me.

It was balmy, with a soft breeze, a sky full of stars, and a bright half moon. The little bit of garden I had out front was in bloom, and scented the air with that waxy smell of flower petals mixed with fresh-cut grass.

And that's when he asked me to marry him, there in my front yard at almost midnight, and me in my purple dress.

I hoped it would wash up all right.

Next time, I'm putting it in my will: Bury me in a dress I don't *like,* I thought.

Eventually, I was able to take in a broader scope of my surroundings.

It was a big graveyard, scattered with full, broad maples bright with fresh spring leaves. There were a few families visiting graves, but none close to where I sat, and they all seemed pretty wrapped up in their own business — not paying any attention to the recently-deceased clawing back out of the grave. Even if they'd looked over, they wouldn't have seen a thing, since there wasn't any earth disturbed from my emersion and I was invisible within the helm.

The tombstone to my right was Uncle Jeff's, and ahead of me, I was pretty sure, were the backs of my great-grandparents' graves. So I was in River Grove Cemetery, where my dad's side of the family was buried.

It was unnerving to see Uncle Jeff's tombstone again. Some

illogical part of my brain was stuck in the habit of mourning his death, as if he'd been torn away from me forever. The knowledge that he continued his existence, that he'd be there when I went back to the Underworld, brought a whole new angle into the picture, but it didn't quite erase the feeling that I'd lost him all over again.

Of course, if Hades caught up with me, I'd be rejoining Uncle Jeff very soon, and *that* was something I wasn't ready for. At the very least, I had to talk to Dominic, face to face.

River Grove Cemetery wasn't too far from home. I could walk it in about an hour, if I weren't wearing stupid shoes — and by that I mean uncomfortable, dressy shoes with heels.

Closer than that, though, was Laura's condo.

It was out of the way, but not by much, and I could wash up there. Even if she were out, I knew where she hid her spare key. I could even borrow a pair of tennis shoes and some clean clothes. Sure, it'd be a little weird for her, coming home to the note I'd leave for her when I was supposed to be dead, but it wasn't as if I hadn't warned her.

And—

Wait a second.

Shouldn't I have all manner of terrible wounds? And you'd think I'd be . . . well . . . stiff, after days of being dead and not moving. And I should be full of embalming fluid.

I stood up, wobbly on my feet (although that could've been the heels).

My dress unzipped at the side, under the arm, so I undid it far enough to bare my stomach. It was healed up.

Not perfect — I could see faint white scars traced there on my skin, like a map of a river and its tributaries, irregular and random. But considering how bad my wounds had been, it seemed negligible.

I knew some bones had broken in the crash, too — I remembered hearing them break, vaguely remembered the pain — but everything seemed in working order now.

This was definitely my body, though. The little light-brown freckle just above my wedding ring on my left hand, the dime-sized birthmark on my side right at the base of the ribs, the scar on my right thumb — they were all old friends, proof of my identity, the most familiar things in the world.

It had to be the scepter, then. It had to have healed my body somehow as it guided me to it from the Underworld.

I should get going; I knew that. Hades could show up any second.

But I *was* wearing the Helm of Darkness, and being alive again was so much more striking than I'd expected. It was much harder to get used to than being dead had been. There was a layer of sheer terror to it — the vulnerability that came with mortality, the awareness of how weak and delicate a human body really is. There was also the distraction of physical reactions and physical needs pulling at me, everything from my shoes being uncomfortable to the thrill of excitement whenever I thought of Dom. He was so close now, so within my reach. I could feel my heart rate increase just thinking about him.

And there was a rush to coming back to life. Every sensation seemed so intense. A breeze against my skin, the feeling of sunlight on my eyelids when I blinked. The scent of warm grass and cut flowers. Songbirds calling each other, their music ringing in my ears along with the sound of the leaves rustling in the same breeze that lifted my hair up away from my neck. Even before my death, it had been a long time since I'd stood still and just taken in the *feeling* of being alive, just soaked up the experience of it.

I could come up with some serious joy-swap material from this kind of thing before I got back to the Underworld.

But.

I *did* need to get moving.

I gave myself a minute or so, giving the world my full attention.

Then, helm in place, invisible, I slipped through the cemetery gates.

Chapter Thirty-Eight

invasion of privacy

The walk to Laura's condo was surprisingly relaxing, despite the uncomfortable shoes and the concern that an angry god might pop out of the ground at any moment and drag me back to the Underworld.

I had the Helm of Darkness, after all — and I was alive now, so maybe Hades couldn't even get to me anymore.

Walking down familiar streets was comforting, especially in the sunshine, with the temperature somewhere between sixty-five and seventy. Even here in the city, the world looked so *green*. The grass and the leaves of the trees I passed seemed almost painfully vibrant against the equally intense blue sky. I felt happy just to be — well, just to *be*.

Laura's car wasn't parked out front, so I let myself in, instantly hyper-aware of how filthy I was amidst her immaculate, expensive possessions.

I lost no time in getting to the shower, partly out of that awareness, partly because I was in a hurry anyway, and (last but not least) because her living room was unnerving to me, seeing as how the last time I'd been in it had been during the séance, and I'd been dead at the time.

Silly as it sounds, that gave me the heebie-jeebies, as if I were afraid of meeting my own ghost.

The shower held no such creepiness for me, however, and I thought of Octavius and his wanting to take a bath as soon as he returned. I wondered if he and Sebastian had managed to get back home, and if so, somewhere in the distant past and an ocean away, whether Octavius, too, was enjoying the sensation of clean, hot water.

It seemed gross not to wash my hair after being dead, but I wasn't sure about removing the helm, even for a couple minutes. I bit my lip, considering. If all I had left in this world were a single conversation with Dom, did I really want to have it with dirty hair? No, I decided, and took off the helm.

Nothing exploded or anything.

I set it between my feet, where it would be easy to grab, and lathered my hair as fast as I could.

I was rinsing when everything twisted. It was like that time Chester had called me up from the Road, back in the Underworld. Like the séance.

I stumbled, caught in the vertigo of being two places at once, and my hand automatically grabbed for the scepter, back in its original form — I'd kept it at arm's length propped against the shower wall, held in place by the soap dish.

There's nothing quite like the vulnerability of being naked — although the part of me that suddenly found itself in the Underworld appeared fully clothed — to hammer it home to you that you are *not*, in fact, in control.

"Hello, Erica." Hades' face was expressionless, and he stood uncomfortably close, towering over me. I was in his study, not far from where I'd stood during my first conversation with him — near the speakers, which were growling out Louis Armstrong.

I gripped the scepter tighter in my physical form, and even in my Underworld self's hand, it felt reassuringly solid.

My body felt unpleasant; weak, tingly, with a deep ache in my stomach from not eating anything in the week or so since my death, and I realized uncomfortably how much better the part of me in the Underworld felt. That part of myself had none of the physical effects of the split across the Void, of course, and there was an odd sense of homecoming, full of relief and even a strange sort of happiness. There was an element of *freedom* to it that I realized I'd been missing desperately ever since my return to the surface.

I wasn't about to let on to Hades, though.

Whatever bizarre allure the Underworld held, I'd come back to the Upper World for a reason, and after all, I'd certainly had little enough time amongst the living. Not even thirty years. That didn't seem like much after having experienced eternity.

"Hello, Hades." I returned his greeting with a slow, lazy blink that was more to steady myself than to feign nonchalance. "Rather an inconvenient time."

"You mortals and your sense of modesty." Hades waved a hand dismissively and moved away, without quite turning his back on me, toward his desk.

Something lay across the polished surface, but I couldn't see what.

"Well, according to the old myths," I said, "you gods are a bunch of skirt-chasers. Don't get all holier-than-thou on me, just because you're a god and I'm human."

He chuckled, which took me less aback than you might think. In his slim, perfectly-tapered fingers, he picked up the object from the desk. It was the copy Uncle Jeff and Latrischa had made of the scepter, held loosely in Hades' grip, as if he were offering it back to me.

"This is a beautiful piece." Hades smiled serenely, leaning in a half-stance, half-perch against his desk.

I secured my hold on the real scepter. "Yes, it is."

"Certainly a flawless representation, at least to the eye." He transferred its weight from one hand to the other, lazily, almost absently.

And yet I knew, as clearly as if he'd said it aloud, that the fake hadn't fooled him for a moment. He didn't even bother to say so.

"Very impressive of you to get the helm, as well." Hades said.

"Thank you." I genuinely meant it, despite the stiff dignity of my tone.

"Unfortunately for you, these items—" he gestured to the scepter and the helm, and his voice took on a dangerous edge, each word delivered with precision — "these items both belong to *me*. Your soul belongs in the Underworld, which also belongs to *me*, and so, you see, in a way, your soul also belongs to *me*." He smiled, looking back at the fake scepter he was toying with.

I glanced at the helm, clumps of dirt loosening away from its surface as the water streamed down over it.

I lunged — the movement gave me horrible vertigo, and my stomach lurched as the part of me attached to my body and the part of me free-form in the Underworld shifted away from each other, out of synch, like I'd taken out one of my eyes but left it still attached to the nerves . . . still transmitting to my brain, but outside my skull. It was a hideous feeling.

Adrenaline spiked up the hairs at the back of my neck and along my arms, thrummed through the veins in my head, and my mind, still not re-adjusted to biology, reeled with trying to process both the internal and external stimuli of the situation.

Hades' eyes widened, a grimace starting to spread across his face as he grabbed for me, but I shoved the helm down over my head in the same moment, and his hand passed right through my arm, closing into an empty fist.

I jerked back, and the Underworld — and Hades — disappeared.

Somehow my Self found its way back into one piece again, and I slumped to the floor of the shower.

I sat there for a long time, just letting the hot water run over me, just feeling my body alive around me, shell-shocked but resilient, soaking up the comfort of the simple and the physical, even with my mind in turmoil.

~*~

I should hurry, I realized at some point, probably ten minutes later. With the helm back in place and the scepter (in pocket knife form) tucked into my jeans, I felt reassured — even cocky. So much for the great god Hades. I'd thwarted him *again*, and without a whole lot of trouble.

I borrowed clothes and makeup from Laura's dressing room, left her a note, and slipped on a pair of her sneakers.

This was all going to freak her out, probably, but I didn't have many other options. If they'd buried me with my wallet and my debit card, none of this would've been necessary.

I was almost out the patio doors when I did a double-take and turned back to the breakfast bar. Laura had a bowl of fresh fruit on the counter, and even from where I stood I could faintly smell the sweet, sharp tang of the oranges. My mouth stung, it started to water so abruptly.

Grabbing an orange, I glanced at the little red-and-white sticker. "Nice," I said, smiling at the California label.

I left the peel in Laura's trash can, and carried the naked orange with me, eating as I walked. It was a perfect orange, too — each wedge crisp and bursting with juice, just tart enough to balance its sweetness, but with no hint of bitterness. Even before I died, an orange like that could send me to a level of optimism bordering on insanity. Post-mortem, it was like a drug.

Chapter Thirty-Nine

the moment i've been waiting for

In comfortable shoes and with food in my system, it was easy to lie to myself about how much Hades' recent appearance had rattled me. *You beat him,* I reminded myself. *If he shows up again, you can beat him again.*

I could hear, on some nearby street, the fanfare of a parade — trumpets and trombones blaring cheerfully, and in the ground, I could feel the booming rhythm section of a marching band. I couldn't help walking to the beat; it was a brisk tempo, and the parade and I seemed to be on a parallel course for the two-mile journey.

Before I knew it, I was on my block.

My heart beat faster, strides growing longer as I craned to see my own house. Two more steps, and I'd be able to see it.

There.

I didn't break stride, but I felt a huge smile cross my face. I loved every slat of fawn-colored siding, the little bricks of the chimney, each slate-blue painted plank of decking across the tiny front porch.

It was about four-thirty — Laura's living room clock had read four, and I figured half an hour for the walk between there and home — and Dom would probably be rummaging around in the kitchen. He always got hungry around this time, although I don't think he'd ever noticed how precise the timing was: always, between four-fifteen and four-thirty, he got a snack and something to drink, no matter when or how much he'd last eaten.

I tried to guess, as I passed our mailbox, what he'd be having today. I decided on iced oatmeal cookies, probably with coffee, and took the two steps up onto the porch.

Automatically, I reached for my pocket to grab the house key, then realized — of course I didn't have it. I fumbled the helm off, but kept it tucked under my arm; the last thing I needed was to freak Dom out by coming back as a disembodied voice.

Heart hammering in my chest, I lifted my arm and knocked, like I always did, five times: two hard hits and three short raps.

I could feel the vibrations of Dom's footsteps in the house before I could even hear them . . . then the muffled squeak of the floorboards in the hallway . . . the handle turned. . . . I wondered for a second if it would be him that answered the door, or if he had company — his parents, an old friend from his music school days, someone I didn't know—

The door swung open and there was Dom, and yes, he was holding a half-eaten oatmeal cookie in one hand.

Time stuttered forward in split-seconds that felt infinite.

In the first instant, I could tell from his face that recognition hadn't hit him yet, and all that happened was that he swallowed the bite of cookie he was working on.

The our-house smell of cinnamon-tinged wood reached out of the doorway as if to embrace me, the familiar song of our front porch wind-chimes just whispering in the barely-there breeze.But before my face could adjust into the smile of delight I was feeling, Dom's expression changed. He stared at me, eyes darting from my face to the space beyond me and back again, unsure. The cookie slipped out of his hand and broke apart as it hit the ground.

"Hey, you," I said softly.

The door swung open wider as Dom let go of the handle. He was breathing hard, like he'd just come up from underwater.

We stared at each other as if we were still in separate worlds, as if the sight of each other were the only thread that could reconnect us.

Dom looked tired, but he'd shaved, and he'd managed to get enough gel into his badly-behaved hair that it wasn't standing up in the back. The sharp, familiar smell of his aftershave brought the hot sting of tears to my eyes. He'd missed a spot shaving, just under his jaw line, halfway between his chin and his ear on the right side — he always had trouble with that spot.

The smile finally burst out of me; everything in my body felt so tight I couldn't contain it . . . I needed to laugh or cry or both. "Dom." My mouth formed the shape of his name, but no sound came out.

Just as suddenly as he'd opened the door, Dom grabbed the door post and clung to it, his fingers white. He made a noise somewhere between choking and groaning, like the breath had gone out of him. Stumbling backward, he fell flat on his ass in the front hall, staring up at me in shock, tears streaming down his reddening face.

"Dom!" I rushed forward to help him, dropping to my knees just inside the threshold.

"Don't!" Dom scrambled away from me, still on the floor. The coat rack crashed down between us as he backed into it.

I dropped the helm and scrambled to recover it; when I looked up, Dom was dog-paddling up the stairs as fast as he could, like a cartoon. My adrenaline level was so high my stomach hurt, and it was weird being able to tell that there were hormones zooming around in my veins. It didn't seem like I should be able to *feel* them, but I could.

Dom slipped out of sight into the bedroom and tried to slam the door. The *whoosh* of air from the room kept the door from catching, and it swung slowly open again.

The rush of being back, being home, seeing Dom, dropped out from under me, like I'd just been cast adrift in a vacuum of my own emotions.

And then I caught a half-sob, half-roar from upstairs, and all I wanted was for Dom to be all right. Everything I'd done since my death was for *Dom to be all right*.

I crept up the stairs, calling his name as gently as my wobbly voice would allow.

"Dom, it's me — it's me, sweetheart."

I took in the room as I made my cautious entry: the furrow in the middle of the bed from where Dom had been sleeping alone all week; the pillows bunched up, blankets twisted around each other from restless sleep; whiskey bottles scattered on the floor, and Dom huddling in the corner with his face buried in his hands, heaving sobs of, "Don't don't don't don't." He'd scraped his arm on something in his panic, one of those rug-burn scrapes that rashes up and then stings like hell.

"It's really me," I said gently. "Dom, it's really me, I promise."

I set the helm aside and knelt by him, whispered to him over and over, "It's okay, it's okay. It's me. I came back. I came back for you. I'm here. It's okay," as I pulled his arms aside and smoothed his hair, caressed his face in my hands and kissed his tear-soaked cheeks.

He struggled against me at first, his pupils huge with panic, sobbing and gritting his teeth around his mantra of "Don't don't don't." Then he was grabbing at my arms, my hands, gripping my face between his hands and staring at me as he sobbed harder and harder in anguish, both of us clammy with tears and sweat, both hot with struggle and fear. "Not real," he whispered, breathless.

"It's real, Dom," I kissed his forehead, ran my hands through his hair. "It's real. It's me. Remember when we met and you were doing that show, that musical downtown — you were playing piano for *Cabaret* — and you got them to let me in backstage that night to watch from the catwalk? Remember that? Or — remember when we went camping and we woke up and the tent was flooded, and you just laughed and laughed . . . and I knew right then that you were right. I didn't tell you then, but that's when I knew, you just . . . made *sense*, and. . . ."

My voice broke as Dom pulled me closer.

"And the time," I went on, choking back sobs, "the time we lost power and we just sat on the living room floor and watched the lightning and stayed up talking all night? I still remember everything — everything we talked about — when you were a little boy, you took your ant farm to school for show and tell and that kid smashed it . . . and all your ants . . . he stepped on all your ants before the teacher could stop him—"

And the words stopped and we were both shaking, drained, frantically clinging to each other, and Dom whispered, *"Erica."*

~*~

"This is so *weird*," Dom kept saying, shaking his head. He was still pale and wobbly from shock, but we were sitting on the bed together, my legs tucked up under me and one of Dom's hands in both of mine. The helm was on the bedside table, within arm's reach, the scepter still in knife form in my pocket. "I mean, you've been dead for almost a week. Your funeral was yesterday. They *buried* you yesterday. I've just been trying to pretend it isn't real . . . but when I *saw you*. . . ."

"I know," I said. "It's like you want something so bad, and then when it happens, it feels like. . . ."

Dom nodded and wrapped my waist in his free arm. "What happened to you? Were you in a coma, or something? Did the doctors make a mistake? Or were you really dead all this time?"

One of the things I really like about Dom is that, unlike most people, he doesn't just choose the most logical explanation and assume it's the real reason behind something. He spins out a whole set of possibilities, and he's no more surprised to find an illogical reason than a logical one. Expecting the unexpected comes naturally to him.

"I was really dead," I said. "I was in Hades."

Dom pulled away to look me in the eye. "You went to *Hell*?"

"No, not Hell. *Hades*. Like in Greek mythology. The Underworld."

"Well, that's . . . not so bad, then. . . ?" Dom raised his eyebrows at me, clearly brimming with questions.

"No," I said. "No, the Underworld was nice, actually." I told him a bit about it, and about Uncle Jeff.

The strike of five from the church bells down the street made me stop mid-sentence. How long did I have before Hades made another appearance? And how long could I hope to fight him off? My stomach flipped at the thought of breaking the news to Dom that I might die again any second. I couldn't linger — things needed to be said, and this could be my only chance.

Without thinking about it, I put my hand palm-up on the bed next to me, and Dom took it — the sort of little gesture you take for granted until you go without it.

"What is it?" Dom asked.

"I came back because I needed to tell you something."

Despite my possibly limited timeframe, I hesitated. Partly because I was nervous about the import of what I had to say. After everything I'd been through to get here, I wanted so badly for this moment to go well, wanted to say the right things to comfort Dom, wanted to feel comforted in return. I'd hung so much on this conversation that now I was afraid to have it. And the other part of what gave me pause was the fact that I didn't want my one conversation with Dom, which I'd kept saying would be enough for me, to be over with. Now that I was here, with him, I knew that no matter what came out of this exchange, I wouldn't want to go back.

"What is it?" Dom looked worried now.

"About that argument — before I . . . well, before I died," I said at last. "It shouldn't have *been* an argument . . . moving or not moving — sure, I care about that, but I care *more* about my life with you. I didn't mean what I said, and I couldn't stand knowing that was the last thing I said to you before the end. I got your message on my cell phone and . . . the crash happened right after."

His grip on my hand tensed, not enough to hurt, but enough that I understood how fresh the pain of my death was to him. I looked down at our interlocked hands as I continued. "I just wanted a chance to apologize to you, and tell you how much I love you." At first, I didn't dare meet his gaze, out of some deep-down fear that he'd still be mad about the fight.

But one glance was enough to dispel that. Dom's a square-jawed, manly sort of guy, but boy, does he have the puppy-dog eyes when he's feeling tender-hearted. He didn't say anything, just hugged me so tight I thought I might die all over again, but it was enough without words. I knew I was forgiven, and also that he had been afraid he *hadn't* been, that he'd been afraid I died hating my life with him.

I had been right. Now that it was said, I was far from prepared for Hades to show up and escort me back to his realm. How could I be okay with another separation from Dom — all the *more* so because all was forgiven between us? I remembered Sebastian explaining that he and Octavius weren't content with a mere moment of life, that they were determined to return to full lives — wives, children, grandchildren, all the love and the heartache of a mortal lifetime. I wondered if they had made it, or if Hades had caught up with them. Or if maybe he was too busy contending with me to go after them yet. I hoped they could cut some kind of deal with him. I hoped *I* could cut some kind of deal with him. I had to stay.

There in Dom's arms, I knew losing his wife wouldn't be any easier just for one apology. This visit would make the loss more difficult than ever. Would he always wonder if I was coming back? Would he waste years of his life hoping I would? If things had been reversed, and Dom had come back from beyond the grave and then returned to it, I knew the answer to those questions. I would always hang back, always hope, always wonder. I'd be torn between wanting to go on and lead a normal life, and wanting every rule of the life-and-death cycle to shatter and allow him to come back to me for keeps. I couldn't leave now. I *wouldn't*.

"Love you," I said, my voice muffled through the hug.

"Love you too," I heard, more through his chest pressed up to my ear than out loud.

I took a deep breath and forced myself to say, "There's something else . . . you should know. . . ."

And then I felt it again — that feeling of being sideswiped, the sudden vertigo starting to pull me out of myself, back into the Underworld. I caught onto the solid, living world as best I could and struggled to stay in it, my hand stretching for the helm.

"Erica, what—" Dom relaxed his grasp around me.

"We need to leave. Now." I grabbed the helm and pulled the pocket-knife scepter out of my jeans.

"Are you—"

"No, not okay." I fought a dizzy spell, focusing on the feel of the bedspread under my free hand, the heat of my own physical body, the rhythm of my own blood. I felt the air expanding my lungs as I inhaled, thought about each cell the oxygen touched, imagined every little molecule affecting every other one. *Stay here*, I told myself.

The scepter shifted back into its true form.

Dom's mouth dropped open. "*What—*"

"I'll explain when I can," I interrupted. "We need to *move*."

"Okay." Dom's jaw clenched shut, determined. I knew that look — he was ready to deal with anything, no matter how messed up he might be feeling.

"Look at me," I said.

He locked his dark blue eyes onto my face.

"Do not freak out. Even if you can't see me, I'll still be here." I held onto one of his hands and ducked into the helm.

Dom stared at where I was standing. He fumbled for my hand, but couldn't actually touch me until I slipped my fingers through his.

"I'm still here," I said. "You just can't see me."

The pressure had lifted; it was easier to concentrate, but I could sense Hades probing around for my mind. It was not a pleasant feeling.

I had no idea how leaving the house would help; it seemed like Hades would be smart enough to know that all he had to do was follow Dominic, and I'd be right alongside. But I was thinking faster than I could process logic, and this was what my instincts told me to do. Instinct had worked for me on the Road — well, and the scepter had guided me, and I had the same resources now as I'd had then.

"You *will* explain all this to me at some point, when you get a chance — right?" Dom said in my general direction.

"'When I get a chance' being the operative phrase," I said. "Come on. Get the car keys."

"Where are we going?"

"Somewhere not here. Hades seems to have caught up with me." I nudged Dom out the bedroom door and into the hallway.

"This doesn't sound good," he commented as we jogged down the stairs. The keys jangled in his hand as he grabbed them from the hook by the front door. "Are you in some kind of trouble, sweetheart?"

"You could say that." I was disturbed and not a little frightened by the situation I'd brought on myself, but at the same time, deep down, I couldn't help being pleased. I've always been a risk-taker, but until I died I'd always tried to keep it in check. Now, somehow, danger didn't seem as constrictive. More like a challenge than a barrier. I felt clever and quick, almost giddy with rebellion. Maybe the helm did more than just hide its wearer.

We ran to the car — Dom's, of course, as mine had been totaled in the wreck that had killed me — our doors closing at almost the same instant, both of us panting for breath.

"Whatever is going on," he told me, "it'll be all right. You tell me how to help, and I'll do anything I can. Just promise me you'll tell me what's going on at some point."

"Fair deal." I squeezed his hand. "Let's go! Get to the highway."

Chapter Forty

hanging on

Once we were on the move, I relaxed a little. Sure, Hades would probably catch on that I wasn't still in our house, and I didn't figure a moving vehicle would pose much of a problem for him, but right now a bit of breathing room (so to speak) was enough for me to unwind.

I took the opportunity to fill Dom in on the fact that Hades was trying to catch up with me and pull me back into the Underworld.

"So, what, you could die again any minute?" He went white, clenching his grip around the steering wheel.

"Well, kind of," I said. "I have a certain amount of leverage in the situation, and besides, he can't just *kill* me now that I'm alive — at least, I don't think he can. I figure he would already have done that, if he could."

Dom was silent for a beat as the scenery zipped by beyond him. "That's not exactly the reassurance I was hoping for."

"It's going to be okay," I said, hoping that was true. "He's going to catch up with me at some point, though. He's way too smart not to. I just figure if we stay on the move long enough for me to think what to do about it, then we'll be in good shape."

"And the helmet that's making you invisible is part of your plan." He glanced sideways to where he knew I was sitting. "I feel like a lunatic, talking to an empty car seat."

"This is *Hades'* helm," I said. "You know, the one he supposedly got during the war between Olympus and the Titans? It renders the wearer not only invisible, but undetectable, even by Hades himself."

"And the shape-shifting walking stick?"

"Hades' scepter. I have no idea what all this thing can do, but it's awesome." I absent-mindedly patted the bird's head that topped the object under discussion. "If I didn't have this, there's no way I would ever have made it back."

"So what you're telling me," Dom said, "is that you're on the run from a god — and you have stolen two incredibly important artifacts from that god. So you're probably on the run from a very *angry* god."

"Well. . . ." I tried to think of a piece of Dom's conclusion that I could argue with, and couldn't find one. "Wait, why are you assuming I stole them?"

"How did you get them, then?"

"Um. I stole them."

For a second, I thought Dom was going to get angry; the way his shoulders tensed and his expression went totally blank — it was the way he looked anytime he was going to blow his stack about something. Instead, he gave a despairing smile to the highway in front of us. "This is the weirdest thing I've ever heard of in my life. So do you have any ideas how to get yourself out of this mess?"

"I didn't really plan this far ahead," I said. "I thought I was just coming back to apologize, but . . . now, that's not enough. I want to stay with *you*."

"And Hades won't let you?"

"That's definitely a no."

Dom's expression hardened. "I can't lose you again, Erica. How do we beat this guy?"

"I wish I knew," I said. "He's getting closer to pinpointing us. I can feel it."

"How can you tell?" Dom asked.

"I don't know." I shifted my weight uncomfortably. "Same way you can tell when someone's watching you."

"You said you were undetectable in that thing," he said.

"I *am*," I said. "But you're not. It was only a matter of time before he decided to lock onto *you* in order to find me."

"Great. And *where* am I supposed to be going?"

That was a good question. There was only one person I could think of that might be able to help me, and I didn't know where he lived. I had no clue how Chester could possibly bail me out of this much trouble with the Other Side, and I felt a pang of guilt about asking Chester to do more than he'd already done for me — after all, he hadn't owed me *anything*, and yet he'd done everything I'd asked of him in our brief acquaintance. But who else could I turn to? If there was such a thing as skill in occult dabblings, Chester had it, and he was the only person I'd ever known who did. "You don't still have Chester's card, do you?"

"The medium. . . ." He swallowed slowly. "You really did send him. That guy that said you were coming back."

I remembered, then, that Dom had torn up the card.

"Oh, crap." Dom ran a hand through his hair, looking guilty. "I threw him out. I was—"

"He lives here in town," I said, "but I don't know where, exactly — he might be able to help."

"Not the usual line for a medium," Dom observed. "Still, at least we know he's not a quack — Damn! If I'd listened to him, I—"

Sure enough, that weird sensation hit me again — that feeling that I was slipping out of myself — and I was watching the highway zip by me, but I was also standing by the riverside in the Underworld. Not where I'd crossed the Styx, but where I'd fought Cerberus.

The hellhound was there, still and silent. It took me a moment to notice Hades, too, was present, and as motionless as a statue. His head was cocked, and leaves had settled around his feet, as if he'd stood through a day's worth of breezes, waiting, listening, searching me out with his mind.

I gasped and gripped Dom's wrist with my own cold hand. Dom yelped.

"Jesus, Erica! You scared the piss out of me!" He hadn't seen me move toward him, of course, and I hadn't thought about how much the sudden icy grip of his week-dead wife would probably shock him. "I'm *driving*, you know!" He squeezed my hand to show me he wasn't upset, just surprised.

My heart was beating so hard it seemed like Hades should be able to hear it, but of course the helm was protecting me from that.

"What's wrong?" Dom asked, his voice sharp with sudden fear.

I was afraid to speak. Hades didn't seem to be sure he'd got hold of me; he hadn't even blinked his lashless eyes since he'd pulled me into his grip.

My Underworld self was steady, but my body was trembling with tension, fight-or-flight kicking all my muscles into overdrive — as if they'd do me any good against the god of the Underworld.

"Erica, what is it?"

I couldn't answer him for fear of alerting Hades to my presence. I was afraid even to struggle my whole self back in one place, because if I fought him, wouldn't that tell Hades exactly what he wanted to know — that he'd gotten through to me?

I stuck the scepter between my knees and grabbed the pen and notepad we kept in the glove compartment for last-minute shopping lists, scribbled furiously, and handed the note to Dom.

Hades has found me. Halfway in the Underworld. Can't talk or he'll know for sure that he's got me. Any suggestions?

"You know how hard it is to read and drive?" Dom muttered as he took the note, but as he read what I'd written, his face became increasingly grim.

I squeezed his hand to communicate, "Well? What now?"

We sat in silence for a few minutes, me watching Hades for the slightest change in expression or stance, anything that said he'd realized how close he was to pulling me back under.

How long could I hold Hades off? How long before he noticed I was standing *right there* in front of him? Even with the helm, I didn't see how he could be fooled for too terribly long.

And then it occurred to me — I wrote a single word and passed it to Dom.

"Laura!" Dom read aloud, and before I knew what he was doing, he'd U-turned across the median and sped off back toward our side of town.

At exactly that moment, Hades blinked.

And then he looked straight at me, poised like a snake about to strike.

He can't possibly see me, I reminded myself, feeling the hair at the nape of my neck rise.

The rate Dom was driving, we'd be at Laura's in less than fifteen minutes, but that seemed like plenty of time for Hades to drag me back to his domain.

Screw that, I thought angrily. *I made it all the way back to the Land of the Living, fought monsters, got the hydra on my side, and dug myself out of my own grave. I can deal with one lousy god.*

Hades was still pushing at my mind, harder now he thought he'd found me.

I pushed back.

"You don't belong among the living," Hades said, his eyes burning into mine, even though I knew he couldn't tell for sure if I was standing there.

"I'm *alive*," I hissed back. "*You're* the one who doesn't belong among the living."

I felt myself slip for a second, almost unaware of my body — like I was only connected by a single, taut thread — and I lashed out at him with the scepter.

My body jerked as I slammed back into it. I hadn't even hit him; he just hadn't expected me to try, and it had broken his concentration for a second.

I pulled off the helm with one hand, keeping my other clenched around the scepter.

"What are you doing?" Dom yelled. "I thought you were *hiding*."

"He knows he's got me," I said. "If I'm going out, you're at least going to know when it happens."

"We're almost there now," he told me. "Just hang on!"

"What?" The stand-off in the Underworld must've pulled me out of linear time again, because there was no way that had taken up ten minutes. But Dom was right, we were coming up to the exit onto Laura's street, turn signal flashing.

Hades was already trying to latch back onto me, but I kept my focus on the physical world. Blue sky dazzling my eyes, the leather seat sticking warm to my clammy palm, the tint of warmth from the sun on my jeans, and the vent blowing cool air through my hair, tickling the skin of my neck. Every subtle hint of my own living body sensing the world around me was a barricade against death, and I clamored to find more.

The click of the turn signal reverberating against my ear drums. The shifting of my weight as the car turned. Dom clutched my free hand in one of his, and I used that, too.

I belong here, I thought at Hades, as hard as I could. *Just because I've been dead, doesn't mean I should have been.*

What would I have done with my last hour of life?

I hadn't had a chance to do it.

But now that I was alive again, there was no way anybody was going to take the opportunity away from me to *stay* alive.

Not even Hades.

Chapter Forty-One

between this world and the next

It was only as Dom pulled onto her street that I wondered if Laura was even home from work yet, and for a second I let myself worry enough that Hades' grip on me tightened. A flash of the Underworld, the stark sunlight gleaming off the river, and Hades standing there like a giant chess piece, immobile and imposing.

I breathed in the scent of the car — air freshener and sun-warmed leather, with a hint of Dom's cologne — and wrenched myself back to the physical world. I focused on the tip of my pinky finger, resting on one of Dom's smooth fingernails, and noticed that the muscles of my jaw were so tense they ached. Purposely relaxing them was another good, solid, physical task.

And Laura's car was in her drive.

Dom parked behind her. "You hanging in there?" He turned to look at me, his blue eyes full of concern.

"That is such a cute expression," I said, grinning weakly.

"Hell of a time to get sappy with me, honey, but thanks." He ran one hand across my forehead to brush my hair back. "You look exhausted."

"It's been quite a day," I said. "Coming back from the dead takes it out of a girl." I didn't mention how hard I was fighting to keep myself there, in the physical world, even as we spoke, but I knew Dom could tell.

"Let's get Laura," he said. "Come on."

He jumped out and opened the door for me, and we walked hand-in-hand to the stoop.

"Maybe I'd better be the first one she sees," Dom said nervously, clearly thinking of his own reaction.

I nodded and stepped a pace behind him as he rang the bell.

"Dominic!" Laura sounded surprised to see him. "I tried to call you at home a couple minutes ago. There's . . . well, something weird happened—"

"It's about Erica, right?"

"How'd you—"

"She's alive," Dom said. "Right here." He pulled me gently forward by the shoulder, and Laura gasped.

"You're really back!" She threw her arms around me. She laughed and cried, turning me in circles. I hugged her and smiled at Dom over her shoulder.

Laura pulled us inside, her grip on my living arm reassuringly solid against the hold of Hades and the Underworld.

"I got that note you left and I — I had no idea what to think," she told me as we sat down. It was still weird to be in that living room again, after the séance.

"I know, I'm sorry," I said.

"Are you okay?" Laura asked, putting her hand over one of mine. "You look — you're so pale."

I probably looked like I had a migraine, given how hard I was concentrating on staying in this conversation, and out of one with Hades.

"I need Chester's phone number," I said. "Dom, can you explain to Laura what's going on, while I call him?"

"Sure thing." Dom gave me one of his lingering, sideways looks, which meant he was worried about me.

Clearly baffled, Laura leaned over the arm of the couch and grabbed her purse. "Here, his number's in there." She handed me her cell phone, with Chester's contact entry pulled up already on the recent calls list.

"Thanks." I listened to the rhythm of Dom's voice as he told Laura the sketchy bits of information I'd given him about my situation, waiting for Chester to pick up.

After three rings, he answered.

"Hello?" I could hear noise in the background, like he was in a moving car, with talk radio on low volume.

"Chester, it's Erica. I'm at Laura's. It's a long story, but I'm back from the Underworld, and I really need your help. Can you come?"

"I — I'm out." His voice was unusually high-pitched with bewilderment. He cleared his throat. "With my son." He added this last with heavy emphasis. "Are you really. . . ? I've never heard of. . . ."

"Chester, I'm sorry to ask you," I said — with all honesty. "I don't know who else to turn to. Please? I need your help. I'll probably be dead again within a few hours otherwise." I'd managed to hold my fear at bay mainly through having too damn much else to think about, but now, saying it aloud, my hands started shaking.

It wasn't going back to the Underworld I was afraid of, or even facing Hades. It was the idea of being torn out of Dom's life all over again, of knowing now how happy Laura was to have me back and knowing how hard it would be on her if I were suddenly gone again. I had no issue with being dead, but there were people who cared about me here among the living. I didn't want to let them down now that I'd made it back to them.

And the actual dying part wasn't something I cared to repeat, either. Like most sudden changes, the transition is the worst part.

"I'll be there as soon as I can," Chester said grimly. Before he hung up, I heard him say to his son, "Garrett, can you turn off here? We've got a stop to make before we go home." Then, there was just a dial tone.

I handed Laura her phone and sat back on the couch, running my palms over the velvet cushion and taking in the scent of her apartment — sweet and spicy, like cedar tinged with vanilla.

"Well?" Dom and Laura looked at me expectantly.

"They're on their way," I said. "Chester and his son."

"His *son*?" Laura repeated. "When he came for the séance, we got to talking after — well, after you disappeared, I was pretty upset. So to calm me down, he got me having a normal conversation, stuff about our families, you know. He said his son was totally set against all this."

I nodded, and then felt myself slip sideways out of my own skull again, the world twisting around me.

I fought it, gritting my teeth and clutching my hands into fists — one of them firmly around the scepter. Dom leapt from his chair at my expression. Beside me, Laura recoiled, her face suddenly drawn and pale.

"Erica — is it happening again?" Dom asked.

"Yes," I said. "I can't—"

And the Underworld solidified around me. I could only dimly see Dom's silhouette, outlined against the light of Laura's arched windows, frozen in place with fear.

"You're right, Erica." Hades' voice came from behind me, silky and indifferent. "You *can't* hang on."

I whipped around. He stood nearby, leaning against a cloudy-grey granite column. We were in a courtyard with a dry fountain in the center, granite cobbles at our feet, and a raised, covered porch lined with arches. I'd never seen the place before, but I sensed it was somewhere within the grounds of Hades' palace — possibly even in the heart of the palace itself.

"I've made it this far," I said.

"You've done what you set out to do." He folded his hands behind his back.

I opened and closed my mouth without speaking. "What difference does it make to you whether I'm in the Underworld now, or in fifty or sixty years, when I've lived a full life? It's not like you have to wait around. There's no such thing as time for you."

"True." He shrugged. "But you have to admit it isn't fair. Maybe it doesn't make a difference to *me*, but why do *you* deserve a full life, when plenty of others die young? Why should *you* return to life, when they remain here?" He swept a hand in a broad gesture — I guessed toward the city of Hades, beyond the walls that surrounded us.

I didn't answer immediately. We stared hard at each other across the grey stones, under a grey sky that cast down a bleak light over us.

"Because I *did* it," I said. "It's not that I *deserve* anything more than anyone else. Anybody could have done what I have — stolen the scepter and the helm, traveled the Road, used your own weapons against you. Anybody can, if they want to badly enough. The only difference is, I *did* it."

"And you expect me to let you get away with it?"

"Why shouldn't you? It wouldn't cost you anything."

"You seem very casual," Hades said, pacing around me in tight, close circles, "for someone who has stolen from, defied, and *threatened* a god."

Something pulled at me, like a harness had wrapped around my soul and someone had started lifting me up, hand over hand. The Underworld dissolved around me, Hades' eyes burning with sudden fury inside the impassive mask of his face.

But then even he faded out of my vision, and I was back in Laura's living room, stretched across the couch, with Dom cradling my head in his hands.

I blinked up at him and then turned to the rest of the room. Laura was sitting in the chair now, tears gleaming wet on her cheeks, with an expression of mingled fear and hope. There was a guy — I recognized him as Garrett — squatted down next to her seat, paused in the middle of patting her consolingly on the arm.

And Chester stood at the end of the couch in a neat blue pin-stripe suit. He looked as if he'd just single-handedly lifted a car — exhausted, but modestly impressed with himself.

"Chester," I said weakly. "You came. Thank you."

Garrett, hearing me speak, stared, not at me, but at Chester, and I couldn't tell if his expression indicated animosity or amazement.

Chester moved to sit on the end of the couch, and I moved my feet aside for him, leaning back on Dom's chest for support.

"Could I please have a glass of water?" the medium requested, of no one in particular, sounding out of breath.

Laura dashed out and back with it so quickly that none of us felt any need to speak in between. I think we were all too shaken by our respective experiences to know *what* to say.

"How did you get me back?" I asked at last, when Chester seemed to have recovered from his exertions.

"Have you ever heard of 'clearing' a house?" Chester asked.

"No," I said. "Is that like an exorcism?"

"Kind of, but not exactly." Chester wiggled one hand to illustrate his two-sided answer. "It's more to do with helping spirits move on — or forcing them to, if that's what's necessary. Not so much on the casting out of demons and so on."

Garrett had taken a chair near Laura's, and at this, his expression changed abruptly from unsettled and unsure to flat-out angry, defiant, and ashamed. Laura and Dom listened with interest, however. Apparently, my sister's skepticism was long gone, what with everything that had happened between her, Chester, and me during the time I'd been dead, and of course Dom was susceptible to this type of thing to begin with.

"Okay, so clearing a house is sort of like getting rid of your drunk friends after the party's over, then," I said to Chester. "Some of them go home when they can tell you're tired, and the rest of them you have to call a cab for, kind of thing?"

"Something like that." Chester half-smiled.

Garrett checked everybody else's reaction to the conversation, found he was the only one not taking his dad seriously — even if I *did* think it was all pretty weird — and looked angrier.

"Well," Chester continued hesitantly, "I decided to try to do the opposite. I tried to pull your spirit *back* here. Not the same as a séance, since you actually have a living body as a receptacle. I tried to think of it as forcing your spirit to possess your body, which, of course, is the opposite of what I'm generally asked to do."

"It worked," I said.

Garrett snorted. "Don't you feel ashamed of yourself, Dad?"

"Why should he?" Dom snapped. I felt his whole frame tighten, and I knew him well enough to know how his face had changed — his usually open, kind-looking face would transform as his jaw jutted out, the tension making the lines of his cheeks suddenly harsh and angular, his eyebrows darkening his gaze to a smoldering glare. "This man just saved my wife."

Garrett didn't even respond to him, but shifted his attention back to his father with a bland, hopeless look. "How can you do this for a living? Going around freaking naive people out and tricking them into thinking you're helping?"

"And how, exactly, could I have faked this?" Chester said, just as calmly and just as hopelessly.

"Ex*cuse* me," Laura said. "I'm not stupid, and I'm not naive. My sister was *dead* for a week. I saw her buried yesterday. Now, you can tell me that there are fake mediums out there, and I'll agree with you. You can tell me none of this makes any sense, and I'll agree with you. But *there* is my sister—" she jabbed a finger in my direction — "and you can see for yourself that she is *alive*. You can take my word for it that she *wasn't* alive yesterday. And she and your father never met before she died. How do you explain the fact that they know each other well enough now that he just dropped everything to come and help her at a moment's notice?"

Dom relaxed a little while Laura's tirade went on, apparently feeling that she was doing a good enough job being angry for both of them.

"I can promise you that your dad didn't trick me into being dead." I chuckled.

I was surprised when Chester joined me in laughing.

Garrett held Laura's gaze for a moment before looking away. "I'm sorry," he said, but he looked unmoved by her argument. He was apologizing for offending her, not for his beliefs about his father's work.

In the silence that followed, I began to feel uneasy — not just because we'd hit an awkward conversation point, but something more than that. Something bad was going to happen. Any moment now.

"Can I get anyone else a drink?" Laura asked suddenly, as if we'd all come over for afternoon tea or something. Poor Laura. She never was good with unpleasant social situations. Or, until now, emergencies. "Or a cookie? I've got—"

The moment came.

This time, it felt like *everything* twisted. Not just the world twisting around me, or me twisting around the world, but everything twisting around everything else.

And I wasn't the only one who'd noticed.

Dom gripped my shoulders, and Laura clung to the arms of her chair. Garrett and Chester both sat bolt upright, their feet braced against the floor.

The room changed, but stayed the same.

We changed, but stayed the same.

We were somewhere else, but we hadn't moved.

And then I realized. The whole room, with us in it, had somehow meshed with the Underworld courtyard where Hades and I had confronted each other a few minutes before.

Hades was standing by the fountain, looking frightfully nonchalant.

It scared me more than if he'd been angry.

"What the hell is going on?" Garrett leapt to his feet.

We were all on our feet by this time, in fact, and the

Underworld was mingling disconcertingly with the Upper World, giving me a weird tingling feeling all over — like the pins-and-needles sensation when your leg falls asleep, but more . . . electric? It's a hard feeling to describe, because it's part physical and part psychological.

"Well," Hades said, ignoring Garrett — ignoring everyone, in fact, except for Dom and me. He slid a lazy gaze over the two of us, Dom with his hands on my upper arms, me poised in front of him with the scepter in both hands, itching to strike if Hades made a move toward us. "So this is your Dominic, the cause of all your troubles . . . and all of mine." One corner of Hades' mouth lifted a fraction of an inch. "There is an easy solution to it all that would give us both what we want, you know."

"Is there?" Fear fluttered in my throat. I knew he had nothing good in mind.

"The answer is simple enough." Hades kept staring past me at Dom with those unnerving, calm, hooded grey eyes. Then he smiled at me. "I just have to kill Dominic."

Chapter Forty-Two

old friends

"Well, don't look so shocked." Hades waved a hand at me dismissively. "What did you expect all this to come to? You tell the ruler of the Underworld that you refuse to stay in his realm because you're determined to be with your husband, who is still among the living. You've certainly proven your determination and cunning by now, and it's only fair I give you what you want, I suppose, after all you've gone through."

"This is *not* what I *want*!" I shoved Dom back with one arm — he'd been trying to step around me, toward Hades.

"You don't want to be with your husband?" Hades affected surprise.

"Yes, I do, but I want us to have a *life* together first! Look, we've got forever to be dead together — you'll have us for eternity here in the Underworld. What difference does it make to you if we *live* first? And anyway," I said, "I thought it was against the rules or something for you to just kill somebody off before their time."

"Rules?" Hades laughed. "Oh, you've already broken so many of those, I'm far beyond the point of being willing to follow them myself. You've disobeyed, lied, stolen, and connived to get what you want. Now you want *me* to follow one . . . tiny . . . pointless . . . rule?"

With each of his last four words, he took a step toward us, his face darkening with each one. Standing over me, he seemed more alien than ever, no matter how human his form might *look*, and his expression eased into a gentle, extremely unnerving smile.

He reached past me, put a hand on Dom's shoulder, pulled him forward so that Dom and I were side by side. His other hand gripped my wrist, and for some reason I didn't move to fight him, although I had the scepter. I just waited to see what would happen — what Hades would do, how he would try to kill us, whether the sky would tear in two and some other god would reach through and punish him for overstepping his bounds.

Nothing intervened, and Hades took a deep breath.

I screamed.

It was like the bird-monsters, back on the Road, when they'd latched onto Sebastian and Octavius and me, pulling at our souls, tearing us out of ourselves.

My body and spirit both reacted instinctively and the scepter seemed to fight of its own accord, breaking Hades' grip on me and slamming into his throat in one fluid motion.

Hades stumbled a pace backward, clutching his throat, but recovered himself almost instantly. He snarled, his face contorted with fury for a fraction of a second before his smile returned. Straightening up again to his full height, he cleared his injured throat. "We don't have to do this the easy way."

My central nervous system thought, "Oh crap, oh crap, oh crap!" My attitude thought, "Bring it on!" Either way, my blood thundered in my veins, the prickle of adrenaline dancing across my skin, dusting me with an instantaneous cold sweat.

At the corner of Hades' mouth, something black gleamed — blood, I thought. But his grin widened as he saw me looking at it, and his teeth parted in a silent laugh. Tumbling out of his mouth, instead of the sound of his laughter, came one of the bird-crea-tures, and then another, and another, and another. They poured out in a horrific cloud around him, and I watched in mind-numbed terror.

He knew . . . he *had* to have known . . . that these things had scared me more than anything else the Road had thrown at me —

that, in fact, they'd been the only thing to defeat me, and if it hadn't been for Sebastian, I would never have made it past them.

I wanted to sink to the courtyard floor, curl up with my hands over my head, and just let whatever was going to happen, happen without me.

But I couldn't do that, not now. They'd kill Dom along with me, and I doubted Hades would lift a finger to keep them away from Laura, Chester, and Garrett, either. I'd dragged all of us into this mess.

The cloud of bird-things gathered, like a single organism taking a deep breath before the plunge. I took that moment to sweep the room with a quick glance, fixing the location of Laura's front door in my mind, even though, in the courtyard, there was just a solid wall there beyond one of the archways.

As one, the creatures attacked.

In the same instant, something thundered through the Underworld walls, bursting into the courtyard. Seven heads blazed fire, cutting great red-and-gold swaths through the black cloud of bird monsters. The hydra's copper claws and barbed tail tore at those creatures unfortunate enough to come within their range, and its own roar drowned out their shrill cries.

Liza-Mae had kept to her word — she really had come back to confront Hades.

"Where the hell did that thing come from?" Dom shouted beside me.

"Discussion later," I yelled back. "This is not a good place to be right now!"

Hades was busy ducking fireballs and swipes from the hydra's tail, but the whole courtyard was a chaos of flame and creatures and claws, and the bird-monsters would get back to us before long.

We had to get out while Hades was distracted.

"Run!" I yelled to the others. "Run, run!" I shoved at Dom, pushed him into Chester until the two of them got it and took off, Garrett hot off the mark just in front of them — he reached back and grabbed Laura's hand, launching her forward along with him — and I kept yelling as we got closer to the door.

"Just go through!" I shouted.

"But there's a wall there," Garrett objected.

"No, there isn't," Chester said, and opened the door.

Of course, the wall still looked like it was there, but outside Laura's condo, you could see the street, with cars swishing gently by, a couple joggers bouncing past with their headphones on, trees bending in a gentle wind. Normal things.

"GO!" I yelled. The bird-creatures were circling above us, squawking to each other, trying to regroup and recover from the hydra's attack.

I didn't dare look back at Hades.

Laura stepped out her front door. She was still holding onto Garrett, and although she looked disconcerted about stepping through the wall, she gave him a gallant smile once she was through — along with his hand, up to the wrist. "Come on through," she said. "Hurry!"

He hesitated for another maddening moment, but at last he stepped through, shuddering as if he'd been doused with dirty ice-water.

Chester had no issue with the Underworld barrier whatsoever. I guess he was used to seeing the difference between the physical plane and the spiritual. It was part of his job description, after all.

Dom went without pause, with a purposely determined stride that told me he was doing so purely on blind faith in my word and Chester's.

I leapt through and, for whatever difference it might make, slammed the door behind us.

If I'd been a cat, my hackles would've been raised down to a bottlebrush tail, knowing those freaking bird-monsters were behind me.

A group of them streamed out of the solid door as if it wasn't there, which, of course, it *wasn't*, for them, gathering like a storm cloud and resuming their circling above us.

"What do we do?" Laura asked me.

"I don't know!" I wailed, but then a thought struck me. "Wait! We've got to move fast, and we should split up. Laura, you go with Chester and Garrett. Dom and I will go in our car. Chester, you can see what's Underworld and what's not, right?"

He nodded.

"Great, then you drive. Just drive *anywhere*, it doesn't matter where. Somewhere you can get a long way away fast. Hades isn't good with real space and real time; he's not used to it." What I didn't say was that the reason I was splitting us up was that I thought Hades would probably leave the three of them alone. I'd gotten Dom into this up to his neck — Hades would go after him no matter what, now — but the other three were just bystanders. The fewer people I had to keep under my wing, the more likely we'd all come out of this alive and intact, I thought.

"If the bird-monsters catch up with you," I said, "use fire. Anybody smoke? Got a lighter?"

Garrett raised his hand sheepishly as his father gave him a disapproving look.

"Good," I said. "Use it if you need to, but I think they'll follow us." I turned to Dom. "I don't want Hades to know where you are. Put the helm on."

He looked at me blankly. "I don't have it. I thought you picked it up."

"You mean it's still on the coffee table — in there?" I felt the blood drain out of my face. "I thought *you* picked it up."

We had lost the helm.

And there was no way we could get it back now.

Chapter Forty-Three

follow the lego brick road

We'd been still too long — just a moment too long. The bird-things screeched down like the heaviest, ugliest raindrops of all time, grabbing at us with their claws, their feathers deceptively soft and smooth.

"Get in the car!" I yelled, to everyone in general.

We scrambled, pulling monsters off our clothing as we ducked into our respective modes of transport. Of course, they flew right into the cars, even after the doors clicked reassuringly shut, but I was figuring on speed saving us, not the physical confines of the car. I hoped it would, since there was no way I could drive while waving a flaming torch around to fend them off.

Dom and I batted away bird-creatures while I backed out of Laura's drive, as I headed the opposite direction from Chester's car, and at the inevitable and obnoxious stop sign at the next intersection.

"Maybe," Dom yelled, over the sound of flapping wings and piercing screeches, "you should think about *not* whapping a god in the face next time!"

"Next time?!"

The conversation ended at that, our concentration taken up with keeping the damn monsters' creepy little mouths away from our poor, tender souls — not to mention I was trying to drive down both Laura's street *and* some random street in the Underworld. I had no idea where in Hades I was.

Trying to ignore Underworld obstacles as I sped toward them,

I headed for the highway, with Dom clutching the armrest and bravely not screaming in terror every time it looked like we were going to hit a wall, statue, child, little old lady, and so on.

"It's okay," I told him. "We'll go right through Underworld stuff."

"How the hell can you tell which is which?" Dom's voice was about an octave higher than usual.

"How can you *not*?" I drove right through an Underworld fountain in the middle of the Upper World street.

We'd cleared the car of monsters by that time, and things were going pretty well, I thought, up until the stoplight at the entrance ramp — the longest light known to mankind.

"Shit!" I said. "Shit, they're going to catch up to us." A cursory glance in the rear-view mirror confirmed it. There they were, a seething black cloud of shrieks and feathers, taking up more and more of the mirror's reflection as they got closer.

My foot desperately wanted to move off the brake and onto the gas pedal. I could swerve right around the line of cars in front of me, dodge between oncoming traffic, and we'd be seventy-five miles an hour from here on out. But then I noticed that, in the Upper World, in the next lane over was a cop car.

I cursed some more.

Meanwhile, the monsters got closer, darkening the sky like a cloud of doubts, worries, fears, and guilt-trips — each individual one was bearable, but together, all hitting home at once, they were enough to tear you apart.

They were almost on top of us when the light turned green.

"Go, go, go, GO!" I literally bounced in my seat waiting for traffic to get the hint and accelerate.

Finally, we burst out onto the highway, swooping over into the leftmost lane and grinding up to seventy-five as fast as Dom's little blue car could manage.

"Jesus, what's *that*?" Dom asked, breaking his silence.

I knew exactly what he meant.

It felt like something in the very air around us was breaking apart, a feeling full of friction and sharp little pellets of discomfort. Like static electricity all around us, only you could *see* it, *hear* it, *smell* it. Even the taste of the air was crackly and sharp, as if the Upper World and Underworld were grating against each other.

The highway seemed okay, but the streets of Hades were — wrong. The false sense of reality was breaking up, and our surroundings were increasingly bizarre. The buildings in the Underworld were made up of thousands of multicolored daisies.

"I don't know," I said, in answer to Dom's question. "I think Hades is having trouble keeping both worlds on a parallel. They usually aren't — I don't think they're supposed to be."

Armchair quantum physics must run in the family. That, or I'd picked it up from Uncle Jeff like a bad habit.

"How close are the bird-monsters?" I asked, not daring a glance in the rear-view. There was way too much to keep track of and mentally process in front of me, let alone bothering with things trying to catch up to us.

"Pretty far back now," Dom said, to my extreme relief.

I couldn't afford to relax, though, because my brain was having trouble keeping up with which obstacles were physical and which ones weren't. That, and just after Dom gave me the good news, the bad news came and squashed it flat.

"Uh. Erica?" He was still turned, looking out the back window.

"What?"

"Hades is behind us."

"*What?*"

"In a really nice car," Dom added, and even now, even faced with death and the unknown and an angry god on the warpath with us in the crosshairs, there was admiration and a trace of jealousy in my husband's voice as he made this observation.

Under better circumstances, I might have teased him about that.

As it was, my nerves were sizzling. Everything seemed, at the same time, to be going too quickly, and not nearly fast enough — like one of those nightmares where your legs don't carry you forward no matter how hard you run.

"How close is he?" I asked.

"Not close, but he's catching up."

I couldn't risk glancing away from the road for even a split-second. We were going too fast in the Upper World, zooming down the fast lane, and in the Underworld everything was a blaze of madness — the street paved with red Lego bricks, soaring high above the ground through a glassed-in overpass, the roads below a dizzying pattern of intersecting lines buzzing with miniature traffic.

And still the two worlds grated against each other, more and more as we tore along, faster and faster. I tried not to think about what would happen if we got pulled over.

"There!" I yelled exuberantly.

"What?" Dom whipped around to see where I was pointing. "Jesus, Erica, get your hand back on the wheel!"

"There, that's the River Styx! And the docks — the carnival!" The river was a blue-grey ribbon glimmering in the distance at the edge of the city, only visible from this far away because the overpass was so high up. Dusk hung over the city like a fog, and in the haze of twilight, the carnival glowed like a beacon. Somewhere down there, in her tent, was Persephone — I hoped.

"We have to get down there," I said.

In the Upper World, a left-hand exit was coming up that would take us off the Interstate and onto the Loop.

The Underworld obligingly answered my expectation and provided a left-hand offshoot from the overpass — and almost immediately, it began the descent back to ground level. Great. So now I had to concentrate on the Upper World's obstacles — not hitting things, not getting pulled over, etc. — *and* concentrate on getting to an actual destination in the Underworld. My poor brain.

"Why the hell are you slowing down?" Dom yelled from the passenger seat.

"I have to!" I wailed. "There's too much going on!"

It still *felt* like we were going insanely fast, though the speedometer told me we'd slowed down to sixty. Careening through the Underworld with no regard for the well-being of the car or the objects it should, technically, be hitting, was all well and good, but I was walking a fine line telling my brain that now, when there were actual, physical cars buzzing alongside me in the Upper World at the same time.

"He's *catching up*!" Dom shouted.

"We're almost there." My hands clenched around the steering wheel so hard it hurt. "Almost there."

Dom didn't bother to ask me where. He seemed beyond caring to know what was going on — he was past that, and into the stage of just wanting it *not* to be going on. I couldn't blame him.

I concentrated on the Upper World, just as if I were trying to pull myself back into it, staring hard at the texture of the road, the colors of the cars around me, the hum and the smell of our car running. After a moment, the physical world looked stronger, clearer, more distinct — the Underworld faded to a dim shadow, a separate layer, washed-out and easy to ignore. Once I had a handle on that, I tried to split my focus. The second part of it was expectation. The Underworld would respond to expectation no matter *what* my eyes actually saw. In the Underworld, technically, any route could take me to the docks, if I honestly believed it would.

Fine. Then the docks were straight ahead. There was an Upper World exit just a half mile away that would put us in a funky shopping district, full of artsy shops and vintage clothing stores. That would do as my focus for a this-world version of the carnival.

I sped up and switched to the exit lane.

Chapter Forty-Four

standoff

We scrambled out of the car without stopping to look for Hades. Now that he had the helm back, it wouldn't do us any good to look, anyway.

Dom slammed his door and ran to take my hand. "Where to?" he asked, breathless with panic.

"This way." I pulled him forward and we jogged down the sunlit street and, at the same time, down the dusky, glittering carnival walkway.

Upper World passersby stared, but compared with being chased down by an angry god, gawking strangers didn't even register on my list of things to care about. Even less so as a ferocious roar shook the air, the ground of the Underworld trembling with it. The canvas tents shivered, but then shouts of fear and glee mingled together afterward, cut through by an amplified voice, muffled through a speaker, and I realized it was just a circus act.

I kept us woven into the crowd, and finally I snuck a glance back the way we'd come.

The crowd behind us parted as if a giant sidewinder was whipping its way through, but at the spear point of the wake was Hades, composed and slate-faced as usual. He touched no one, spoke only softly as he passed, but they moved aside as if he were roiling with flames or exuding plague fumes. He was only thirty yards behind us, at best, and moving much more quickly. He wasn't even *bothering* with the helm — either that, or Liza-Mae had it, which might be even scarier.

"Where?" Dom asked me desperately. I'd paused to stare in horror as Hades gained on us, and I was glad Dom pulled me back to the task at hand — escaping.

"Shortcut," I whispered, and tugged him under a tent flap. "We'll go through this way. The fortune-teller's tent is just through the other side of this one."

In the Upper World, we'd entered a little family-run bakery, and the family turned abruptly toward the employees-only entrance we'd come through.

"You lost?" the owner, a native African I knew by sight if not by name, asked, his arms crossed over his chest.

"Sorry," I said. "Just got turned around."

In the Underworld, we were in a tent full of funnel cakes and cotton candy, and the few occupants seemed not the least bit fazed that I was talking to someone they couldn't see, hear, or otherwise perceive.

The owner of the bakery exchanged a look with his wife, and they, along with their grown daughter, shook their heads and spoke to each other quietly in a rapid-fire language, probably speculating about our sanity and sobriety.

I hurried Dom out through the front entrance — also known as the Underworld's concession stand doorway.

Straight ahead was the fortune-teller's tent. In the Land of the Living, it was a New Age shop, its front windows full of crystals and amulets. We ducked inside, neither of us daring to look back to check Hades' progress.

"Upstairs," I whispered to Dom, and under the disinterested eye of the cashier, we slunk into the unpopulated upper floor of the New Age shop. The Underworld equivalent was moving out of the dark entryway into the little pool of light around Persephone's velvet-covered table.

"Anatol!" For a moment, all fear forgotten, I rushed forward to hug him. Dom hung onto my hand, and Anatol leapt from his seat across from Persephone and met me halfway.

"Erica, what are you doing back here?" Anatol asked, his voice boisterous.

Then he noticed Dominic.

Persephone didn't move from her seat, her sea-glass eyes inscrutable as she looked at us. She didn't seem put out that we'd interrupted her fortune-telling session with Anatol — maybe because *he* didn't mind.

"I'm . . . uh . . . on the run from Hades, actually," I said. "I made it back to the Land of the Living, but he caught up with me and now—" I stopped short, not wanting to say it aloud. "Now Hades is trying to kill us *both*." Dom squeezed my hand.

"That's why we're here." I looked past Anatol and into the pale green eyes of Persephone. "We need your help. He'll be here any second."

"Anatol, perhaps you should go," Persephone said softly.

He looked back over his shoulder as he left, but hurried away.

There was an abrupt change in the air, as if the Underworld itself had taken a breath. The canvas around us rippled, crackling against the metal poles that supported it.

I clutched Dom closer to me, half because I wanted him to protect me, and half because I wanted to protect him.

I expected Hades, in his human form, to walk in glowering, but he'd found my weak spot. Of course he would use whatever terrified me the most, all the more because I didn't terrify easily.

I recognized the squawking, prehistoric noises only a split-second before the entryway erupted with a mass of feathery, black wings.

Mid-scream, I pushed Dom to the ground, kneeling over him to shield him as best I could while I batted the bird-monsters with the scepter. It's hard to cower and fight at the same time, but I was managing.

"Dom, your lighter!" I yelled over the thunder of flapping wings.

He hadn't quite caught up to current events, so it took him a moment to dig into his pocket.

"Light something — *anything!*"

Claws ripped at my hands and hair. One of the creatures burrowed into the hair that fell across the back of my neck, wriggling to try and reach the flesh beneath. I screamed again and fought the urge to whack at the thing with the scepter. Knocking myself out right now was tempting, but probably not a good idea if I wanted both Dom and myself to live.

It was then I realized Dom wasn't safely beneath my crouched form anymore — he'd crawled away somewhere.

I had time for one panic-stricken moment before the tent caught fire.

The flames roared to life, and the bird-things screeched, retreating. The one in my hair struggled for escape, its high-pitched wails piercingly close. I cringed, but then felt the creature slip away.

"Dom!" I stayed where I was, cowering on the ground — below the smoke and the heat of the flames. I choked as I called out to him again.

I felt his hand slide into my own, and together we slunk out from under the flaming canvas. Persephone was waiting outside, looking on without concern as her tent burned, the metal framework just a hot skeleton now, with only the top still blazing.

"Sorry, Persephone," I said quietly, standing next to her.

"*Persephone?*" Dom stared not at her, but at me. "You mean I just set fire to a tent that belonged to the wife of the god who's trying to kill us?"

"Yup," I said.

Persephone smiled at him.

"This has been . . . a strange day," Dom commented.

"Where's Hades?" My voice shook on me unexpectedly.

"Behind you," Hades said.

I spun around with — I confess — a quaking squeak of surprise.

Hades was less than two feet behind Dom and me, his long-fingered hands clasped behind his back, his expression serene but threatening at the same time.

"You know," Persephone said thoughtfully, "I really hate it when you do that thing where monsters come out of your mouth. It's . . . unattractive."

Hades apologized in an impressively gallant fashion, and then, unfortunately, returned his attention to us.

"Look," I said, swallowing a lump in my throat. "If you want me back in the Underworld that much, then fine. I did what I went back to do, and it's not bad being dead. Just leave Dominic out of it. If you'll let him go, I'll come back."

Hades smiled toothily. "There are two problems with your logic. One, you are in no position to bargain, since you have no real control in the situation at hand. And two, you are offering no more than what I demanded in the first place, before you caused a great deal of trouble for me."

"Three problems," Dom said stiffly. "*I'm* not going anywhere if it means Erica will die all over again."

I elbowed him in the ribs and whispered, "Shut up!"

"*Au contraire.*" Hades smiled more widely. "You act as if death is something that can be avoided. Put off. Conveniently set aside for a rainy day, as it were. Erica has already died. She has no place in the Land of the Living, even if she currently occupies a living body. But in a sense, you're correct in your statement that you aren't going anywhere. After all—" Hades spread his arms wide to indicate the city around us — "you've already arrived at your final destination. Here you are! Now all you have to do is stay."

"Ex*cuse* me. I'm not agreeing to any of this — with either of you." I shot Dom the most smoldering glare I'm capable of. "And I *do* have some leverage." I raised the scepter in both hands, tapping it in my left palm for emphasis. "If you could just grab this back from me, I'm guessing you would've by now. And if I didn't have it, I figure you could've grabbed *us* by now." I dashed a glance at Persephone, who was trying to hide a smile behind her hand, that familiar mischievous glint brightening her pale eyes.

Hades' smile stayed in place, but only in that his features didn't shift position. The spark had gone out of it. "You are making dangerous assumptions, Erica."

I shrugged. "Convictions carry a lot of weight here in your little realm. I'm pretty damn sure I'm right. Reality will bend around that."

"Even if that's so, do you want to pit *your* convictions against *mine*? Or don't you think mine might carry a great deal more weight than yours?"

"According to you, the two of us are dead no matter what," I pointed out. "What've we got to lose?"

"Maybe you shouldn't piss him off," Dom whispered in my ear. "Or give him ideas."

"I have your scepter," I said to Hades, ignoring my husband's interjection. "Would you rather have it back after I've had a long, natural, healthy life, or would you rather I just hung onto it? It's already been with me across the void twice without changing hands. I'm pretty sure I could hang onto it if I kept my wits about me. Which I will. In that case, either way, Dom and I get to live. The question is, do you lose most of your power to a mortal, or do you get it back when she dies? To *you*, the time is negligible. You won't even miss it." I tapped the scepter in my palm again.

"Are you trying to *bargain* with me?" Hades snarled.

"The Greeks did it all the time." I waved a hand dismissively, despite the trembling in my knees.

"It's true," Persephone said casually from behind him.

Hades glared at her for a moment before turning back to me. "Fine. We'll write an official contract, then."

"We — we will?" I stammered over the words, simple as they were.

He smiled and inclined his head to indicate the affirmative.

He *had* to be up to something. Dom must've agreed with me, because he squeezed my hand in a silent warning.

"Will he honor a contract with me?" I asked Persephone.

"He'll keep his word," she assured me, her tone implying that he'd be sorry if he didn't live up to her expectation.

"Can I name the person who'll draw up the contract?" I turned back to Hades.

"I don't see why not. It makes no difference to me." He spread his hands and laughed. "It's not as if I have my own personal lawyer."

"He'll cheat us somehow," Dom whispered to me. "It's like the evil genie in a bottle thing — he'll twist any wish you ask for, make the worst of it any way he can. What are you *doing*?"

"Calling Laura," I said, pulling Dom's cell phone out of his jeans pocket.

He smiled.

In that smile, I could read his thoughts exactly.

No mortal, genie, or god can outfox Laura. We're saved!

Chapter Forty-Five

until we meet again

Laura, along with Chester and Garrett, were on their way to the New Age shop that was currently linked to the Underworld. From all Dom and I could tell, nobody had noticed anything odd going on — none of our shouts or arson had taken place in the Upper World, and we'd gotten so wrapped up in being on the flip side that our bodies had sort of slipped into stasis. If anything, we probably looked like we were in some kind of mutual trance. They probably saw weirder stuff than that all the time in a New Age shop. Especially since they sold bongs as well as crystals and pendants and all that jazz.

Once we'd ascertained that nobody was going to be arrested in the immediate future, it was just a matter of waiting for the others to show up.

Dom and I wandered away from Hades and Persephone, still in line of sight, but far enough away to feel more comfortable. The carnival was beautiful in the rich blue of the night, all glitter and glam, and Dom looked around eagerly. "Wow. This is — not what I expected."

"I know," I said, half-smiling. It felt like showing someone your hometown for the first time, being here with him. All the associations coming back to me, the strange combination of familiarity and freshness — knowing I knew the place inside and out, but seeing it through new eyes.

"I guess I always thought of death as more of a . . . well . . . *formal* occasion." Dom put his arm around my shoulder, holding me in a comfortable half-hug.

"Only for the living," I said.

The Styx glittered with stars and carnival lights, and drifting toward us was the ferry, jazz band in full swing, the music gentle with distance. Faint laughter and the drone of voices rose to carry above the music. Carnies' cries and calliope numbers cut through and broke off at will.

"It doesn't seem like death," Dom said, his voice marveling. "It all seems so *vibrant.*"

"What'd you expect? *Waiting for Godot*?" I laughed.

"I don't know. I believed in *an* afterlife. I guess I never gave much thought to what *kind* of afterlife until now." He pulled away enough to look me in the eye. "I didn't realize I had so many preconceived notions about it."

"I felt the same way, at first." I thought about explaining to him about reality and belief and expectation, how all of it worked down here, but there was music and dancing and a carnival all around us, and for a moment I missed being part of this world. There would be plenty of time to talk about it when we were topside. Only this instant could be *experienced* together. Dom seemed content to bask in the present with me, his eyes tracing the unfamiliar constellations that dusted the crisp, clear sky above us.

"I could really get used to this place," he murmured.

"Not a bad place to retire to," I agreed. "And there's so much more. A whole world this side of the void. Other cities to explore, the wilderness in between." I could definitely picture us venturing into the wild together sometime, leaving behind all constraints of reality — at least long enough to say we'd done it, even though we'd probably come back to Hades afterward. Funny, having things like "long enough" and "afterward" in my mental vocabulary again. Just six hours ago my body had been a corpse in the ground, and I'd had no thought of anything like hours. The whole idea of time had seemed so foreign to me. How easily we physical beings slipped back into comfortable old habits.

"Are you sure you want to come back?" Dom asked me, not taking his eyes off the stars.

"You trying to get rid of me?" I teased, and planted a noisy kiss on his cheek.

"I think we're a two-for-one deal now." Dom glanced behind us to where Hades and Persephone stood talking, Hades with his hands folded behind his back, pacing, and his wife leaning against a nearby lamppost, looking serenely amused as usual.

"Think how our families would feel," I said, and Dom made an "ouch" face with an exaggerated wince. "Besides, I wouldn't give Hades the satisfaction — not after everything he's thrown at me."

Dom laughed.

"Erica!" someone shouted, and I turned back toward the Styx. Running up the dock toward me, waving excitedly, was Latrischa, my Uncle Jeff in tow, and Anatol strolling along behind them with cigar smoke curling out of his smile.

It was surprising, but nice, to see Latrischa sans cynicism. You knew you'd been genuinely missed when someone as prickly as Latrischa threw her arms around you and hopped up and down upon reuniting.

Uncle Jeff was quick to grab a hug from me, too, and Anatol smiled on benevolently. Clearly, he'd gone to fetch them from somewhere.

"You must be Dominic." Uncle Jeff gave Dom a once-over, seemed to approve, and shook his hand.

"You *have* to be Jeffrey Shaw." Dom smiled. "Erica takes after her dad's side of the family."

Briefly, I was tempted, like Dom had been a moment ago, to throw life to the wind and just dive back into my afterlife. Uncle Jeff and Dom, my two musicians and my two favorite people to spend time with, both in one place for the first time. All these years I'd thought about how well they would've gotten along, if only Uncle Jeff had still been around. They'd have fun talking about technical music stuff I didn't understand, maybe show off a little, but in a friendly way.

But again, we had forever for that.

Uncle Jeff pulled Latrischa forward with an arm around her shoulders. "And this," he said to Dom, "is Latrischa Blake . . . my . . ." he hesitated and flicked a glance to me ". . . my fiancée."

"Your *what*?" It took me a second to realize the half-question, half-exclamation had come from me.

Latrischa beamed.

Uncle Jeff did too, but he looked a little sheepish. "Sorry, Erica — I wanted to tell you, but you'd already left, and I figured you'd be away up there living your whole life before you'd be back to hear the news. I hope — I hope you don't mind that — well, she's your friend, and your age, too, and—"

Latrischa snorted. "Like *age* has any bearing when you're *dead*." She went right back to beaming. "Erica's happy for us — you can see it in her face. If she'd close her damn mouth and stop gawking."

I stuck my tongue out at her and then grinned. "I *am* happy for you," I assured Uncle Jeff. "You just surprised me, that's all. Bachelor-man."

He laughed as I mock-punched his arm, and then hugged him.

"It would appear Hades is ready to return to the matter at hand." Anatol pointed with his cigar, and we all turned.

Laura, Chester, and Garrett had arrived, looking eerily fragile next to Hades' towering form. Only Chester seemed as physically formidable. Garrett looked like you'd expect from a young man whose entire world view was in the process of crumbling out from under him. He stood in his father's shadow, with an attitude halfway between protectiveness and desperation.

My sister had on her Business face, smooth and impassive as any poker player — no, not quite, because she also looked a tiny bit imperious, like she knew something you didn't. She carried it as well as Hades carried his mask when she greeted him, shaking his hand as if he were really no more than a business client.

"We'll be back," I told Latrischa, Uncle Jeff, and Anatol, and Dom and I went to join the others.

Anatol stopped us with one hand. "One thing first. I was told if I saw you again, to let you know that Sebastian and Octavius made it back to their lives."

"How—" I began the question, but Anatol pointed his cigar toward the impatiently-waiting Hades, and Dom and I moved on.

I felt better, knowing that my former companions were safe. I didn't know how the two brothers had made it out, or how Anatol could possibly know about it if they had, but right now was not the time to sort all that out.

"Thanks for coming, guys," Dom said to Laura and the Wilkinses.

"Let's talk contracts," Laura said crisply, and from her purse pulled a legal pad and a black fine-tip pen.

Poor Hades. For a moment I actually pitied him.

"It seems like this is all going to work out fine," Dom said happily as he and I, along with the Wilkinses, strolled off to leave Laura some alone time for writing up the contract. She'd actually shooed Hades and Persephone away, as well — *shooed* the god of the Underworld and his wife.

Dom, Chester, Garrett, and I found Anatol, Uncle Jeff, and Latrischa playing ski-ball. I made introductions hastily, hoping Latrischa wouldn't mention that I'd believed Chester was crazy for a while. She didn't, but I wouldn't have put it past her to grin and say something like, "Oh, so this is the crazy medium. Nice to meet you."

"So," I said to Anatol, once everyone was settled into either the ski-ball game or the nearby benches overlooking the starlit Styx. "How did you know about Sebastian and Octavius?"

"Persephone. She intervened for them with Hades. Of course, she knew they were under your wing, and she knew you'd be worried about them, so she told me. Maybe she thought I'd see you on the ferry before she saw you at the carnival. She isn't wrong very often."

"Why'd she interfere for us? *Any* of us?" I asked. It seemed like there was genuine affection between Persephone and her husband, which weakened my previous theory that vengeance was her motive. Still, her smile pegged her as a trouble-maker at heart, and I wondered if it wasn't some kind of kick for her to drive Hades nuts now and then — a way to tease him, or some odd little game she played against him.

Anatol shrugged and blew a smoke ring. "Everybody's gotta have a hobby. Who knows?"

"Funny how many questions she answers, and then how many she *doesn't*." I quirked a half-smile and accepted a drag from Anatol's cigar. "How did she get Hades to agree to let them go?"

"They cut some kind of deal. I don't know the specifics, just that they agreed to talk up how fearsome and vengeful Hades is to anyone who tries to escape him. They're supposed to go around making up terrible punishments that supposedly await them when they get back to the Underworld." Anatol took his cigar back. "I don't know. Hades says fear works best on older cultures. Not so much for people from your time."

"Fear tends to just piss us off," I commented cheerfully.

Anatol grinned at me. "I've noticed."

"Any news on your sweetheart?" I asked him.

He shook his head. "It's all right, though. She'll be along."

I was distracted by trying very hard not to notice Uncle Jeff and Latrischa exchanging a kiss by the ski-ball booth, so I looked away to where Garrett leaned against the splintery dockside railing. Chester and Dom sat on a bench a few feet away from us, alternately talking and taking in the scene, both of them looking a little nervous but a lot curious. Garrett, however, looked like a guy trying to pick up the pieces of a shattered world — not self-pitying or even *sad* really, just steeled for the task and none too pleased about it. It couldn't be easy for him, I thought sympathetically. He'd been so sure there was a strict logic to the way things worked, and that it was quantifiable. I'd been that way, too, before I'd died, but at least I'd had the worst of my shock over with. Once you were *dead*, it was pretty easy to accept anything, just because it was a relief that there was still an *anything* to accept.

Then again, I thought, looking over at Dom and Chester, some people were just interested to know what there was, whether it was easy to believe or not. True, Dom was sometimes *too* eager to believe things — Tarot readings and horoscopes were nothing to base your life plans on, in my book — but at least when he was faced with new information, he didn't choke. It had always annoyed me, in a protective sort of way, that he was so gullible. Nice to think that maybe it had a flip side, too — that sometimes, his gullibility was good for him.

"Ski-ball?" I asked Anatol.

"Why not?" he agreed.

I picked Dom up on the way to the booth, giving him my hand and a sly smile that, even though he couldn't have known its cause, seemed to make him happy.

I invited Chester, too, but he shook his head, throwing a glance at his son, and I understood that he wanted to keep Garrett company and, hopefully, have a good conversation with him, as well.

Uncle Jeff and Latrischa traipsed off briefly and brought back elephant ears and popcorn and root beer floats, and after a few games of ski-ball, we all ended up sitting on the sandy ground by the benches, talking and laughing and enjoying the snacks. Even Garrett seemed more cheerful, whether it was the distraction or something Chester had said to him.

The religious trio passed us, and the minister waved, looking oddly pleasant.

"Dead again already?" the priest called to me.

"Nope," I called back. "Just visiting. Hey, I thought you went to Hell?"

The reverend tipped his hat to us.

"Didn't like it." The minister Doom and Gloom actually smiled. "Thanks for the return ticket!"

Before I could find out more, they burst out laughing, and walked on together.

"Wow, I had no idea he *could* laugh. Where's Matt?" I asked Anatol.

"The thrill park. He just finished his first batch of zombie pellets." Latrischa rolled her eyes.

"Tell him I'm sorry I missed him." I was fleetingly grateful that Hades had chased me down and dragged me back here for this — for another visit to the carnival, a chance to say "goodbye for now" to Anatol, Uncle Jeff, and Latrischa.

Then Persephone was looking down at me. "Laura is finished," she said. "Hades is reading the contract now."

Dom and I leapt up almost in unison and helped the others to their feet.

"Then what?" I asked nervously.

"Then you'll both read the contract, and then you'll both sign it." Persephone smiled. "Then you'll both return to the Upper World, along with those you brought with you." She inclined her head toward the Wilkinses, nodded toward where we'd left Laura working on the deal. "You may bring the others as witnesses to the agreement."

The whole group followed her back to where Hades and Laura waited.

As we came around one of the tents, I saw Hades pacing around where Laura sat at the table in the ruins of Persephone's tent. He was holding the legal pad and looking increasingly upset.

"... anything wrong ... wording?" I caught only fragments of Laura's question, the rest lost in the distance between us.

Hades thrust his hands down at his sides, fingers still balled into fists. All I heard of his reply was, ". . . *no loopholes!*"

I couldn't stop the smug smile that crept across my face. "Love you, Laura," I said under my breath.

"There are *no loopholes*!" Hades repeated, swinging around toward us with undisguised fury burning in his features.

"You agreed to the terms," Laura pointed out calmly.

"Yes, you did." Persephone patted his arm as if he were a petulant toddler.

Hades spluttered angrily, but scrawled his name across the bottom of the last page. The signature went through the next several pages of the notepad.

Anatol handed him a cigar and offered him a light.

Hades accepted both.

Chapter Forty-Six

life will never be the same

We were glad to discover that nothing in the Upper World shop had been affected as a result of our escapade. The cashier rolled his eyes as we left and muttered something about "hippie nut job customers," but if that was the worst repercussion coming to me after all the speeding, reckless driving, and general mayhem today, I considered myself lucky.

Chester and Garrett parted ways with us, and Dom drove Laura and me back to the condo. I had the scepter propped between my knees again — it was officially in my possession until the end of my natural life. By natural, I mean, as per the contract, that no nasty "accidents" courtesy of Hades would befall us. We were still two for one, as Hades had demanded, which meant that when one of us died, Hades would come fetch the other the same day. He'd been pleased with himself for getting that clause in, but Dom and I were actually okay with the idea.

"I think it's time I went home and got some rest," was my answer to Laura's hesitant invitation to come in. She was about as exhausted as I was, I knew. The day had taken a lot out of everyone involved. "After all," I joked, "I've been mostly dead all day."

She half-laughed, half-sobbed, and squeezed me in a long hug. "I missed you, Erica. God, today's been weird, but I'm glad you're back."

"I know," I said. "Me too. And thank you. I wouldn't be here if it weren't for you." I gave her a heartfelt peck on the cheek and slid back into the passenger seat of Dom's car.

"Who's telling Mom and Dad?" Laura asked, just as I was about to close the door.

"I think," I said, after careful consideration, "that it would probably freak them out if *I* called, since I'm certifiably dead. Possibly Dad would have a heart attack and Mom would die of shock. At the very least, I bet Mom will pass out if she sees me," I mused. "If Dom gives them the good news, they may think he's gone off the eccentric end of being a musician."

"Oh, thanks very much," Dom grumbled from the driver's seat, but he smiled.

"You, however," I said to my sister, "are a practical, rational, down-to-earth girl whose tact is unmatched in this world or the next."

Laura rolled her eyes. "Don't think I can't tell when I'm being buttered up."

"Please?" I clasped my hands and smiled as angelically as I could manage.

She sighed, which I took as an agreement.

"Thanks, Laura," Dom called, waving to her through the windshield.

And off we went . . . toward home.

My shoes ticked a cheerful rhythm on the hospital tiles as I walked back to the waiting room from the doctor's office.

I waved to my parents — seated next to each other in two uncomfortable-looking chairs upholstered in Easter-egg hues of plastic — and paid my co-pay to a nasal little blonde lady at the desk. She had long, creepy fake nails that clicked against my debit card when she took it.

While she processed my payment and did her thing with the paperwork, I looked around the room thoughtfully. People coughing, holding their congested chests. People doubled over upset stomachs. People bent with age, frail and pained, clutching walkers or canes. People with casts over shattered bones. Some of these people might find out today that they just had a cold or the flu or pneumonia. Or they might need surgery. It might be an organ gone bad, a terminal illness, cancer. Our contract with Hades bought Dom and me a full lifetime, but there was nothing that would protect us from the weakness of being alive. Organic bodies are dangerous places to exist.

Nothing's perfect, not life or death or the places in between. My best reassurance to myself as the fear of living suddenly gripped me, was that at least, for once, I had thought out the consequences before I took the risk. Maybe I hadn't been altogether prepared for the Road, but I had *known* about becoming mortal again. They say the first step to recovery is admitting you have a problem — well, let this be my admission. I have a problem with doing crazy stuff.

But I was okay with the consequences of being alive. Scared of the renewed vulnerability it brought, yeah, but that's just life.

My mom was at my elbow then. "Well?"

Once Laura had convinced her I really was alive, my mom's first response was a demand that I make a doctor's appointment. I could see her point, although I knew I was okay. Whatever Hades' scepter had done when I'd re-emerged into the Land of the Living, it had healed everything that had contributed to my death.

But my dad backed up the necessity of a doctor's visit, something I never thought I'd live to see. Laura had weighed in with an agreement, too. When my brother Tyler called me and told me to stop being stupid and go to the doctor already, I'd decided to comply.

"Well???" My mom poked me gently with her elbow.

"I'm fine." I shook off my morbid thoughts. I took my card back from the clicking woman, and my dad joined us at the door. "I'm fine," I repeated. "Doctor figures I must've slipped into some kind of deep coma and then came out of it somehow on my own."

"Can that *happen*?" my mom asked, clearly appalled. After

all, from the doctor's point of view — and my parents' — I'd been buried alive. "You were *embalmed*. Don't they take out your blood and everything for that?"

I shrugged. "He seemed pretty amazed by it, too, but that's the only explanation he could think of." It didn't make sense to anyone who didn't know about my week in the Underworld, but it's hard for a doctor to ignore the fact that someone who *should* be dead is alive enough to walk into their office for a check-up.

"But there're no lasting effects, right?" my dad asked.

"Nope. I'm fine."

We emerged into the sunlight of a breezy spring day, and I couldn't help but stop and let the sun soak into my skin. The air smelled like fresh leaves and new flowers, the colors of everything sharp and clear after last night's rain.

I hurried to catch up to my parents, who'd kept walking. They were both angry with the medical staff who'd been on duty when I'd died, with the mortician, with the funeral home. I tried to calm them down, but my mom was having none of it.

"They *buried* my daughter alive!" she cried. "The least I can do is sue the pants off them."

"We don't hold with suing over trifles," Dad added for my benefit. "But this isn't small beans, Erica! This is a case of life and death."

"Tell me about it," I muttered.

"What if they make a mistake with someone else?" my mom demanded.

My dad unlocked the car, and I got in the back seat.

"Oh!" Mom exclaimed. "I forgot my purse!"

"You want me to run back for it?" Dad offered.

"No, no, I know just where I left it," she said, and hurried away, as fast as she could in high heels.

Dad took his seat behind the wheel, leaving the door open to let the spring air into the car. "Hope we're not late to your party."

Tyler and his wife, Maci, were hosting an all-day get-together in honor of my return, starting at noon.

"Dad," I said hesitantly. "There's something I need to tell you. You and Mom are upset with the doctors, I get that, but . . . I wouldn't be too hard on them. Some weird stuff happened while I was . . . gone."

I met his gaze via the rear-view mirror. He looked confused.

"You tried to get Uncle Jeff to come down off the roof that day," I said. "He was trying to fix the satellite dish when you got there, but he fell when he tried to get to the ladder. You were watching when it happened."

Dad's expression changed — his features didn't move, but his eyes looked different.

"He wanted me to tell you that it wasn't your fault and you couldn't have done anything to save him," I went on. "He's happy — I promise, Dad. He told me to tell you that the only thing he worries about is that you might still be upset about his death."

We didn't say anything for a long time, but I knew Dad believed me.

"Can you try to explain to Mom?" I asked at last. "About leaving the doctors and everyone alone, I mean?"

Dad nodded. "It's pretty irregular. They may still get called out by the medical board or something, but. . . ." he glanced at me in the rear-view, ". . . well, we won't press any claims."

"Thanks, Dad."

He put a hand on the back of his seat and I put mine over his. "He's happy?" Dad asked.

"Very happy." I thought of the look on his face when he'd introduced Latrischa as his fiancée. I smiled — Dad saw it, and joined me. He looked relieved, like he'd been carrying a cloud with him for years, and now it had finally passed.

Chapter Forty-Seven

beyond the grave

I'd just bought my new cell phone when it rang for the first time.

It was Chester.

"Hi." I got in my rental car and headed for home.

"Hello, Erica," Chester rumbled. There was an awkward silence before he spoke again. "I just wanted to thank you."

"For?" I said, after a confused pause.

"Garrett."

"He finally believes you," I guessed.

"Yes, he does. He's not that happy about it, but he's adjusting," Chester said.

"I'm happy for you," I said. "It's great that you two can finally be okay with each other. That he can finally. . . ." I hesitated.

". . . Respect me," Chester finished, the exact wording I'd been thinking. "If it hadn't been for what happened — if it hadn't been for you — I don't think he would ever have come around."

"Well, I'm glad it worked out. I did feel bad for dragging you into all of it."

"I'm glad you did," Chester said gruffly. "Although I certainly didn't think I'd be saying that, at the time."

"Thank *you*," I said. "I owe you . . . everything."

We exchanged our goodbyes and hung up.

~*~

That evening, I sat on the porch, waiting impatiently for Dom to get home from a piano lesson.

The stars were just starting to appear in the middle of the sky, the horizon glowing faintly still. I thought of the twilights I'd seen in the Underworld.

Tomorrow there would be the task of looking into a new car for me, since mine had been totaled. There would be legal issues surrounding the fact that I was certified dead, and we'd have to clear those up. At some point, I wanted a better job. Dom wanted to move, and *he* wanted a better job. We'd have to figure out a new budget, move out of Uncle Jeff's — which was no longer as heart-wrenching to me — settle into a new place. Basic, everyday stuff for a real live mortal person.

That was okay.

Even tedious details were an experience, a part of being alive. A moment in time, in a finite world where things went in a certain order. I wouldn't always have to put up with things like reality, so I felt more at ease with the things I used to find exasperating even to think about. And Dom would be here with me, and I would be here with him.

I watched the headlights of a car pulling into the drive, watched the driver get out and close the door behind him, watched him avoid stepping on any of the cracks in the pavement between the car and the porch steps.

Yeah, the more things change, the more they stay the same, I thought, but even so, I knew that everything, for me, was different, and that it would be from now on. I was not quite the same person who had died a week ago, and I never would be again.

"I should've known you'd come back this week," Dom said, as we sat down together on the couch.

"Other than me sending a medium over to tell you, how could you possibly have known I'd come back from the dead?"

"Your horoscope in yesterday's paper." Dom was completely

serious, his conviction increasing as he went on. "It said this would be a week of homecoming and resolution, overcoming obstacles and miscommunications."

I opened my mouth to say something about how generic that prediction was, stopped, and smiled. "That sounds like this week, all right," I said. "Did your horoscope say anything to prepare you?"

He stared into my eyes and smiled. "I don't think *anything* could've prepared me for yesterday."

"Make me a celebratory rum and coke?" I asked happily.

Dom obliged me, and we kicked back together with my legs across his lap, each with a glass in hand, the ice rattling comfortably whenever one of us took a drink.

"What a week," Dom said softly, interrupting the drifting thoughts that swirled around in my head.

"Yeah," I agreed.

"It's amazing. I finally know what comes next." He drank the last of his rum and coke. "Want another?" he offered.

I handed over my glass and let him up, pulling my knees up and curling against the arm of the couch. "It's good to know it's nice, right?" I said. "The afterlife."

"Yeah." More ice clinked into the empty glasses. "But just *knowing* . . . I mean, it's supposed to be the unknown, right? For the living, at least. Now we know, for certain, that there's an afterlife, what it consists of. We know that there's a god."

I scoffed at that. "Please. Hades? He's *something*, that's for sure — more than just a regular human being — but . . . he's self-centered, vain, subjective, and at least as flawed as most people I know, probably more."

"He's still a god." Dom handed me a full glass. He took his place next to me again and I put my legs back across his lap.

"A god should be more than just some jerk with superpowers." I made a face. "Hades is to divinity what a pissed-off spider-monkey is to humanity."

Wrapped up in the moment, I forgot all about the little detail of alcohol tolerance. I was used to drinking as much as I had a taste for in Hades, and coming away none the worse for wear. Not so with a physical state of affairs.

"Oh, God, I feel terrible," I moaned, two hours and four drinks later.

"You're okay," Dom said soothingly, holding me upright so I could brush my teeth before he put me to bed.

"If the room would stop spinning," I mumbled, "*then* I would be okay."

"I know, sweetie, I know." Dom rubbed my back with the palm of his hand.

"This is *not* a good thing to be alive for." Then I apologized, because I realized that at least Dom was here with me for it, and he was trying to make it as easy on me as possible.

"It's okay," he said.

"I'm sorry," I said.

"It's okay," Dom repeated.

"No, I meant about . . . the fight." I looked at him guiltily, and we both knew what argument I was talking about.

"That's okay, too," he said.

"I mean — are you sure it — " I hesitated and bit my lip. "I didn't want to be that girl, you know. I never wanted to hold you back, keep you from living out any of your ambitions or dreams."

"You weren't — aren't — that girl," Dom assured me, holding me steady as I wobbled my way to our room.

I plopped down without dignity on my side of the bed.

"But you want that job in Chicago, and I *still* don't want to move to Chicago," I said fuzzily. "Maybe — maybe you would've been better off if I'd just stayed dead." It was shocking to me how quickly the tears sprung up, how hot they were against my cheeks. So many of them all at once. I hadn't expected that. I hadn't even known what I was thinking until I'd said it out loud to Dom.

He looked up at me from where he knelt on the floor next to the bed. He clenched his teeth for a second, then said firmly, "No."

He took a moment before he went on. "No, I would *not* have been better off. And I turned the job down two days ago."

My reaction was delayed by the alcohol, but eventually I got around to gasping. "*Why?*"

"Two reasons. One, I was busy wallowing in pain over the death of my wife—" he paused to touch my cheek— "and two, well . . . I didn't want to move to Chicago, either."

"But your career—" I protested.

"—Can start elsewhere," Dom interrupted. "I wanted something closer, same as you. Nothing's come up for *me* yet, but. . . ."

"What do you mean?" I asked, registering something in his expression.

"Well, I got a letter in the mail yesterday. I haven't gotten around to writing anything back. Now that you're not dead, I guess you'll have to take care of it."

"What kind of letter?" I asked, not wanting to get my hopes up but knowing it was too late not to.

"Oh, just a graduate program at NYU. Something about historical architecture. Something about sustainable restorations of historic buildings? I can't think *who* could have sent your application to them, because I *know* if you'd been trying to get me to move to New York City, you'd have mentioned applying to school there." Dom played nonchalant.

I flushed and stammered. "Well," I finally managed, "I didn't think I'd get *in*. And I *did* suggest Manhattan. It's close enough for lots of visits, and big enough for your music career. Better than Chicago for a music career, even." All of this was slurred, and I knew it, but I was thinking more clearly than it sounded from my voice.

Dom chuckled and swept my hair off my forehead. "Maybe we should talk about this more when you're *not* drunk off your ass. Right now, you look like you need some sleep."

"I'm fine," I said petulantly, crossing my arms.

"Are you?" He kissed me.

"Yes," I said when we were finished.

"How fine?" He kissed me again.

"Are you taking advantage of me when I'm drunk, buster?" I did my best to raise one eyebrow and lower the other, probably not very successfully.

"I don't know. Am I?"

"I didn't say I objected." I giggled drunkenly.

Yes, things were going to work out fine, I thought. I'd even have a career at last — once I got through grad school — and one that wouldn't (I hoped) get boring anytime soon. Dom could work his way up to the swankiest concert halls of New York, and I could still see my family on the weekends. It would only be a day trip to make the drive.

One less car crash in my life, and I could've been here when the acceptance letter had arrived. Problem solved, no death necessary.

Still, I couldn't bring myself to regret my sojourn into the world beyond the grave. Too many good things had happened there, too many friendships had formed. Life seemed easier, knowing there was something to look forward to — that Uncle Jeff would still be there waiting to hang out, that somehow I'd meet up with Sebastian and Octavius again, that Anatol, Latrischa, and Matt would greet me with open arms, and that Dom and I would have a whole world to explore, free of concerns about shelter and money and other annoying physical needs. Anything life might throw at me was just temporary, after all. No point worrying about it, really. I was just back this side for kicks and rebellion, so I might as well enjoy it, regardless of the curveballs.

These thoughts flitted through my head for a second, and then I was too distracted to bother with any of it.

Eventually, we did get to sleep.

About the Author

Sara Marian was raised in the woods by wild English teachers, and has been writing for as long as she can remember. She is an avid reader of a wide range of fiction, especially classic literature, fantasy, and historical fiction mysteries. She is pursuing a degree in anthropology from University of Louisville (minoring in Russian studies), with plans for a career in archaeology.